A Handful of

Evelyn Waugh was born in Hampstead in 1903, second son of
Arthur Waugh, publisher and literary critic, and brother of Alec
Waugh, the popular novelist. He was educated at Lancing and
Hertford College, Oxford, where he read Modern History. In 1928
he published his first work, a life of Dante Gabriel Rossetti, and his
first novel, *Decline and Fall*, which was soon followed by *Vile Bodies*
(1930), *Black Mischief* (1932), *A Handful of Dust* (1934) and *Scoop* (1938).
During these years he travelled extensively in most parts of
Europe, the Near East, Africa and tropical America, and published
a number of travel books, including *Labels* (1930), *Remote People*
(1931), *Ninety-Two Days* (1934) and *Waugh in Abyssinia* (1936). In 1939
he was commissioned in the Royal Marines and later transferred
to the Royal Horse Guards, serving in the Middle East and in
Yugoslavia. In 1942 he published *Put Out More Flags* and then in
1945 *Brideshead Revisited*. *When the Going Was Good* and *The Loved One*
preceded *Men at Arms*, which came out in 1952, the first volume in
the *Sword of Honour* trilogy, and won the James Tait Black
Memorial Prize. The other volumes, *Officers and Gentlemen* and
Unconditional Surrender followed in 1955 and 1961. *The Ordeal of Gilbert
Pinfold* appeared in 1957, the *Life of Ronald Knox* in 1959 and *A Little
Learning*, Waugh's last book and the first volume of a projected
autobiography, in 1964. Evelyn Waugh was received into the
Roman Catholic Church in 1930 and his biography of the
Elizabethan Jesuit martyr, *Edmund Campion*, was awarded the
Hawthornden Prize in 1936. For many years he lived with his wife
and six children in the West Country. He died in 1966.

Waugh said of his work: 'I regard writing not as investigation of
character but as an exercise in the use of language, and with this I
am obsessed. I have no technical psychological interest. It is drama,
speech and events that interest me.' Mark Amory called Evelyn
Waugh 'one of the five best novelists in the English language this
century', while Harold Acton described him as having 'the sharp
eye of a Hogarth alternating with that of the Ancient Mariner'.

Robert Murray Davis is Professor Emeritus of English at the University of Oklahoma. His books include *Evelyn Waugh, Writer* (1981), *Evelyn Waugh and the Forms of His Time* (1989), *Brideshead Revisited: The Past Redeemed* (1990), *Outside the Lines: Poems* (1990), *Playing Cowboys: Low Culture and High Art in the Western* (1992), *Mid-Lands: A Family Album* (1992) and *Mischief in the Sun: The Making and Unmaking of 'The Loved One'* (1999). His prose and poetry have been published in England, Canada, France, Hungary and Slovakia as well as the USA. He has also compiled bibliographies of Evelyn Waugh (1972; 1981; 1986) and Donald Barthelme (1977), and the collections: *Evelyn Waugh* (1969), *The Novel: Modern Essays in Criticism* (1969), *Modern British Short Novels* (1972), *John Steinbeck* (1972), *Evelyn Waugh, Apprentice: The Early Writing (1910–1927)* (1985) and *Owen Wister's West* (1987).

EVELYN WAUGH

A Handful of Dust

Edited with an Introduction and Notes by
ROBERT MURRAY DAVIS

PENGUIN BOOKS

PENGUIN BOOKS

Published by the Penguin Group
Penguin Books Ltd, 80 Strand, London WC2R 0RL, England
Penguin Putnam Inc., 375 Hudson Street, New York, New York 10014, USA
Penguin Books Australia Ltd, 250 Camberwell Road, Camberwell, Victoria 3124, Australia
Penguin Books Canada Ltd, 10 Alcorn Avenue, Toronto, Ontario, Canada M4V 3B2
Penguin Books India (P) Ltd, 11 Community Centre, Panchsheel Park, New Delhi – 110 017, India
Penguin Books (NZ) Ltd, Cnr Rosedale and Airborne Roads, Albany, Auckland, New Zealand
Penguin Books (South Africa) (Pty) Ltd, 24 Sturdee Avenue, Rosebank 2196, South Africa

Penguin Books Ltd, Registered Offices: 80 Strand, London WC2R 0RL, England

www.penguin.com

First published by Chapman and Hall 1934
Published in Penguin Books 1951
This annotated edition published 1997
Reprinted in Penguin Classics 2000

17

Copyright © Evelyn Waugh, 1934
Introduction and notes copyright © Robert Murray Davis, 1997
All rights reserved

The moral right of the editor has been asserted

Typeset in 10.5 / 12.5 pt Monotype Baskerville
Typeset by Rowland Phototypesetting Ltd, Bury St Edmunds, Suffolk
Printed in England by Clays Ltd, St Ives plc

ISBN-13: 978–0–141–18396–1

www.greenpenguin.co.uk

Penguin Books is committed to a sustainable future
for our business, our readers and our planet.
The book in your hands is made from paper
certified by the Forest Stewardship Council.

CONTENTS

Bibliographical Note	vii
Introduction	ix
Further Reading	xxviii
Note on the Text	xxx
A HANDFUL OF DUST	I
Notes	229
Appendix I: Alternative Ending	241
Appendix II: Variant Readings	252

BIBLIOGRAPHICAL NOTE

The following is a list of abbreviated titles used in this edition:

HD: *A Handful of Dust*, first British edition (Chapman and Hall, 1934).

Diaries: The Diaries of Evelyn Waugh, ed. Michael Davie (Weidenfeld and Nicolson, 1976).

Letters: The Letters of Evelyn Waugh, ed. Mark Amory (Weidenfeld and Nicolson, 1980).

Essays: The Essays, Articles and Reviews of Evelyn Waugh, ed. Donat Gallagher (Methuen, 1983).

CH: Evelyn Waugh: The Critical Heritage, ed. Martin Stannard (Routledge and Kegan Paul, 1984).

INTRODUCTION

Evelyn Waugh's fourth novel, *A Handful of Dust*, takes its title from T. S. Eliot's quintessentially modernist poem *The Waste Land*.[1] While less aggressively experimental in technique and less comprehensive in thematic and historical range than the poem, the novel is in some ways a deeper indictment of contemporary civilization because it chronicles social and moral disintegration so pervasive that the characters are unaware of it and the omniscient authorial voice reveals it primarily through implication. The result is a book that Frank Kermode has called 'one of the most distinguished novels of the century'.[2]

In retrospect, it is less surprising that Waugh completed work of this stature by the time he was thirty than that he wrote at all. Seven years earlier Waugh had been fired from the last of a series of dismal teaching jobs and, 'feeling rather like a housemaid who has been caught stealing gloves', concluded that 'the time has arrived to set about being a man of letters'.[3] By the time he was ready to begin writing *A Handful of Dust*, he had published six books in five years and had a seventh nearly ready to go to press. His opinions were widely disseminated and well remunerated by the daily newspapers. Rebecca West and other critics spoke highly of his books and even more highly of his future.[4]

Waugh was far from solemn about his career, but he conducted it efficiently and, if an early article based on his own experience is credible, almost cynically. 'Art', he wrote, especially literature, 'offers scope for profound and prolonged laziness, and in the event of success gives rewards quite out of proportion to industry.'[5]

In fact he worked very hard, but in military terms he was a good tactician with little grasp of strategy. In 1928, a year after his reluctant decision to become a writer, he published a centenary biography of Dante Gabriel Rossetti. *Decline and Fall*, a novel very loosely based on his first teaching job in Wales, followed six months later. It is far more light-hearted than the title from Gibbon suggests. In fact, Waugh felt it necessary to point out in the Author's Note to the first edition that the novel was supposed to be funny.[6]

He also married Evelyn Gardner and engaged A. D. Peters as his literary agent. The second was the wiser move. At this point Waugh needed money so badly that he was even willing to write about cricket, which he hated, or about anything else which could find a market. When an editor read 'mothers' for 'manners' in accepting Waugh's offer to write about 'Matter-of-Fact Manners of the New Age', he dutifully wrote about mothers. Peters and his associates were able to sell most of the 'STUFF' that Waugh sent them and very ably managed Waugh's campaign to become a spokesman for the younger generation.[7]

That campaign culminated in the extremely successful novel *Vile Bodies* (1930), a *roman-à-clef* about the Bright Young People among whom Waugh had moved in London. This novel reflected its title – from Philippians 3:21 and the Anglican burial service – somewhat more accurately than *Decline and Fall* had done with Gibbon. This was due in part to the collapse of his marriage, and in part to the sense that he belonged to 'a crazy and sterile generation'.[8] However, there is little sense of this theme in *Labels* (1930), the travel book based on his belated honeymoon trip to the Mediterranean. In fact, the book contains no mention of Evelyn Gardner, and the American edition of the book was called *A Bachelor Abroad*.

The success of *Vile Bodies* made Waugh's 'STUFF' much more profitable, but he still seemed to have very little sense of direction, as a man of letters, and he was writing about his life almost as fast as he could live it. Clearly he was in need not just of tactics but of a strategy. For the next few years he was in the process of finding one. In September 1930 he was received into the Roman Catholic Church and shortly thereafter left for Ethiopia to attend the coronation of Emperor Haile Selassie. The travel book, *Remote People* (1931), and the novel, *Black Mischief* (1932), which resulted from that trip both reveal a concern for style and a seriousness of purpose new for Waugh. He began to find the stance of spokesman for youth increasingly awkward and turned his coat to advantage in an article titled, 'Why Glorify Youth?' He admitted that 'The Youth boom has been very convenient for young men like myself who have made a living out of it, but it seems to me time that criticism adopted some more significant standard.'[9]

In December 1932, perhaps in search of that standard, Waugh embarked on a three-month trip to what was then British Guiana with ill-defined or at any rate unexplained purposes. On the journey to the interior, he encountered a man named Christie who professed to see the auras of his visitors, viewed the choir of the blessed singing before the throne of God, and confidently predicted the end of the world. A little later, Waugh found himself stranded in Boa Vista, the inaptly named town in Brazil which he had idealized as a centre of ease and civilization and was to transmute into Tony's 'City' in *A Handful of Dust*. There he wrote 'The Man Who Liked Dickens', a story about an explorer imprisoned to read to a madman in the jungle. He wrote to his agent that it was 'first-rate' and should command a large fee in America – which it duly received.[10]

By the time he returned to England Waugh had discovered a theme to give some coherence to his body of work. In *Ninety-Two Days*, the travel book he wrote before beginning *A Handful of Dust*, he denied that he had taken the trip for specifically literary purposes.

> One does not travel, any more than one falls in love, to collect material. It is simply part of one's life . . . for myself and many better than me, there is a fascination in distant and barbarous places, and particularly in the borderlands of conflicting cultures and states of development, where ideas, uprooted from their traditions, become oddly changed in transplantation. It is there that I find the experiences vivid enough to demand translation into literary form.[11]

This passage illustrates Waugh's ability to describe a temporary arrangement as if it were chiselled in stone. This was in fact only his second trip to 'distant and barbarous places', and his efforts to secure commissions from editors make it obvious that he intended to write about it.

However, he had recently been forced by a Catholic editor's attack on *Black Mischief* to reconsider not only that novel but his position as a Catholic writer. In a letter to the Cardinal Archbishop of Westminster defending himself against charges of obscenity and blasphemy, he argued that 'The story deals with the conflict of civilization, with all its attendant and deplorable ills, and barbarism.'[12]

He rather overstates the novel's case for civilization, but the apologia may have given him the idea for 'Out of Depth', a story he wrote before he finished *Ninety-Two Days*. Rip Van Winkle, the central character of the story, is displaced from his sterile and fashionable existence forward in time to a shattered London whose inhabitants have degenerated into barbarism. Submerged in delirium more fully rendered than the explorer's in 'The Man Who Liked Dickens', Rip emerges only after perceiving 'a shape in chaos' at a Roman Catholic Mass.[13] The religious theme is at most implied in *A Handful of Dust*, but the fantastic story anticipates a major theme in the novel.

Of course, Waugh could draw on more than the trip to British Guiana and his growing interest in the theme of civilization versus barbarism. As in his first three novels, Waugh drew incidents and characters from his experience and circle of acquaintances. Readers familiar with Waugh's life have assumed that Brenda's affair with Beaver is based on Evelyn Gardner's with John Heygate. Four decades after the novel was published, Heygate wrote that 'One realizes one was the rather feeble villain in *A Handful of Dust*.'[14] Heygate may have underestimated the incidence of adultery in Waugh's circle. As Waugh began the novel, he said that it was 'first about sponger [Murrough O'Brien] and then about some imaginary people who are happy to be married but not for long'.[15] He worried that Lord Brownlow 'will think it is about him – it isn't but bits of it are like'. He did admit that Marjorie's Pekinese was drawn directly from Phillis de Janzé's.[16]

Furthermore, though Waugh was far from being a social realist, his work shows that he was aware of economic and political developments. In 1932 he had published a short story first titled 'The Patriotic Honeymoon' (that is, taken at home rather than abroad) and then 'Love in the Slump'. The story presents the marriage of Tom and Angela Trench-Troubridge as 'completely typical of all that is most unremarkable in modern social conditions'.[17] The two marry out of a sense of desperation on her side, and bewildered acquiescence to 'one of the few bright fragments remaining from his glamorous [undergraduate] past'[18] on his. They are separated by accident, and Tom discovers the pleasures of hunting on his host's new mare, while Angela has very satisfactory sex with the same man – who gives them a cottage near his estate which 'would be such a good place for her to go sometimes when she wanted a change'.[19] In retrospect, the story is almost a negative image of *A Handful of Dust*. Tom, the Beaverish Londoner with neither qualities nor prospects, is cuckolded by a lively country squire, a counter-Tony, in a cottage which, like Mrs Beaver's flat, is 'very suitable for base love'.

Even Waugh's most feckless social butterflies can be vaguely aware of social and economic conditions. One of the Londoners in *Black Mischief* remarks to a character just returned from abroad that 'Everyone's got very poor and it makes them duller,' and mentions 'something about a gold standard'.[20] She is talking about England's going off the gold standard in 1931.

In *A Handful of Dust*, economic conditions strongly affect the plot, though they do not drive it. John Beaver is 'London's only spare man' because the slump ended his job with an advertising agency and, 'Since then no one had been able to find anything for him to do.' The necessity of paying death duties has left Tony's estate in relatively straitened circumstances, and a second imposition of these taxes after Tony is declared legally dead leaves the heirs only a little less impoverished than they had always been.

Even the trip to Brazil has analogues outside Waugh's direct experience. Peter Fleming had already made an expedition to Brazil to search for a lost English explorer, described in *Brazilian Adventure*. Before Waugh left for South America, he consulted Fleming about 'equipment for forests'.[21] After returning he praised Fleming's book, though he objected to the author's 'awareness that the spirit of adventure often results in literary trash'.[22] Perhaps Waugh had cured himself with his own very early illustrated story about a rescue from the Brazilian jungle, 'In Quest of Thomas Lee'.[23]

*

By the end of 1933 Waugh had assembled the materials from which to shape his novel and he had settled in Fez, Morocco, to begin work on the book for which he had no definite title or plot. His account of the composition of *A Handful of Dust* is much clearer than the actual process seems to have been. The novel, he said, 'began at the end' with 'The Man Who Liked Dickens'. But later:

> the idea kept working in my mind. I wanted to discover how the prisoner got there, and eventually the thing grew into a study of other sorts of savages at home and the civilized man's helpless plight among them.[24]

In the long view, this statement is probably true, but it is certainly misleading. Ten months after writing the short story, he wrote to A. D. Peters that, though he might use the story, he had no idea how the novel would end.[25] In fact, he did not yet have a title: the manuscript is headed 'NOVEL (as yet unnamed)'.[26] Even after finishing the draft through to the end of what is now 'English Gothic – II', he was not sure what would happen in the next half.[27]

For the most part, however, his spirits were high. In rather pious letters to Katharine Asquith and overtly bawdy letters to Lady Mary Lygon he commented on the progress of the novel. It seemed 'faultless of its kind', he commented to Mrs Asquith, but 'Very difficult to write because for the first time I am trying to deal with normal people instead of eccentrics. Comic English character parts too easy when one gets to be thirty.'[28] He told Lady Mary that his 'filthy novel' was 'excellent – very grim'; later he called it 'My good taste book'.[29]

At this point in Waugh's career his lack of a clear goal was no deterrent to progress. Years later, he said that early in his career he 'had the facility . . . to sit down at my table, set a few characters on the move, write 3,000 words a day, and note with surprise what happened'.[30] By the time he had finished John Andrew's death scene he was complaining that 'The novel drags on at 10,000 words a week'.[31] In late January, a typescript of what is now chapters one and two reached Peters, and by 6 February Peters had received typescript up to the point of Mrs Rattery's arrival at Hetton. By 10 February Waugh had finished what was then called Book I –

through to the end of 'English Gothic – II' – and instructed Peters to inquire about serialization, offering to write another 5,000 words to round off the story.[32]

Two weeks later Waugh was back in England, announcing his intention to remain at the Easton Court Hotel, Chagford (for some years Waugh's favourite refuge for writing), until he finished the novel. By then it had a title – or two titles: 'A Handful of Ashes' and, in a postscript to the same letter, 'A Handful of Dust'.[33] He said nothing about his plans for the rest of the novel, but by this time he must have had them clearly in mind, for the manuscript of the last three parts is very clean, with just enough revision to indicate that it was not recopied.

His contention that the novel was written to lead into the short story was by this time obviously true, for he used the typescript of 'The Man Who Liked Dickens' for major portions of the manuscript of chapter six. He probably finished the brief chapter seven in March, for by mid-April he had corrected proofs of the first half. By early May he had written the ending for the serial (titled 'A Flat in London'), printed at the end of this volume and at the end of the 1964 Uniform Edition.[34]

The serial differs from the novel in tone and in many details, most obviously in the conclusion. One might ask why Waugh bothered to reprint the alternative ending, which seems to have been written out of financial rather than artistic necessity. He provided one answer in the 1964 Preface: it was 'a curiosity'. Other motives are possible. The 'alternative ending', and indeed the whole serial version, may have represented to Waugh a kind of alternative fictional universe to *A Handful of Dust*.[35] 'A Flat in London', in the body as well as the conclusion of the story, embodies a system of values and sanctions which, ironically, show English society decaying more sordidly, if less spectacularly, than in the novel or in Eliot's poem.[36]

In some ways, the novel embodied a bleaker vision than the poem, which ends with the Sanskrit words 'Shantih shantih shantih', implying at least the possibility of salvation. The novel rejects even that faint consolation. Waugh may have been drawing upon the whole story of the Cumean Sybil, merely referred to in Eliot's epigraph from the *Satyricon* of Petronius, who asked Apollo for the same number of years of life as the number of grains of dust (or sand) that she could hold in her hand. The wish was granted, but she forgot to ask for eternal youth and was condemned to dwindle, with age, into little more than a voice. That version of the story comes from Ovid's *Metamorphoses* (XII, 115-82). The Sybil's fate anticipates that of Tony, condemned to read aloud until his voice is extinguished.

This conclusion is harsher than Eliot's, perhaps because Waugh had a more coherent view of theology than Eliot did before his own conversion. Writing after the Second World War, at a period when he was more overtly concerned with religious values, Waugh commented that *A Handful of Dust* 'dealt entirely with behaviour. It was humanist and said all I had to say about humanism.'[37] Readers for whom 'humanism' is an honorific term may be confused by this remark; the tone of the novel is certain to bewilder them. For example, Waugh regarded his friend Cyril Connolly as an archetype of the liberal humanist, and while Connolly thought *A Handful of Dust* Waugh's finest novel to date, he complained that it was 'the first of Evelyn Waugh's to have a bore for a hero'.[38] The anonymous reader of a library copy of the novel had similar expectations about what the central character should be like and wrote 'Hurrah! At last' in the margin when Tony finally asserts himself and refuses to sell Hetton in order to buy Beaver for Brenda. It is easy to see why readers sympathize with Tony, and in the Preface to the 1964 edition Waugh referred to him as a 'betrayed romantic'. David Bittner goes even further, arguing not only that 'Tony is a hapless victim and that he is a good character' but that, when imprisoned by Mr Todd, 'it is Tony's heroic faith which helps him accept his fate for the foreseeable future'.[39] For that matter, he is the only character in the novel who gives evidence of having virtue, of any sort. If everyone else is wrong, then Tony must be right.

The flaw in this reasoning comes from a problem of definition. For Waugh, humanism is antithetical to the religious view of life.[40]

Writing just after his conversion to Roman Catholicism, he asserted that 'in the present phase of European history the essential issue is no longer between Catholicism, on one side, and Protestantism, on the other, but between Christianity and Chaos'. Further, 'civilization' – by which he meant European civilization – 'has not in itself the power of survival. It came into being through Christianity, and without it has no significance or power to command allegiance.'[41]

Christianity is not entirely missing from the novel, but it is clearly vestigial. The chief symbol of this decline is Hetton Abbey, 'formerly one of the notable houses of the county', until it was razed and rebuilt by Tony's great-grandfather – as the American edition puts it – 'in the late generation of the Gothic revival, when the movement had lost its fantasy and become structurally logical and stodgy'.[42] Waugh does not specifically identify the original structure as medieval; his point is not merely that a building of historical and aesthetic significance has been destroyed and replaced by a grotesque version of little historic value, but that the religious heritage of the building, and by extension of England itself, has been lost. Waugh may have admired aspects of Ruskin's thought, but his comment that the way to beautify Oxford was to dynamite many of the buildings shows that he deplored at least some of its effects.[43]

Tony's Victorian ancestor destroyed the building. Tony ends the practice of holding daily prayers in the chapel, and at church his attention shifts easily from divine judgement to renovations in Hetton's plumbing. Even when confronted with the death of his son, he remarks that 'the last thing one wants to talk about at a time like this is religion'. Nor are traditional virtues much regarded – the bedroom named after Sir Galahad, purest of Arthur's knights, is so uncomfortable that it is reserved for the most unwelcome guests.

Tony is faithful to his vision of Hetton, but that vision is based upon a false and sentimental conception. Readers can sympathize with Tony's personal unhappiness when his 'whole Gothic world had come to grief', but in the context of Hetton, made inescapable by the names of the bedrooms, Tony is a very feeble imitation of King Arthur – though his dalliance with Thérèse de Vitré is more in the spirit of Malory than of Tennyson – and John Beaver is unrecognizable as Lancelot. There is no Round Table, and Tony goes in quest not of the Holy Grail but of another way of escaping the politely savage world of Brenda's London. Brenda's infidelity destroys Hetton as Guinevere's did Camelot, but only for Tony.

Oddly enough, Brenda's 'Thank God' at learning that her child, not her lover, has died does not wholly destroy sympathy for her. Jock and the reader know what she said, but later Waugh describes her at Hetton, moving slowly and expressionlessly up the stairs, 'the stained glass windows glowing and sparkling all about her', in an echo of the scene in which John Beaver first sees her, to look out at 'the naked tossing trees' and 'the maelstroms of dust and leaf' in 'the troubled landscape'. And when Beaver abandons her, she may have received her deserts, but, the repetition of the line she used twice in chapter two, 'Me? Oh, I'm all right', indicates that she is forlorn.

If readers cannot entirely sympathize with Tony or condemn Brenda, conventional morality and religion offer no reliable clues to the novel's tone and scale of values. Perhaps, as Waugh said in 1947, only 'behaviour' is left, and when he wrote *A Handful of Dust* he was still trying 'to distil comedy and sometimes tragedy from the knockabout farce of people's outward behaviour'. However, he denied that he was a satirist because:

> Satire is a matter of period. It flourishes in a stable society and presupposes homogeneous moral standards . . . It is aimed at inconsistency and hypocrisy. It exposes polite cruelty and folly by exaggerating them. It seeks to produce shame. All this has no place . . . where vice no longer pays lip service to virtue.[44]

In Waugh's London, the distinction between vice and virtue no longer exists for the background chorus of gossips. Waugh had said that he was giving up 'comic character parts', but many of the characters are defined by and limited to their names. Some characters partake of but transcend the label assigned to them, like Tony Last and Mr Todd, a name which can refer to Beatrix Potter's fox or to the German word for 'death'.[45] Others, like the surprisingly

American Souki de Foucauld-Esterhazy, are merely names. Even
when characters are more developed, it is impossible to take ser-
iously someone named Polly Cockpurse – especially in view of her
former profession as a procuress – and the way in which she is
introduced parenthetically puts her firmly outside any possible
moral scheme:

> ... her first steps to eminence had been in circles so obscure that
> they had made her no enemies in the world to which she aspired;
> some time ago she had married a good-natured Earl, whom nobody
> else happened to want at the time; since then she had scaled all but
> the highest peaks of every social mountain.

Waugh had been tempted to go still further. In a manuscript passage which survived into the serial version, he continued with:

> She enjoyed herself hugely and did very little harm to anyone else.
> But men, except the very young and the very old for whom she had
> the glamour of the reputation she was trying to shed, mostly found
> her a bore.[46]

However, he deleted the passage before book publication, possibly
to avoid making her merely comic.

The same motive seems to have operated when Waugh trimmed
back the first description of the Old Hundredth. He retained the
club's eventful history, and in manuscript and serial continued,
after 'an unimpeded flow of dubious, alcoholic preparations', with:

> Mrs Weybridge, founder and martyr of its fortunes, is dead, but she
> has left behind her a vast and handsome progeny to carry on her work;
> while some married into the aristocracy and limited their interest in
> the concern, others grew up to take their places, and it was a younger
> son, still wearing the short black coat in which during the day he
> practised as a barrister, who admitted Tony and Jock to the ram-
> shackle building.[47]

By cutting this passage and adding the information that the patrons
are frequently robbed, the novel emphasizes the pathos of Tony's
attempt to enjoy himself and the essential sordidness of still another
aspect of life in London.[48]

The London characters have no taste, only an eye for fashion, and no morals whatever. Adultery is not a sin or even an indiscretion. 'Old Sybil' is the woman of first choice for a liaison, however brief, and she refuses to help Tony provide divorce evidence only because it is momentarily inconvenient. Adultery helps Mrs Beaver to let her flats, gives John Beaver new status, and provides the gossips with a new and welcome topic, far more interesting than if Brenda 'had at last broken away with Jock Grant-Menzies or Robin Beaseley or any other young buck with whom nearly everyone had had a crack one time or another'. Brenda begins the affair partly out of boredom and partly because Beaver seems indifferent to her. She rubs against Beaver's cheek, 'in the way she had', in the same manner and in the same words as she had done with Tony.

At times, the characters employ the vocabulary associated with traditional standards, but it has been emptied of content. 'Hell' is invoked almost a dozen times in the course of the novel, but it is used to describe minor inconveniences or, at worst, the embarrassment of faked adultery. On the first page, Mrs Beaver remarks that 'The fire never reached the bedrooms, I am afraid', and then encourages her son to eat yoghurt which she describes as nasty. Brenda characterizes Tony's response to betrayal as 'brooding'.

The inversion of traditional labels is strongest in 'English Gothic – II'. Tony's divorce lawyer 'had not had Tony's opportunities to contract the habit of loving and trusting Brenda', in a phrase echoed from the end of the previous chapter. One of the detectives hired to provide evidence of Tony's infidelity complains, 'Sets a nasty, respectable note bringing a kid into it.' One of the bar girls says of Milly that 'Lots of the girls here are all right to have a lark with in town, but you have to have a *lady* for a divorce.' Later the appalling Dan confides that Milly attracts a higher class of people 'like you and me'. Dan's friend is by Tony's usual standards incredibly vulgar, but Tony wonders 'whether he was as amiable when people he did not know were brought over unexpectedly to Hetton', without staying for the obvious answer in the negative. Brenda's brother finds 'even the Christian era full of significance'. No one else seems to find significance in anything.

*

Even those readers accustomed to discerning a structure of values in the most experimental fiction are sometimes puzzled by novels like *A Handful of Dust*. If the characters have no values, or only shallow ones, and the narrator seems to refuse to provide them, then two alternatives are left: either the story has no inherent structure and meaning, or these principles of coherence are established through other means.

One way of discovering these principles is to look at the differences between serial and novel versions. The fact that it was possible for Waugh to alter not only plot, but tone and theme, casually and significantly raises useful questions about the construction of the book. Critics have argued that, as Rose Macaulay put it, the serial ending 'has a closer coherence with the rest of the book',[49] and generations of students startled by the shift of setting from England to South America have felt that the novel breaks in half.

Two novelists whose work Waugh praised highly have objected to the South American episodes without, apparently, knowing anything about the serial. P. G. Wodehouse huffed, 'What a snare this travelling business is to the young writer. He goes to some blasted jungle or other and imagines that everybody will be interested in it.'[50] Henry Yorke, better known as the novelist Henry Green, objected more to the shift in tone. He praised the English scenes for presenting 'a real picture of people one has met and may at any moment meet again', but felt that 'the end is so fantastic that it throws the rest out of proportion'.

Waugh's response seems to have more to do with theme than with structure. He agreed that:

> the Todd episode is fantastic. It is a 'conceit' in the Webster manner – wishing to bring Tony to a sad end I made it an elaborate and improbable one. I think too the sentimental episode with Thérèse in the ship is probably a mistake. But the Amazon stuff had to be there. The scheme was a Gothic man in the hands of savages – first Mrs Beaver etc. then the real ones, finally the silver foxes at Hetton. All that quest for a city seems to me justifiable symbolism.[51]

Waugh had attempted to embody this intention in the novel's external structure. In this, as in most of his novels, he made final decisions about chapter divisions and titles after he completed at least one draft and, in the case of *Brideshead Revisited*, fifteen years after the first edition appeared. He experimented with various principles of division as he wrote the novel. By the time he reached what is now chapter five he had settled on its title, 'In Search of a City', though he numbered it 'Book Two'. 'À Côté de Chez Todd' (in Waugh's fractured French) and 'English Gothic – III' followed.

The current divisions and titles support his theme. The first and sixth chapters describe two strongholds of barbarism, and Waugh clearly expects the reader to compare their essential heartlessness, materialism and lack of values. 'Hard Cheese on Tony' and 'In Search of a City' show the death of two versions of a dream. The second, fourth and seventh chapters use the words 'English Gothic' in their titles, but the meaning changes significantly in each repetition. At first, the words seems merely to describe the architecture of Hetton, but as chapter two develops, they encompass Tony's way of life and that of his class. The second use of the title apparently describes English divorce proceedings of the period, in which absurd chivalry and ritual adultery render divorce respectable, formalized and dull. The third use refers to Hetton again, but a Hetton occupied by Tony's worthy but deluded successors.

For purposes of mathematical symmetry, chapters six and seven should be reversed. Thematically the current order seems to offer consolation: Tony's living death is followed by the heirs' plans for the future. The final chapter demonstrates that, unlike characters in tragedy, the Lasts have learned nothing; that delusions as well as property are handed down; and that the process of social entropy continues.

Waugh did not rely solely on external structural devices to give coherence to the novel. Well before he formulated the chapter titles, he had carefully interwoven parallel scenes, characters and verbal motifs to provide an internal structure to the novel. Most of these also reinforce the novel's ironic tone. For example, the visit to Hetton of Mrs Rattery, cool, reflective, reserved and controlled, is parallel to that of the emotionally extravagant Jenny Adbul Akbar. Jenny unwittingly prophesies the succession of Teddy

Last when she gets Tony's name wrong. Mrs Rattery, like Mme Sosostris in *The Waste Land*, has a 'wicked pack of cards' (1.46), but she uses them in an attempt to console rather than fraudulently to predict.

Perhaps the most startling use of the device is in the pairing of John Andrew Last and John Beaver, not only for the confusion in their first names but in Brenda's maternal failure towards the first and quasi-maternal interest in the second. John Andrew is also paired with Winnie, not merely because one falls from a horse and the other from her fairy bicycle, but because both are literal-minded enough to ask very inconvenient questions. John Andrew's death causes his parents' marriage to fail and Winnie's surprise appearance prevents it from being dissolved.

In chapters five and six, the comparisons become more obvious and painfully ironic as Waugh uses the apparent differences of Brazil to emphasize the realities behind the pretensions in the manners and language of the English. For example in chapter five pigs are hunted and eaten in the jungle. In England, in Jock's question about the basic pig in Parliament, they are merely a paper concept.

Characters and situations are not only paired, as in the counterpoint of Brenda's and Tony's increasing isolation, but conflated, as in Tony's delirium. Unlike Winnie at Brighton, John Beaver is allowed to bathe, 'for the time is different in Brazil'. Brenda appears in a gown like Rosa's which has been obtained from Polly. The bus that occasioned John Andrew's death merges with the mechanical mice which frightened the Macushi Indians and, in chapter six, Brenda. And it is in delirium, and only there, that Tony is able to formulate, to an unseen audience of Londoners 'walking round in a circle' as in Eliot's poem, his understanding of what has happened:

> I know you are friends of my wife and that is why you will not listen to me. But be careful. She will say nothing cruel, she will not raise her voice, there will be no hard words. She hopes you will be great friends afterwards as before. But she will leave you. She will go away quietly during the night. She will take her hammock and her rations of farine . . . Listen to me. I know I am not clever but that is no reason why we should forget all courtesy. Let us kill in the gentlest manner. I will tell you what I have learned in the forest, where time is different. There is no

City. Mrs Beaver has covered it with chromium plating and converted it into flats. Three guineas a week with a separate bathroom. Very suitable for base love. And Polly will be there. She and Mrs Beaver under the fallen battlements . . .

Cured of his fever by Mr Todd's medicines, Tony relapses into his usual state of dulled acceptance of the unfamiliar. Like many readers of the novel, he does not realize the most devastating parallel in the novel: himself and Mr Todd. Instead of 'a trans-figured Hetton', he finds Mr Todd's house, where, eating farine and tasso, he is condemned to 'recklessly mixing starch and protein' in defiance of his and Brenda's diet at the beginning of the novel. There he is forced to read aloud, as earlier he had unwittingly forced Brenda to listen and then failed to listen to her. He is kept captive. Brenda, at least in the imaginations of the London gossips, had been 'the imprisoned princess of fairy story'. Most significantly, by juxtaposing Tony's hallucination at the end of chapter five and the drab reality of Todd's place, Waugh emphasizes the emptiness of Tony's ideal and presents not a sentimental, Ruskinian, Gothic estate but an irreducibly feudal community, based on Todd's real patriarchal authority and upon force. Years later, in *Helena*, one of the characters speaks of power without grace.[52] That is what Tony finds in the Brazilian jungle: secular feudalism unredeemed by the saving grace of Christianity, without which, to use Waugh's com-ment on his conversion, 'it has no significance or power to com-mand allegiance'. The only spirit informing Todd's clearing is a limited and sentimental understanding of Dickens, whose writings Waugh regarded as limited and sentimental.

Ironically, therefore, Tony has found the reality behind the delus-ive object of his quest. Having sought the form without awareness of spiritual content, an embroidered Camelot rather than the Grail, he is left bound in undifferentiated time. He is, like Ovid's Sybil, reduced to a voice, without hope of rescue or redemption.

In the final chapter, the wisdom of the children of Mammon is proven correct. Jock's satisfaction at having done something for his constituents has kept him in Parliament. Brenda marries Jock Grant-Menzies, as 'Everybody thought she would.' As Jenny had unconsciously predicted, Teddy Last will be master of an imitation Gothic Hetton reduced still further by death duties. And all of the characters more or less get what they wanted all along, whether or not they realize it.

Notes

1. The title is taken from lines 27–30 of T. S. Eliot's *The Waste Land* (Faber and Faber, 1922), which serve as the epigraph to the novel.
2. Frank Kermode, *Puzzles and Epiphanies* (Chilmark, 1962), p. 171.
3. *Diaries*, 20 and 21 February 1927, p. 281.
4. Rebecca West, 'A Letter from Abroad', *Bookman*, vol. 71 (March 1930), pp. 83–6; reprinted in *Ending in Earnest* (Doran, Doubleday, 1931). For other contemporary estimates of Waugh's books, see *CH*.
5. *Essays*, p. 49.
6. *Decline and Fall* (Chapman and Hall, 1928).
7. Letters to A. D. Peters and W. N. Roughead, *Letters*, p. 30. Waugh's letters to the same men, October 1928 to January 1929, are summarized in *Catalogue*, E85–96. 'Matter-of-Fact Mothers of the New Age', *Evening Standard*, 8 April 1929, p. 7.
8. 'The War and the Younger Generation', *Essays*, pp. 61–3.
9. *Essays*, pp. 125–8.
10. Waugh, letter to A. D. Peters, 15 February 1933. The story appeared in *Hearst's International* combined with *Cosmopolitan*, vol. 95 (September 1933), pp. 54–7, 127–30. The story was reprinted, with minor variations, in the November *Nash's Pall Mall Magazine*.
11. *Ninety Two Days*, p. 6. In 1946 Waugh put the idea more bluntly: 'If you hear a novelist say he needs to collect "copy", be sure he is no good'. *Essays*, p. 301.
12. *Essays*, p. 77.
13. *Mr Loveday's Little Outing and Other Sad Stories* (Chapman and Hall, 1936), p. 136.
14. *Diaries*, p. 796.
15. *Letters*, p. 83.
16. *Letters*, p. 85.
17. *Mr Loveday's Little Outing and Other Sad Stories* (Chapman and Hall, 1936), p. 167.
18. *Ibid*, p. 170.
19. *Ibid*, p. 183.
20. *Black Mischief* (Chapman and Hall, 1962), p. 233.
21. *Diaries*, p. 355.
22. *Essays*, 136. See also A. S. G. Edwards, 'A Source for Waugh's *A Handful of Dust*', *Modern Fiction Studies* vol. 22 no. 2. (Summer 1976), pp. 242–4.
23. Robert Murray Davis, *A Catalogue of the Evelyn Waugh Collection at the Humanities Research Center*, The University of Texas at Austin (Whitston, 1981), A3.
24. 'Fan-Fare', *Essays*, p. 303.

25. Letter to A. D. Peters, early 1934. See *Catalogue*, E234.

26. The manuscript of *A Handful of Dust* is now at the Humanities Research Center of the University of Texas at Austin. *Catalogue*, A12.

27. Letter to A. D. Peters, *c.* 10 February 1934. *Catalogue*, E235.

28. *Letters*, p. 84.

29. *Letters*, pp. 84, 85.

30. *Vile Bodies* (Chapman and Hall, 1965), Preface, p. 7.

31. Letter to Katharine Asquith, *c.* 10 February 1934, *Letters*, p. 85.

32. *Catalogue*, E235.

33. Letter to A. D. Peters, *c.* 27 February 1934, *Letters*, p. 87, where Mark Amory dates it '[March? 1934]'.

34. Letter to A. D. Peters, *c.* 12 April 1934, *Catalogue*, E239. For the serial ending, letters to A. D. Peters, *c.* 27 February and *c.* 30 April 1934, E236, E240.

35. The 1988 motion picture of *A Handful of Dust* offers another vision of the novel. It is a thorough and honourable attempt to do justice to the novel, but it cannot reflect the complexity of the novel's themes, particularly the Gothic/religious theme.

36. For a discussion of the text of the entire serial version, see Robert Murray Davis, '*Harper's Bazaar* and *A Handful of Dust*' in *Philological Quarterly* vol. 48, no. 4 (1969), pp. 508–16. Waugh revised the serial ending for inclusion in *Mr Loveday's Little Outing and Other Sad Stories* (Chapman and Hall, 1936). See Robert Murray Davis, ' "A Flat in London" and "By Special Request": Some Variant Readings', *Papers of the Bibliographical Society of America*, vol. 69 (1975), pp. 565–8.

37. *Essays*, p. 304.

38. Cyril Connolly, 'The Novel-Addict's Cupboard' in *The Condemned Playground* (Macmillan, 1946), p. 116. The essay was originally published in January 1936.

39. David Bittner, 'Tony as Hero of *A Handful of Dust* or "Last" But Not Least', *Evelyn Waugh Newsletter and Studies* No. 1, vol. 28 (Spring 1994), p. 5. In 'Tony Last's Search for Order and Justice in *A Handful of Dust* ', *Evelyn Waugh Newsletter* No. 1, vol. 18 (Spring 1984), pp. 6–7, Pamela Johnson maintains that Tony 'is a sensitive, sharing, and gentle man' who searches for 'order and justice', however naïvely. Johnson also gives a useful summary of the comparisons and contrasts between Tony and Todd.

40. Waugh's essay on George Orwell, 'A New Humanism', is almost contemporaneous with his comment on *A Handful of Dust*. *Essays*, pp. 304–7.

41. *Essays*, pp. 103, 104.

42. *A Handful of Dust* (Farrar, Rinehart, 1934), p. 44.

43. *Letters*, p. 49.

44. *Essays*, pp. 303, 304.

45. Eric Korn, 'Remainders', *Times Literary Supplement*, 23–8 July 1988, p. 803.

46. 'A Flat in London', *Harper's Bazaar* June 1934, p. 138.

47. 'A Flat in London', *Harper's Bazaar* August 1934, p. 96.

48. A comparison of the Old Hundredth in this novel with the club of the same

name in *Brideshead Revisited* illustrates some of the ways in which setting helps to establish tone and character.

49. Rose Macaulay, 'Evelyn Waugh', *Horizon*, vol. 14 (December 1946); reprinted in *CH*, p. 158. Richard Wasson develops the point more fully in '*A Handful of Dust*: Critique of Victorianism' (*Modern Fiction Studies*, vol. 7, no. 4 (1961–2), pp. 327ff.), reprinted in James F. Carens, *Critical Essays on Evelyn Waugh* (G. K. Hall, 1987).

50. Quoted in Frances Donaldson, *P. G. Wodehouse* (Weidenfeld and Nicolson, 1982), p. 155.

51. Letter to Henry Yorke, September 1934, *Letters*, p. 88. Yorke's criticism is quoted in a note to Waugh's response.

52. *Helena* (Chapman and Hall, 1950), p. 198.

FURTHER READING

Two reference works offer a place to begin the study of Waugh and *A Handful of Dust: A Bibliography of Evelyn Waugh*, by Robert Murray Davis, Paul A. Doyle, Donat Gallagher, Charles E. Linck, Jr., and Winnifred M. Bogaards (Whitston, 1986) and *Evelyn Waugh: A Reference Guide*, by Margaret Morriss and D. J. Dooley (G. K. Hall, 1984). Lists of material published in the years since these books were completed can be found in *Evelyn Waugh Newsletter and Studies* as well as more general serial bibliographies. Stannard's *CH* reprints important early reviews and some later material on the novel.

There are at present three biographies: Christopher Sykes's *Evelyn Waugh: A Biography* (Collins, 1975), which is sketchy on the facts, and Martin Stannard's two volumes, *Evelyn Waugh: The Early Years, 1903–1939* (Dent, 1986) and *Evelyn Waugh: No Abiding City, 1939–1966* (Dent, 1992), which have more facts and interpretations than Sykes's biography, although both have been challenged by other students of Waugh's life and career. There is also Selina Hastings's *Evelyn Waugh: A Biography* (Sinclair-Stevenson, 1994).

Frederick J. Stopp's *Evelyn Waugh: Portrait of an Artist* (Chapman and Hall, 1958) is sensible and as thorough as a first book on an author can be. For a discussion of the composition of *HD* and other Waugh novels, see Robert Murray Davis, *Evelyn Waugh, Writer* (Pilgrim, 1981). Jeffrey Heath's *The Picturesque Prison: Evelyn Waugh and His Writing* (McGill-Queens, 1982) traces symbolic and thematic patterns in the novel. George McCartney's *Confused Roaring: Evelyn Waugh and the Modernist Tradition* (Indiana, 1987) deals with Waugh's ambivalence towards modernist literature and philosophy.

Leszek Kolek's ' "Uncinematic Devices" in Evelyn Waugh's *A Handful of Dust*' (*Literatur in Wissenschaft und Unterricht*, vol. 15, December 1982, pp. 353–65) and Robert Frick's 'Style and Structure in the Early Novels of Evelyn Waugh' (*Papers on Language and*

Literature, vol. 28, no. 4 (Fall 1992), pp. 417–41) explore narrative technique in the novel.

Richard Wasson's '*A Handful of Dust*: Critique of Victorianism' (*Modern Fiction Studies*, vol. 7, no. 2 (Winter 1961–2), pp. 327–37) deals with that broad theme. Wasson's insights are expanded in Peter Firchow's 'In Search of *A Handful of Dust*: The Literary Background of Evelyn Waugh's Novel' (*Journal of Modern Literature*, vol. 2, no. 3 (1971–2), pp. 406–16), in Nicholas Joost's '*A Handful of Dust*: Evelyn Waugh and the Novel of Manners' (*Papers on Language and Literature*, vol. 12, no. 2 (Spring 1976), pp. 177–96) and in Brooke Allen's 'The Man Who Didn't Like Dickens: Evelyn Waugh and Boz' (*Dickens Quarterly*, vol. 8 (December 1991), 155–62). Ann Pasternak Slater's 'Waugh's *A Handful of Dust*: Right Things in Wrong Places' (*Essays in Criticism*, vol. 32 (January 1982), pp. 48–68) traces the theme of misplaced things and values, especially the values of humanism.

NOTE ON THE TEXT

The text of this edition of *A Handful of Dust*, with minor emendations, is that of the first British edition, published by Chapman and Hall on 3 September 1934. Four more impressions were issued that month and another in October. The novel was reissued in the Chapman and Hall Modern Library in 1936 without alteration of type. A limited edition – twelve copies – was 'Reset and Reprinted, October 1937'. Subsequently the novel was issued in the Uniform Edition of 1948 and in the second Uniform Edition of 1964. The author's preface and 'Alternative Ending' were included in that edition; these texts are followed in the current edition. However, the 1964 edition introduced a number of errors and failed to correct at least one other – the 'John nodded' of all editions published during Waugh's lifetime should be 'Jock nodded' – and though the punctuation is heavier and more conventionally correct, notably in the dialogue, it seems less likely to represent Waugh's sense of rhythm and intonation than the first edition.

Farrar and Rinehart published the first American edition in 1934. The text, unaltered except for the correction of 'À Côté' to 'Du Côté' in the titles and running heads of chapters one and six, was issued by Little, Brown in 1944 and subsequently. The American edition varies from the first British edition in a number of ways, and probably derives from an earlier typescript version or from uncorrected proofs of the British first edition. The major variants are listed in the Appendix.

The manuscript of the novel, now at the Humanities Research Center of the University of Texas at Austin, is, if Waugh followed his usual practice of correcting heavily in first typescript, at least two typescript versions removed from the first British edition, with the exception of chapter six, which incorporates, with corrections, the carbon typescript of 'The Man Who Liked Dickens'. See my *Evelyn Waugh, Writer* for details about the process of composition.

For further details about the manuscript, see Robert Murray Davis, *A Catalogue of the Evelyn Waugh Collection at the Humanities Research Center, The University of Texas at Austin* (Whitston, 1981). For further details about paperback and other editions of the novel, see the *Bibliography*.

A HANDFUL OF DUST

BY

EVELYN WAUGH

'. . . I will show you something different from either
Your shadow at morning striding behind you
Or your shadow at evening rising to meet you ;
I will show you fear in a handful of dust.'

The Waste Land.

CHAPMAN AND HALL LTD.
LONDON

HETTON ABBEY

~ ·:· the seat of ·+·+·+· ~

ANTHONY LAST, ESQ^{re}

Contents

Chapter One
DU CÔTÉ DE CHEZ BEAVER   5

Chapter Two
ENGLISH GOTHIC   15

Chapter Three
HARD CHEESE ON TONY   65

Chapter Four
ENGLISH GOTHIC – II   127

Chapter Five
IN SEARCH OF A CITY   155

Chapter Six
DU CÔTÉ DE CHEZ TODD   207

Chapter Seven
ENGLISH GOTHIC – III   223

Chapter One

DU CÔTÉ DE CHEZ BEAVER

'Was anyone hurt?'

'No one I am thankful to say,' said Mrs Beaver, 'except two housemaids who lost their heads and jumped through a glass roof into the paved court. They were in no danger. The fire never reached the bedrooms I am afraid. Still, they are bound to need doing up, everything black with smoke and drenched in water and luckily they had that old-fashioned sort of extinguisher that ruins *everything*. One really cannot complain. The chief rooms were *completely* gutted and everything was insured. Sylvia Newport knows the people. I must get on to them this morning before that ghoul Mrs Shutter snaps them up.'

Mrs Beaver stood with her back to the fire, eating her morning yoghurt. She held the carton close under her chin and gobbled with a spoon.

'Heavens, how nasty this stuff is. I wish you'd take to it, John. You're looking so tired lately. I don't know how I should get through my day without it.'

'But, mumsy, I haven't as much to do as you have.'

'That's true, my son.'

John Beaver lived with his mother at the house in Sussex Gardens[1] where they had moved after his father's death. There was little in it to suggest the austerely elegant interiors which Mrs Beaver planned for her customers. It was crowded with the unsaleable furniture of two larger houses, without pretension to any period, least of all to the present. The best pieces and those which had sentimental interest for Mrs Beaver were in the L shaped drawing room upstairs.

Beaver had a dark little sitting room (on the ground floor, behind the dining room) and his own telephone. The elderly parlourmaid looked after his clothes. She also dusted, polished and maintained in symmetrical order on his dressing table and on the top of his chest of drawers, the collection of sombre and bulky objects that had stood in his father's dressing room; indestructible presents for his wedding and twenty-first birthday, ivory, brass bound, covered in pigskin, crested and gold mounted, suggestive of expensive Edwardian masculinity – racing flasks and hunting flasks, cigar cases, tobacco jars, jockeys,[2] elaborate meerschaum pipes, button hooks and hat brushes.

There were four servants, all female and all, save one, elderly.

When anyone asked Beaver why he stayed there instead of setting up on his own, he sometimes said that he thought his mother liked having him there (in spite of her business she was lonely); sometimes that it saved him at least five pounds a week.

His total income varied around six pounds a week, so this was an important saving.

He was twenty-five years old. From leaving Oxford until the beginning of the slump[3] he had worked in an advertising agency. Since then no one had been able to find anything for him to do. So he got up late and sat near his telephone most of the day, hoping to be rung up.

Whenever it was possible, Mrs Beaver took an hour off in the middle of the morning. She was always at her shop punctually at nine, and by half past eleven she needed a break. Then, if no important customer was imminent, she would get into her two-seater and drive home to Sussex Gardens. Beaver was usually dressed by then and she had grown to value their morning interchange of gossip.

'What was your evening?'

'Audrey rang up at eight and asked me to dinner. Ten of us at the Embassy, rather dreary. Afterwards we all went on to a party given by a woman called de Trommet.'

'I know who you mean. American. She hasn't paid for the toile-de-jouy chaircovers we made her last April. I had a dull time too; didn't hold a card all the evening and came away four pounds ten to the bad.'

'Poor mumsy.'

'I'm lunching at Viola Chasm's.[4] What are you doing? I didn't order anything here I'm afraid.'

'Nothing so far. I can always go round to Brat's.'

'But that's so expensive. I'm sure if we ask Chambers she'll be able to get you something in. I thought you were certain to be out.'

'Well, I still may be. It isn't twelve yet.'

(Most of Beaver's invitations came to him at the last moment; occasionally even later, when he had already begun to eat a solitary meal from a tray . . . 'John, darling, there's been a muddle and Sonia has arrived without Reggie. Could you be an angel and help me out? Only be quick, because we're going in now' . . . Then he would go headlong for a taxi and arrive, with apologies, after the first course . . . One of his few recent quarrels with his mother had occurred when he left a luncheon party of hers in this way.)

'Where are you going for the weekend?'

'Hetton.'

'Who's that? I forget.'

'Tony Last.'

'Yes, of course. She's lovely, he's rather a stick. I didn't know you knew them.'

'Well, I don't really. Tony asked me in Brat's the other night. He may have forgotten.'

'Send a telegram and remind them. It is far better than ringing up. It gives them less chance to make excuses. Send it tomorrow just before you start. They owe me for a table.'

'What's their dossier?'

'I used to see her quite a lot before she married. She was Brenda Rex, Lord St Cloud's daughter, very fair, underwater look. People used to be mad about her when she was a girl. Everyone thought she would marry Jock Grant-Menzies at one time. Wasted on Tony Last, he's a prig. I should say it was time she began to be bored. They've been married five or six years. Quite well off but everything goes in keeping up the house. I've never seen it but I've an idea it's huge and quite hideous. They've got one child at least, perhaps more.'

'Mumsy, you are wonderful. I believe you know about everyone.'

'It's a great help. All a matter of paying attention while people are talking.'

Mrs Beaver smoked a cigarette and then drove back to her shop. An American woman bought two patchwork quilts at thirty guineas each, Lady Metroland telephoned about a bathroom ceiling, an unknown young man paid cash for a cushion; in the intervals between these events, Mrs Beaver was able to descend to the basement where two dispirited girls were packing lampshades. It was cold down there in spite of a little oil stove, and the walls were always damp. The girls were becoming quite deft, she noticed with pleasure, particularly the shorter one who was handling the crates like a man.

'That's the way,' she said, 'you are doing very nicely, Joyce. I'll soon get you on to something more interesting.'

'Thank you, Mrs Beaver.'

They had better stay in the packing department for a bit, Mrs Beaver decided; as long as they would stand it. They had neither of them enough chic to work upstairs. Both had paid good premiums to learn Mrs Beaver's art.

Beaver sat on beside his telephone. Once it rang and a voice said, 'Mr Beaver? Will you please hold the line, sir, Mrs Tipping would like to speak to you.'

The intervening silence was full of pleasant expectation. Mrs Tipping had a luncheon party that day, he knew; they had spent some time together the evening before and he had been particularly successful with her. Someone had chucked . . .

'Oh, Mr Beaver, I *am* so sorry to trouble you. I was wondering, could you *possibly* tell me the name of the young man you introduced to me last night at Madame de Trommet's? The one with the reddish moustache. I think he was in Parliament.'

'I expect you mean Jock Grant-Menzies.'

'Yes, that's the name. You don't by any chance know where I can find him, do you?'

'He's in the book but I don't suppose he'll be at home now. You might be able to get him at Brat's at about one. He's almost always there.'

'Jock Grant-Menzies, Brat's Club. Thank you so *very* much. It *is* kind of you. I hope you will come and see me some day. *Goodbye.*' After that the telephone was silent.

At one o'clock Beaver despaired. He put on his overcoat, his gloves, his bowler hat and with neatly rolled umbrella set off to his club, taking a penny bus as far as the corner of Bond Street.[5]

The air of antiquity pervading Brat's, derived from its elegant Georgian façade and finely panelled rooms, was entirely spurious, for it was a club of recent origin, founded in the burst of bonhomie immediately after the war. It was intended for young men, to be a place where they could straddle across the fire and be jolly in the card room without incurring scowls from older members. But now these founders were themselves passing into middle age; they were heavier, balder and redder in the face than when they had been demobilized,[6] but their joviality persisted and it was their turn now to embarrass their successors, deploring their lack of manly and gentlemanly qualities.

Six broad backs shut Beaver from the bar. He settled in one of the armchairs in the outer room and turned over the pages of the *New Yorker*,[7] waiting until someone he knew should turn up.

Jock Grant-Menzies came upstairs. The men at the bar greeted him saying, 'Hullo, Jock old boy, what are you drinking?' or, more simply, 'Well, old boy?' He was too young to have fought in the war but these men thought he was all right; they liked him far more than they did Beaver, who, they thought, ought never to have got into the club at all. But Jock stopped to talk to Beaver. 'Well, old boy,' he said. 'What are you drinking?'

'Nothing so far.' Beaver looked at his watch. 'But I think it's time I had one. Brandy and ginger ale.'

Jock called to the barman and then said:

'Who was the old girl you wished on me at that party last night?'

'She's called Mrs Tipping.'

'I thought she might be. That explains it. They gave me a message downstairs that someone with a name like that wanted me to lunch with her.'

'Are you going?'

'No, I'm no good at lunch parties. Besides I decided when I got up that I'd have oysters here.'

The barman came with the drinks.

'Mr Beaver, sir, there's ten shillings against you in my books for last month.'

'Ah, thank you, Macdougal, remind me sometime, will you?'

'Very good, sir.'

Beaver said, 'I'm going to Hetton tomorrow.'

'Are you now? Give Tony and Brenda my love.'

'What's the form?'

'Very quiet and enjoyable.'

'No paper games?'[8]

'Oh, no, nothing like that. A certain amount of bridge and backgammon and low poker with the neighbours.'

'Comfortable?'

'Not bad. Plenty to drink. Rather a shortage of bathrooms. You can stay in bed all the morning.'

'I've never met Brenda.'

'You'll like her, she's a grand girl. I often think Tony Last's one of the happiest men I know. He's got just enough money, loves the place, one son he's crazy about, devoted wife, not a worry in the world.'

'Most enviable. You don't know anyone else who's going, do you? I was wondering if I could get a lift down there.'

'I don't, I'm afraid. It's quite easy by train.'

'Yes, but it's more pleasant by road.'

'And cheaper.'

'Yes, and cheaper I suppose . . . well, I'm going down to lunch. You won't have another?'

Beaver rose to go.

'Yes, I think I will.'

'Oh, all right. Macdougal. Two more, please.'

Macdougal said, 'Shall I book them to you, sir?'

'Yes, if you will.'

Later, at the bar, Jock said, 'I made Beaver pay for a drink.'

'He can't have liked that.'

'He nearly died of it. Know anything about pigs?'

'No. Why?'

'Only that they keep writing to me about them from my constituency.'

Beaver went downstairs but before going into the dining room he told the porter to ring up his home and see if there was any message for him.

'Mrs Tipping rang up a few minutes ago and asked whether you could come to luncheon with her today.'

'Will you ring her up and say that I shall be delighted to, but that I may be a few minutes late?'

It was just after half past one when he left Brat's and walked at a good pace towards Hill Street.[9]

Chapter Two

ENGLISH GOTHIC

One

Between the villages of Hetton and Compton Last lies the extensive park of Hetton Abbey.[1] *This, formerly one of the notable houses of the county, was entirely rebuilt in 1864 in the Gothic style and is now devoid of interest. The grounds are open to the public daily until sunset and the house may be viewed on application by writing. It contains some good portraits and furniture. The terrace commands a fine view.*

This passage from the county Guide Book did not cause Tony Last any serious annoyance. Unkinder things had been said. His aunt Frances, embittered by an upbringing of unremitting severity, remarked that the plans of the house must have been adapted by Mr Pecksniff[2] from one of his pupils' designs for an orphanage. But there was not a glazed brick or encaustic tile that was not dear to Tony's heart. In some ways, he knew, it was not convenient to run; but what big house was? It was not altogether amenable to modern ideas of comfort; he had many small improvements in mind, which would be put into effect as soon as the death duties[3] were paid off. But the general aspect and atmosphere of the place; the line of its battlements against the sky; the central clock tower where quarterly chimes disturbed all but the heaviest sleepers; the ecclesiastical gloom of the great hall, its ceiling groined[4] and painted in diapers[5] of red and gold, supported on shafts of polished granite with vine-wreathed capitals, half-lit by day through lancet windows[6] of armorial stained glass, at night by a vast gasolier of brass and wrought iron, wired now and fitted with twenty electric bulbs; the blasts of hot air that rose suddenly at one's feet, through grills of cast-iron trefoils from the antiquated heating apparatus below; the cavernous chill of the more remote corridors where, economising in coke, he had had the pipes shut off; the dining hall with its hammer-beam roof and pitch-pine minstrels' gallery; the bedrooms with their brass bedsteads, each with a frieze of Gothic text, each named from Malory,[7] Yseult, Elaine, Mordred and Merlin,

Gawaine and Bedivere, Lancelot, Perceval, Tristram, Galahad, his own dressing room, Morgan le Fay, and Brenda's Guinevere, where the bed stood on a dais, the walls hung with tapestry, the fireplace like a tomb of the thirteenth century, from whose bay window one could count, on days of exceptional clearness, the spires of six churches – all these things with which he had grown up were a source of constant delight and exultation to Tony; things of tender memory and proud possession.

They were not in the fashion, he fully realized. Twenty years ago people had liked half timber and old pewter; now it was urns and colonnades; but the time would come, perhaps in John Andrew's day, when opinion would reinstate Hetton in its proper place. Already it was referred to as 'amusing,' and a very civil young man had asked permission to photograph it for an architectural review.

The ceiling of Morgan le Fay was not in perfect repair. In order to make an appearance of coffered wood, moulded slats had been nailed in a chequer across the plaster. They were painted in chevrons of blue and gold. The squares between were decorated alternately with Tudor roses and fleurs-de-lis. But damp had penetrated into one corner, leaving a large patch where the gilt had tarnished and the colour flaked away; in another place the wooden laths had become warped and separated from the plaster. Lying in bed, in the grave ten minutes between waking and ringing, Tony studied these defects and resolved anew to have them put right. He wondered whether it would be easy, nowadays, to find craftsmen capable of such delicate work.

Morgan le Fay had been his room since he left the night nursery. He had been put there so that he would be within calling distance of his parents (inseparable in Guinevere), for until quite late in his life he was subject to nightmares. He had taken nothing from the room since he had slept there, but every year added to its contents, so that it now formed a gallery representative of every phase of his adolescence – the framed picture of a dreadnought (a coloured supplement from *Chums*[8]), all its guns spouting flame and smoke; a photographic group of his private school; a cabinet called 'the

Museum,' filled with the fruits of a dozen desultory hobbies, eggs, butterflies, fossils, coins; his parents, in the leather diptych which had stood by his bed at school; Brenda, eight years ago when he had been trying to get engaged to her; Brenda with John, taken just after the christening; an aquatint of Hetton, as it had stood until his great-grandfather demolished it; some shelves of books, *Bevis*,[9] *Woodwork at Home, Conjuring for All, The Young Visiters*,[10] *The Law of Landlord and Tenant, Farewell to Arms*.[11]

All over England people were waking up, queasy and despondent. Tony lay for ten minutes very happily planning the renovation of his ceiling. Then he rang the bell.

'Has her ladyship been called yet?'

'About quarter of an hour ago, sir.'

'Then I'll have breakfast in her room.'

He put on his dressing gown and slippers and went through into Guinevere.

Brenda lay on the dais.

She had insisted on a modern bed. Her tray was beside her and the quilt was littered with envelopes, letters and the daily papers. Her head was propped against a very small blue pillow; clean of make-up, her face was almost colourless, rose-pearl, scarcely deeper in tone than her arms and neck.

'Well?' said Tony.

'Kiss.'

He sat by the tray at the head of the bed; she leant forward to him (a nereid[12] emerging from fathomless depths of clear water). She turned her lips away and rubbed against his cheek like a cat. It was a way she had.

'Anything interesting?'

He picked up some of the letters.

'No. Mama wants nanny to send John's measurements. She's knitting him something for Christmas. And the mayor wants me to open something next month. I needn't, need I?'

'I think you'd better, we haven't done anything for him for a long time.'

'Well, you must write the speech. I'm getting too old for the

girlish one I used to give them all. And Angela says, will we stay
for the New Year?'

'That's easy. Not on her life, we won't.'

'I guessed not . . . though it sounds an amusing party.'

'You go if you like. I can't possibly get away.'

'That's all right. I knew it would be "no" before I opened the
letter.'

'Well, what sort of pleasure can there be in going all the way to
Yorkshire in the middle of winter?'

'Darling, don't be cross. I know we aren't going. I'm not making
a thing about it. I just thought it might be fun to eat someone
else's food for a bit.'

Then Brenda's maid brought in the other tray. He had it put
by the window seat, and began opening his letters. He looked out
of the window. Only four of the six church towers were visible that
morning. Presently he said, 'As a matter of fact I probably *can*
manage to get away that weekend.'

'Darling, are you sure you wouldn't hate it?'

'I daresay not.'

While he ate his breakfast Brenda read to him from the papers.
'Reggie's been making another speech . . . There's such an extraordinary picture of Babe and Jock . . . a woman in America has
had twins by two different husbands. Would you have thought that
possible? . . . Two more chaps in gas ovens . . . a little girl has been
strangled in a cemetery with a bootlace . . . that play we went to
about a farm is coming off.' Then she read him the serial. He lit
his pipe. 'I don't believe you're listening. Why doesn't Sylvia want
Rupert to get the letter?'

'Eh? Oh well, you see, she doesn't really trust Rupert.'

'I *knew* it. There's no such character as Rupert in the story. I
shall never read to you again.'

'Well, to tell you the truth I was just thinking.'

'Oh.'

'I was thinking how delightful it is, that it's Saturday morning
and we haven't got anyone coming for the weekend.'

'Oh, you thought that?'

'Don't you?'

'Well, it sometimes seems to me rather pointless keeping up a house this size if we don't now and then ask some other people to stay in it.'

'*Pointless?* I can't think what you mean. I don't keep up this house to be a hostel for a lot of bores to come and gossip in. We've always lived here and I hope John will be able to keep it on after me. One has a duty towards one's employees, and towards the place too. It's a definite part of English life which would be a serious loss if . . .' Then Tony stopped short in his speech and looked at the bed. Brenda had turned on her face and only the top of her head appeared above the sheets.

'Oh God,' she said into the pillow. 'What have I done?'

'I say, am I being pompous again?'

She turned sideways so that her nose and one eye emerged. 'Oh no, darling, not *pompous*. You wouldn't know how.'

'Sorry.'

Brenda sat up. 'And, please, I didn't mean it. I'm jolly glad too, that no one's coming.'

(These scenes of domestic playfulness had been more or less continuous in Tony and Brenda's life for seven years.)

Outside, it was soft English weather; mist in the hollows and pale sunshine on the hills; the coverts had ceased dripping, for there were no leaves to hold the recent rain, but the undergrowth was wet, dark in the shadows, iridescent where the sun caught it; the lanes were soggy and there was water running in the ditches.

John Andrew sat on his pony, solemn and stiff as a Life-Guard,[13] while Ben fixed the jump. Thunderclap had been a present on his sixth birthday from Uncle Reggie. It was John who had named her, after lengthy consultation. Originally she had been called Christabelle[14] which, as Ben said, was more the name for a hound than a horse. Ben had known a strawberry roan called Thunderclap who killed two riders and won the local point-to-point four years running. He had been a lovely little horse, said Ben, till he staked himself in the guts, hunting, and had to be shot. Ben knew stories about a great many different horses. There was one called Zero on whom he had won five Jimmy-o-goblins[15] at ten to three at Chester one year. And there was a mule he had known during the war, called Peppermint, who had died of drinking the company's rum ration. But John was not going to name his pony after a drunken mule. So in the end they had decided on Thunderclap, in spite of her imperturbable disposition.

She was a dark bay, with long tail and mane. Ben had left her legs shaggy. She cropped the grass, resisting John's attempts to keep her head up.

Before her arrival riding had been a very different thing. He had jogged round the paddock on a little Shetland pony called Bunny, with his nurse panting at the bridle. Now it was a man's business. Nanny sat at a distance, crocheting, on her camp stool; out of earshot. There had been a corresponding promotion in Ben's position. From being the hand who looked after the farm horses, he was now, perceptibly, assuming the air of a stud groom. The handkerchief round his neck gave place to a stock with a fox-head pin. He was a man of varied experience in other parts of the country.

Neither Tony or Brenda hunted but they were anxious that John should like it. Ben foresaw the time when the stables would be full and himself in authority; it would not be like Mr Last to get anyone in from outside.

Ben had got two posts bored for iron pegs, and a whitewashed rail. With these he erected a two foot jump in the middle of the field.

'Now take it quite easy. Canter up slow and when she takes off lean forward in the saddle and you'll be over like a bird. Keep her head straight at it.'

Thunderclap trotted forwards, cantered two paces, thought better of it and, just before the jump, fell into a trot again and swerved round the obstacle. John recovered his balance by dropping the reins and gripping the mane with both hands; he looked guiltily at Ben, who said, 'What d'you suppose your bloody legs are for? Here take this and just give her a tap when you get up to it.' He handed John a switch.

Nanny sat by the gate re-reading a letter from her sister.

John took Thunderclap back and tried the jump again. This time they made straight for the rail.

Ben shouted 'Legs!' and John kicked sturdily, losing his stirrups. Ben raised his arms as if scaring crows. Thunderclap jumped; John rose from the saddle and landed on his back in the grass.

Nanny rose in alarm. 'Oh, what's happened, Mr Hacket, is he hurt?'

'He's all right,' said Ben.

'I'm all right,' said John, 'I think she put in a short step.'

'Short step my grandmother. You just opened your bloody legs and took an arser. Keep hold on to the reins next time. You can lose a hunt that way.'

At the third attempt John got over and found himself, breathless and insecure, one stirrup swinging loose and one hand grabbing its old support in the mane, but still in the saddle.

'There, how did that feel? You just skimmed over like a swallow. Try it again?'

Twice more John and Thunderclap went over the little rail, then nanny called that it was time to go indoors for his milk. They walked the pony back to the stable. Nanny said, 'Oh dear, look at all the mud on your coat.'

Ben said, 'We'll have you riding the winner at Aintree[16] soon.'

'Good morning, Mr Hacket.'

'Good morning, miss.'

'Goodbye, Ben, may I come and see you doing the farm horses this evening?'

'That's not for me to say. You must ask nanny. Tell you what though, the grey carthorse has got worms. Would you like to see me give him a pill.'

'Oh yes; please nanny, may I?'

'You must ask mother. Come along now, you've had quite enough of horses for one day.'

'Can't have enough of horses,' said John, 'ever.' On the way back to the house, he said, 'Can I have my milk in mummy's room?'

'That depends.'

Nanny's replies were always evasive, like that – 'We'll see' or

'That's asking' or 'Those that ask no questions, hear no lies' – altogether unlike Ben's decisive and pungent judgments.

'What does it depend on?'

'Lots of things.'

'Tell me one of them.'

'On your not asking a lot of silly questions.'

'Silly old tart.'

'*John!* How dare you? What do you mean?'

Delighted by the effect of this sally, John broke away from her hand and danced in front of her, saying, 'Silly old tart, silly old tart' all the way to the side entrance. When they entered the porch his nurse silently took off his leggings; he was sobered a little by her grimness.

'Go straight up to the nursery,' she said. 'I am going to speak to your mother about you.'

'Please, nanny. I don't know what it means, but I didn't mean it.'

'Go straight to the nursery.'

Brenda was doing her face.

'It's been the same ever since Ben Hacket started teaching him to ride, my lady, there's been no doing anything with him.'

Brenda spat in the eye black. 'But nanny, what exactly did he say?'

'Oh, I couldn't repeat it, my lady.'

'Nonsense, you must tell me. Otherwise I shall be thinking it something far worse than it was.'

'It couldn't have been worse ... he called me a silly old tart, my lady.'

Brenda choked slightly into her face towel. 'He said *that?*'

'Repeatedly. He danced in front of me all the way up the drive, *singing it.*'

'I see ... well you were quite right to tell me.'

'Thank you, my lady, and since we are talking about it I think I ought to say that it seems to me that Ben Hacket is making the child go ahead far too quickly with his riding. It's very dangerous. He had what might have been a serious fall this morning.'

24

'All right, nanny, I'll speak to Mr Last about it.'

She spoke to Tony. They both laughed about it a great deal. 'Darling,' she said, '*you* must speak to him. You're so much better at being serious than I am.'

'I should have thought it was very nice to be called a tart,' John argued, 'and anyway it's a word Ben often uses about people.'

'Well, he's got no business to.'

'I like Ben more than anyone in the world. And I should think he's cleverer too.'

'Now you know you don't like him more than your mother.'

'Yes I do. *Far* more.'

Tony felt that the time had come to cut out the cross talk and deliver the homily he had been preparing. 'Now, listen, John. It was very wrong of you to call nanny a silly old tart. First, because it was unkind to her. Think of all the things she does for you every day.'

'She's paid to.'

'Be quiet. And secondly because you were using a word which people of your age and class do not use. Poor people use certain expressions which gentlemen do not. You are a gentleman. When you grow up all this house and lots of other things besides will belong to you. You must learn to speak like someone who is going to have these things and to be considerate to people less fortunate than you, particularly women. Do you understand?'

'Is Ben less fortunate than me?'

'That has nothing to do with it. Now you are to go upstairs and say you are sorry to nanny and promise never to use that word about anyone again.'

'All right.'

'And because you have been so naughty today you are not to ride tomorrow.'

'Tomorrow's Sunday.'

'Well, next day then.'

'But you said "tomorrow." It isn't fair to change now.'

'John, don't argue. If you are not careful I shall send Thunderclap back to Uncle Reggie and say that I find you are not a good enough boy to keep it. You wouldn't like that, would you?'

'What would Uncle Reggie do with her? She couldn't carry him. Besides, he's usually abroad.'

'He'd give it to some other little boy. Anyway that's got nothing to do with it. Now run off and say you're sorry to nanny.'

At the door John said, 'It's all right about riding on Monday, isn't it? You did *say* "tomorrow." '

'Yes, I suppose so.'

'Hooray. Thunderclap went very well today. We jumped a big post and rail. She refused first time but went like a bird after that.'

'Didn't you come off?'

'Yes, once. It wasn't Thunderclap's fault. I just opened my bloody legs and cut an arser.'

'How did the lecture go?' Brenda asked.

'Bad. Rotten bad.'

'The trouble is that nanny's jealous of Ben.'

'I'm not sure we shan't both be soon.'

They lunched at a small, round table in the centre of the dining hall. There seemed no way of securing an even temperature in that room; even when one side was painfully roasting in the direct blaze of the open hearth, the other was numbed by a dozen converging draughts. Brenda had tried numerous experiments with screens and a portable, electric radiator, but with little success. Even today, mild elsewhere, it was bitterly cold in the dining hall.

Although they were both in good health and of unexceptional figure, Tony and Brenda were on a diet. It gave an interest to their meals and saved them from the two uncivilized extremes of which solitary diners are in danger – absorbing gluttony or an irregular régime of scrambled eggs and raw beef sandwiches. Under their present system they denied themselves the combination of protein and starch[17] at the same meal. They had a printed catalogue telling them which foods contained protein and which starch. Most normal dishes seemed to be compact of both, so that it was fun for Tony and Brenda to choose the menu. Usually it ended by their declaring some food 'joker.'

'I'm sure it does me a great deal of good.'

'Yes, darling, and when we get tired of it we might try an alphabetical diet, having things beginning with a different letter every day. J would be hungry, nothing but jam and jellied eels . . . What are your plans for the afternoon?'

'Nothing much. Carter's coming up at five to go over a few things. I may go to Pigstanton after luncheon. I think we've got a tenant for Lowater Farm but it's been empty some time and I ought to see how much needs doing to it.'

'I wouldn't say "no" to going in to the "movies."'

'All right. I can easily leave Lowater till Monday.'

'And we might go to Woolworth's afterwards, eh?'

What with Brenda's pretty ways and Tony's good sense, it was not surprising that their friends pointed to them as a pair who were preeminently successful in solving the problem of getting along well together.

The pudding, without protein, was unattractive.

Five minutes afterwards a telegram was brought in. Tony opened it and said 'Hell.'

'Badders?'[18]

'Something too horrible has happened. Look at this.'

Brenda read. *Arriving 3.18 so looking forward visit. Beaver.* And asked, 'What's Beaver?'

'It's a young man.'

'That sounds all right.'

'Oh no it's not. Wait till you see him.'

'What's he coming here for? Did you ask him to stay?'

'I suppose I did in a vague kind of way. I went to Brat's one evening and he was the only chap there so we had some drinks and he said something about wanting to see the house . . .'

'I suppose you were tight.'

'Not really, but I never thought he'd hold it against me.'

'Well, it jolly well serves you right. That's what comes of going up to London on business and leaving me alone here . . . Who is he anyway?'

'Just a young man. His mother keeps that shop.'

'I used to know her. She's hell. Come to think of it we owe her some money.'

'Look here, we must put a call through and say we're ill.'

'Too late, he's in the train now, recklessly mixing starch and protein in the Great Western[19] three and sixpenny lunch . . . Anyway he can go into Galahad. No one who sleeps there ever comes again – the bed's agony I believe.'

'What on earth are we going to do with him? It's too late to get anyone else.'

'You go over to Pigstanton. I'll look after him. It's easier alone. We can take him to the movies tonight, and tomorrow he can see over the house. If we're lucky he may go up by the evening train. Does he have to work on Monday morning?'

'I shouldn't know.'

Three-eighteen was far from being the most convenient time for arrival. One reached the house at about a quarter to four and if, like Beaver, one was a stranger, there was an awkward time until tea; but without Tony there to make her self-conscious, Brenda could carry these things off quite gracefully and Beaver was so seldom wholly welcome anywhere that he was not sensitive to the slight constraint of his reception.

She met him in what was still called the smoking room; it was in some ways the least gloomy place in the house. She said, 'It is nice that you were able to come. I must break it to you at once that we haven't got a party. I'm afraid you'll be terribly bored . . . Tony had to go out but he'll be in soon . . . was the train crowded? It often is on Saturdays . . . would you like to come outside? It'll be dark soon and we might get some of the sun while we can . . .' and so on. If Tony had been there it would have been difficult, for she would have caught his eye and her manner as châtelaine would have collapsed. Beaver was well used to making conversation, so they went out together through the French windows on to the terrace, down the steps, into the Dutch garden, and back round the orangery without suffering a moment's real embarrassment. She even heard herself telling Beaver that his mother was one of her oldest friends.

Tony returned in time for tea. He apologized for not being at home to greet his guest and almost immediately went out again to interview the agent in his study.

Brenda asked about London and what parties there were. Beaver was particularly knowledgeable.

'Polly Cockpurse is having one soon.'

'Yes, I know.'

'Are you coming up for it?'

'I don't expect so. We never go anywhere nowadays.'

The jokes that had been going round for six weeks were all new to Brenda; they had become polished and perfected with repetition and Beaver was able to bring them out with good effect. He told her of numerous changes of alliance among her friends.

'What's happening to Mary and Simon?'

'Oh, didn't you know? That's broken up.'

'When?'

'It began in Austria this summer ...'

'And Billy Angmering?'

'He's having a terrific walk out with a girl called Sheila Shrub.'

'And the Helm-Hubbards?'

'That marriage isn't going too well either ... Daisy has started a new restaurant. It's going very well ... and there's a new night club called the Warren ...'

'Dear me,' Brenda said at last. 'What fun everyone seems to be having.'

After tea John Andrew was brought in and quickly usurped the conversation. 'How do you do?' he said. 'I didn't know you were coming. Daddy said he had a weekend to himself for once. Do you hunt?'

'Not for a long time.'

'Ben says it stands to reason everyone ought to hunt who can afford to, for the good of the country.'

'Perhaps I can't afford to.'

'Are you poor?'

'Please, Mr Beaver, you mustn't let him bore you.'

'Yes, very poor.'

'Poor enough to call people tarts?'

'Yes, quite poor enough.'

'How did you get poor?'

'I always have been.'

'Oh.' John lost interest in this topic. 'The grey horse at the farm has got worms.'

'How do you know?'

'Ben says so. Besides you've only got to look at his dung.'

'Oh dear,' said Brenda, 'what would nanny say if she heard you talking like that?'

'How old are you?'

'Twenty-five. How old are you?'

'What do you do?'

'Nothing much.'

'Well if I was you I'd do something and earn some money. Then you'd be able to hunt.'

'But I shouldn't be able to call people tarts.'

'I don't see any point in that anyway.'

(Later in the nursery, while he was having supper, John said: 'I think Mr Beaver's a very silly man, don't you?'

'I'm sure I don't know,' said nanny.

'I think he's the silliest man who's ever been here.'

'Comparisons are odious.'

'There just isn't anything nice about him. He's got a silly voice and a silly face, silly eyes and silly nose,' John's voice fell into a liturgical sing-song, 'silly feet and silly toes, silly head and silly clothes . . .'

'Now you eat up your supper,' said nanny.)

That evening before dinner Tony came up behind Brenda as she sat at her dressing table and made a face over her shoulder in the glass.

'I feel rather guilty about Beaver – going off and leaving you like that. You were heavenly to him.'

She said, 'Oh it wasn't bad really. He's rather pathetic.'

Further down the passage Beaver examined his room with the care of an experienced guest. There was no reading lamp. The ink pot was dry. The fire had been lit but had gone out. The bathroom, he had already discovered, was a great distance away, up a flight of turret steps. He did not at all like the look or feel of the bed; the springs were broken in the centre and it creaked ominously when he lay down to try it. The return ticket, third class, had been eighteen shillings. Then there would be tips.

Owing to Tony's feeling of guilt they had champagne for dinner, which neither he nor Brenda particularly liked. Nor, as it happened, did Beaver, but he was glad that it was there. It was decanted into a tall jug and was carried round the little table, between the three of them, as a pledge of hospitality. Afterwards they drove into Pigstanton to the Picturedrome, where there was a film Beaver had seen some months before. When they got back there was a grog tray[20] and some sandwiches in the smoking room. They talked about the film but Beaver did not let on that he had seen it. Tony took him to the door of Sir Galahad.

'I hope you sleep well.'

'I'm sure I shall.'

'D'you like to be called in the morning?'

'May I ring?'

'Certainly. Got everything you want?'

'Yes thanks. Goodnight.'

'Goodnight.'

But when he got back he said, 'You know, I feel awful about Beaver.'

'Oh Beaver's all right,' said Brenda.

But he was far from being comfortable and as he rolled patiently about the bed in quest of a position in which it was possible to go to sleep, he reflected that, since he had no intention of coming to the house again, he would give the butler nothing and only five shillings to the footman who was looking after him. Presently he adapted himself to the rugged topography of the mattress and dozed, fitfully, until morning. But the new day began dismally with the information that all the Sunday papers had already gone to her ladyship's room.

*

Tony invariably wore a dark suit on Sundays and a stiff white collar. He went to church, where he sat in a large pitch pine pew, put in by his great grandfather at the time of rebuilding the house, furnished with very high crimson hassocks and a fireplace, complete with iron grate and a little poker which his father used to rattle when any point in the sermon excited his disapproval. Since his father's day a fire had not been laid there; Tony had it in mind to revive the practice next winter. On Christmas Day and Harvest Thanksgiving Tony read the lessons from the back of the brass eagle.

When service was over he stood for a few minutes at the porch chatting affably with the vicar's sister and the people from the village. Then he returned home by a path across the fields which led to a side door in the walled garden; he visited the hot houses and picked himself a buttonhole, stopped by the gardeners' cottages for a few words (the smell of Sunday dinners rising warm and overpowering from the little doorways) and then, rather solemnly, drank a glass of sherry in the library. That was the simple, mildly ceremonious order of his Sunday morning, which had evolved, more or less spontaneously, from the more severe practices of his parents; he adhered to it with great satisfaction. Brenda teased him whenever she caught him posing as an upright, God-fearing gentleman of the old school and Tony saw the joke, but this did not at all diminish the pleasure he derived from his weekly routine, or his annoyance when the presence of guests suspended it.

For this reason his heart sank when, emerging from his study into the great hall at quarter to eleven, he met Beaver already dressed and prepared to be entertained; it was only a momentary vexation, however, for while he wished him good morning he noticed that his guest had an *A.B.C.*[21] in his hands and was clearly looking out a train.

'I hope you slept all right?'

'Beautifully,' said Beaver, though his wan expression did not confirm the word.

'I'm so glad. I always sleep well here myself. I say, I don't like the look of that train guide. I hope you weren't thinking of leaving us yet?'

'Alas, I've got to get up tonight I'm afraid.'

'Too bad. I've hardly seen you. The trains aren't very good on Sundays. The best leaves at five-fortyfive and gets up about nine. It stops a lot and there's no restaurant car.'

'That'll do fine.'

'Sure you can't stay until tomorrow?'

'Quite sure.'

The church bells were ringing across the park.

'Well, I'm just off to church. I don't suppose you'd care to come.'

Beaver always did what was expected of him when he was staying away, even on a visit as unsatisfactory as the present one. 'Oh yes. I should like to very much.'

'No, really, I shouldn't, if I were you. You wouldn't enjoy it. I only go because I more or less have to. You stay here. Brenda will be down directly. Ring for a drink when you feel like it.'

'Oh, all right.'

'See you later then.' Tony took his hat and stick from the lobby and let himself out. 'Now I've behaved inhospitably to that young man again,' he reflected.

The bells were clear and clamorous in the drive and Tony walked briskly towards them. Presently they ceased and gave place to a single note, warning the village that there was only five minutes to go before the organist started the first hymn.

He caught up nanny and John, also on their way to church. John was in one of his rare, confidential moods; he put his small gloved hand into Tony's and, without introduction, embarked upon a story which lasted them all the way to the church door; it dealt with the mule Peppermint who had drunk the company's rum ration, near Wipers in 1917; it was told breathlessly, as John trotted to keep pace with his father. At the end, Tony said, 'How very sad.'

'Well, *I* thought it was sad too, but it isn't. Ben said it made him laugh fit to bust his pants.'

The bell had stopped and the organist was watching from behind his curtain for Tony's arrival. He walked ahead up the aisle, nanny and John following. In the pew he occupied one of the armchairs; they sat on the bench at his back. He leant forward for half a minute with his forehead on his hand, and as he sat back, the organist played the first bars of the hymn.

'Enter not into judgment with Thy servant, O Lord . . .'[23] The service followed its course. As Tony inhaled the agreeable, slightly musty atmosphere and performed the familiar motions of sitting, standing, and leaning forward, his thoughts drifted from subject to subject, among the events of the past week and his plans for the future. Occasionally some arresting phrase in the liturgy would recall him to his surroundings, but for the most part that morning he occupied himself with the question of bathrooms and lavatories, and of how more of them could best be introduced without disturbing the character of his house.

The village postmaster took round the collecting bag. Tony put in his half-crown;[24] John and nanny their pennies.

The vicar climbed, with some effort, into the pulpit. He was an elderly man who had served in India most of his life. Tony's father had given him the living at the instance of his dentist. He had a noble and sonorous voice and was reckoned the best preacher for many miles around.

His sermons had been composed in his more active days for delivery at the garrison chapel; he had done nothing to adapt them to the changed conditions of his ministry and they mostly concluded with some reference to homes and dear ones far away. The villagers did not find this in any way surprising. Few of the things said in church seemed to have any particular reference to themselves. They enjoyed their vicar's sermons very much and they knew that when he began about their distant homes, it was time to be dusting their knees and feeling for their umbrellas.

'. . . And so as we stand here bareheaded at this solemn hour of the week,' he read, his powerful old voice swelling up for the peroration, 'let us remember our Gracious Queen Empress[25] in whose service we are here, and pray that she may long be spared to send us at her bidding to do our duty in the uttermost parts of the earth;[26] and let us think of our dear ones far away and the homes we have left in her name, and remember that though miles of barren continent and leagues of ocean divide us, we are never so near to them as on these Sunday mornings, united with them across dune and mountain in our loyalty to our sovereign and thanksgiving for her welfare; one with them as proud subjects of her sceptre and crown.'

('The Reverend Tendril[27] e do speak uncommon igh of the Queen,' a gardener's wife had once remarked to Tony.)

After the choir had filed out, during the last hymn, the congregation crouched silently for a few seconds and then made for the door. There was no sign of recognition until they were outside among the graves; then there was an exchange of greetings, solicitous, cordial, garrulous.

Tony spoke to the vet's wife and Mr Partridge from the shop; then he was joined by the vicar.

'Lady Brenda is not ill, I hope?'

'No, nothing serious.' This was the invariable formula when he appeared at Church without her. 'A most interesting sermon, vicar.'

'My dear boy, I'm delighted to hear you say so. It is one of my favourites. But have you never heard it before?'

'No, I assure you.'

'I haven't used it here lately. When I am asked to supply elsewhere it is the one I invariably choose. Let me see now, I always make a note of the times I use it.' The old clergyman opened the manuscript book he was carrying. It had a limp black cover and the pages were yellow with age. 'Ah yes, here we are. I preached it first in Jellalabad[28] when the Coldstream Guards[29] were there; then I used it in the Red Sea coming home from my fourth leave; then at Sidmouth[30]... Mentone ... Winchester ... to the Girl Guides at their summer rally in 1921 ... the Church Stage Guild at Leicester ... twice at Bournemouth during the winter of 1926 when poor Ada was so ill ... No, I don't seem to have used it here since 1911 when you would have been too young to enjoy it ...'

The vicar's sister had engaged John in conversation. He was telling her the story of Peppermint: '... he'd have been all right, Ben says, if he had been able to cat[31] the rum up, but mules can't cat, neither can horses ...'

Nanny grasped him firmly and hurried him towards home. 'How

many times have I told you not to go repeating whatever Ben Hacket tells you? Miss Tendril didn't want to hear about Peppermint. And don't ever use that rude word "cat" again.'

'It only means to be sick.'

'Well, Miss Tendril isn't interested in being sick . . .'

As the gathering between porch and lych gate[32] began to disperse, Tony set off towards the gardens. There was a good choice of buttonholes in the hot houses; he picked lemon carnations with crinkled, crimson edges for himself and Beaver and a camellia for his wife.

Shafts of November sunshine streamed down from lancet and oriel,[33] tinctured in green and gold, gules[34] and azure[35] by the emblazoned coats, broken by the leaded devices into countless points and patches of coloured light. Brenda descended the great staircase step by step through alternations of dusk and rainbow. Both hands were occupied, holding to her breast a bag, a small hat, a half finished panel of petit-point embroidery and a vast, disordered sheaf of Sunday newspapers, above which only her eyes and forehead appeared as though over a yashmak.[36] Beaver emerged from the shadows below and stood at the foot of the stairs looking up at her.

'I say, can't I carry something?'

'No thanks, I've got everything safe. How did you sleep?'

'Beautifully.'

'I bet you didn't.'

'Well, I'm not a very good sleeper.'

'Next time you come you shall have a different room. But I daresay you won't ever come again. People so seldom do. It is very sad because it's such fun for us having them and we never make any new friends living down here.'

'Tony's gone to church.'

'Yes, he likes that. He'll be back soon. Let's go out for a minute or two, it looks lovely.'

When Tony came back they were sitting in the library. Beaver was telling Brenda's fortune with cards. '. . . Now cut to me again,' he was saying, 'and I'll see if it's any clearer . . . Oh yes . . . there is going to be a sudden death which will cause you great pleasure and profit. In fact you are going to kill someone. I can't tell if it's a man or a woman ... yes, a woman ... then you are going to go on a long journey across the sea, marry six dark men and have eleven children, grow a beard and die.'

'Beast. And all this time I've been thinking it was serious. Hullo, Tony, jolly church?'

'Most enjoyable; how about some sherry?'

When they were alone together, just before luncheon, he said, 'Darling, you're being heroic with Beaver.'

'Oh, I quite enjoy coping – in fact I'm bitching[37] him rather.'

'So I saw. Well, I'll look after him this afternoon and he's going this evening.'

'Is he? I'll be quite sorry. You know that's a difference between us, that when someone's awful you just run away and hide, while I actually enjoy it – making up to them and showing off to myself how well I can do it. Besides, Beaver isn't so bad. He's quite like us in some ways.'

'He's not like me,' said Tony.

After luncheon Tony said, 'Well, if it would really amuse you, we might go over the house. I know it isn't fashionable to like this sort of architecture now – my Aunt Frances says it is an authentic Pecksniff – but I think it's good of its kind.'

It took them two hours. Beaver was well practised in the art of being shown over houses; he had been brought up to it in fact, ever since he had begun to accompany his mother, whose hobby it had always been, and later, with changing circumstances, profession. He made apt and appreciative comments and greatly enhanced the pleasure Tony always took in exposing his treasures.

They saw it all: the shuttered drawing room, like a school speech-hall, the cloistral passages, the dark inner courtyard, the chapel where, until Tony's succession, family prayers had been daily read to the assembled household, the plate room and estate office, the bedrooms and attics, the water-tank concealed among the battle-ments.[38] They climbed the spiral staircase into the works of the clock and waited to see it strike half past three. Thence they descended with ringing ears to the collections – enamel, ivories, seals, snuff boxes, china, ormolu,[39] cloisonné;[40] they paused before each picture in the oak gallery and discussed its associations; they took out the more remarkable folios in the library and examined prints of the original buildings, manuscript account books of the old Abbey, travel journals of Tony's ancestors. At intervals Beaver would say, 'The So-and-sos have got one rather like that at Such-and-such a place,' and Tony would say, 'Yes, I've seen it but I think mine is the earlier.' Eventually they came back to the smoking room and Tony left Beaver to Brenda.

She was stitching away at the petit point, hunched in an armchair. 'Well,' she asked, without looking up from her needlework, 'what did you think of it?'

'Magnificent.'

'You don't have to say that to me, you know.'

'Well, a lot of the things are very fine.'

'Yes, the *things* are all right I suppose.'

'But don't you like the house?'

'Me? I *detest* it . . . at least I don't mean that really, but I do wish sometimes that it wasn't *all*, every bit of it, so appallingly ugly. Only I'd die rather than say that to Tony. We could never live anywhere else, of course. He's crazy about the place . . . It's funny. None of us minded very much when my brother Reggie sold *our* house – and that was built by Vanbrugh,[41] you know . . . I suppose we're lucky to be able to afford to keep it up at all. Do you know how much it costs just to live here? We should be quite rich if it wasn't for that. As it is we support fifteen servants indoors, besides gardeners and carpenters and a night watchman and all the people at the farm and odd little men constantly popping in to wind the clocks and cook the accounts and clean the moat, while Tony and I have to fuss about whether it's cheaper to take a car up to London for the night or buy an excursion ticket . . . I shouldn't feel so badly about it if it were a really lovely house – like my home for instance . . . but of course Tony's been brought up here and sees it all differently . . .'

*

Tony joined them for tea. 'I don't want to seem inhospitable, but if you're going to catch that train, you ought really to be getting ready.'

'That's all right. I've persuaded him to stay on till tomorrow.'

'If you're sure you don't . . .'

'Splendid. I *am* glad. It's beastly going up at this time, particularly by that train.'

When John came in he said, 'I thought Mr Beaver was going.'

'Not till tomorrow.'

'Oh.'

After dinner Tony sat and read the papers. Brenda and Beaver were on the sofa playing games together. They did a cross word. Beaver said 'I've thought of something,' and Brenda asked him questions to find what it was. He was thinking of the rum Peppermint drank. John had told him the story at tea. Brenda guessed it quite soon. Then they played 'Analogies'[42] about their friends and finally about each other.

They said goodbye that night because Beaver was catching the 9.10.

'Do let me know when you come to London.'

'I may be up this week.'

Next morning Beaver tipped both butler and footman ten shillings each. Tony, still feeling rather guilty in spite of Brenda's heroic coping, came down to breakfast to see his guest off. Afterwards he went back to Guinevere.

'Well, that's the last of *him*. You were superb, darling. I'm sure he's gone back thinking that you're mad about him.'

'Oh, he wasn't too awful.'

'No. I must say he took a very intelligent interest when we went round the house.'

Mrs Beaver was eating her yoghurt when Beaver reached home. 'Who was there?'

'No one.'

'No one? My poor boy.'

'They weren't expecting me. It was awful at first but got better.

They were just as you said. She's very charming. He scarcely spoke.'

'I wish I saw her sometimes.'

'She talked of taking a flat in London.'

'*Did* she?' The conversion of stables and garages was an important part of Mrs Beaver's business. 'What does she want?'

'Something quite simple. Two rooms and a bath. But it's all quite vague. She hasn't said anything to Tony yet.'

'I am sure I shall be able to find her something.'

Two

If Brenda had to go to London for a day's shopping, hair-cutting, or bone-setting[43] (a recreation she particularly enjoyed), she went on Wednesday, because the tickets on that day were half the usual price. She left at eight in the morning and got home soon after ten at night. She travelled third class and the carriages were often full, because other wives on the line took advantage of the cheap fare. She usually spent the day with her younger sister Marjorie, who was married to the prospective Conservative candidate for a South London constituency of strong Labour sympathies.[44] She was more solid than Brenda. The newspapers used always to refer to them as 'the lovely Rex sisters.' Marjorie and Allan were hard up and popular; they could not afford a baby; they lived in a little house in the neighbourhood of Portman Square,[45] very convenient for Paddington Station.[46] They had a Pekingese dog named Djinn.[47]

Brenda had come on impulse, leaving the butler to ring up and tell Marjorie of her arrival. She emerged from the train, after two hours and a quarter in a carriage crowded five a side, looking as fresh and fragile as if she had that moment left a circle of masseuses, chiropodists, manicurists and coiffeuses in an hotel suite. It was an aptitude she had, never to look half finished; when she was really exhausted, as she often was on her return to Hetton after these days in London, she went completely to pieces quite suddenly and became a waif; then she would sit over the fire with a cup of bread and milk, hardly alive, until Tony took her up to bed.

Marjorie had her hat on and was sitting at her writing table puzzling over her cheque book and a sheaf of bills.

'Darling, what *does* the country do to you? You look like a thousand pounds. Where *did* you get that suit?'

'I don't know. Some shop.'

'What's the news at Hetton?'

'All the same. Tony madly feudal. John Andrew cursing like a stable boy.'

'And you?'

'Me? Oh, I'm all right.'

'Who's been to stay?'

'No one. We had a friend of Tony's called Mr Beaver last weekend.'

'John Beaver? . . . How very odd. I shouldn't have thought he was at all Tony's ticket.'

'He wasn't . . . What's he like?'

'I hardly know him. I see him at Margot's sometimes. He's a great one for going everywhere.'

'I thought he was rather pathetic.'

'Oh, he's *pathetic* all right. D'you fancy him?'

'Heavens, no.'

They took Djinn for a walk in the Park. He was a very unrepaying dog who never looked about him and had to be dragged along by his harness; they took him to Watts's *Physical Energy*;[48] when loosed he stood perfectly still, gazing moodily at the asphalt until they turned towards home; only once did he show any sign of emotion, when he snapped at a small child who attempted to stroke him; later he got lost and was found a few yards away, sitting under a chair and staring at a shred of waste paper. He was quite colourless, with pink nose and lips and pink circles of bald flesh round his eyes. 'I don't believe he has a spark of human feeling,' said Marjorie.

They talked about Mr Cruttwell,[49] their bone-setter, and Marjorie's new treatment. 'He's never done that to me,' said Brenda enviously; presently, 'What do you suppose is Mr Beaver's sex life?'

'I shouldn't know. Pretty dim, I imagine . . . You *do* fancy him?'

'Oh well,' said Brenda, 'I don't see such a lot of young men . . .'

They left the dog at home and did some shopping – towels for the nursery, pickled peaches, a clock for one of the lodge-keepers who was celebrating his sixtieth year of service at Hetton, a pot of Morecambe Bay[50] shrimps as a surprise for Tony; they made an appointment with Mr Cruttwell for that afternoon. They talked about Polly Cockpurse's party. 'Do come up for it. It's certain to be amusing.'

'I might . . . if I can find someone to take me. Tony doesn't like her . . . I can't go to parties alone at my age.'

They went out to luncheon, to a new restaurant in Albemarle Street[51] which a friend of theirs named Daisy had recently opened. 'You're in luck,' said Marjorie, as soon as they got inside the door, 'there's your Mr Beaver's mother.'

She was entertaining a party of eight at a large round table in the centre of the room; she was being paid to do so by Daisy, whose restaurant was not doing all she expected of it – that is to say the luncheon was free and Mrs Beaver was getting the order, should the restaurant still be open, for its Spring redecorations. It was, transparently, a made-up party, the guests being chosen for no mutual bond – least of all affection for Mrs Beaver or for each other – except that their names were in current use – an accessible but not wholly renegade Duke, an unmarried girl of experience, a dancer and a novelist and a scene designer, a shamefaced junior minister who had not realised what he was in for until too late, and Lady Cockpurse. 'God, what a party,' said Marjorie, waving brightly to them all.

'You're both coming to my party, darlings?' Polly Cockpurse's strident tones rang across the restaurant. 'Only don't tell anyone about it. It's just a very small, secret party. The house will only hold a few people – just old friends.'

'It would be wonderful to see what Polly's *real* old friends were like,' said Marjorie. 'She hasn't known anyone more than five years.'

'I wish Tony could see her point.'

(Although Polly's fortune was derived from men, her popularity was chiefly among women, who admired her clothes and bought them from her second-hand at bargain prices; her first steps to eminence had been in circles so obscure that they had made her no enemies in the world to which she aspired; some time ago she had married a good-natured Earl, whom nobody else happened to want at the time; since then she had scaled all but the highest peaks of every social mountain.)

After luncheon Mrs Beaver came across to their table. 'I *must* just come and speak to you, though I'm in a great hurry. It's *so* long since we met and John has been telling me about a *delightful* weekend he had with you.'

'It was very quiet.'

'That's just what he *loves*. Poor boy, he gets rushed off his feet in London. Tell me, Lady Brenda, is it true you are looking for a flat, because I think I've got just the place for you? It's being done up now and will be ready well before Christmas.' She looked at her watch. 'Oh dear, I must fly. You couldn't possibly come in for a cocktail, this evening? Then you could hear all about it.'

'I *could* . . .' said Brenda doubtfully.

'Then *do*. I'll expect you about six. I daresay you don't know where I live?' She told her and left the table.

'What's all this about a flat?' Marjorie asked.

'Oh just something I thought of . . .'

That afternoon, as she lay luxuriously on the osteopath's table, and her vertebræ, under his strong fingers, snapped like patent fasteners, Brenda wondered whether Beaver would be at home that evening. 'Probably not, if he's so keen on going about,' she thought, 'and, anyhow, what's the sense? . . .'

But he was there, in spite of two other invitations.

She heard all about the maisonette. Mrs Beaver knew her job. What people wanted, she said, was somewhere to dress and telephone. She was subdividing a small house in Belgravia[52] into six flats at three pounds a week, of one room each and a bath; the bathrooms were going to be slap-up,[53] with limitless hot water and every transatlantic refinement; the other room would have a large built-in wardrobe with electric light inside, and space for a bed. It would fill a long felt need, Mrs Beaver said.

'I'll ask my husband and let you know.'

'You *will* let me know soon, won't you, because *everyone* will be wanting one.'

'I'll let you know very soon.'

When she had to go, Beaver came with her to the station. She usually ate some chocolate and buns in her carriage; they bought them together at the buffet. There was plenty of time before the train left and the carriage was not yet full. Beaver came in and sat with her.

'I'm sure you want to go away.'

'No, really.'

'I've got lots to read.'

'I *want* to stay.'

'It's very sweet of you.' Presently she said, rather timidly, for she was not used to asking for that sort of thing, 'I suppose you wouldn't like to take me to Polly's party, would you?'

Beaver hesitated. There would be several dinner parties that evening and he was almost certain to be invited to one or other of them . . . if he took Brenda out it would mean the Embassy or some smart restaurant . . . three pounds at least . . . and he would be responsible for her and have to see her home . . . and if, as she said, she really did not know many people nowadays (why indeed should she have asked him if that were not true?) it might mean tying himself up for the whole evening . . . 'I wish I could,' he said, 'but I've promised to dine out for it.'

Brenda had observed his hesitation. 'I was afraid you would have.'

'But we'll meet there.'

'Yes, if I go.'

'I wish I could have taken you.'

'It's quite all right . . . I just wondered.'

The gaiety with which they had bought the buns was all gone now. They were silent for a minute. Then Beaver said, 'Well, I think perhaps I'll leave you now.'

'Yes, run along. Thank you for coming.'

He went off down the platform. There were still eight minutes to go. The carriage suddenly filled up and Brenda felt tired out.

'Why *should* he want to take me, poor boy?' she thought. 'Only he might have done it better.'

'Barnardo case?'[54]

Brenda nodded. 'Down and out,' she said, 'sunk, right under.' She sat nursing her bread and milk, stirring it listlessly. Every bit of her felt good for nothing.

'Good day?'

She nodded. 'Saw Marjorie and her filthy dog. Bought some things. Lunched at Daisy's new joint. Bone-setter. That's all.'

'You know I wish you'd give up these day trips to London. They're far too much for you.'

'Me? Oh, I'm all right. Wish I was dead, that's all . . . and please, please, darling Tony, don't say anything about bed, because I can't move.'

Next day a telegram came from Beaver. *Have got out of dinner 16th. Are you still free.*

She replied: *Delighted. Second thoughts always best. Brenda.*

Up till then they had avoided Christian names.

'You seem in wonderful spirits today,' Tony remarked.

'I feel big. I think it's Mr Cruttwell. He puts all one's nerves right and one's circulation and everything.'

Three

'Where's mummy gone?'

'London.'

'Why?'

'Someone called Lady Cockpurse is giving a party.'

'Is she nice?'

'Mummy thinks so. I don't.'

'Why?'

'Because she looks like a monkey.'

'I should love to see her. Does she live in a cage? Has she got a tail? Ben saw a woman who looked like a fish, with scales all over instead of skin. It was in a circus in Cairo. Smelt like a fish too, Ben says.'

They were having tea together on the afternoon of Brenda's departure. 'Daddy, what does Lady Cockpurse eat?'

'Oh, nuts and things.'

'Nuts and what things?'

'Different kinds of nuts.'

For days to come the image of this hairy, mischievous Countess occupied John Andrew's mind. She became one of the inhabitants of his world, like Peppermint, the mule who died of rum. When kindly people spoke to him in the village he would tell them about her and how she swung head down from a tree throwing nutshells at passers-by.

'You mustn't say things like that about real people,' said nanny. 'Whatever would Lady Cockpurse do if she heard about it?'

'She'd gibber and chatter and lash round with her tail, and then I expect she'd catch some nice, big, juicy fleas and forget all about it.'

Brenda was staying at Marjorie's for the night. She was dressed first and came into her sister's room. 'Lovely, darling. New?'

'Fairly.'

Marjorie was rung up by the woman at whose house she was dining. ('Look here, are you absolutely sure you can't make Allan come tonight?' 'Absolutely. He's got a meeting in Camberwell.[55] He may not even come to Polly's.' 'Is there *any* man you can bring?' 'Can't think of anybody.' 'Well, we shall have to be one short, that's all. I can't think what's happened tonight. I rang up John Beaver but even *he* won't come.')

'You know,' said Marjorie, putting down the telephone, 'you're causing a great deal of trouble. You've taken London's only spare man.'

'Oh dear, I didn't realize . . .'

Beaver arrived at quarter to nine in a state of high self-approval; he had refused two invitations to dinner while dressing that evening; he had cashed a cheque for ten pounds at his club; he had booked a divan table at Espinosa's. It was almost the first time in his life that he had taken anyone out to dinner, but he knew perfectly well how it was done.

'I must see your Mr Beaver properly,' said Marjorie. 'Let's make him take off his coat and drink something.'

The two sisters were a little shy as they came downstairs, but Beaver was perfectly at his ease. He looked very elegant and rather more than his age.

'Oh, he's not so bad, your Mr Beaver,' Marjorie's look seemed to say, 'not by any means,' and he, seeing the two women together, who were both beautiful, though in a manner so different that, although it was apparent that they were sisters, they might have belonged each to a separate race, began to understand what had perplexed him all the week; why, contrary to all habit and principle, he had telegraphed to Brenda asking her to dine.

'Mrs Jimmy Deane's very upset that she couldn't get you for tonight. I didn't give away what you were doing.'

'Give her my love,' said Beaver. 'Anyway we'll all meet at Polly's.'

'I must go, we're dining at nine.'

'Stay a bit,' said Brenda. 'She's sure to be late.'

Now that it was inevitable, she did not want to be left alone with Beaver.

'No, I must go. Enjoy yourselves, bless you both.' She felt as though she were the elder sister, seeing Brenda timid and expectant at the beginning of an adventure.

They were awkward when Marjorie left, for in the week that they had been apart, each had, in thought, grown more intimate with the other than any actual occurrence warranted. Had Beaver been more experienced, he might have crossed to where Brenda was sitting on the arm of a chair, and made love[56] to her at once; and probably he would have got away with it. Instead he remarked in an easy manner, 'I suppose we ought to be going too.'

'Yes, where?'

'I thought Espinosa's.'

'Yes, lovely. Only listen. I want you to understand right away that it's *my* dinner.'

'Of course not . . . nothing of the sort.'

'Yes it is. I'm a year older than you and an old married woman and quite rich, so, please, I'm going to pay.'

Beaver continued protesting to the taxi door.

But there was still a constraint between them and Beaver began to wonder, 'Does she expect me to pounce?' So, as they waited in a traffic block by the Marble Arch,[57] he leaned forward to kiss her; when he was quite near, she drew back. He said, '*Please*, Brenda,' but she turned away and looked out of the window, shaking her head several times quickly. Then, her eyes still fixed on the window, she put out her hand to his and they sat in silence till they reached the restaurant.

Beaver was thoroughly puzzled.

Once they were in public again, his confidence returned. Espinosa led them to their table; it was the one by itself on the right of the door, the only table in the restaurant at which one's conversation was not overheard. Brenda handed him the card. 'You choose. Very little for me, but it must only have starch, no protein.'

The bill at Espinosa's was, as a rule, roughly the same whatever one ate, but Brenda would not know this, so, since it was now understood that she was paying, Beaver felt constrained from ordering anything that looked obviously expensive. However, she insisted on champagne, and later a ballon of liqueur brandy for him. 'You can't think how exciting it is for me to take a young man out. I've never done it before.'

They stayed at Espinosa's until it was time to go to the party, dancing once or twice, but most of the time sitting at the table, talking. Their interest in each other had so far outdistanced their knowledge that there was a great deal to say.

Presently Beaver said, 'I'm sorry I was an ass in the taxi just now.'

'Eh?'

He changed it and said, 'Did you mind when I tried to kiss you just now?'

'Me? No, not particularly.'

'Then why wouldn't you let me?'

'Oh dear, you've got a lot to learn.'

'How d'you mean?'

'You mustn't ever ask questions like that. Will you try and remember?'

Then he was sulky. 'You talk to me as if I was an undergraduate having his first walk out.'[58]

'Oh, is this a walk out?'

'Not as far as I am concerned.'

There was a pause in which Brenda said, 'I am not sure it hasn't been a mistake, taking you out to dinner. Let's ask for the bill and go to Polly's.'

But they took ten minutes to bring the bill, and in that time Beaver and Brenda had to say something, so he said he was sorry.

'You've got to *learn* to be nicer,' she said soberly. 'I don't believe you'd find it impossible.' When the bill eventually came, she said, 'How much do I tip him?' and Beaver showed her. 'Are you sure that's enough? I should have given twice as much.'

'It's exactly right,' said Beaver, feeling older again, just as Brenda had meant him to feel.

When they sat in the taxi Beaver knew at once that Brenda wished him to make love to her. But he decided it was time she took the lead. So he sat at a distance from her and commented on an old house that was being demolished to make way for a block of flats.

'Shut up,' said Brenda. 'Come here.'

When he had kissed her, she rubbed against his cheek in the way she had.

Polly's party was exactly what she wished it to be, an accurate replica of all the best parties she had been to in the last year; the same band, the same supper, and, above all, the same guests. Hers was not the ambition to create a sensation, to have the party talked about in months to come for any unusual feature, to hunt out shy celebrities or introduce exotic strangers. She wanted a perfectly straight, smart party and she had got it. Practically everyone she asked had come. If there were other, more remote worlds upon which she did not impinge, Polly did not know about them. These were the people she was after, and here they were. And looking round on her guests, with Lord Cockpurse, who was for the evening loyally putting in one of his rare appearances, at her side, she was able to congratulate herself that there were very few people present whom she did not want. In other years people had taken her hospitality more casually and brought on with them anyone with whom they happened to have been dining. This year, without any conscious effort on her part, there had been more formality. Those who wanted to bring friends had rung up in the morning and asked whether they might do so, and on the whole they had been cautious of even so much presumption. People who, only eighteen months before, would have pretended to be ignorant of her existence, were now crowding up her stairs. She had got herself in line with the other married women of her world.

As they started to go up, Brenda said, 'You're not to leave me, please. I'm not going to know anybody,' and Beaver again saw himself as the dominant male.

They went straight through to the band and began dancing, not talking much except to greet other couples whom they knew. They danced for half an hour and then she said, 'All right, I'll give you a rest. Only don't let me get left.'

She danced with Jock Grant-Menzies and two or three old friends and did not see Beaver again until she came on him alone in the bar. He had been there a long time, talking sometimes to the couples who came in and out, but always ending up alone. He was not enjoying the evening and he told himself rather resentfully that it was because of Brenda; if he had come there in a large party it would have been different.

Brenda saw he was out of temper and said, 'Time for supper.'

It was early, and the tables were mostly empty except for earnest couples sitting alone. There was a large round table between the windows, with no one at it; they sat there.

'I don't propose to move for a long time, d'you mind?' She wanted to make him feel important again, so she asked him about the other people in the room.

Presently their table filled up. These were Brenda's old friends, among whom she used to live when she came out and in the first two years of her marriage, before Tony's father died; men in the early thirties, married women of her own age, none of whom knew Beaver or liked him. It was by far the gayest table in the room. Brenda thought 'How my poor young man must be hating this'; it did not occur to her that, from Beaver's point of view, these old friends of hers were quite the most desirable people at the party, and that he was delighted to be seen at their table. 'Are you dying of it?' she whispered.

'No, indeed, never happier.'

'Well, I am. Let's go and dance.'

But the band was taking a rest and there was no one in the ballroom except the earnest couples who had migrated there away from the crowd and were sitting huddled in solitude round the walls, lost in conversation. 'Oh dear,' said Brenda, 'now we're done. We can't go back to the table . . . it almost looks as though we should have to go home.'

'It's not two.'

'That's late for me. Look here, don't you come. Stay and enjoy yourself.'

'Of course I'll come,' said Beaver.

It was a cold, clear night. Brenda shivered and he put his arm round her in the taxi. They did not say much.

'There already?'

They sat for a few seconds without moving. Then Brenda slipped free and Beaver got out.

'I am afraid I can't ask you in for a drink. You see it isn't my house and I shouldn't know where to find anything.'

'No, of course not.'

'Well, goodnight, my dear. Thank you a thousand times for looking after me. I'm afraid I rather bitched your evening.'

'No, of course not,' said Beaver.

'Will you ring me in the morning . . . promise?' She touched her hand to her lips and then turned to the key hole.

Beaver hesitated a minute whether he should go back to the party, but decided not to. He was near home, and everyone at Polly's would have settled down by now; so he gave his address in Sussex Gardens, and went up to bed.

Just as he was undressed he heard the telephone ringing

downstairs. It was his telephone. He went down, two flights in the cold. It was Brenda's voice.

'Darling, I was just going to ring off. I thought you must have gone back to Polly's. Is the telephone not by your bed?'

'No, it's on the ground floor.'

'Oh dear, then it wasn't a very good idea to ring up, was it?'

'Oh, I don't know. What is it?'

'Just to say "goodnight".'

'Oh, I see, well – goodnight.'

'And you'll ring me in the morning?'

'Yes.'

'Early, before you've made any plans.'

'Yes.'

'Then goodnight, bless you.'

Beaver went up the two flights of stairs again, and got into bed.

'. . . going away in the middle of the party.'

'I can't tell you how innocent it was. He didn't even come in.'

'No one is going to know that.'

'And he was furious when I rang him up.'

'What does he think of you?'

'Simply can't make me out at all . . . terribly puzzled, and rather bored in bits.'

'Are you going to go on with it?'

'I shouldn't know.' The telephone rang. 'Perhaps that's him.' But it was not.

Brenda had come into Marjorie's room and they were having breakfast in bed. Marjorie was more than ever like an elder sister that morning. 'But really, Brenda, he's such a *dreary* young man.'

'I know it all. He's second rate and a snob and, I should think, as cold as a fish, but I happen to have a fancy for him, that's all . . . besides I'm not sure he's *altogether* awful . . . he's got that odious mother whom he adores . . . and he's always been very poor. I don't think he's had a fair deal. I heard all about it last night. He got engaged once but they couldn't get married because of money

and since then he's never had a proper affair with anyone decent
. . . he's got to be taught a whole lot of things. That's part of his
attraction.'

'Oh dear, I see you're very serious.'

The telephone rang.

'Perhaps *that's* him.'

But a familiar voice rang out from the instrument so that Brenda
too could hear it, 'Good-morning, darling, what's the dirt today?'

'Oh, Polly, what a good party last night.'

'Not so bad for the old girl, was it? I say, what about your sister
and Mr Beaver?'

'What about them?'

'How long has *that* been on?'

'There's nothing doing there, Polly.'

'Don't you tell me. They were well away last night. How's the
boy managed it? That's what I want to know. He must have
something we didn't know about . . .'

'So Polly's on to your story. She'll be telling everyone in London
at this moment.'

'How I wish there was anything to tell! The cub hasn't even
rung me up . . . Well, I'll leave him in peace. If he doesn't do
anything about me, I'll go down to Hetton this afternoon. Perhaps
that's him.' But it was only Allan from the Conservative Central
Office,[59] to say how sorry he had been not to get to the party the
night before. 'I hear Brenda disgraced herself,' he said.

'Goodness,' said Brenda. 'People do think that young men are
easily come by.'

'I scarcely saw you at Polly's last night,' said Mrs Beaver. 'What
became of you?'

'We went early. Brenda Last was tired.'

'She was looking lovely. I am so glad you've made friends with
her. When are you going to see her again?'

'I said I'd ring up.'

'Well, why don't you?'

'Oh, mumsy, what's the use? I can't afford to start taking about
women like Brenda Last. If I ring up she'll say, what are you doing,

and I shall have to ask her to something, and it will be the same thing every day. I simply haven't the money.'

'I know, my son. It's very difficult for you . . . and you're wonderful about money. I ought to be grateful that I haven't a son always coming to me with debts. Still, it doesn't do to deny yourself *everything*, you know. You're getting to be an old bachelor already at twenty-five. I could see Brenda liked you, that evening she came here.'

'Oh, she likes me all right.'

'I hope she makes up her mind about that flat. They're going like hot cakes. I shall have to look about for another suitable house to split up. You'd be surprised who've been taking them – quite a number of people with houses in London already . . . Well, I must be getting back to work. I'm away for two nights by the way. See that Chambers looks after you properly. There are some Australians Sylvia Newport discovered who want to take a house in the country, so I'm driving them round to one or two that might do for them. Where are you lunching?'

'Margot's.'

By one o'clock, when they came back from taking Djinn to the Park, Beaver had not rung up. 'So that's that,' said Brenda, 'I daresay I'm glad really.' She sent a telegram to Tony to expect her by the afternoon train and, in a small voice, ordered her things to be packed. 'I don't seem to have anywhere to lunch,' she said.

'Why don't you come to Margot's? I know she'd love it.'

'Well, ring up and ask her.'

So she met Beaver again.

He was sitting some way from her and they did not speak to each other until everyone was going. 'I kept trying to get through to you this morning,' he said, 'but the line was always engaged.'

'Oh come on,' said Brenda, 'I'll sock[60] you a movie.'

Later she wired to Tony: *Staying with Marjorie another day or two all love to you both.*

Four

'Is mummy coming back today?'

'I hope so.'

'That monkey-woman's party has lasted a long time. Can I come in to the station and meet her?'

'Yes, we'll both go.'

'She hasn't seen Thunderclap for four days. She hasn't seen me jump the new post and rail, has she, daddy?'

She was coming by the 3.18. Tony and John Andrew were there early. They wandered about the station looking at things, and bought some chocolate from a slot machine. The stationmaster came out to talk to them. 'Her ladyship coming back today?' He was an old friend of Tony's.

'I've been expecting her every day. You know what it is when ladies get to London.'

'Sam Brace's wife went to London and he couldn't get her back. Had to go up and fetch her himself. And then she give him a hiding.'

Presently the train came in and Brenda emerged exquisitely from her third class carriage. 'You've *both* come. What angels you are. I don't at all deserve it.'

'Oh mummy, have you brought the monkey-lady?'

'What *does* the child mean?'

'He's got it into his head that your chum Polly has a tail.'

'Come to think of it, I shouldn't be surprised if she had.'

Two little cases held all her luggage. The chauffeur strapped them on behind the car, and they drove to Hetton.

'What's all the news?'

'Ben's put the rail up ever so high and Thunderclap and I jumped it six times yesterday and six times again today and two more of the fish in the little pond are dead, floating upside down all swollen and nanny burnt her finger on the kettle yesterday and daddy and I saw a fox just as near as anything and he sat quite still and then went away into the wood and I began drawing a picture of a battle only I couldn't finish it because the paints weren't right and the grey carthorse the one that had worms is quite well again.'

'Nothing much has happened,' said Tony. 'We've missed you. What did you find to do in London all this time?'

'Me? Oh I've been behaving rather badly to tell you the truth.'

'Buying things?'

'Worse. I've been carrying on madly with young men and I've spent heaps of money and I've enjoyed it very much indeed. But there's one awful thing.'

'What's that?'

'No, I think it had better keep. It's something you won't like at all.'

'You've bought a Pekingese.'

'Worse, far worse. Only I haven't done it yet. But I *want* to dreadfully.'

'Go on.'

'Tony, I've found a flat.'

'Well, you'd better lose it again, quick.'

'All right. I'll attack you about it again later. Meanwhile try not to brood about it.'

'I shan't give it another thought.'

'What's a flat, daddy?'

Brenda wore pyjamas at dinner, and afterwards sat close to Tony on the sofa and ate some sugar out of his coffee cup.

'I suppose all this means that you're going to start again about your flat?'

'Mmmm.'

'You haven't signed any papers yet, have you?'

'Oh no.' Brenda shook her head emphatically.

'Then no great harm's done.' Tony began to fill his pipe.

Brenda knelt on the sofa, sitting back on her heels. 'Listen, you haven't been brooding?'

'No.'

'Because, you see, when you say "flat" you're thinking of something quite different to me. *You* mean by a flat, a lift and a man in uniform, and a big front door with knobs, and an entrance hall and doors opening in all directions, with kitchens and sculleries

and dining rooms and drawing rooms and servants' bathrooms . . .
don't you, Tony?'

'More or less.'

'*Exactly*. Now *I* mean just a bedroom and a bath and a telephone.
You see the difference? Now a woman I know –'

'Who?'

'Just a woman – has fixed up a whole house like that off Belgrave
Square and they are three pounds a week, no rates and taxes,
constant hot water and central heating, woman comes in to make
the bed when required, what d'you think of that?'

'I see.'

'Now this is how I look at it. What's three pounds a week? Less
than nine bob a night. Where could one stay for less than nine
bob a night with all those advantages? You're always going to the
club, and that costs more, and I can't stay often with Marjorie
because it's hell for her having me, and anyway she's got that dog,
and you're always saying when I come back in the evenings after
shopping, "Why didn't you stay the night," you say, "instead of
killing yourself?" Time and again you say it. I'm sure we spend
much more than three pounds a week through not having a flat.
Tell you what, I'll give up Mr Cruttwell. How's that?'

'D'you really want this thing?'

'Mmm.'

'Well, I'll have to see. We *might* manage it, but it'll mean putting
off the improvements down here.'

'I don't really deserve it,' she said, clinching the matter. 'I've
been carrying on *anyhow* this week.'

Brenda's stay at Hetton lasted only for three nights. Then she
returned to London, saying that she had to see about the flat. It
did not, however, require very great attention. There was only the
colour of the paint to choose and some few articles of furniture.
Mrs Beaver had them ready for her inspection, a bed, a carpet, a
dressing-table and chair – there was not room for more. Mrs Beaver
tried to sell her a set of needlework pictures for the walls, but these
she refused, also an electric bed warmer, a miniature weighing
machine for the bathroom, a frigidaire, an antique grandfather

clock, a backgammon set of looking-glass and synthetic ivory, a set of prettily bound French eighteenth century poets, a massage apparatus, and a wireless set fitted in a case of Regency lacquer, all of which had been grouped in the shop for her as a 'suggestion.' Mrs Beaver bore Brenda no ill will for the modesty of her requirements; she was doing very well on the floor above with a Canadian lady who was having her walls covered with chromium plating at immense expense.

Meanwhile Brenda stayed with Marjorie, on terms which gradually became acrimonious. 'I'm sorry to be pompous,' she said one morning, 'but I just don't want your Mr Beaver hanging about the house all day and calling me Marjorie.'

'Oh well, the flat won't be long now.'

'And I shall go on saying that I think you're making a ridiculous mistake.'

'It's just that you don't like Mr Beaver.'

'It isn't only that. I think it's hard cheese on Tony.'

'Oh, Tony's all right.'

'And if there's a row –'

'There won't be a row.'

'You never know. If there is, I don't want Allan to think I've been helping to arrange things.'

'I wasn't so disagreeable to you about Robin Beaseley.'

'There was never much in that,' said Marjorie.

But with the exception of her sister's, opinion was greatly in favour of Brenda's adventure. The morning telephone buzzed with news of her; even people with whom she had the barest acquaintance were delighted to relate that they had seen her and Beaver the evening before at a restaurant or cinema. It had been an autumn of very sparse and meagre romance; only the most obvious people had parted or come together, and Brenda was filling a want long felt by those whose simple, vicarious pleasure it was to discuss the subject in bed over the telephone. For them her circumstances shed peculiar glamour; for five years she had been a legendary, almost ghostly name, the imprisoned princess of fairy story, and now that she had emerged there was more enchantment in the occurrence than in the mere change of habit of any other circumspect wife. Her very choice of partner gave the affair an appropriate touch of fantasy; Beaver, the joke figure they had all known and despised, suddenly caught up to her among the luminous clouds of deity. If, after seven years looking neither to right or left, she had at last broken away with Jock Grant-Menzies or Robin Beaseley or any other young buck with whom nearly everyone had had a crack one time or another, it would have been thrilling no doubt, but straightforward, drawing-room comedy. The choice of Beaver raised the whole escapade into a realm of poetry for Polly and Daisy and Angela and all the gang of gossips.

Mrs Beaver made no bones about her delight. 'Of course the subject has not been mentioned between John and myself, but if what I hear is true, I think it will do the boy a world of good. Of course he's always been very much in demand and had a great number of friends, but *that isn't the same thing*. I've felt for a long time a Lack of Something in him, and I think that a charming and experienced woman like Brenda Last is just the person to help him. He's got a *very* affectionate nature, but he's so sensitive that he hardly ever lets it appear . . . to tell you the truth I felt something of the kind was in the air last week, so I made an excuse to go away for a few days. If I had been there things might never have come to anything. He's very shy and reserved even to me. I'll have the chess-men done up and sent round to you this afternoon. Thank you so much.'

And Beaver, for the first time in his life, found himself a person of interest and, almost, of consequence. Women studied him with a new scrutiny, wondering what they had missed in him; men treated him as an equal, even as a successful fellow competitor. 'How on earth has *he* got away with it?' they may have asked themselves, but now, when he came into Brat's, they made room for him at the bar and said, 'Well old boy, how about one?'

Brenda rang up Tony every morning and evening. Sometimes John Andrew spoke to her, too, as shrill as Polly Cockpurse; quite unable to hear her replies. She went to Hetton for the weekend, and then back to London, this time to the flat where the paint was already dry, though the hot water was not yet in perfect working order; everything smelt very new – walls, sheets, curtains – and the new radiators gave off a less agreeable reek of hot iron.

That evening as usual she telephoned to Hetton. 'I'm talking from the flat.'

'Oh, ah.'

'*Darling*, do try to sound interested. It's very exciting for me.'

'What's it like?'

'Well, there are a good many smells at present and the bath makes odd sounds and when you turn on the hot tap there's just a rush of air and that's all, and the cold tap keeps dripping and the water is rather brown and the cupboard doors are jammed and the curtains won't pull right across so that the street lamp shines in all night . . . but it's *lovely*.'

'You don't say so.'

'Tony, you must be nice about it. It's all so exciting – front door and a latch key and all . . . And someone sent me a lot of flowers today – so many that there's hardly room for them and I've had to put them in the basin on account of having no pots. It wasn't you, was it?'

'Yes . . . as a matter of fact.'

'Darling, I did so hope it was . . . how like you.'

'Three minutes please.'

'Must stop now.'

'When are you coming back?'

'Almost at once. Goodnight, my sweet.'

'What a lot of talk,' said Beaver.

All the time that she was speaking, she had been kept busy with one hand warding him off the telephone, which he threatened playfully to disconnect.

'Wasn't it sweet of Tony to send those flowers?'

'I'm not awfully fond of Tony.'

'Don't let that worry you, my beauty, he doesn't like you *at all*.'

'*Doesn't* he? Why not?'

'No one does except me. You must get that clear . . . it's very odd that *I* should.'

*

60

Beaver and his mother were going to Ireland for Christmas, to stay with cousins. Tony and Brenda had a family party at Hetton: Marjorie and Allan, Brenda's mother, Tony's Aunt Frances and two families of impoverished Lasts, humble and uncomplaining victims of primogeniture, to whom Hetton meant as much as it did to Tony. There was a little Christmas tree in the nursery for John Andrew and a big one downstairs in the central hall which was decorated by the impoverished Lasts and lit up for half an hour after tea (two footmen standing by with wet sponges on the end of poles, to extinguish the candles which turned turtle and threatened to start a fire). There were presents for all the servants, of value strictly graded according to their rank, and for all the guests (cheques for the impoverished Lasts). Allan always brought a large croûte[61] of foie gras, a delicacy of which he was particularly fond. Everyone ate a great deal and became slightly torpid towards Boxing Day evening; silver ladles of burning brandy went round the table, crackers[62] were pulled and opened; paper hats, indoor fireworks, mottoes. This year, everything happened in its accustomed way; nothing seemed to menace the peace and stability of the house. The choir came up and sang carols in the pitch pine gallery, and later devoured hot punch and sweet biscuits. The vicar preached his usual Christmas sermon. It was one to which his parishioners were greatly attached.

'How difficult it is for us,' he began, blandly surveying his congregation, who coughed into their mufflers and chafed their chilblains under their woollen gloves, 'to realize that this is indeed Christmas. Instead of the glowing log fire and windows tight shuttered against the drifting snow, we have only the harsh glare of an alien sun; instead of the happy circle of loved faces, of home and family, we have the uncomprehending stares of the subjugated, though no doubt grateful, heathen. Instead of the placid ox and ass of Bethlehem,' said the vicar, slightly losing the thread of his comparisons, 'we have for companions the ravening tiger and the exotic camel, the furtive jackal and the ponderous elephant . . .' And so on, through the pages of faded manuscript. The words had temporarily touched the heart of many an obdurate trooper, and hearing them again, as he had heard them year after year since

Mr Tendril had come to the parish, Tony and most of Tony's guests felt that it was an integral part of their Christmas festivities; one with which they would find it very hard to dispense. 'The ravening tiger and the exotic camel' had long been bywords in the family, of frequent recurrence in all their games.

These games were the hardest part for Brenda. They did not amuse her and she still could not see Tony dressed up for charades[63] without a feeling of shyness. Moreover, she was tortured by the fear that any lack of gusto on her part might be construed by the poor Lasts as superiority. These scruples, had she known it, were quite superfluous, for it never occurred to her husband's relatives to look on her with anything but cousinly cordiality and a certain tolerance, for, as Lasts, they considered they had far more right in Hetton than herself. Aunt Frances, with acid mind, quickly discerned the trouble and attempted to reassure her, saying, 'Dear child, all these feelings of delicacy are valueless; only the rich realize the gulf that separates them from the poor,' but the uneasiness persisted, and night after night she found herself being sent out of the room, asking or answering questions, performing actions in uncouth manners, paying forfeits, drawing pictures, writing verses, dressing herself up and even being chased about the house, and secluded in cupboards, at the will of her relatives. Christmas was on a Friday that year, so the party was a long one, from Thursday until Monday.

She had forbidden Beaver to send her a present or to write to her; in self protection, for she knew that whatever he said would hurt her by its poverty, but in spite of this she awaited the posts nervously, hoping that he might have disobeyed her. She had sent him to Ireland a ring of three interlocked hoops of gold and platinum. An hour after ordering it she regretted her choice. On Tuesday a letter came from him thanking her. *Darling Brenda*, he wrote. *Thank you so very much for the charming Christmas present. You can imagine my delight when I saw the pink leather case and my surprise at opening it. It really was sweet of you to send me such a charming present. Thank you again very much for it. I hope your party is being a success. It is rather dull here. The others went hunting yesterday. I went to the meet. They did not have a good day. Mother is here too and sends you her love. We shall be leaving tomorrow or the day after. Mother has got rather a cold.*

It ended there at the bottom of a page. Beaver had been writing it before dinner and later had put it in the envelope without remembering to finish it.

He wrote a large, school-girlish hand with wide spaces between the lines.

Brenda felt a little sick when she read this letter but she showed it to Marjorie, saying, 'I can't complain, he's never pretended to like me much. And anyway it was a damned silly present.'

Tony had become fretful about his visit to Angela's. He always hated staying away.

'Don't come, darling. I'll make it all right with them.'

'No, I'll come. I haven't seen so much of you in the last three weeks.'

They had the whole of Wednesday alone together. Brenda exerted herself and Tony's fretfulness subsided. She was particularly tender to him at this time and scarcely teased him at all.

On Thursday they went North to Yorkshire. Beaver was there. Tony discovered him in the first half hour and brought the news to Brenda upstairs.

'I'll tell you something very odd,' he said. 'Who do you think is here?'

'Who?'

'Our old friend Beaver.'

'Why's that odd particularly?'

'Oh, I don't know. I'd forgotten all about him, hadn't you? D'you think he sent Angela a telegram as he did to us?'

'I daresay.'

Tony supposed Beaver must be fairly lonely and took pains to be agreeable to him. He said, 'All kinds of changes since we saw you last. Brenda's taken a flat in London.'

'Yes, I know.'

'How?'

'Well, my mother let it to her, you know.'

Tony was greatly surprised and taxed Brenda with this. 'You never told me who was behind your flat. I might not have been so amiable if I'd known.'

'No, darling, that's why.'

Half the house party wondered why Beaver was there; the other half knew. As a result of this he and Brenda saw each other very little, less than if they had been casual acquaintances, so that Angela remarked to her husband, 'I daresay it was a mistake to ask him. It's so hard to know.'

Brenda never started the subject of the half finished letter, but she noticed that Beaver was wearing his ring, and had already acquired a trick of twisting it as he talked.

On New Year's Eve there was a party at a neighbouring house. Tony went home early and Beaver and Brenda returned together in the back of a car. Next morning, while they were having breakfast, she said to Tony, 'I've made a New Year resolution.'

'Anything to do with spending more time at home?'

'Oh no, *quite* the reverse. Listen, Tony, it's serious. I think I'll take a course of something.'

'Not bone-setters again? I thought that was over.'

'No, something like economics. You see, I've been thinking. I don't really *do* anything at all at present. It's absurd to pretend I'm any use to John. The house runs itself. It seems to me time I *took* to something. Now you're always talking about going into Parliament. Well, if I had done a course of economics I could be some use canvassing and writing speeches and things – you know, the way Marjorie did when Allan was standing on the Clydeside.[64] There are all sorts of lectures in London, to do with the University, where girls go. Don't you think it's rather a good idea?'

'It's one better than the bone-setters,' Tony admitted.

That was how the New Year began.

Chapter Three

HARD CHEESE ON TONY

One

It is not uncommon at Brat's Club, between nine and ten in the evening, to find men in white ties and tail coats sitting by themselves and eating, in evident low spirits, large and extravagant dinners. They are those who have been abandoned at the last minute by their women. For twenty minutes or so they have sat in the foyer of some restaurant, gazing expectantly towards the revolving doors and alternately taking out their watches and ordering cocktails, until at length a telephone message has been brought them that their guests are unable to come. Then they go to Brat's, half hoping to find friends but, more often than not, taking a melancholy satisfaction in finding the club deserted or peopled by strangers. So they sit there, round the walls, morosely regarding the mahogany tables before them, and eating and drinking heavily.

It was in this mood and for this reason that, one evening towards the middle of February, Jock Grant-Menzies arrived at the club.

'Anyone here?'

'Very quiet tonight, sir. Mr Last is in the dining room.'

Jock found him seated in a corner; he was in day clothes; the table and the chair at his side were littered with papers and magazines; one was propped up in front of him. He was half way through dinner and three quarters of the way through a bottle of Burgundy.

'Hullo,' he said. 'Chucked?[1] Come and join me.'

It was some time since Jock had seen Tony; the meeting embarrassed him slightly, for like all his friends, he was wondering how Tony felt and how much he knew about Brenda and John Beaver. However, he sat down at Tony's table.

'Been chucked?' asked Tony again.

'Yes, it's the last time I ask that bitch out.'

'Better have a drink. I've been drinking a whole lot.[2] Much the best thing.'

67

They took what was left of the Burgundy and ordered another bottle.

'Just come up for the night,' said Tony. 'Staying here.'

'You've got a flat now, haven't you?'

'Well, Brenda has. There isn't really room for two . . . we tried it once and it wasn't a success.'

'What's she doing tonight?'

'Out somewhere. I didn't let her know I was coming . . . silly not to, but you see I got fed up with being alone at Hetton and thought I'd like to see Brenda, so I came up suddenly on the spur of the moment, just like that. Damned silly thing to do. Might have known she'd be going out somewhere . . . she's very high-principled about chucking . . . so there it is. She's going to ring me up here later, if she can get away.'

They drank a lot.

Tony did most of the talking. 'Extraordinary idea of hers, taking up economics,' he said. 'I never thought it would last, but she seems really keen on it . . . I suppose it's a good plan. You know there wasn't really much for her to do all the time at Hetton. Of course she'd rather die than admit it, but I believe she got a bit bored there sometimes. I've been thinking it over and that's the conclusion I came to. Brenda must have been bored . . . Daresay she'll get bored with economics some time . . . Anyway she seems cheerful enough now. We've had parties every weekend lately . . . I wish you'd come down sometimes, Jock. I don't seem to get on with Brenda's new friends.'

'People from the school of economics?'

'No, but ones I don't know. I believe I bore them. Thinking it over that's the conclusion I've come to. I bore them. They talk about me as "the old boy." John heard them.'

'Well, that's friendly enough.'

'Yes, that's friendly.'

They finished the Burgundy and drank some port. Presently Tony said, 'I say, come next weekend, will you?'

'I think I'd love to.'

'Wish you would. I don't see many old friends . . . Sure to be lots of people in the house, but you won't mind that, will you? . . .

68

sociable chap, Jock . . . doesn't mind people about. *I* mind it like hell.' They drank some more port. Tony said, 'Not enough bathrooms, you know . . . but of course you know. You've been there before, often. Not like the new friends who think me a bore. You don't think I'm a bore, do you?'

'No, old boy.'

'Not even when I'm tight, like this? . . . There would have been bathrooms. I had the plans out. Four new ones. A chap down there made the plans . . . but then Brenda wanted the flat, so I had to postpone them as an economy . . . I say, that's funny. We had to economize because of Brenda's economics.'

'Yes, that's funny. Let's have some port.'

Tony said, 'You seem pretty low tonight.'

'I am rather. Worried about the Pig Scheme.³ Constituents keep writing.'

'*I* felt low, *bloody* low, but I'm all right again now. The best thing is to get tight. That's what I did and I don't feel low any more . . . discouraging to come to London and find you're not wanted. Funny thing, *you* feel low because your girl's chucked, and *I* feel low because mine won't chuck.'

'Yes, that's funny.'

'But you know I've felt low for weeks now . . . bloody low . . . how about some brandy?'

'Yes, why not? After all there are other things in life besides women and pigs.'

They had some brandy and after a time Jock began to cheer up.

Presently a page came to their table to say, 'A message from Lady Brenda, sir.'

'Good, I'll go and speak to her.'

'It's not her ladyship speaking. Someone was sending a message.'

'I'll come and speak to her.'

He went to the telephone in the lobby outside. 'Darling,' he said.

'Is that Mr Last? I've got a message here, from Lady Brenda.'

'Right, put me through to her.'

'She can't speak herself, but she asked me to give you this

message, that she's very sorry but she cannot join you tonight. She's very tired and has gone home to bed.'

'Tell her I want to speak to her.'

'I can't I'm afraid, she's gone to bed. She's very tired.'

'She's very tired and she's gone to bed?'

'That's right.'

'Well, I want to speak to her.'

'Goodnight,' said the voice.

'The old boy's plastered,' said Beaver as he rang off.

'Oh, dear. I feel rather awful about him. But what *can* he expect, coming up suddenly like this? He's got to be taught not to make surprise visits.'

'Is he often like that?'

'No, it's quite new.'

The telephone bell rang. 'D'you suppose that's him again? I'd better answer it.'

'I want to speak to Lady Brenda Last.'

'Tony, darling, this *is* me, Brenda.'

'Some damn fool said I couldn't speak to you.'

'I left a message from where I was dining. Are you having a lovely evening?'

'Hellish. I'm with Jock. He's worried about the Pig Scheme. Shall we come round and see you?'

'No, not now, darling, I'm terribly tired and just going to bed.'

'We'll come and see you.'

'Tony, are you a tiny bit tight?'

'Stinking. Jock and I'll come and see you.'

'*Tony*, you're *not* to. D'you hear? I can't have you making a brawl. The flats are getting a bad name anyhow.'

'Their name'll be mud when Jock and I come.'

'Tony, listen, will you please not come, not tonight. Be a good boy and stay at the club. Will you *please* not?'

'Shan't be long.' He rang off.

'Oh God,' said Brenda. 'This isn't the least like Tony. Ring up Brat's and get on to Jock. He'll have more sense.'

*

'That was Brenda.'

'So I gathered.'

'She's at the flat. I said that we'd go round.'

'Splendid. Haven't seen her for weeks. Very fond of Brenda.'

'So am I. Grand girl.'

'Grand girl.'

'A lady on the telephone for you, Mr Grant-Menzies.'

'Who?'

'She didn't give a name.'

'All right. I'll come.'

Brenda said to him, 'Jock, what *have* you been doing to my husband?'

'He's a bit tight, that's all.'

'He's roaring. Look here, he threatens to come round. I simply can't face him tonight in that mood, I'm tired out. You understand, don't you?'

'Yes, I understand.'

'So, will you, *please*, keep him away? Are you tight too?'

'A little bit.'

'Oh dear, can I trust you?'

'I'll try.'

'Well, it doesn't sound too good. Goodbye' . . . 'John, you've got to go. Those hooligans may turn up at any moment. Have you got your taxi fare? You'll find some change in my bag.'

'Was that your girl?'

'Yes.'

'Made it up?'

'Not exactly.'

'Far better to make it up. Shall we have some more brandy or go round to Brenda straight away?'

'Let's have some more brandy.'

'Jock, you aren't still feeling low, are you? Doesn't do to feel low. *I'm* not feeling low. I *was*, but I'm not any more.'

'No, I'm not feeling low.'

'Then we'll have some brandy and then go to Brenda's.'

'All right.'

Half an hour later they got into Jock's car. 'Tell you what, I shouldn't drive if I were you.'

'Not drive?'

'No, I shouldn't drive. They'd say you were drunk.'

'Who would?'

'Anyone you ran over. They'd say you were drunk.'

'Well, so I am.'

'Then I shouldn't drive.'

'Too far to walk.'

'We'll take a taxi.'

'Oh hell, I can drive.'

'Or let's not go to Brenda's at all.'

'We'd better go to Brenda's,' said Jock. 'She's expecting us.'

'Well, I can't walk all that way. Besides I don't think she really wanted us to come.'

'She'll be pleased when she sees us.'

'Yes, but it's a long way. Let's go some other place.'

'I'd like to see Brenda,' said Jock. 'I'm very fond of Brenda.'

'She's a grand girl.'

'She's a grand girl.'

'Well, let's take a taxi to Brenda's.'

But half way Jock said, 'Don't let's go there. Let's go some other place. Let's go to some low joint.'

'All the same to me. Tell him to go to some lousy joint.'

'Go to some lousy joint,' said Jock, putting his head through the window.

The cab wheeled round and made towards Regent Street.[4]

'We can always ring Brenda from the lousy joint.'

'Yes, I think we ought to do that. She's a grand girl.'

'Grand girl.'

The cab turned into Golden Square[5] and then down Sink Street, a dingy little place inhabited for the most part by Asiatics.

'D'you know, I believe he's taking us to the Old Hundredth.'

'Can't still be open? Thought they closed it down years ago.'

But the door was brightly illumined and a seedy figure in peaked cap and braided overcoat stepped out to open the taxi for them.

The Old Hundredth has never been shut. For a generation,

while other night clubs have sprung into being, with various names and managers, and various pretensions to respectability, have enjoyed a precarious and brief existence, and come to grief at the hands either of police or creditors, the Old Hundredth has maintained a solid front against all adversity. It has not been immune from persecution; far from it. Times out of number, magistrates have struck it off, cancelled its licence, condemned its premises; the staff and proprietor have been constantly in and out of prison; there have been questions in the House and committees of enquiry, but whatever Home Secretaries[6] and Commissioners of Police have risen into eminence and retired discredited, the doors of the Old Hundredth have always been open from nine in the evening until four at night, and inside there has been an unimpeded flow of dubious, alcoholic preparations. A kindly young lady admitted Tony and Jock to the ramshackle building.

'D'you mind signing in?' Tony and Jock inscribed fictitious names at the foot of a form which stated, *I have been invited to a Bottle Party at 100 Sink Street[7] given by Captain Weybridge.*

'That's five bob each please.'

It is not an expensive club to run, because none of the staff, except the band, receive any wages; they make what they can by going through the overcoat pockets and giving the wrong change to drunks. The young ladies get in free but they have to see to it that their patrons spend money.

'Last time I was here, Tony, was the bachelor party before your wedding.'

'Tight that night.'

'Stinking.'

'I'll tell you who else was tight that night – Reggie. Broke a fruit gum machine.'

'Reggie was stinking.'

'I say, you don't still feel low about that girl?'

'I don't feel low.'

'Come on, we'll go downstairs.'

The dance-room was fairly full. An elderly man had joined the band and was trying to conduct it. 'I like this joint,' said Jock. 'What'll we drink?'

'Brandy.'

They had to buy the bottle. They filled in an order form to the Montmorency Wine Company and paid two pounds. When it came there was a label saying *Very Old Liqueur Fine Champagne. Imported by the Montmorency Wine Co.* The waiter brought ginger ale and four glasses. Two young ladies came and sat with them. They were called Milly and Babs. Milly said, 'Are you in town for long?' Babs said, 'Have you got such a thing as a cigarette?'

Tony danced with Babs. She said, 'Are you fond of dancing?'

'No, are you?'

'So-so.'

'Well, let's sit down.'

The waiter said, 'Will you buy a ticket in a raffle for a box of chocolates?'

'No.'

'Buy one for me,' said Babs.

Jock began to describe the specifications of the Basic Pig.

. . . Milly said, 'You're married, aren't you?'

'No,' said Jock.

'Oh, I can always tell,' said Milly. 'Your friend is too.'

'Yes, *he* is.'

'You'd be surprised how many gentlemen come here just to talk about their wives.'

'He hasn't.'

Tony was leaning across the table and saying to Babs, 'You see the trouble is my wife is studious. She's taking a course in economics.'

Babs said, 'I think it's nice for a girl to be interested in things.'

The waiter said, 'What will you be taking for supper?'

'Why, we've only just had dinner.'

'How about a nice haddock?'

'I tell you what I must do, is to telephone. Where is it?'

'D'you mean really the telephone or the gentlemen's?' Milly asked.

'No, the telephone.'

'Upstairs in the office.'

Tony rang up Brenda. It was some time before she answered, then, 'Yes, who is it?'

'I have a message here from Mr Anthony Last and Mr Jocelyn Grant-Menzies.'

'Oh it's you, Tony. Well, what do you want?'

'You recognized my voice?'

'I did.'

'Well, I only wanted to give a message but as I am speaking to you I can give it myself, can't I?'

'Yes.'

'Well, Jock and I are terribly sorry but we can't come round this evening after all.'

'Oh.'

'You don't think it very rude, I hope, but we have a lot to attend to.'

'That's all right, Tony.'

'Did I wake you up by any chance?'

'That's all right, Tony.'

'Well, goodnight.'

'Goodnight.'

Tony went down to the table. 'I've been talking to Brenda. She sounded rather annoyed. D'you think we *ought* to go round there?'

'We promised we would,' said Jock.

'You should never disappoint a lady,' said Milly.

'Oh, it's too late now.'

Babs said, 'You two are officers, aren't you?'

'No, why?'

'I thought you were.'

Milly said, 'I like business gentlemen best, myself. They've more to say.'

'What d'you do?'

'I design postmen's hats,' said Jock.

'Oh, go on.'

'And my friend here trains sea-lions.'

'Tell us another.'

Babs said, 'I've got a gentleman friend who works on a newspaper.'

After a time Jock said, 'I say, ought we to do something about Brenda?'

'I told her we weren't coming, didn't I?'

'Yes . . . but she might still be *hoping*.'

'I tell you what, you go and ring her up and find out if she really wants us.'

'All right.' He came back ten minutes later. '*I* thought she sounded rather annoyed,' he reported. 'But I said in the end we wouldn't come.'

'She may be tired,' said Tony. 'Has to get up early to do economics. Now I come to think of it someone *did* say she was tired, earlier on in the evening.'

'I say, what's this frightful piece of fish?'

'The waiter said you ordered it.'

'Perhaps I did.'

'I'll give it to the club cat,' said Babs, 'she's a dear called Blackberry.'

They danced once or twice. Then Jock said, 'D'you think we ought to ring up Brenda again?'

'Perhaps we ought. She sounded annoyed with us.'

'Let's go now and ring her up on the way out.'

'Aren't you coming home with us?' said Babs.

'Not tonight, I'm afraid.'

'Be a sport,' said Milly.

'No, we can't, really.'

'All right. Well, how about a little present? We're professional dancing partners, you know,' said Babs.

'Oh yes, sorry, how much?'

'Oh, we leave that to the gentlemen.'

Tony gave them a pound. 'You might make it a bit more,' said Babs. 'We've sat with you two hours.'

Jock gave another pound. 'Come and see us again one evening when you've more time,' said Milly.

'I'm feeling rather ill,' said Tony on the way upstairs. 'Don't think I shall bother to ring up Brenda.'

'Send a message.'

'That's a good idea . . . Look here,' he said to the seedy commissionaire. 'Will you ring up this Sloane number[8] and speak to her ladyship and say Mr Grant-Menzies and Mr Last are very sorry but they cannot call this evening? Got that?' He gave the man half a crown and they sauntered out into Sink Street. 'Brenda can't expect us to do more than that,' he said.

'I tell you what I'll do. I go almost past her door, so I'll ring the bell a bit just in case she's awake and still waiting up for us.'

'Yes, you do that. What a good friend you are, Jock.'

'Oh, I'm fond of Brenda . . . a grand girl.'

'Grand girl . . . I wish I didn't feel ill.'

Tony was awake at eight next morning, miserably articulating in his mind the fragmentary memories of the preceding night. The more he remembered, the baser his conduct appeared to him. At nine he had his bath and some tea. At ten he was wondering whether he should ring Brenda up when the difficulty was solved by her ringing him.

'Well, Tony, how do you feel?'

'Awful. I *was* tight.'

'You were.'

'I'm feeling pretty guilty too.'

'I'm not surprised.'

'I don't remember everything very clearly but I have the impression that Jock and I were rather bores.'

'You were.'

'Are you in a rage?'

'Well, I was last night. What made you do it, Tony, grown up men like you two?'

'We felt low.'

'I bet you feel lower this morning . . . A box of white roses has just arrived from Jock.'

'I wish I'd thought of that.'

'You're such infants, both of you.'

'You aren't really in a rage?'

'Of course I'm not, darling. Now just you go straight back to the country. You'll feel all right again tomorrow.'

'Am I not going to see you?'

'Not today, I'm afraid. I've got lectures all the morning and I'm lunching out. But I'll be coming down on Friday evening or anyway Saturday morning.'

'I see. You couldn't possibly chuck lunch or one of the lectures?'

'Not possibly, darling.'

'I see. You are an angel to be so sweet about last night.'

'Nothing could have been more fortunate,' Brenda said. 'If I know Tony, he'll be tortured with guilt for weeks to come. It was maddening last night but it was worth it. He's put himself so much in the wrong now that he won't dare to *feel* resentful, let alone say anything, whatever I do. And he hasn't really enjoyed himself at all, the poor sweet, so *that's* a good thing too. He had to learn not to make surprise visits.'

'You are one for making people learn things,' said Beaver.

Tony emerged from the 3.18 feeling cold, tired, and heavy with guilt. John Andrew had come in the car to meet him. 'Hullo, daddy, had a good time in London? You didn't mind me coming to the station, did you? I *made* nanny let me.'

'Very pleased to see you, John.'

'How was mummy?'

'She sounded very well. I didn't see her.'

'But you *said* you were going to see her.'

'Yes, I thought I was, but I turned out to be wrong. I talked to her several times on the telephone.'

'But you can telephone her from here, can't you, daddy? Why did you go all the way to London to telephone her? . . . *Why*, daddy?'

'It would take too long to explain.'

'Well tell me some of it . . . *Why*, daddy?'

'Look here, I'm tired. If you don't stop asking questions I shan't let you ever come and meet the train again.'

John Andrew's face began to pucker. 'I thought you'd *like* me to come and meet you.'

'If you cry I shall put you in front with Dawson. It's absurd to cry at your age.'

'I'd *sooner* go in front with Dawson,' said John Andrew between his tears.

Tony picked up the speaking tube to tell the chauffeur to stop, but he could not make him hear. So he hitched the mouthpiece back on its hook and they drove on in silence, John Andrew leaning against the window and snivelling slightly. When they got to the house, he said, 'Nanny, I don't want John to come to the station in future unless her ladyship or I specially say he can.'

'No, sir, I wouldn't have let him go today, only he went on so. Come along now, John, and take off your coat. Goodness, child, where's your handkerchief?'

Tony went and sat alone in front of the library fire. 'Two men of thirty,' he said to himself, 'behaving as if they were up for the night from Sandhurst[9] getting drunk and ringing people up and dancing with tarts at the Old Hundredth . . . And it makes it all the worse that Brenda was so nice about it.' He dozed a little; then he went up to change. At dinner he said, 'Ambrose, when I'm alone I think in future I'll have dinner in the library.' Afterwards he sat with a book in front of the fire, but he was unable to read. At ten o'clock he scattered the logs in the fireplace before going upstairs. He fastened the library windows and turned out the lights. That night he went into Brenda's empty room to sleep.

Two

That was Wednesday; on Thursday Tony felt well again. He had a meeting of the county council[10] in the morning. In the afternoon he went down to the home farm and discussed a new kind of tractor with his agent. From then onwards he was able to say to himself, 'This time tomorrow Brenda and Jock will be here.' He dined in front of the fire in the library. He had given up the diet some weeks ago. ('Ambrose, when I'm alone I don't really need a long dinner. In future I'll just have two courses.') He looked over some accounts his agent had left for him and then went to bed, saying to himself, 'When I wake up it will be the weekend.'

But there was a telegram for him next morning from Jock, saying, *Weekend impossible have to go to constituency how about one after next.* He wired back, *Delighted any time always here.* 'I suppose he's made it up with that girl,' Tony reflected.

There was also a note from Brenda, written in pencil:

Coming Sat. with Polly and a friend of Polly's called Veronica in P.'s car. Perhaps Daisy Maids and luggage on 3.18. Will you tell Ambrose and Mrs Mossop. We had better open Lyonesse for Polly you know what she is about comfort. Veronica can go anywhere – not Galahad. Polly says she's v. amusing. Also Mrs Beaver coming, please don't mind it is only on business, she thinks she can do something to morning room. Polly bringing chauffeur. By the way I'm leaving Grimshawe at Hetton next week tell Mrs Mossop. It's a bore and expense boarding her out in London. In fact I think I might do without her altogether what do you think? except she's useful for sewing. Longing to see John again. All going back Sunday evening. Keep sober darling. Try.

x x x x x x

B.

Tony found very little to occupy his time on Friday. His letters were all finished by ten o'clock. He went down to the farm but they had no business for him there. The duties which before had seemed so multifarious, now took up a very small part of his day; he had not realized how many hours he used to waste with Brenda. He watched John riding in the paddock. The boy clearly bore him ill will for their quarrel on Wednesday; when he applauded a jump, John said, 'She usually does better than this.' Later, 'When's mummy coming down?'

'Not till tomorrow.'

'Oh.'

'I've got to go over to Little Bayton this afternoon. Would you like to come too and perhaps we could see the kennels?'

John had for weeks past been praying for this expedition. 'No, thank you,' he said. 'I want to finish a picture I'm painting.'

'You can do that any time.'

'I want to do it this afternoon.'

When Tony had left them Ben said, 'Whatever made you speak

to your dad like that for? You've been going on about seeing the kennels since Christmas.'

'Not with *him*,' said John.

'You ungrateful little bastard, that's a lousy way to speak of your dad.'

'And you ought not to say bastard or lousy in front of me, nanny says not.'

So Tony went over alone to Little Bayton where he had some business to discuss with Colonel Brink. He hoped they would ask him to stay on, but the Colonel and his wife were themselves going out to tea, so he drove back in the dusk to Hetton.

A thin mist lay breast high over the park; the turrets and battlements of the abbey stood grey and flat; the boiler man was hauling down the flag on the main tower.

'My poor Brenda, it's an appalling room,' said Mrs Beaver.

'It's not one we use a great deal,' said Tony very coldly.

'I should think not,' said the one they called Veronica.

'I can't see much wrong with it,' said Polly, 'except it's a bit mouldy.'

'You see,' Brenda explained, not looking at Tony. 'What I thought was that I must have *one* habitable room downstairs. At present there's only the smoking room and the library. The drawing room is vast and quite out of the question. I thought what I needed was a small sitting room more or less to myself. Don't you think it has possibilities?'

'But, my angel, the *shape's* all wrong,' said Daisy, 'and that chimney piece – what is it made of, pink granite, and all the plaster work and the dado.[11] *Everything's* horrible. It's so *dark*.'

'I know exactly what Brenda wants,' said Mrs Beaver more moderately. 'I don't think it will be impossible. I must think about it. As Veronica says, the structure does rather limit one . . . you know I think the only thing to do would be to disregard it altogether and find some treatment so definite that it *carried* the room, if you see what I mean . . . supposing we covered the walls with white chromium plating and had natural sheepskin carpet . . . I wonder if that would be running you in for more than you meant to spend?'

'I'd blow the whole thing sky-high,' said Veronica.
Tony left them to their discussion.

'D'you really want Mrs Beaver to do up the morning-room?'
'Not if you don't, sweet.'
'But can you imagine it – white chromium plating?'
'Oh, that was just an idea.'
Tony walked in and out between Morgan le Fay and Guinevere as he always did while they were dressing. 'I say,' he said, returning with his waistcoat. 'You aren't going away tomorrow too, are you?'
'Must.'
He went back to Morgan le Fay for his tie and bringing it to Brenda's room again, sat by her side at the dressing table to fasten it.
'By the way,' said Brenda, 'what did you think about keeping on Grimshawe? – it seems rather a waste.'
'You used always to say you couldn't get on without her.'
'Yes, but now I'm living at the flat everything's so simple.'
'*Living?* Darling, you talk as though you had settled there for good.'
'D'you mind moving a second, sweet? I can't see properly.'
'Brenda, how long are you going on with this course of economics?'
'Me? I don't know.'
'But you must have some idea?'
'Oh it's surprising what a lot there is to learn ... I was so backward when I started ...'
'Brenda ...'
'Now run and put on your coat. They'll all be downstairs waiting for us.'
That evening Polly and Mrs Beaver played backgammon.[12] Brenda and Veronica sat together on the sofa sewing and talking about their needlework; occasionally there were bursts of general conversation between the women; they had the habit of lapsing into a jargon of their own which Tony did not understand; it was a thieves' slang, by which the syllables of each word were transposed. Tony sat just outside the circle, reading under another lamp.

That night when they went upstairs, the guests came to sit in Brenda's room and talk to her while she went to bed. Tony could hear their low laughter through the dressing-room door. They had boiled water in an electric kettle and were drinking Sedobrol[13] together.

Presently, still laughing, they left, and Tony went into Brenda's room. It was in darkness, but hearing him come and seeing the square of light in the doorway, she turned on the little lamp by the bedside.

'Why, Tony,' she said.

She was lying on the dais with her head deep back in the pillows; her face was shining with the grease she used for cleaning it; one bare arm on the quilted eiderdown, left there from turning the switch. 'Why, Tony,' she said, 'I was almost asleep.'

'Very tired?'

'Mm.'

'Want to be left alone?'

'So tired . . . and I've just drunk a lot of that stuff of Polly's.'

'I see . . . well, goodnight.'

'Goodnight . . . don't mind, do you? . . . so tired.'

He crossed to the bed and kissed her; she lay quite still, with closed eyes. Then he turned out the light and went back to the dressing room.

'Lady Brenda not ill, I hope?'

'No, nothing serious, thank you very much. She gets rather done up in London, you know, during the week, and likes to take Sunday quietly.'

'And how are the great studies progressing?'

'Very well, I gather. She seems keen on it still.'

'Splendid. We shall all be coming to her soon to solve our economic problems. But I daresay you and John miss her?'

'Yes, we do rather.'

'Well, please give her my kindest regards.'

'I will indeed. Thank you so much.'

Tony left the church porch and made his accustomed way to the hot houses; a gardenia for himself; some almost black carnations for the ladies. When he reached the room where they were sitting there was a burst of laughter. He paused on the threshold, rather bewildered.

'Come in, darling, it isn't anything. It's only we had a bet on what coloured buttonhole you'd be wearing and none of us won.'

They still giggled a little as they pinned on the flowers he had brought them; all except Mrs Beaver, who said, 'Any time you are buying cuttings or seeds do get them through me. I've made quite a little business of it, perhaps you didn't know . . . all kinds of rather unusual flowers. I do everything like that for Sylvia Newport and all sorts of people.'

'You must talk to my head man about it.'

'Well, to tell you the truth I *have* – this morning while you were in church. He seems quite to understand.'

They left early, so as to reach London in time for dinner. In the car Daisy said, 'Golly, what a house.'

'Now you can see what I've been through all these years.'

'My poor Brenda,' said Veronica, unpinning her carnation and throwing it from the window into the side of the road.

'You know,' Brenda confided next day, 'I'm not *absolutely* happy about Tony.'

'What's the old boy been up to?' asked Polly.

'Nothing much yet, but I do see it's pretty boring for him at Hetton all this time.'

'I shouldn't worry.'

'Oh, I'm not *worrying*. It's only, supposing he took to drink or something. It would make everything very difficult.'

'I shouldn't have said that was his thing . . . We must get him interested in a girl.'

'If only we could . . . Who is there?'

'There's always old Sybil.'[14]

'Darling, he's known her all his life.'

'Or Souki de Foucauld-Esterhazy.'

'He isn't his best with Americans.'

'Well, we'll find him someone.'

'The trouble is that I've become such a habit with him – he

won't take easily to a new one . . . ought she to be like me, or quite different?'

'I'd say, different, but it's hard to tell.'

They discussed this problem in all its aspects.

Three

Brenda wrote:

Darling Tony,

Sorry not to have written or rung up but I've had such a busy time with himetallism.[15] V complicated.

Coming down Saturday with Polly again. Good her coming twice – Lyonesse can't be as beastly as most of the rooms, can it?

Also charming girl I have taken up with who I want us to be kind to. She's had a terrible life and she lives in one of these flats, called Jenny Abdul Akbar. Not black but married one. Get her to tell you. She'll come by train 3.18 I expect. Must stop now and go to lecture.

Keep away from the Demon Rum.

x x x x x

Brenda.

Saw Jock last night at Café de Paris with shameless blonde. Who?

Gin. No, Djin how? – has rheumatism and Marjorie is v. put out about it. She thinks his pelvis is out of place and Cruttwell won't do him which is pretty mean considering all the people she has brought there.

'Are you *certain* Jenny will be Tony's tea?'

'You can't ever be certain,' said Polly. 'She bores my pants off, but she's a good trier.'

'Is mummy coming down today, daddy?'

'Yes.'

'Who else?'

'Someone called Jenny Abdul Akbar.'

'What a silly name. Is she foreign?'

'I don't know.'

'Sounds foreign, doesn't she, daddy? D'you think she won't be able to talk any English? Is she black?'

'Mummy says not.'

'Oh . . . who else?'

'Lady Cockpurse.'

'The monkey-woman. You know she wasn't a bit like a monkey except perhaps her face and I don't think she had a tail because I looked as close as anything . . . unless perhaps she has it rolled up between her legs. D'you think she has, daddy?'

'I shouldn't be surprised.'

'*Very* uncomfortable.'

Tony and John were friends again; but it had been a leaden week.

It was part of Polly Cockpurse's plan to arrive late at Hetton. 'Give the girl a chance to get down to it,' she said. So she and Brenda did not leave London until Jenny was already on her way from the station. It was a day of bitter cold and occasional rain. The resolute little figure huddled herself in the rugs until she reached the gates. Then she opened her bag, tucked up her veil, shook out her powder puff and put her face to rights. She licked the rouge from her finger with a sharp red tongue.

Tony was in the smoking room when she was announced; the library was now too noisy during the daytime, for there were men at work on the walls of the morning room next door, tearing down the plaster tracery.

'Princess Abdul Akbar.'

He rose to greet her. She was preceded by a heavy odour of musk.

'Oh, Mr Last,' she said, 'what a sweet old place this is.'

'I'm afraid it's been restored a great deal,' said Tony.

'Ah, but its *atmosphere*. I always think that's what counts in a house. Such dignity, and repose. But of course you're used to it. When you've been very unhappy as I have, you appreciate these things.'

Tony said, 'I'm afraid Brenda hasn't arrived yet. She's coming by car with Lady Cockpurse.'

'Brenda's been *such* a friend to me.' The Princess took off her furs and sat down on the stool before the fire, looking up at Tony. 'D'you mind if I take off my hat?'

'No, no . . . of course.'

She threw it on to the sofa and shook out her hair, which was dead black and curled. 'D'you know, Mr Last, I'm going to call you Teddy[16] right away. You don't think that very fresh of me? And you must call me Jenny. "Princess" is so formal, isn't it, and suggests tight trousers and gold braid . . . Of course,' she went on, stretching out her hands to the fire and letting her hair fall forwards a little across her face, 'my husband was not called "Prince" in Morocco; his title was Moulay[17] – but there's no proper equivalent for a woman, so I've always called myself Princess in Europe . . . Moulay is *far* higher really . . . my husband was a descendant of the Prophet. Are you interested in the East?'

'No . . . yes. I mean I know very little about it.'

'It has an uncanny fascination for me. You must go there, Teddy. I know you'd like it. I've been saying the same to Brenda.'

'I expect you'd like to see your room,' said Tony. 'They'll bring tea soon.'

'No, I'll stay here. I like just to curl up like a cat in front of the fire, and if you're nice to me I'll purr, and if you're cruel I shall pretend not to notice – just like a cat . . . Shall I purr, Teddy?'

'Er . . . yes . . . do, please, if that's what you like doing.'

'Englishmen are so gentle and considerate. It's wonderful to be back among them . . . mine own people. Sometimes when I look back at my life, especially at times like this among lovely old English things and kind people, I think the whole thing must be a frightful nightmare . . . then I remember my *scars* . . .'

'Brenda tells me you've taken one of the flats in the same house as hers. They must be very convenient.'

'How English you are, Teddy – so shy of talking about personal things, intimate things . . . I like you for that, you know. I love everything that's solid and homely and *good* after . . . after all I've been through.'

'You're not studying economics too, are you, like Brenda?'

'No; is Brenda? She never told me. What a wonderful person she is. When *does* she find the time?'

'Ah, here comes tea at last,' said Tony. 'I hope you allow yourself to eat muffins. So many of our guests nowadays are on a diet. I think muffins one of the few things that make the English winter endurable.'

'Muffins stand for so much,' said Jenny.

She ate heartily; often she ran her tongue over her lips, collecting crumbs that had become embedded there and melted butter from the muffin. One drop of butter fell on her chin and glittered there unobserved except by Tony. It was a relief to him when John Andrew was brought in.

'Come and be introduced to Princess Abdul Akbar.'

John Andrew had never before seen a Princess; he gazed at her fascinated.

'Aren't you going to give me a kiss?'

He walked over to her and she kissed him on the mouth.

'Oh,' he said, recoiling and rubbing away the taste of the lipstick; and then 'What a beautiful smell.'

'It's my last link with the East,' she said.

'You've got butter on your chin.'

She reached for her bag, laughing. 'Why, so I have. Teddy, you *might* have told me.'

'Why do you call daddy Teddy?'

'Because I hope we are going to be great friends.'

'What a funny reason.'

John stayed with them for an hour, and all the time watched her fascinated. 'Have you got a crown?' he asked. 'How did you learn to speak English? What is that big ring made of? Did it cost much? Why are your nails that colour? Can you ride?'

She answered all his questions, sometimes enigmatically with an eye on Tony. She took out a little heavily scented handkerchief and showed John the monogram. 'That is my only crown . . . now,' she said. She told him about the horses she used to have – glossy black, with arched necks; foam round their silver bits; plumes tossing on their foreheads; silver studs on the harness, crimson saddle cloths. 'On the Moulay's birthday –'

'What's the Moulay?'

'A beautiful and a very bad man,' she said gravely, 'and on his birthday all his horsemen used to assemble round a great square,

88

with all their finest clothes and trappings and jewels, with long swords in their hands. The Moulay used to sit on a throne under a great crimson canopy.'

'What's a canopy?'

'Like a tent,' she said more sharply, and then, resuming her soft voice, 'and all the horsemen used to gallop across the plain, in a great cloud of dust, waving their swords, straight towards the Moulay. And everyone used to hold their breath, thinking the horsemen were bound to ride right on top of the Moulay, but when they were a few feet away, as near as I am to you, galloping at full speed, they used to rein their horses back, up on to their hind legs and salute –'

'Oh, but they *shouldn't*,' said John. 'It's *very* bad horsemanship indeed. Ben says so.'

'They're the most wonderful horsemen in the world. Everyone knows that.'

'Oh, no, they can't be, if they do *that*. It's one of the *worst* things. Were they natives?'

'Yes, of course.'

'Ben says natives aren't humans at all really.'

'Ah, but he's thinking of negroes, I expect. These are pure Semitic type.'

'What's that?'

'The same as Jews.'

'Ben says Jews are worse than natives.'

'Oh dear, what a very severe boy you are. I was like that once. Life teaches one to be tolerant.'

'It hasn't taught Ben,' said John. 'When's mummy coming? I thought she'd be here, otherwise I wouldn't have stopped painting my picture.'

But when nanny came to fetch him, John, without invitation, went over and kissed Jenny goodnight. 'Goodnight, Johnny-boy,' she said.

'What did you call me?'

'Johnny-boy.'

'You are funny with names.'

Upstairs, meditatively splashing his spoon in the bread and milk, he said, 'Nanny, I do think that Princess is beautiful, don't you?'

Nanny sniffed. 'It would be a dull world if we all thought alike,' she said.

'She's more beautiful than Miss Tendril, even. I think she's the most beautiful lady I've ever seen . . . D'you think she'd like to watch me have my bath?'

Downstairs, Jenny said, 'What a heavenly child . . . I love children. That has been my great tragedy. It was when he found I couldn't have children that the Moulay first showed the Other Side of his Nature. It wasn't my fault . . . you see my womb is out of place . . . I don't know why I'm telling you all this, but I feel you'll understand. It's such a *waste of time*, isn't it, when one knows one is going to like someone and one goes on *pretending* . . . I know at once if someone is going to be a real friend . . .'

Polly and Brenda arrived just before seven. Brenda went straight up to the nursery. 'Oh mummy,' said John, 'there's such a beautiful lady downstairs. Do ask her to come and say goodnight. Nanny doesn't think she'd want to.'

'Did daddy seem to like her?'

'He didn't talk much . . . She doesn't know anything about horses or natives but she *is* beautiful. Please tell her to come up.'

Brenda went downstairs and found Jenny with Polly and Tony in the smoking room. 'You've made a wild success with John Andrew. He won't go to sleep until he's seen you again.'

They went up together, and Jenny said, 'They're both such dears.'

'Did you and Tony get on? I was so sorry not to be here when you arrived.'

'He was *so* sympathetic and gentle . . . and so wistful.'

They sat on John's small bed in the night-nursery. He threw the clothes back and crawled out, nestling against Jenny. 'Back to bed,' she said, 'or I shall spank you.'

'Would you do it hard? I shouldn't mind.'

'Oh dear,' said Brenda, 'what a terrible effect you seem to have. He's never like this as a rule.'

When they had gone nanny threw open another window. 'Poof!' she said, 'making the whole place stink.'

'Don't you like it? *I* think it's lovely.'

Brenda took Polly up to Lyonesse. It was a large suite, fitted up with satin wood for King Edward when, as Prince of Wales, he was once expected at a shooting party; he never came.

'How's it going?' she asked anxiously.

'Too soon to tell. I'm sure it will be all right.'

'She's got the wrong chap. John Andrew's mad about her . . . quite embarrassing.'

'I should say Tony was a slow starter. It's a pity she's got his name wrong. Ought we to tell her?'

'No, let's leave it.'

When they were dressing, Tony said, 'Brenda, who *is* this joke-woman?'

'Darling, don't you like her?'

The disappointment and distress in her tone were so clear that Tony was touched. 'I don't know about not liking her exactly. She's just a joke, isn't she?'

'Is she . . . oh, dear . . . She's had a terrible life, you know.'

'So I gathered.'

'Be nice to her, Tony, please.'

'Oh, I'll be nice to her. Is she a Jewess?'

'I don't know. I never thought. Perhaps she is.'

Soon after dinner Polly said she was tired and asked Brenda to come with her while she undressed. 'Leave the young couple to it,' she whispered outside the door.

'My dear, I don't believe it's going to be any good . . . the poor old boy's got *some* taste you know, and a sense of humour.'

'She didn't show up too well at dinner, did she?'

'She will *go on* so . . . and after all, Tony's been used to me for seven years. It's rather a sudden change.'

'Tired?'

'Mmm. Little bit.'

'You gave me a pretty long bout of Abdul Akbar.'

'I know. I'm sorry, darling, but Polly takes so long to get to bed . . . Was it awful? I wish you liked her more.'

'She's awful.'

'One has to make allowances . . . she's got the most terrible scars.'

'So she told me.'

'I've seen them.'

'Besides I hoped to see something of you.'

'Oh.'

'Brenda, you aren't angry still about my getting tight that night and waking you up?'

'No, sweet, do I seem angry?'

'. . . I don't know. You do rather . . . Has it been an amusing week?'

'Not amusing, very hard work. Bimetallism, you know.'

'Oh, yes . . . well, I suppose you want to go to sleep.'

'Mm . . . so tired. Goodnight, darling.'

'Goodnight.'

'Can I go and say good-morning to the Princess, mummy?'

'I don't expect she's awake yet.'

'Please, mummy, may I go and see? I'll just peep and, if she's asleep, go away.'

'I don't know what room she's in.'

'Galahad, my lady,' said Grimshawe, who was putting out her clothes.

'Oh dear, why was she put there?'

'It was Mr Last's orders, my lady.'

'Well, she's probably awake, then.'

John slipped out of the room and trotted down the passage to Galahad. 'May I come in?'

'Hullo, Johnny-boy. Come in.'

He swung on the handles of the door, half in, half out of the room. 'Have you had breakfast? Mummy said you wouldn't be awake.'

'I've been awake a long time. You see I was once very badly hurt, and now I don't always sleep well. Even the softest beds are too hard for me now.'

'Ooh. What did you do? Was it a motor car accident?'

'Not an accident, Johnny-boy, not an accident . . . but come in.

92

It's cold with the door open. Look, there are some grapes here. Would you like to eat them?'

Johnny climbed on to the bed. 'What are you going to do today?'

'I don't know yet. I haven't been told.'

'Well, I'll tell you. We'll go to Church in the morning because I have to and then we'll go and look at Thunderclap and I'll show you the place we jump and then you can come with me while I have dinner because I have it early and afterwards we can go down to Bruton Wood and we needn't take nanny because it makes her so muddy and you can see where they dug out a fox in the drain just outside the wood, he nearly got away, and then you can come and have tea in the nursery and I've got a little gramophone Uncle Reggie gave me for Christmas and it plays "When Father Papered the Parlour," do you know that song? Ben can sing it and I've got some books to show you and a picture I did of the battle of Marston Moor.'[18]

'I think that sounds a lovely day. But don't you think I ought to spend some time with daddy and mummy and Lady Cockpurse?'

'Oh, *them* . . . besides it's all my foot about Lady Cockpurse having a tail. Please you *will* spend the day with me?'

'Well, we'll see.'

'She's gone to Church with him. That's a good sign, isn't it?'

'Well, not really, Polly. He likes going alone, or with me. It's the time he gossips to the village.'

'She won't stop him.'

'I'm afraid you don't understand the old boy altogether. He's much odder than you'd think.'

'I could see from your sermon that you knew the East, Rector.'

'Yes, yes, most of my life.'

'It has an uncanny fascination, hasn't it?'

'Oh, come on,' said John, pulling at her coat. 'We must go and see Thunderclap.'

So Tony returned alone with the buttonholes.

After luncheon Brenda said, 'Why don't you show Jenny the house?'

'Oh yes, *do.*'

When they reached the morning-room he said, 'Brenda's having it done up.'

There were planks and ladders and heaps of plaster about.

'Oh Teddy, what a shame. I do hate seeing things modernized.'

'It isn't a room we used very much.'

'No, but still . . .' She stirred the mouldings of fleurs-de-lis that littered the floor, fragments of tarnished gilding and dusty stencilwork. 'You know, Brenda's been a wonderful friend to me. I wouldn't say anything against her . . . but ever since I came here I've been wondering whether she really understands this beautiful place and all it means to you.'

'Tell me more about your terrible life,' said Tony, leading her back to the central hall.

'You *are* shy of talking about yourself, aren't you, Teddy? It's a mistake, you know, to keep things bottled up. I've been very unhappy too.'

Tony looked about him desperately in search of help; and help came. 'Oh there you are,' said a firm, child's voice. 'Come on. We're going down to the woods now. We must hurry, otherwise it will be dark.'

'Oh Johnny-boy, must I really? I was just talking to daddy.'

'*Come on.* It's all arranged. And afterwards you're to be allowed to have tea with me upstairs.'

Tony crept into the library, habitable today, since the workmen were at rest. Brenda found him there two hours later. '*Tony,* here all alone? We thought you were with Jenny. What have you done with her?'

'John took her off . . . just in time before I said something rude.'

'Oh dear . . . well there's only me and Polly in the smoking room. Come and have some tea. You look all funny – have you been asleep?'

'We must write it down a failure, definitely.'

'What *does* the old boy expect? It isn't as though he was everybody's money.'

'I daresay it would all have been all right, if she hadn't got his name wrong.'

'Anyway, this lets _you_ out. You've done far more than most wives would to cheer the old boy up.'

'Yes, that's certainly true,' said Brenda.

Four

Another five days; then Brenda came to Hetton again. 'I shan't be here next weekend,' she said, 'I'm going to stay with Veronica.'

'Am I asked?'

'Well, you _were_, of course, but I refused for you. You know you always hate staying away.'

'I wouldn't mind coming.'

'Oh, darling, I wish I'd known. Veronica would have loved it so ... but I'm afraid it will be too late now. She's only got a tiny house ... to tell you the truth I didn't think you liked her much.'

'I hated her like hell.'

'Well then . . . ?'

'Oh, it doesn't matter. I suppose you must go back on Monday? The hounds are meeting here on Wednesday, you know.'

'Are we giving them a lawner?'[19]

'Yes, darling, you know we do every year.'

'So we do.'

'You couldn't stay down till then?'

'Not possibly, darling. You see if I miss one lecture I get right behind and can't follow the next. Besides I am not mad keen to see the hounds.'

'Ben was asking if we'd let John go out.'

'Oh, he's far too young.'

'Not to hunt. But I thought he might bring his pony to the meet and ride with them to the first covert. He'd love it so.'

'Is it quite safe?'

'Oh, yes, surely?'

'Bless his heart, I wish I could be here to see him.'

'Do change your mind.'

95

'Oh no, that's quite out of the question. Don't make a thing about it, Tony.'

That was when she first arrived; later everything got better. Jock was there that weekend, also Allan and Marjorie and another married couple whom Tony had known all his life. Brenda had arranged the party for him and he enjoyed it. He and Allan went out with rook rifles and shot rabbits in the twilight; after dinner the four men played billiard fives while one wife watched. 'The old boy's happy as a lark,' said Brenda to Marjorie. 'He's settling down wonderfully to the new régime.'

They came in breathless and rather flushed for whisky and soda.

'Tony nearly had one through the window,' said Jock.

That night Tony slept in Guinevere.

'Everything *is* all right, isn't it?' he said once.

'Yes, of course, darling.'

'I get depressed down here all alone and imagine things.'

'You aren't to *brood*, Tony. You know that's one of the things that aren't allowed.'

'I won't brood any more,' said Tony.

Next day Brenda came to Church with him. She had decided to devote the weekend wholly to him; it would be the last for some time.

'And how are the abstruse sciences, Lady Brenda?'

'Absorbing.'

'We shall all be coming to you for advice about our overdrafts.'

'Ha, ha.'

'And how's Thunderclap?' asked Miss Tendril.

'I'm taking her out hunting on Wednesday,' said John. He had forgotten Princess Abdul Akbar in the excitement of the coming meet. 'Please God make there be a good scent. Please God make me see the kill. Please God don't let me do anything wrong. God bless Ben and Thunderclap. Please God make me jump an enormous great oxer,'[20] he had kept repeating throughout the service.

Brenda did the round with Tony of cottages and hot houses; she helped him choose his buttonhole.

Tony was in high spirits at luncheon. Brenda had begun to forget how amusing he could be. Afterwards he changed into other clothes and went with Jock to play golf. They stayed some time at the club house. Tony said, 'We've got the hounds meeting at Hetton on Wednesday. Couldn't you stay down till then.'

'Must be back. There's going to be a debate on the Pig Scheme.'

'I wish you'd stay. Look here, why don't you ask that girl down? Everyone goes tomorrow. You could ring her up, couldn't you?'

'I *could*.'

'Would she hate it? She could have Lyonesse – Polly slept there two weekends running, so it can't be too uncomfortable.'

'She'd probably love it. I'll ring up and ask her.'

'Why don't you hunt too? There's a chap called Brinkwell who's got some quite decent hirelings, I believe.'

'Yes, I might.'

'Jock's staying on. He's having the shameless blonde down. You don't mind?'

'Me? Of course not.'

'This *has* been a jolly weekend.'

'I thought you were enjoying it.'

'Just like old times – before the economics began.'

Marjorie said to Jock, 'D'you think Tony knows about Mr Beaver?'

'Not a thing.'

'I haven't mentioned it to Allan. D'you suppose he knows?'

'I doubt it.'

'Oh Jock, how d'you think it'll end?'

'She'll get bored with Beaver soon enough.'

'The trouble is that he doesn't care for her in the least. If he did, it would soon be over ... What an ass she is being.'

'I should say she was managing it unusually well, if you asked me.'

The other married couple said to each other, 'D'you think Marjorie and Allan know about Brenda?'

'I'm sure they don't.'

*

Brenda said to Allan, 'Tony's as happy as a sandboy, isn't he?'

'Full of beans.'

'I was getting worried about him ... You don't think he's got any idea about my goings on?'

'Lord no. It's the last thing that would come into his head.'

Brenda said, 'I don't want him to be unhappy, you know ... Marjorie's been frightfully governessy about the whole thing.'

'Has she? I haven't discussed it with her.'

'How did *you* hear?'

'My dear girl, until this minute I didn't know you had any goings on. And I'm not asking any questions about them now.'

'Oh ... I thought everyone knew.'

'That's always the trouble with people when they start walking out. They either think no one knows, or everybody. The truth is that a few people like Polly and Sybil make a point of finding out about everyone's private life; the rest of us just aren't interested.'

'Oh.'

Later he said to Marjorie, 'Brenda tried to be confidential about Beaver this evening.'

'I didn't know you knew.'

'Oh, I knew all right. But I wasn't going to let her feel important by talking about it.'

'I couldn't disapprove more of the whole thing. Do you know Beaver?'

'I've seen him about. Anyway, it's her business and Tony's, not ours.'

Five

Jock's blonde was called Mrs Rattery. Tony had conceived an idea of her from what he overheard of Polly's gossip and from various fragments of information let fall by Jock. She was a little over thirty. Somewhere in the Cottesmore country[21] there lived a long-legged, slightly discredited Major Rattery, to whom she had once been married. She was American by origin, now totally dena-tionalized, rich, without property or possessions, except those that would pack in five vast trunks. Jock had had his eye on her last summer at Biarritz[22] and had fallen in with her again in London where she played big bridge, very ably, for six or seven hours a day and changed her hotel, on an average, once every three weeks. Periodically she was liable to bouts of morphine; then she gave up her bridge and remained for several days at a time alone in her hotel suite, refreshed at intervals with glasses of cold milk.

She arrived by air on Monday afternoon. It was the first time that a guest had come in this fashion and the household was appreciably excited. Under Jock's direction the boiler man and one of the gardeners pegged out a dust sheet in the park to mark a landing for her and lit a bonfire of damp leaves to show the direction of the wind. The five trunks arrived in the ordinary way by train, with an elderly, irreproachable maid. She brought her own sheets with her in one of the trunks; they were neither silk nor coloured, without lace or ornament of any kind, except small, plain monograms.

Tony, Jock and John went out to watch her land. She climbed out of the cockpit, stretched, unbuttoned the flaps of her leather helmet, and came to meet them. 'Forty-two minutes,' she said, 'not at all bad with the wind against me.'

She was tall and erect, almost austere in helmet and overalls; not at all as Tony had imagined her. Vaguely, at the back of his mind he had secreted the slightly absurd expectation of a chorus girl, in silk shorts and brassiere, popping out of an immense be-ribboned Easter Egg with a cry of 'Whoopee, boys.' Mrs Rattery's greetings were deft and impersonal.

'Are you going to hunt on Wednesday?' asked John. 'They're meeting here, you know.'

'I might go out for half the day, if I can find a horse. It'll be the first time this year.'

'It's my first time too.'

'We shall both be terribly stiff.' She spoke to him exactly as though he were a man of her own age. 'You'll have to show me the country.'

'I expect they'll draw Bruton Wood first. There's a big fox there, daddy and I saw him.'

*

99

When they were alone together, Jock said, 'It's delightful your coming down. What d'you think of Tony?'

'Is he married to that rather lovely woman we saw at the Café de Paris?'

'Yes.'

'The one you said was in love with that young man?'

'Yes.'

'Funny of her . . . What's this one's name again?'

'Tony Last. It's a pretty ghastly house, isn't it?'

'Is it? I never notice houses much.'

She was an easy guest to entertain. After dinner on Monday she produced four packs of cards and laid out for herself on the smoking room table a very elaborate patience, which kept her engrossed all the evening. 'Don't wait up for me,' she said. 'I shall stay here until it comes out. It often takes several hours.'

They showed her where to put the lights out and left her to it.

Next day Jock said, 'Have you got any pigs at the farm?'

'Yes.'

'Would you mind if I went to see them?'

'Not the least – but why?'

'And is there a man who looks after them, who will be able to explain about them?'

'Yes.'

'Well, I think I'll spend the morning with him. I've got to make a speech about pigs, fairly soon.'

They did not see Mrs Rattery until luncheon. Tony assumed she was asleep until she appeared in overalls from the morning room. 'I was down early,' she explained, 'and found the men at work stripping the ceiling. I couldn't resist joining in. I hope you don't mind.'

In the afternoon they went to a neighbouring livery stables to look for hirelings. After tea Tony wrote to Brenda; he had taken to writing letters in the past few weeks.

How enjoyable the weekend was, he wrote. *Thank you a thousand times for all your sweetness. I wish you were coming down next weekend, or that you had been able to stay on a little, but I quite understand.*

The Shameless Blonde is not the least what we expected – very serene and distant. Not at all like Jock's usual taste. I am sure she hasn't any idea where she is or what my name is.

The work in the morning room is going on well. The foreman told me today he thought he would begin on the chromium plating by the end of the week. You know what I think about that.

John can talk of nothing except his hunting tomorrow. I hope he doesn't break his neck. Jock and his S.B. are going out too.

Hetton lay near the boundary of three packs; the Pigstanton, who hunted it, had, in the division of territory, come off with the worst country and they cherished a permanent resentment about some woods near Bayton. They were a somewhat ill-tempered lot, contemptuous of each other's performance, hostile to strangers, torn by internal rancour, united only in their dislike of the Master. In the case of Colonel Inch this unpopularity, traditional to the hunt, was quite undeserved; he was a timid, inconspicuous man who provided the neighbourhood with sport of a kind at great personal expense. He himself was seldom in sight of hounds and could often be found in another part of the country morosely nibbling ginger nut biscuits in a lane or towards the end of the day cantering heavily across country, quite lost, a lonely scarlet figure against the ploughed land, staring about him in the deepening twilight and shouting at yokels for information. The only pleasure he gained from his position, but that a substantial one, was in referring to it casually at Board Meetings of the various companies he directed.

The Pigstanton met twice a week. There was seldom a large field on Wednesdays, but the Hetton meet was popular; it lay in their best country and the prospect of stirrup cups had drawn many leathery old ladies from the neighbouring packs. There were also followers on foot and in every kind of vehicle, some hanging back diffidently, others, more or less known to Tony, crowding round the refreshment table. Mr Tendril had a niece staying with him, who appeared on a motor bicycle.

John stood beside Thunderclap, solemn with excitement. Ben had secured a powerful, square-headed mare from a neighbouring farmer; he hoped to have a hunt after John had been taken home; at John's earnest entreaty nanny was confined indoors, among the housemaids whose heads obtruded at the upper windows; it was not her day. She had been out of temper while dressing him. 'If I'm in at the death I expect Colonel Inch will blood me.'

'You won't see any death,' said nanny.

Now she stood with her eyes at an arrow slit gazing rather resentfully at the animated scene below. 'It's all a lot of nonsense of Ben Hacket's,' she thought. She deplored it all, hounds, Master, field, huntsman and whippers-in, Mr Tendril's niece in her mackintosh, Jock in a rat-catcher,[23] Mrs Rattery in tall hat and cutaway coat, oblivious of the suspicious glances of the subscribers, Tony smiling and chatting to his guests, the crazy old man with the terriers, the Press photographer, pretty Miss Ripon in difficulties with a young horse, titupping sideways over the lawn, the grooms and second horses, the humble, unknown followers in the background – it was all a lot of nonsense of Ben Hacket's. 'It was after eleven before the child got to sleep last night,' she reflected, 'he was that over-excited.'

Presently they moved off towards Bruton Wood. The way lay down the south drive through Compton Last, along the main road for half a mile, and then through fields. 'He can ride with them as far as the covert,' Tony had said.

'Yes, sir, and there'd be no harm in his staying a bit to see hounds working, would there?'

'No, I suppose not.'

'And if he breaks away towards home, there'd be no harm in our following a bit, if we keeps to the lanes and gates, would there, sir?'

'No, but he's not to stay out more than an hour.'

'You wouldn't have me take him home with hounds running, would you, sir?'

'Well, he's got to be in before one.'

'I'll see to that, sir.' 'Don't you worry, my beauty,' he said to John, 'you'll get a hunt right enough.'

They waited until the end of the line of horses and then trotted soberly behind them. Close at their heels followed the motor-cars, at low gear, in a fog of exhaust gas. John was breathless and slightly dizzy. Thunderclap was tossing her head and worrying at her snaffle. Twice while the field was moving off, she had tried to get away and had taken John round in a little circle, so that Ben had said, 'Hold on to her, son,' and had come up close beside him so as to be able to catch the reins if she looked like bolting. Once, boring forwards with her head, she took John by surprise and pulled him forwards out of his balance; he caught hold of the front of the saddle to steady himself and looked guiltily at Ben. 'I'm afraid I'm riding very badly today. D'you think anyone has noticed?'

'That's all right, son. You can't keep riding-school manners when you're hunting.'

Jock and Mrs Rattery trotted side by side. 'I rather like this absurd horse,' she said. She rode astride and it was evident from the moment she mounted that she rode extremely well.

The members of the Pigstanton noted this with ill-concealed resentment, for it disturbed their fixed opinion according to which, while all fellow members of the hunt were clowns and poltroons, strangers were, without exception, mannerless lunatics, and a serious menace to anyone within quarter of a mile of them.

Half way through the village Miss Ripon had difficulties in getting past a stationary baker's van. Her horse plunged and reared, trembling all over, turning about, and slipping frantically over the tarmac. They rode round her, giving his heels the widest berth, scowling ominously and grumbling about her. They all knew that horse. Miss Ripon's father had been trying to sell him all the season, and had lately come down to eighty pounds. He was a good jumper on occasions but a beast of a horse to ride. Did Miss Ripon's father really imagine he was improving his chances of a sale by letting Miss Ripon make an exhibition of herself? It was like that skinflint, Miss Ripon's father, to risk Miss Ripon's neck for eighty pounds. And anyway Miss Ripon had no business out on *any* horse . . .

Presently she shot past them at a gallop; she was flushed in the face and her bun was askew; she leant back, pulling with all her weight. 'That girl will come to no good,' said Jock.

They encountered her later at the covert. Her horse was sweating and lathered at the bridle but temporarily at rest cropping the tufts of sedge that lay round the woods. Miss Ripon was much out of breath, and her hands shook as she fiddled with veil, bun and bowler. John rode up to Jock's side.

'What's happening, Mr Grant-Menzies?'

'Hounds are drawing the covert.'

'Oh.'

'Are you enjoying yourself?'

'Oh yes. Thunderclap's terribly fresh. I've never known her like this.'

There was a long wait as the horn sounded in the heart of the wood. Everyone stood in the corner of the big field, near a gate. Everyone, that is to say, except Miss Ripon, who some minutes ago had disappeared suddenly, indeed in the middle of a sentence, at full gallop towards Hetton Hills. After half an hour Jock said, 'They're calling hounds off.'

'Does that mean it's a blank?'

'I'm afraid so.'

'I hate this happening in *our* woods,' said Ben. 'Looks bad.'

Indeed the Pigstanton were already beginning to forget their recent hospitality and to ask each other what did one expect when Last did not hunt himself, and to circulate dark reports of how one of the keepers had been observed last week burying Something late in the evening.

They moved off again, away from Hetton. Ben began to feel his responsibility. 'D'you think I ought to take the young gentleman home, sir?'

'What did Mr Last say?'

'He said he could go as far as the covert. He didn't say which, sir.'

'I'm afraid it sounds as if he ought to go.'

'*Oh, Mr Menzies!*'

'Yes, come along, Master John. You've had enough for today.'

'But I haven't had *any*.'

'If you come back in good time today your dad will be all the more willing to let you come out another day.'

'But there mayn't *be* another day. The world may come to an end. *Please*, Ben. *Please*, Mr Menzies.'

'It is a shame they shouldn't have found,' said Ben. 'He's been looking forward to it.'

'Still, I think Mr Last would want him to go back,' said Jock.

So John's fate was decided; hounds went in one direction, he and Ben in another. John was very near tears as they reached the main road.

'Look,' said Ben, to encourage him. 'Here comes Miss Ripon on that nappy bay. Seems as if she's going in, too. Had a fall by the looks of her.'

Miss Ripon's hat and back were covered with mud and moss. She had had a bad twenty minutes after her disappearance. 'I'm taking him away,' she said. 'I can't do anything with him this morning.' She jogged along beside them towards the village. 'I thought perhaps Mr Last would let me come up to the house and telephone for the car. I don't feel like hacking him home in his present state. I can't think what's come over him,' she added loyally. 'He was out on Saturday. I've never known him like this before.'

'He wants a man up,' said Ben.

'Oh, he's no better with the groom, and daddy won't go near him,' said Miss Ripon, stung to indiscretion. 'At least . . . I mean . . . I don't think that they'd be any better with him in this state.'

He was quiet enough at that moment, keeping pace with the other horses. They rode abreast, she on the outside with John's pony between her and Ben.

Then this happened: they reached a turn in the road and came face to face with one of the single-decker country buses that covered that neighbourhood. It was not going fast and, seeing the horses, the driver slowed down still further and drew into the side. Mr Tendril's niece, who had also despaired of the day's sport, was following behind them at a short distance on her motor bicycle; she too slowed down and, observing that Miss Ripon's horse was likely to be difficult, stopped.

Ben said, 'Let me go first, Miss. He'll follow. Don't hold too hard on his mouth and just give him a tap.'

Miss Ripon did as she was told; everyone in fact behaved with complete good-sense.

They drew abreast of the omnibus. Miss Ripon's horse did not like it, but it seemed as though he would get by. The passengers watched with amusement. At that moment the motor bicycle, running gently in neutral gear, fired back into the cylinder with a sharp detonation.

For a second Miss Ripon's horse stood rigid with alarm; then, menaced in front and behind, he did what was natural to him and shied sideways, cannoning violently into the pony at his side. John was knocked from the saddle and fell on the road while Miss Ripon's bay, rearing and skidding, continued to plunge away from the bus.

'Take a hold of him, Miss. Use your whip,' shouted Ben. 'The boy's down.'

She hit him and the horse collected himself and bolted up the road into the village, but before he went one of his heels struck out and sent John into the ditch, where he lay bent double, perfectly still.

Everyone agreed that it was nobody's fault.[24]

It was nearly an hour before the news reached Jock and Mrs Rattery, where they were waiting beside another blank covert. Colonel Inch stopped hunting for the day and sent the hounds back to the kennels. The voices were hushed which, five minutes before, had been proclaiming that they knew it for a fact, Last had given orders to shoot every fox on the place. Later, after their baths, they made up for it in criticism of Miss Ripon's father, but at the moment everyone was shocked and silent. Someone lent Jock and Mrs Rattery a car to get home in, and a groom to see to the hirelings.

'It's the most appalling thing,' said Jock in the borrowed car. 'What on earth are we going to say to Tony?'

'I'm the last person to have about on an occasion like this,' said Mrs Rattery.

They passed the scene of the accident; there were still people hanging about, talking.

There were people hanging about, talking, in the hall at the house. The doctor was buttoning up his coat, just going.

'Killed instantly,' he said. 'Took it full on the base of the skull. Very sad, awfully fond of the kid. No one to blame though.'

Nanny was there in tears; also Mr Tendril and his niece; a policeman and Ben and two men who had helped bring up the body were in the servants' hall. 'It wasn't the kid's fault,' said Ben.

'It wasn't anyone's fault,' they said.

'He'd had a lousy day too, poor little bastard,' said Ben. 'If it was anyone's fault it was Mr Grant-Menzies making him go in.'

'It wasn't anyone's fault,' they said.

Tony was alone in the library. The first thing he said, when Jock came in was, 'We've got to tell Brenda.'

'D'you know where to get her?'

'She's probably at that school . . . But we can't tell her over the telephone . . . Anyway Ambrose has tried there and the flat but he can't get through . . . What on earth are we going to say to her?'

Jock was silent. He stood in the fireplace with his hands in the pockets of his breeches, with his back to Tony. Presently Tony said, 'You weren't anywhere near, were you?'

'No, we'd gone on to another covert.'

'That niece of Mr Tendril's told me first . . . then we met them coming up, and Ben told me all that happened . . . It's awful for the girl.'

'Miss Ripon?'

'Yes, she's just left . . . she had a nasty fall too, just after. Her horse slipped up in the village . . . she was in a terrible state, poor child, what with that and . . . John. She didn't know she'd hurt him until quite a time afterwards . . . she was in the chemist's shop having a bandage put on her head, when they told her. She cut it falling. She was in a terrible state. I sent her back in the car . . . it wasn't her fault.'

'No, it wasn't anybody's fault. It just happened.'

'That's it,' said Tony. 'It just happened . . . how are we going to tell Brenda?'

'One of us will have to go up.'

'Yes . . . I think I shall have to stay here. I don't know why really, but there will be things to see to. It's an awful thing to ask anyone to do . . .'

'I'll go,' said Jock.

'There'll be things to see to here . . . there's got to be an inquest the doctor says. It's purely formal of course, but it will be ghastly for that Ripon girl. She'll have to give evidence . . . she was in a terrible state. I hope I was all right to her. They'd just brought John in and I was rather muddled. She looked awful. I believe her father's bloody to her . . . I wish Brenda had been here. She's so good with everyone. I get in a muddle.'

The two men stood in silence. Tony said, 'Can you really face going up and seeing Brenda?'

'Yes, I'll go,' said Jock.

Presently Mrs Rattery came in. 'Colonel Inch has been here,' she said. 'I talked to him. He wanted to give you his sympathy.'

'Is he still here?'

'No, I told him you'd probably prefer to be left alone. He thought you'd be glad to hear he stopped the hunt.'

'Nice of him to come . . . Were you having a good day?'

'No.'

'I'm sorry. We saw a fox in Bruton Wood last week, John and I . . . Jock's going up to London to fetch Brenda.'

'I'll take him in the aeroplane. It'll be quicker.'

'Yes that will be quicker.'

'I'll go and change now. I won't be ten minutes.'

'I'll change too,' said Jock.

When he was alone Tony rang the bell. A young footman answered; he was quite young and had not been long at Hetton.

'Will you tell Mr Ambrose that Mrs Rattery is leaving today. She is flying up with Mr Grant-Menzies. Her ladyship will probably be coming by the evening train.'

'Very good, sir.'

'They had better have some luncheon before they go. I will have it with them . . . And will you put a call through to Colonel Inch and thank him for coming? Say I will write. And to Mr Ripon's to enquire how Miss Ripon is? And to the vicarage and ask Mr Tendril if I can see him this evening? He's not here still?'

'No, sir, he left a few minutes ago.'

'Tell him I shall have to discuss arrangements with him.'

'Very good, sir.'

Mr Last was very matter of fact about everything, the footman reported later.

It was perfectly quiet in the library, for the workmen in the morning room had laid aside their tools for the day.

Mrs Rattery was ready first.

'They're just getting luncheon.'

'We shan't want any,' she said. 'You forget we were going hunting.'

'Better have something,' said Tony, and then, 'It's awful for Jock, having to tell Brenda. I wonder how long it will be before she arrives.'

There was something in Tony's voice as he said this which made Mrs Rattery ask, 'What are you going to do while you're waiting?'

'I don't know. I suppose there will be things to see to.'

'Look here,' said Mrs Rattery, 'Jock had better go up by car. I'll stay here until Lady Brenda comes.'

'It would be awful for you.'

'No, I'll stay.'

Tony said, 'I suppose it's ridiculous of me, but I wish you would ... I mean, won't it be awful for you? I am all in a muddle. It's so hard to believe yet, that it really happened.'

'It happened all right.'

The footman came to say that Mr Tendril would call after tea that day; that Miss Ripon had gone straight to bed and was asleep.

'Mr Grant-Menzies is going up in his car. He may be back tonight,' said Tony. 'Mrs Rattery is waiting until her ladyship arrives.'

'Very good, sir. And Colonel Inch wanted to know whether you would care to have the huntsman blow "Gone to ground" at the funeral.'

'Say that I'll write to him,' and, when the footman had left the room, Tony said, 'An atrocious suggestion.'

'Oh, I don't know. He's very anxious to be helpful.'

'They don't like him much as Master.'

Jock left soon after half past two. Tony and Mrs Rattery had coffee in the library.

'I'm afraid this is a very difficult situation,' said Tony. 'After all we scarcely know each other.'

'You don't have to think about me.'

'But it must be awful for you.'

'And you must stop thinking that.'

'I'll try . . . the absurd thing is that I'm not thinking it, just saying it . . . I keep thinking of other things all the time.'

'I know. You don't have to say anything.'

Presently Tony said, 'It's going to be so much worse for Brenda. You see she'd got nothing else, much, except John. I've got her, and I love the house . . . but with Brenda John always came first . . . naturally . . . And then you know she's seen so little of John lately. She's been in London such a lot. I'm afraid that's going to hurt her.'

'You can't ever tell what's going to hurt people.'

'But, you see, I know Brenda so well.'

Six

The library windows were open and the clock, striking the hour, high overhead among its crockets[25] and finials,[26] was clearly audible in the quiet room. It was some time since they had spoken. Mrs Rattery sat with her back to Tony; she had spread out her intricate four pack patience on a card table; he was in front of the fire, in the chair he had taken after lunch.

'Only four o'clock?' he said.

'I thought you were asleep.'

'No, just thinking . . . Jock will be more than half way there by now, about Aylesbury or Tring.'[27]

'It's a slow way to travel.'

'It's less than four hours ago that it happened . . . it's odd to think that this is the same day; that it's only five hours ago they were all here at the meet having drinks.' There was a pause in which Mrs Rattery swept up the cards and began to deal them again. 'It was twenty eight minutes past twelve when I heard. I looked at my watch . . . It was ten to one when they brought John in . . . just over three hours ago . . . It's almost incredible, isn't it, everything becoming absolutely different, suddenly like that?'

'It's always that way,' said Mrs Rattery.

'Brenda will hear in an hour now . . . if Jock finds her in. Of course she may very likely be out. He won't know where to find her, because there's no one else in the flat. She leaves it locked up, empty, when she goes out . . . and she's out half the day. I know because I sometimes ring up and can't get an answer. He may not find her for hours . . . It may be as long again as the time since it happened. That would only make it eight o'clock. It's quite likely she won't come in until eight . . . Think of it, all the time between now and when it happened, before Brenda hears. It's scarcely credible, is it? And then she's got to get down here. There's a train that leaves at nine something. She might get that. I wonder if I ought to have gone up too . . . I didn't like to leave John.'

(Mrs Rattery sat intent over her game, moving little groups of cards adroitly backwards and forwards about the table like shuttles across a loom; under her fingers order grew out of chaos; she established sequence and precedence; the symbols before her became coherent, interrelated.)

'. . . Of course she may be at home when he arrives. In that case she can get the evening train she used always to come by, when she went to London for the day, before she got the flat . . . I'm trying to see it all, as it's going to happen, Jock coming and her surprise at seeing him, and then his telling her . . . It's awful for Jock . . . She may know at half past five or a bit earlier.'

'It's a pity you don't play patience,' said Mrs Rattery.

'In a way I shall feel happier when she knows . . . it feels all wrong as it is at present, having it as a secret that Brenda doesn't know . . . I'm not sure how she fits in her day. I suppose her last lecture is over at about five . . . I wonder if she goes home first to change if she's going out to tea or cocktails. She can't sit about much in the flat, it's so small.'

Mrs Rattery brooded over her chequer of cards and then drew them towards her into a heap, haphazard once more and without meaning; it had nearly come to a solution that time, but for a six of diamonds out of place, and a stubbornly congested patch at one corner, where nothing could be made to move. 'It's a heartbreaking game,' she said.

The clock struck again.

'Is that only quarter past? . . . You know I think I should have gone off my head if I were alone. It's nice of you to stay with me.'

'Do you play bezique?'[28]

'I'm afraid not.'

'Or piquet?'[29]

'No. I've never been able to learn any card game except animal snap.'

'Pity.'

'There's Marjorie and several people I ought to wire to, but I'd better wait until I know that Jock has seen Brenda. Suppose she was with Marjorie when the telegram arrived.'

'You've got to try and stop thinking about things. Can you throw craps?'

'No.'

'That's easy; I'll show you. There'll be some dice in the back-gammon board.'

'I'm all right, really. I'd sooner not play.'

'You get the dice and sit up here at the table. We've got six hours to get through.'

She showed him how to throw craps. He said, 'I've seen it on the cinema – pullman porters and taxi men.'

'Of course you have, it's easy . . . there you see you've won, you take all.'

Presently Tony said, 'I've just thought of something.'

'Don't you ever take a rest from thinking?'

'Suppose the evening papers have got hold of it already. Brenda may see it on a placard, or just pick up a paper casually and there it will be . . . perhaps with a photograph.'

'Yes, I thought of that just now, when you were talking about telegraphing.'

'But it's quite likely, isn't it? They get hold of everything so quickly. What can we do about it?'

'There isn't anything we can do. We've just got to wait . . . Come on, boy, throw up.'

'I don't want to play any more. I'm worried.'

'I know you're worried. You don't have to tell me . . . you aren't going to give up playing just when the luck's running your way?'

'I'm sorry . . . it isn't any good.'

He walked about the room, first to the window, then to the fireplace. He began to fill his pipe. 'At least we can find out whether the evening papers have got it in. We can ring up and ask the hall porter at my club.'

'That's not going to prevent your wife reading it. We've just got to wait. What was the game you said you knew? Animal something?'

'Snap.'

'I'll buy it.'

'It's just a child's game. It would be ridiculous with two.'

'Show me.'

'Well each of us chooses an animal.'

'All right, I'm a dog and you're a hen. Now what?'

Tony explained.

'I'd say it was one of those games that you have to feel pretty good first, before you can enjoy them,' said Mrs Rattery. 'But I'll try anything.'

They each took a pack and began dealing. Soon a pair of eights appeared. 'Bow-wow,' said Mrs Rattery, scooping in the cards.

Another pair. 'Bow-wow,' said Mrs Rattery. 'You know you aren't putting your heart into this.'

'Oh,' said Tony. 'Coop-coop-coop.'

Presently he said again, 'Coop-coop-coop.'

'Don't be dumb,' said Mrs Rattery, 'that isn't a pair . . .'

They were still playing when Albert came in to draw the curtains. Tony had only two cards left which he turned over regularly; Mrs Rattery was obliged to divide hers, they were too many to hold. They stopped playing when they found that Albert was in the room.

'What must that man have thought?' said Tony, when he had gone out.

('Sitting there clucking like a 'en,' Albert reported, 'and the little fellow lying dead upstairs.')

'We'd better stop.'

'It wasn't a very good game. And to think it's the only one you know.'

She collected the cards and began to deal them into their proper packs. Ambrose and Albert brought in tea. Tony looked at his watch. 'Five o'clock. Now that the shutters are up we shan't hear the chimes. Jock must be in London by now.'

Mrs Rattery said, 'I'd rather like some whisky.'

Jock had not seen Brenda's flat. It was in a large, featureless house, typical of the district. Mrs Beaver deplored the space wasted by the staircase well and empty, paved hall. There was no porter; a woman came three mornings a week with bucket and mop. A board painted with the names of the tenants informed Jock that Brenda was IN. But he put little reliance on this information, knowing that Brenda was not one to remember, as she came in and out, to change the indicator. He found her front door on the second floor. After the first flight the staircase changed from marble to a faded carpet that had been there before Mrs Beaver undertook the reconstruction. Jock pressed the bell and heard it ringing just inside the door. Nobody came to open it. It was ten past five, and he had not expected to find Brenda at home. He had decided on the road up that after trying the flat, he would go to his club and ring up various friends of Brenda's who might know where she was. He rang again, from habit, and waited a little; then turned to go. But at that moment the door next to Brenda's opened and a dark lady in a dress of crimson velvet looked out at him; she wore very large earrings of oriental filigree, set with bosses of opaque, valueless stone.

'Are you looking for Lady Brenda Last?'

'I am. Is she a friend of yours?'

'Oh, *such* a friend,' said Princess Abdul Akbar.

'Then perhaps you can tell me where I can find her?'

'I think she's bound to be at Lady Cockpurse's. I'm just going there myself. Can I give her any message?'

'I had better come and see her.'

'Well, wait five minutes and you can go with me. Come inside.'

The Princess's single room was furnished promiscuously and with truly Eastern disregard of the right properties of things; swords meant to adorn the state robes of a moorish caid were swung from the picture rail; mats made for prayer were strewn on the divan; the carpet on the floor had been made in Bokhara[30] as a wall covering; while over the dressing table was draped a shawl made in Yokohama[31] for sale to cruise-passengers; an octagonal table from Port Said[32] held a Tibetan Buddha of pale soapstone; six ivory elephants from Bombay[33] stood along the top of the radiator. Other cultures, too, were represented by a set of Lalique[34] bottles and powder boxes, a phallic fetish from Senegal,[35] a Dutch copper bowl, a waste-paper basket made of varnished aquatints, a golli-wog[36] presented at the gala dinner of a seaside hotel, a dozen or so framed photographs of the Princess, a garden scene ingeniously constructed in pieces of coloured wood, and a radio set in fumed oak,[37] Tudor[38] style. In so small a room the effect was distracting. The princess sat at the looking glass, Jock behind her on the divan.

'What's your name?' she asked over her shoulder. He told her. 'Oh, yes, I've heard them mention you. I was at Hetton the week-end before last . . . such a quaint old place.'

'I'd better tell you. There's been a frightful accident there this morning.'

Jenny Abdul Akbar spun round on the leather stool; her eyes were wide with alarm, her hand pressed to her heart. 'Quick,' she whispered, '*Tell me*. I can't bear it. Is it *death*?'

Jock nodded. 'Their little boy . . . kicked by a horse.'

'*Little Jimmy*.'

'John.'

'John . . . *dead*. It's *too* horrible.'

'It wasn't anybody's fault.'

'Oh yes,' said Jenny. 'It was. It was *my* fault. I ought never to have gone there . . . a terrible curse hangs over me. Wherever I go I bring nothing but sorrow . . . if only it was *I* that was dead . . . I shall never be able to face them again. I feel like a murderess . . . that brave little life snuffed out.'

'I say you know, really, I shouldn't take that line about it.'

'It isn't the first time it's happened ... always, anywhere, I am hunted down ... without remorse. O God,' said Jenny Abdul Akbar. 'What have I done to deserve it?'

She rose to leave him; there was nowhere she could go except the bathroom. Jock said, through the door, 'Well I must go along to Polly's and see Brenda.'

'Wait a minute and I'll come too.' She had brightened a little when she emerged. 'Have you got a car here,' she asked, 'or shall I ring up a taxi?'

After tea Mr Tendril called. Tony saw him in his study and was away half an hour. When he returned he went to the tray, which, on Mrs Rattery's instructions, had been left in the library, and poured himself out whisky and ginger ale. Mrs Rattery had resumed her patience. 'Bad interview?' she asked without looking up.

'Awful.' He drank the whisky quickly and poured out some more.

'Bring me one too, will you?'

Tony said, 'I only wanted to see him about arrangements. He tried to be comforting. It was very painful ... after all the last thing one wants to talk about at a time like this is religion.'

'Some like it,' said Mrs Rattery.

'Of course,' Tony began, after a pause, 'when you haven't got children yourself –'

'I've got two sons,' said Mrs Rattery.

'Have you? I'm so sorry. I didn't realize ... we know each other so little. How very impertinent of me.'

'That's all right. People are always surprised. I don't see them often. They're at school somewhere. I took them to the cinema last summer. They're getting quite big. One's going to be good looking, I think. His father is.'

'Quarter past six,' said Tony. 'He's bound to have told her by now.'

There was a little party at Lady Cockpurse's, Veronica and Daisy and Sybil, Souki de Foucauld-Esterhazy, and four or five others, all women. They were there to consult a new fortune-teller called

Mrs Northcote. Mrs Beaver had discovered her and for every five guineas that she earned at her introduction Mrs Beaver took a commission of two pounds twelve and sixpence. She told fortunes in a new way, by reading the soles of the feet. They waited their turn impatiently. 'What a time she is taking over Daisy.'

'She is very thorough,' said Polly, 'and it tickles rather.'

Presently Daisy emerged. 'What was she like?' they asked.

'I mustn't tell or it spoils it all,' said Daisy.

They had dealt cards for precedence. It was Brenda's turn now. She went next door to Mrs Northcote, who was sitting at a stool beside an armchair. She was a dowdy, middle-aged woman with a slightly genteel accent. Brenda sat down and took off her shoe and stocking. Mrs Northcote laid the foot on her knee and gazed at it with great solemnity; then she picked it up and began tracing the small creases of the sole with the point of a silver pencil case.[39] Brenda wriggled her toes luxuriously and settled down to listen.

Next door they said, 'Where's her Mr Beaver today?'

'He's flown over to France with his mother to see some new wall papers. She's been worrying all day thinking he's had an accident.'

'It's all very touching, isn't it? Though I can't see his point myself . . .'

'You must never do anything on Thursdays,' said Mrs Northcote.

'Nothing?'

'Nothing important. You are intellectual, imaginative, sympathetic, easily led by others, impulsive, affectionate. You are highly artistic and are not giving full scope to your capabilities.'

'Isn't there anything about love?'

'I am coming to love. All these lines from the great toe to the instep represent lovers.'

'Yes, go on some more about that . . .'

Princess Abdul Akbar was announced. 'Where's Brenda?' she said. 'I thought she'd be here.'

'Mrs Northcote's doing her now.'

'Jock Menzies wants to see her. He's downstairs.'

'Darling Jock . . . Why on earth didn't you bring him up?'

'No, it's something terribly important. He's got to see Brenda alone.'

'My dear, how mysterious. Well, she won't be long now. We can't disturb them. It would upset Mrs Northcote.'

Jenny told them her news.

On the other side of the door, Brenda's leg was beginning to feel slightly chilly. 'Four men dominate your fate,' Mrs Northcote was saying, 'one is loyal and tender but he has not yet disclosed his love, one is passionate and overpowering, you are a little afraid of him.'

'Dear me,' said Brenda. 'How very exciting. Who *can* they be?'

'One you must avoid; he bodes no good for you, he is steely hearted and rapacious.'

'I bet that's my Mr Beaver, bless him.'

Downstairs Jock sat waiting in the small front room where Polly's guests usually assembled before luncheon. It was five past six.

Soon Brenda pulled on her stocking, stepped into her shoe, and joined the ladies. '*Most* enjoyable,' she pronounced. 'Why, how odd you all look.'

'Jock Grant-Menzies wants to see you downstairs.'

'Jock? How very extraordinary. It isn't anything awful, is it?'

'You better go and see him.'

Suddenly Brenda became frightened by the strange air of the room and the unfamiliar expression in her friends' faces. She ran down stairs to the room where Jock was waiting.

'What is it, Jock? Tell me quickly, I'm scared. It's nothing awful, is it?'

'I'm afraid it is. There's been a very serious accident.'

'John?'

'Yes.'

'Dead?'

He nodded.

She sat down on a hard little Empire chair[40] against the wall, perfectly still with her hands folded in her lap, like a small well-brought-up child introduced into a room full of grown-ups. She said, 'Tell me what happened. Why do you know about it first?'

'I've been down at Hetton since the weekend.'

'Hetton?'

'Don't you remember? John was going hunting today.'

She frowned, not at once taking in what he was saying. 'John ... John Andrew ... I ... Oh thank God[41] ...' Then she burst into tears.

She wept helplessly, turning round in the chair and pressing her forehead against its gilt back.

Upstairs Mrs Northcote had Souki Foucauld-Esterhazy by the foot and was saying, 'There are four men dominating your fate. One is loyal and tender but has not yet disclosed his love ...'

In the silence of Hetton, the telephone rang near the house-keeper's room and was switched through to the library. Tony answered it.

'This is Jock speaking. I've just seen Brenda. She's coming down by the seven o'clock train.'

'Is she terribly upset?'

'Yes, naturally.'

'Where is she now?'

'She's with me. I'm speaking from Polly's.'

'Shall I talk to her?'

'Better not.'

'All right ... I'll meet that train. Are you coming too?'

'No.'

'Well, you've been wonderful. I don't know what I should have done without you and Mrs Rattery.'

'Oh, that's all right. I'll see Brenda off.'

She had stopped crying and sat crouched in the chair. She did not look up while Jock telephoned. Then she said, 'Yes, I'll go by that train.'

'We ought to start. I suppose you will have to get some things from the flat.'

'My bag ... upstairs. You get it. I can't go in there again.'

She did not speak on the way to her flat. She sat beside Jock as he drove, looking straight ahead. When they arrived she unlocked her door and led him in. The room was extremely empty of furniture. She sat down in the only chair. 'There's plenty of time really. Tell me exactly what happened.'

Jock told her.

'Poor little boy,' she said. 'Poor little boy.'

Then she opened her cupboard and began to put a few things into a suit case; she went in and out from the bathroom once or twice. 'That's everything,' she said. 'There's still too much time.'

'Would you like anything to eat?'

'Oh no, nothing to eat.' She sat down again and looked at herself in the glass. She did not attempt to do anything to her face. 'When you first told me,' she said, 'I didn't understand. I didn't know what I was saying.'

'I know.'

'I didn't say anything, did I?'

'You know what you said.'

'Yes, I know . . . I didn't mean . . . I don't think it's any good trying to explain.'

Jock said, 'Are you sure you've got everything?'

'Yes, that's everything,' she nodded towards the little case on the bed. She looked quite hopeless.

'Well, we'd better go to the station.'

'All right. It's early. But it doesn't matter.'

Jock took her to the train. As it was Wednesday the carriages were full of women returning after their day's shopping.

'Why not go first class?'

'No, no. I always go third.'

She sat in the middle of a row. The women on either side looked at her curiously wondering if she were ill.

'Don't you want anything to read?'

'Nothing to read.'

'Or eat?'

'Or eat.'

'Then I'll say good bye.'

'Good bye.'

Another woman pushed past Jock into the carriage, laden with light parcels.

When the news became known Marjorie said to Allan, 'Well, anyway, this will mean the end of Mr Beaver.'

But Polly Cockpurse said to Veronica, 'That's the end of Tony so far as Brenda is concerned.'

The impoverished Lasts were stunned by the telegram. They lived on an extensive but unprofitable chicken farm near Princes Risborough.[42] It did not enter the heads of any of them that now, if anything happened, they were the heirs to Hetton. Had it done so, their grief would have been just as keen.

Jock drove from Paddington to Brat's. One of the men by the bar said, 'Ghastly thing about Tony Last's boy.'

'Yes, I was there.'

'No, were you? What a ghastly thing.'

Later a telephone message came: 'Princess Abdul Akbar wishes to know whether you are in the club.'

'No, no, tell her I'm not here,' said Jock.

Seven

The inquest was held at eleven o'clock next morning; it was soon over. The doctor, the bus-driver, Ben and Miss Ripon gave evidence. Miss Ripon was allowed to remain seated. She was very white and spoke in a trembling voice; her father glared at her from a nearby seat; under her hat was a small bare patch, where they had shaved off the hair to clean her cut. In his summary the coroner remarked that it was clear from the evidence that nobody was in any way to blame for the misadventure; it only remained to express the deep sympathy of the court to Mr Last and Lady Brenda in their terrible loss. The people fell back to allow Tony and Brenda to leave the room. Colonel Inch and the hunt secretary were both present. Everything was done with delicacy and to show respect for their sorrow.

Brenda said, 'Wait a minute. I must just speak to that poor Ripon girl.'

She did it charmingly. When everyone had gone, Tony said, 'I wish you had been here yesterday. There were so many people about and I didn't know what to say to them.'

'What did you do all day?'

'There was the shameless blonde . . . we played animal snap some of the time.'

'Animal snap? Was that any good?'

'Not much . . . It's odd to think that yesterday this time it hadn't happened.'

'Poor little boy,' said Brenda.

They had scarcely spoken to each other since Brenda's arrival. Tony had driven to the station to meet her; by the time they reached the house Mrs Rattery had gone to bed; that morning she left in her aeroplane without seeing either of them. They heard the machine pass over the house, Brenda in her bath, Tony downstairs in his study attending to the correspondence that had become necessary.

A day of fitful sunshine and blustering wind; white and grey clouds were scarcely moving, high overhead, but the bare trees round the house swayed and shook and there were swift whirlpools of straw in the stable yard. Ben changed from the Sunday suit he had worn at the inquest and went about his duties. Thunderclap, too, had been kicked yesterday and was very slightly lame in the off fore.

Brenda took off her hat and threw it down on a chair in the hall. 'Nothing to say, is there?'

'There's no need to talk.'

'No. I suppose there'll have to be a funeral.'

'Well, of course.'

'Yes; tomorrow?'

She looked into the morning room. 'They've done quite a lot, haven't they?'

All Brenda's movements were slower than usual and her voice was flat and expressionless. She sank down into one of the arm chairs in the centre of the hall, which nobody ever used. She sat there doing nothing. Tony put his hand on her shoulder but she said 'Don't,' not impatiently or nervously but without any expression. Tony said, 'I'll go and finish those letters.'

'Yes.'

'See you at luncheon.'

'Yes.'

She rose, looked round listlessly for her hat, found it and went very slowly upstairs, the sunlight through the stained glass windows[43] glowing and sparkling all about her.

In her room she sat on the window seat, looking out across the meadows and dun ploughland, the naked tossing trees, the church towers, the maelstroms of dust and leaf which eddied about the terrace below; she still held her hat and fidgeted with her fingers on the brooch which was clipped to one side of it.

Nanny knocked at the door and came in, red eyed. 'If you please, my lady, I've been going through John's things. There's this handkerchief doesn't belong to him.'

The heavy scent and crowned cypher at the corner proclaimed its origin.

'I know whose it is. I'll send it back to her.'

'Can't think how it came to be there,' said nanny.

'Poor little boy. Poor little boy,' said Brenda to herself, when nanny had left her, and gazed out across the troubled landscape.

'I was thinking about the pony, sir.'

'Oh yes, Ben?'

'Will you want to be keeping her now?'

'I hadn't thought . . . no, I suppose not.'

'Mr Westmacott over at Restall was asking about her. He thought she might do for his little girl.'

'Yes.'

'How much shall we be asking?'

'Oh, I don't know . . . whatever you think is right.'

'She's a good little pony and she's always been treated well. I don't think she ought to go under twenty-five quid, sir.'

'All right Ben, you see about it.'

'I'll ask thirty, shall I, sir, and come down a bit?'

'Do just what you think best.'

'Very good, sir.'

*

At luncheon Tony said, 'Jock rang up. He wanted to know if there was anything he could do.'

'How sweet of him. Why don't you have him down for the weekend?'

'Would you like that?'

'I shan't be here. I'm going to Veronica's.'

'You're going to Veronica's?'

'Yes, don't you remember?'

There were servants in the room so that they said nothing more until later, when they were alone in the library. Then, 'Are you really going away?'

'Yes. I can't stay here. You understand that, don't you?'

'Yes, of course. I was thinking we might both go away, abroad somewhere.'

Brenda did not answer him but continued in her own line. 'I couldn't stay here. It's all over, don't you see, our life down here.'

'Darling, what *do* you mean?'

'Don't ask me to explain . . . not just now.'

'But Brenda, sweet, I don't understand. We're both young. Of course, we can never forget John. He'll always be our eldest son but . . .'

'Don't go on, Tony, please don't go on.'

So Tony stopped and after a time said, 'So you're going to Veronica's tomorrow?'

'Mmmm.'

'I think I will ask Jock to come.'

'Yes, I should.'

'And we can think about plans later when we've got more used to things.'

'Yes, later.'

Next morning.

'A sweet letter from mother,' said Brenda, handing it across. Lady St Cloud had written:

. . . I shall not come down to Hetton for the funeral, but I shall be thinking of you both all the time and of my dear grandson. I shall think of you as I saw you all three, together, at Christmas. Dear children, at a time like this

only yourselves can be any help to each other. Love is the only thing that is
stronger than sorrow . . .

'I got a telegram from Jock,' said Tony, 'he *can* come.'

'It's really rather embarrassing for us all, Brenda coming,' said
Veronica. 'I do think she might have chucked. I shan't in the least
know what to say to her.'

Tony said to Jock, as they sat alone after dinner, 'I've been
trying to understand, and I think I do now. It's not how I feel
myself but Brenda and I are quite different in lots of ways. It's
because they were strangers and didn't know John, and were never
in our life here, that she wants to be with them. That's it, don't
you think? She wants to be absolutely alone and away from everything that reminds her of what has happened . . . all the same I
feel awful about letting her go. I can't tell you what she was like
here . . . quite mechanical. It's so much worse for her than it is for
me, I see that. It's so terrible not being able to do anything to
help.'

Jock did not answer.

Beaver was staying at Veronica's. Brenda said to him, 'Until
Wednesday, when I thought something had happened to you, I
had no idea that I loved you.'

'Well you've said it often enough.'

'I'm going to make you understand,' said Brenda. 'You clod.'

On Monday morning Tony found this letter on his breakfast
tray.

Darling Tony,

I am not coming back to Hetton. Grimshawe can pack everything and bring
it to the flat. Then I shan't want her any more.

You must have realized for some time that things were going wrong.

I am in love with John Beaver and I want to have a divorce and marry
him. If John Andrew had not died things might not have happened like this.
I can't tell. As it is, I simply can't begin over again. Please do not mind too

much. I suppose we shan't be allowed to meet while the case is on but I hope afterwards we shall be great *friends. Anyway I shall always look on you as one whatever you think of me.*

> Best love from
> Brenda.

When Tony read this his first thought was that Brenda had lost her reason. 'She's only seen Beaver twice to my knowledge,' he said.

But later he showed the letter to Jock, who said, 'I'm sorry it should have happened like this.'

'But it's not true, is it?'

'Yes, I'm afraid it is. Everyone has known for some time.'

But it was several days before Tony fully realized what it meant. He had got into a habit of loving and trusting Brenda.

Chapter Four

ENGLISH GOTHIC — II

One

'How's the old boy taking it?'

'Not so well. It makes me feel rather a beast,' said Brenda. 'I'm afraid he minds a lot.'

'Well, you wouldn't like it if he didn't,' said Polly to console her.

'No, I suppose not.'

'I shall stick by you whatever happens,' said Jenny Abdul Akbar.

'Oh everything is going quite smoothly now,' said Brenda. 'There was a certain amount of *gêne*[1] with relatives.'

Tony had been living with Jock for the last three weeks. Mrs Rattery had gone to California and he was grateful for company. They dined together most evenings. They had given up going to Brat's; so had Beaver; they were afraid of meeting each other. Instead Tony and Jock went to Brown's, where Beaver was not a member. Beaver was continually with Brenda nowadays, at one of half a dozen houses.

Mrs Beaver did not like the turn things had taken; her workmen had been sent back from Hetton with their job unfinished.

In the first week Tony had had several distasteful interviews. Allan had attempted to act as peacemaker.

'You just wait a few weeks,' he had said. 'Brenda will come back. She'll soon get sick of Beaver.'

'But I don't want her back.'

'I know just how you feel, but it doesn't do to be medieval about it. If Brenda hadn't been upset at John's death this need never have come to a crisis. Why last year Marjorie was going everywhere with that ass Robin Beaseley. She was mad about him at the time, but I pretended not to notice and it all blew over. If I were you I should refuse to recognize that anything has happened.'

Marjorie had said, 'Of *course* Brenda doesn't love Beaver. How could she? . . . And if she thinks she does at the moment, I think it's your duty to prevent her making a fool of herself. You must refuse to be divorced – anyway until she has found someone more reasonable.'

Lady St Cloud had said, 'Brenda has been very, very foolish. She always was an excitable girl, but I am sure there was never anything *wrong*, quite sure. *That* wouldn't be like Brenda at all. I haven't met Mr Beaver and I do not wish to. I understand he is unsuitable in every way. Brenda would never want to marry anyone like that. I will tell you exactly how it happened, Tony. Brenda must have felt a tiny bit neglected – people often do at that stage of marriage. I have known countless cases – and it was naturally flattering to find a young man to beg and carry for her. That's all it was, nothing *wrong*. And then the terrible shock of little John's accident unsettled her and she didn't know what she was saying or writing. You'll both laugh over this little fracas in years to come.'

Tony had not set eyes on Brenda since the afternoon of the funeral. Once he spoke to her over the telephone.

It was during the second week when he was feeling most lonely and bewildered by various counsels. Allan had been with him urging a reconciliation. 'I've been talking to Brenda,' he had said. 'She's sick of Beaver already. The one thing she wants is to go back to Hetton and settle down with you again.'

While Allan was there, Tony resolutely refused to listen, but later the words, and the picture they evoked, would not leave his mind. So he rang her up and she answered him calmly and gravely.

'Brenda, this is Tony.'

'Hullo Tony, what is it?'

'I've been talking to Allan. He's just told me about your change of mind.'

'I'm not sure I know what you mean.'

'That you want to leave Beaver and come back to Hetton.'

'Did Allan say that?'

'Yes, isn't it true?'

'I'm afraid it's not. Allan is an interfering ass. I had him here this afternoon. He told me that you didn't want a divorce but that you were willing to let me stay on alone in London and do as I liked provided there was no public scandal. It seemed a good idea and I was going to ring you up about it. But I suppose that's just his diplomacy too. Anyway I'm afraid there's no prospect of my coming back to Hetton just at present.'

'Oh I see. I didn't think it was likely . . . I just rang you up.'

'That's all right. How are you, Tony?'

'All right, thanks.'

'Good, so am I. Goodbye.'

That was all he had heard of her. Both avoided places where there was a likelihood of their meeting.

It was thought convenient that Brenda should appear as the plaintiff. Tony did not employ the family solicitors in the matter but another, less reputable firm who specialized in divorce. He had steeled himself to expect a certain professional gusto, even levity, but found them instead disposed to melancholy and suspicion.

'I gather Lady Brenda is being far from discreet. It is quite likely that the King's Proctor[2] may intervene . . . Moreover there is the question of money. You understand that by the present arrangement since she is the innocent and injured party she will be entitled to claim substantial alimony from the courts.'

'Oh that's all right,' said Tony. 'I've been into all that with her brother-in-law and have decided to make a settlement of five hundred a year. She has four hundred of her own and I understand Mr Beaver has something.'

'It's a pity we can't put it in writing,' said the solicitor, 'but that might constitute Conspiracy.'

'Lady Brenda's word is quite good enough,' said Tony.

'We like to protect our clients against even the most remote contingencies,' said the lawyer with an air of piety, for he had not had Tony's opportunities to contract the habit of loving and trusting Brenda.

The fourth weekend after Brenda's departure from Hetton was fixed for Tony's infidelity. A suite was engaged at a seaside hotel ('We always send our clients there. The servants are well

accustomed to giving evidence') and private detectives were noti-
fied. 'It only remains to select a partner,' said the solicitor; no hint
of naughtiness lightened his gloom. 'We have on occasions been
instrumental in accommodating our clients but there have been
frequent complaints, so we find it best to leave the choice to them.
Lately we had a particularly delicate case involving a man of very
rigid morality and a certain diffidence. In the end his own wife
consented to go with him and supply the evidence. She wore a red
wig. It was quite successful.'

'I don't think that would do in this case.'

'No. Exactly. I was merely quoting it as a matter of interest.'

'I expect I shall be able to find someone,' said Tony.

'I have no doubt of it,' said the solicitor, bowing politely.

But when he came to discuss the question later with Jock, it did
not seem so easy. 'It's not a thing one can ask every girl to do,' he
said, 'whichever way you put it. If you say it is merely a legal form
it is rather insulting, and if you suggest going the whole hog it's
rather fresh – suddenly, I mean, if you've never paid any particular
attention to her before and don't propose to carry on with it afterwards . . . Of course there's always old Sybil.'

But even Sybil refused. 'I'd do it like a shot any other time,' she
said, 'but just at the moment it wouldn't suit my book. There's a
certain person who might hear about it and take it wrong . . .
There's an awfully pretty girl called Jenny Abdul Akbar. I wonder
if you've met her.'

'Yes, I've met her.'

'Well, won't she do?'

'No.'

'Oh dear, I don't know who to suggest.'

'We'd better go and study the market at the Old Hundredth,'
said Jock.

They dined at Jock's house. Lately they had found it a little
gloomy at Brown's, for people tended to avoid anyone they knew
to be unhappy. Though they drank a magnum of champagne they
could not recapture the light hearted mood in which they had last
visited Sink Street. And then Tony said, 'Is it any good going there
yet?'

'We may as well try. After all we aren't going there for enjoyment.'

'No, indeed.'

The doors were open at a Hundred Sink Street and the band was playing to an empty ballroom. The waiters were eating at a little table in the corner. Two or three girls were clustered round the Jack-Pot machine, losing shillings hard and complaining about the cold. They ordered a bottle of the Montmorency Wine Company's brandy and sat down to wait.

'Any of those do?' asked Jock.

'I don't much care.'

'Better get someone you like. You've got to put in a lot of time with her.'

Presently Milly and Babs came downstairs.

'How are the postman's hats?' said Milly.

They could not recognize the allusion.

'You are the two boys who were here last month, aren't you?'

'Yes. I'm afraid we were rather tight.'

'You don't say?' It was very seldom that Milly and Babs met anyone who was quite sober during their business hours.

'Well, come and sit down. How are you both?'

'I think I'm starting a cold,' said Babs. 'I feel awful. Why can't they heat this hole, the mean hounds?'

Milly was more cheerful and swayed in her chair to the music. 'Care to dance?' she said, and she and Tony began to shuffle across the empty floor.

'My friend is looking for a lady to take to the seaside,' said Jock.

'What, this weather? That'll be a nice treat for a lonely girl.' Babs sniffed into a little ball of handkerchief.

'It's for a divorce.'

'Oh, I see. Well, why doesn't he take Milly? She doesn't catch cold easy. Besides she knows how to behave at an hotel. Lots of the girls here are all right to have a lark with in town, but you have to have a *lady* for a divorce.'

'D'you often get asked to do that?'

'Now and then. It's a nice rest – but it means so much *talking* and the gentlemen will always go on so about their wives.'

While they were dancing Tony came straight to business. 'I suppose you wouldn't care to come away for the weekend?' he asked.

'Shouldn't mind,' said Milly. 'Where?'

'I thought of Brighton.'

'Oh . . . Is it for a divorce?'

'Yes.'

'You wouldn't mind if I brought my little girl with us? She wouldn't be any trouble.'

'Yes.'

'You mean you wouldn't mind?'

'I mean I should mind.'

'Oh . . . You wouldn't think I had a little girl of eight, would you?'

'No.'

'She's called Winnie. I was only sixteen when I had her. I was the youngest of the family and our stepfather wouldn't leave any of us girls alone. That's why I have to work. She lives with a lady at Finchley.³ Twenty-eight bob a week it costs me, not counting her clothes. She does like the seaside.'

'No,' said Tony. 'I'm sorry but it would be quite impossible. We'll get a lovely present for you to take back to her.'

'All right . . . One gentleman gave her a fairy cycle⁴ for Christmas. She fell off and cut her knee . . . When do we start?'

'Would you like to go by train or car?'

'Oh, train. Winnie's sick if she goes in a car.'

'Winnie's not coming.'

'No, but let's go by train anyway.'

So it was decided that they should meet at Victoria on Saturday afternoon.

Jock gave Babs ten shillings and he and Tony went home. Tony had not slept much lately. He could not prevent himself, when alone, from rehearsing over and over in his mind all that had happened since Beaver's visit to Hetton; searching for clues he had missed at the time; wondering where something he had said or done might have changed the course of events; going back further to his earliest acquaintance with Brenda to find indications that should have made him more ready to understand the change that had come over her; reliving scene after scene in the last eight years of his life. All this kept him awake.

Two

There was a general rendezvous at the first class booking office. The detectives were there earliest, ten minutes before their time. They had been pointed out to Tony at the solicitor's office so that he should not lose them. They were cheerful middle-aged men in soft hats and heavy overcoats. They were looking forward to their weekend, for most of their daily work consisted in standing about at street corners watching front doors and a job of this kind was eagerly competed for in the office. In more modest divorces the solicitors were content to rely on the evidence of the hotel servants. The detectives were a luxury and proposed to treat themselves as such.

There was a slight fog in London that day. The station lamps were alight prematurely.

Tony came next, with Jock at his side, loyally there to see him off. They bought the tickets and waited. The detectives, sticklers for professional etiquette, made an attempt at self effacement, studying the posters on the walls and peering from behind a pillar.

'This is going to be hell,' said Tony.

It was ten minutes before Milly came. She emerged from the gloom with a porter in front carrying her suitcase and a child dragging back on her arm behind her. Milly's wardrobe consisted mainly of evening dresses, for during the day she usually spent her time sitting before a gas fire in her dressing gown. She made an insignificant and rather respectable appearance.

'Sorry if I'm late,' she said. 'Winnie here couldn't find her shoes. I brought her along too. I knew you wouldn't mind really. She travels on a half ticket.'

Winnie was a plain child with large gold-rimmed spectacles. When she spoke she revealed that two of her front teeth were missing.

'I hope you don't imagine she's coming with us.'

'Yes that's the idea,' said Milly. 'She won't be any trouble – she's got her puzzle.'

Tony bent down to speak to the little girl. 'Listen,' he said. 'You don't want to come to a nasty big hotel. You go with this kind gentleman here. He'll take you to a shop and let you choose the biggest doll you can find and then he'll drive you back in his motor to your home. You'll like that, won't you?'

'No,' said Winnie. 'I want to go to the seaside. I won't go with that man. I don't want a doll. I want to go to the seaside with my mummy.'

Several people besides the detectives were beginning to take notice of the oddly assorted group.

'Oh God!' said Tony, 'I suppose she's got to come.'

The detectives followed at a distance down the platform. Tony settled his companions in a pullman car. 'Look,' said Milly, 'we're travelling first class. Isn't that fun? We can have tea.'

'Can I have an ice?'

'I don't expect they've got an ice. But you can have some nice tea.'

'But I want an ice.'

'You shall have an ice when you get to Brighton. Now be a good girl and play with your puzzle or mother won't take you to the seaside again.'

'The Awful Child of popular fiction,' said Jock as he left Tony.

Winnie sustained the part throughout the journey to Brighton. She was not inventive but she knew the classic routine thoroughly, even to such commonplace but alarming devices as breathing heavily, grunting and complaining of nausea.

Rooms at the hotel had been engaged for Tony by the solicitors. It was therefore a surprise to the reception clerk when Winnie arrived. 'We have reserved in your name double and single communicating rooms, bathroom and sitting-room,' he said. 'We did not understand you were bringing your daughter. Will you require a further room?'

'Oh, Winnie can come in with me,' said Milly.

The two detectives who were standing nearby at the counter exchanged glances of disapproval.

Tony wrote *Mr and Mrs Last* in the Visitors' Book.

'And daughter,' said the clerk with his finger on the place.

Tony hesitated. 'She is my niece,' he said, and inscribed her name on another line, as *Miss Smith*.

The detective, registering below, remarked to his colleague, 'He got out of that all right. Quite smart. But I don't like the look of this case. Most irregular. Sets a nasty, respectable note bringing a kid into it. We've got the firm to consider. It doesn't do them any good to get mixed up with the King's Proctor.'

'How about a quick one?' said his colleague indifferently.

Upstairs, Winnie said, 'Where's the sea?'

'Just there across the street.'

'I want to go and see it.'

'But it's dark now, pet. You shall see it tomorrow.'

'I want to see it tonight.'

'You take her to see it now,' said Tony.

'Sure you won't be lonely?'

'Quite sure.'

'We won't be long.'

'That's all right. You let her see it properly.'

Tony went down to the bar where he was pleased to find the two detectives. He felt the need of male company. 'Good evening,' he said.

They looked at him askance. Everything in this case seemed to be happening as though with deliberate design to shock their professional feelings. 'Good evening,' said the senior detective. 'Nasty, raw evening.'

'Have a drink.'

Since Tony was paying their expenses in any case, the offer seemed superfluous but the junior detective brightened instinctively and said, 'Don't mind if I do.'

'Come and sit down. I feel rather lonely.'

They took their drinks to a table out of hearing of the barman. 'Mr Last, sir, this is all *wrong*,' said the senior detective. 'You haven't no business to recognize us at all. I don't know what they'd say at the office.'

'Best respects,' said the junior detective.

'This is Mr James, my colleague,' said the senior detective. 'My name is Blenkinsop. James is new to this kind of work.'

'So am I,' said Tony.

'A pity we've such a nasty weekend for the job,' said Blenkinsop, 'very damp and blowy. Gets me in the joints.'

'Tell me,' said Tony. 'Is it usual to bring children on an expedition of this kind?'

'It is *not*.'

'I thought it couldn't be.'

'Since you ask me, Mr Last, I regard it as most irregular and injudicious. It looks wrong, and cases of this kind depend very much on making the right impression. Of course as far as James and me are concerned, the matter is O.K. There won't be a word about it in our evidence. But you can't trust the servants. You might very likely happen to strike one who was new to the courts, who'd blurt it out, and then where would we be? I don't like it, Mr Last, and that's the truth.'

'You can't feel more strongly about it than I do.'

'Fond of kids myself,' said James, who was new to this kind of work. 'How about one with us?'

'Tell me,' said Tony, when they had been at their table some little time. 'You must have observed numerous couples in your time, qualifying for a divorce; tell me, how do they get through their day?'

'It's easier in the summer,' said Blenkinsop, 'the young ladies usually bathe and the gentlemen read the papers on the esplanade; some goes for motor drives and some just hangs around the bar. They're mostly glad when Monday comes.'

Milly and her child were in the sitting-room when Tony came up.

'I've ordered an ice,' said Milly.

'Quite right.'

'I want late dinner. I want late dinner.'

'No, dear, not late dinner. You have an ice up here.'

Tony returned to the bar. 'Mr James,' he said. 'Did I understand you to say you were fond of children.'

'Yes, in their right place.'

'You wouldn't I suppose consider dining tonight with the little girl who has accompanied me? I should take it as a great kindness.'

'Oh no, sir, hardly that.'

'You would not find me ungrateful.'

'Well, sir, I don't like to appear unobliging, but it's not part of my duties.'

He seemed to be wavering but Blenkinsop interposed. 'Quite out of the question, sir.'

When Tony left them Blenkinsop spoke from the depth of his experience; it was the first job that he and James had been on together, and he felt under some obligation to put his junior wise. 'Our trouble is always the same – to make the clients realize that divorce is a serious matter.'

Eventually extravagant promises for the morrow, two or three ices and the slight depression induced by them, persuaded Winnie to go to bed.

'How are we going to sleep?' asked Milly.

'Oh, just as you like.'

'Just as *you* like.'

'Well, perhaps Winnie would be happier with you . . . she'll have to go into the other room tomorrow morning when they bring in breakfast, of course.'

So she was tucked up in a corner of the double bed and to Tony's surprise was asleep before they went down to dinner.

A change of clothes brought to both Tony and Milly a change of temper. She, in her best evening frock, backless and vermilion, her face newly done and her bleached curls brushed out, her feet in high red shoes, some bracelets on her wrists, a dab of scent behind the large sham pearls in her ears, shook off the cares of domesticity and was once more in uniform, reporting for duty, a legionary ordered for active service after the enervating restraints of a winter in barracks; and Tony, filling his cigar case before the mirror, and slipping it into the pocket of his dinner jacket, reminded himself that phantasmagoric, and even gruesome as the situation might seem to him, he was nevertheless a host, so that he knocked at the communicating door and passed with a calm manner into his guest's room; for a month now he had lived in a world suddenly bereft of order; it was as though the whole reasonable and decent constitution of things, the sum of all he had experienced or learned to expect, were an inconspicuous, inconsiderable object mislaid somewhere on the dressing table; no outrageous circumstance in which he found himself, no new, mad thing brought to his notice, could add a jot to the all encompassing chaos that shrieked about his ears. He smiled at Milly from the doorway. 'Charming,' he said, 'perfectly charming. Shall we go down to dinner?'

Their rooms were on the first floor. Step by step, with her hand on his arm, they descended the staircase into the bright hall below.

'Cheer up,' said Milly. 'You have a tongue sandwich. That'll make you talk.'

'Sorry, am I being a bore?'

'I was only joking. You are a serious boy, aren't you?'

In spite of the savage weather the hotel seemed full of weekend visitors. More were arriving through the swing doors, their eyes moist and their cheeks rigid from the icy cold outside.

'Yids,' explained Milly superfluously. 'Still it's nice to get a change from the club once in a while.'

One of the new arrivals was a friend of Milly's. He was supervising the collection of his luggage. Anywhere else he would have been a noticeable figure, for he wore a large fur coat and a béret; under the coat appeared tartan stockings and black and white shoes. 'Take em up and get em unpacked and quick about it,' he said. He was a stout little young man. His companion, also in furs, was staring resentfully at one of the showcases that embellished the hall.

'Oh for Christ's sake,' she said.

Milly and the young man greeted each other. 'This is Dan,' she said.

'Well, well, well,' said Dan, 'what next?'

'Do I get a drink?' said Dan's girl.

'Baby, you do, if I have to get it myself. Won't you two join us, or are we de trop?'

They went together into the glittering lounge. 'I'm cold like hell,' said Baby.

Dan had taken off his great coat and revealed a suit of smooth, purplish plus fours, and a silk shirt of a pattern Tony might have chosen for pyjamas. 'We'll soon warm you up,' he said.

'This place stinks of yids,' said Baby.

'I always think that's the sign of a good hotel, don't you?' said Tony.

'Like hell,' said Baby.

'You mustn't mind Baby, she's cold,' Dan explained.

'Who wouldn't be, in your lousy car?'

They had some cocktails. Then Dan and Baby went to their room; they must doll up, they explained, as they were going to a party given by a friend of Dan's, at a place of his near there. Tony and Milly went in to dinner. 'He's a very nice boy,' she said, 'and comes to the club a lot. We get all sorts there, but Dan's one of the decent ones. I was going to have gone abroad with him once but in the end he couldn't get away.'

'His girl didn't seem to like us much.'

'Oh, she was cold.'

Tony did not find conversation easy at dinner. At first he commented on their neighbours as he would have done if he had been dining with Brenda at Espinosa's. 'That's a pretty girl in the corner.'

'I wonder you don't go and join her, dear,' said Milly testily.

'Look at that woman's diamonds. Do you think they can be real?'

'Why don't you ask her, if you're so interested?'

'That's an interesting type – the dark woman dancing.'

'I'm sure she'd be delighted to hear it.'

Presently Tony realized that it was not etiquette in Milly's world, to express interest in women, other than the one you were with.

They drank champagne. So also, Tony noticed with displeasure, did the two detectives. He would have something to say about that when their bill for expenses came in. It was not as though they had been accommodating in the matter of Winnie. All the time, at the back of his mind, he was worrying with the problem of what they could possibly do after dinner, but it was solved for him, just as he was lighting his cigar, by the appearance of Dan from the other side of the dining room. 'Look here,' he said, 'if you two aren't doing anything special, why don't you join up with us and come to the party at my friend's place. You'll like it. He always gives one the best of everything.'

'Oh do let's,' said Milly.

Dan's evening clothes were made of blue cloth that was supposed to appear black in artificial light; for some reason, however, they remained very blue.

So Milly and Tony went to Dan's friend's place and had the best of everything. There was a party of twenty or thirty people, all more or less like Dan. Dan's friend was most hospitable. When he was not fiddling with the wireless, which gave trouble off and on throughout the evening, he was sauntering among his guests refilling their glasses. 'This stuff's all right,' he said, showing the label, 'it won't hurt you. It's the right stuff.'

They had a lot of the right stuff.

Quite often Dan's friend noticed that Tony seemed to be out of the party. Then he would come across and put his hand on Tony's shoulder. 'I'm so glad Dan brought you,' he would say. 'Hope you're getting all you want. Delighted to see you. Come again when there isn't a crowd and see over the place. Interested in roses?'

'Yes, I like them very much.'

'Come when the roses are out. You'd like that if you're interested in roses. Damn that radio, it's going wonky again.'

Tony wondered whether he was as amiable when people he did not know were brought over unexpectedly to Hetton.

At one stage in the evening he found himself sitting on a sofa with Dan, who said, 'Nice kid, Milly.'

'Yes.'

'I'll tell you a thing I've noticed about her. She attracts quite a different type from the other girls. People like you and me.'

'Yes.'

'You wouldn't think she had a daughter of eight, would you?'

'No, it's very surprising.'

'I didn't know for ages. Then I was taking her to Dieppe[5] for the weekend and she wanted to bring the child along too. Of course that put the kybosh on it,[6] but I've always liked Milly just the same. You can trust her to behave anywhere.' He said this with a sour glance towards Baby, who was full of the right stuff and showing it.

It was after three before the party broke up. Dan's friend renewed his invitation to come again when the roses were out. 'I doubt if you'll find a better show of roses anywhere in the south of England,' he said.

Dan drove them back to the hotel. Baby sat beside him in front, disposed to be quarrelsome. 'Where were you?' she kept asking. 'Never saw you all the evening. Where did you get to? Where were you hiding? I call it a lousy way to take a girl out.'

Tony and Milly sat at the back. From habit and exhaustion she put her head on his shoulder and her hand in his. When they reached their rooms, however, she said, 'Go quietly. We don't want to wake Winnie.'

For an hour or so Tony lay in the warm little bedroom, reviewing over and over again the incidents of the last three months; then he too fell asleep.

He was awakened by Winnie. 'Mother's still asleep,' she said.

Tony looked at his watch. 'So I should think,' he said. It was quarter past seven. 'Go back to bed.'

'No, I'm dressed. Let's go out.'

She went to the window and pulled back the curtains, filling the room with glacial morning light. 'It's hardly raining at all,' she said.

'What do you want to do?'

'I want to go on the pier.'

'It won't be open yet.'

'Well, I want to go down to the sea. Come on.'

Tony knew that he would not get to sleep again that morning. 'All right. You go and wait while I dress.'

'I'll wait here. Mother snores so.'

Twenty minutes later they went downstairs into the hall where aproned waiters were piling up the furniture and brushing the carpets. A keen wind met them as they emerged from the swing door. The asphalt promenade was wet with spray and rain. Two or three female figures were scudding along, bowed to the wind, prayer books clutched in their gloved hands. Four or five rugged old men were hobbling down to bathe, hissing like ostlers.[7] 'Oh come on,' said Winnie.

They went down to the beach and stumbled painfully across the shingle to the margin of the sea. Winnie threw some stones. The bathers were in the water now; some of them had dogs who swam snorting beside them.

'Why don't you bathe?' asked Winnie.

'Far too cold.'

'But *they're* bathing. I want to.'

'You must ask your mother.'

'I believe you're afraid. Can you swim?'

'Yes.'

'Well, why don't you? Bet you can't.'

'All right. I can't.'

'Then why did you say you could? Fibber.'

They walked along the shingle. Winnie slithered about astride a backwater. 'Now my knickers are wet,' she said.

'Better come back and change.'

'It feels horrible. Let's go and have breakfast.'

The hotel did not, as a rule, cater for guests who breakfasted downstairs at eight o'clock on Sunday morning. It took a long time before anything could be got ready. There were no ices, much to Winnie's annoyance. She ate grape fruit and kippers and scrambled eggs on toast, complaining fitfully about her wet clothing. After breakfast Tony sent her upstairs to change and, himself, smoked a pipe in the lounge and glanced over the Sunday papers. Here at nine o'clock he was interrupted by the arrival of Blenkinsop. 'We missed you last night,' he said.

'We went to a party.'

'You shouldn't have done that – not strictly, but I daresay no harm will come of it. Have you had your breakfast?'

'Yes, in the dining room with Winnie.'

'But Mr Last, what are you thinking of? You've got to get evidence from the hotel servants.'

'Well, I didn't like to wake Milly.'

'She's paid for it, isn't she? Come, come, Mr Last, this won't do at all. You'll never get your divorce if you don't give your mind to it more.'

'All right,' said Tony. 'I'll have breakfast again.'

'In bed, mind.'

'In bed.' And he went wearily upstairs to his rooms.

Winnie had drawn the curtains but her mother was still asleep. 'She woke up once and then turned over. Do get her to come out. I want to go on the pier.'

'Milly,' said Tony firmly. 'Milly.'

'Oh,' she said. 'What time is it?'

'We've got to have breakfast.'

'Don't want any breakfast. I think I'll sleep a little.'

'You've had breakfast,' said Winnie.

'Come on,' said Tony. 'Plenty of time to sleep afterwards. This is what we came for.'

Milly sat up in bed. 'O.K.,' she said. 'Winnie darling, give mother her jacket off the chair.' She was a conscientious girl, ready to go through with her job, however unattractive it might seem. 'But it's early.'

Tony went into his room and took off his shoes, collar and tie, coat and waistcoat, and put on a dressing gown.

'You are greedy,' said Winnie, 'eating two breakfasts.'

'When you're a little older you'll understand these things. It's the Law. Now I want you to stay in the sitting room for quarter of an hour very quietly. Promise? And afterwards you can do exactly what you like.'

'Can I bathe?'

'Yes certainly, if you're quiet now.'

Tony got into bed beside Milly and pulled the dressing gown tight round his throat. 'Does that look all right?'

'Love's young dream,' said Milly.

'All right then. I'll ring the bell.'

When the tray had been brought Tony got out of bed and put

on his things. 'So much for my infidelity,' he said. 'It is curious to reflect that this will be described in the papers as "intimacy." '

'Can I bathe now?'

'Certainly.'

Milly turned over to sleep again. Tony took Winnie to the beach. The wind had got up and a heavy sea was pounding on the shingle.

'This little girl would like to bathe,' said Tony.

'No bathing for children today,' said the beach attendant.

'The very idea,' said various onlookers. 'Does he want to drown the child?' 'He's no business to be trusted with children.' '*Unnatural beast.*'

'But I *want* to bathe,' said Winnie. 'You said I could bathe if you had two breakfasts.'

The people who had clustered round to witness Tony's discomfort looked at one another askance. 'Two breakfasts? Wanting to let the child bathe? The man's balmy.'

'Never mind,' said Tony. 'We'll go on the pier.'

Several of the crowd followed them round the slots, curious to see what new enormity this mad father might attempt. 'There's a man who's eaten two breakfasts and tries to drown his little girl,' they informed other spectators, sceptically observing his attempts to amuse Winnie with skee-ball. Tony's conduct confirmed the view of human nature derived from the weekly newspapers which they had all been reading that morning.

'Well,' said Brenda's solicitor. 'We have our case now, all quite regular and complete. I don't think it can come on until next term – there's a great rush at the moment, but there's no harm in you having your own evidence ready. I've got it typed out for you. You'd better keep it by you and get it clear in your mind.'

'. . . *My marriage was an ideally happy one,*' she read, '*until shortly before Christmas last year when I began to suspect that my husband's attitude had changed towards me. He always remained in the country when my studies took me to London. I realized that he no longer cared for me as he used to. He began to drink heavily and on one occasion made a disturbance at our flat in London, constantly ringing up when drunk and sending a drunken friend round to knock on the door.* Is that necessary?'

'Not strictly, but it is advisable to put it in. A great deal depends on psychological impression. Judges in their more lucid moments sometimes wonder why perfectly respectable, happily married men go off for weekends to the seaside with women they do not know. It is always helpful to offer evidence of general degeneracy.'

'I see,' said Brenda. *'From then onwards I had him watched by private agents and as a result of what they told me, I left my husband's house on April 5th.* Yes, that all seems quite clear.'

Three

Lady St Cloud preserved an atavistic[8] faith in the authority and preternatural good judgment of the Head of the Family; accordingly her first act, on learning from Marjorie of Brenda's wayward behaviour, was to cable for Reggie's return from Tunisia where he was occupied in desecrating some tombs. His departure, like all his movements, was leisurely. He did not take the first available boat or the second, but eventually he arrived in London on the Monday after Tony's visit to Brighton. He held a family conclave in his library, consisting of his mother, Brenda, Marjorie, Allan and the solicitor; later he discussed the question fully with each of them severally; he took Beaver out to luncheon; he dined with Jock; he even called on Tony's Aunt Frances. Finally on Thursday evening he arranged to meet Tony for dinner at Brown's.

He was eight years older than Brenda; very occasionally a fugit-ive, indefinable likeness was detectable between him and Marjorie, but both in character and appearance he was as different from Brenda as it was possible to imagine. He was prematurely, unnat-urally stout, and he carried his burden of flesh as though he were not yet used to it; as though it had been buckled on to him that morning for the first time and he were still experimenting for its better adjustment; there was an instability in his gait and in his eyes a furtive look as though he were at any moment liable to ambush and realized that he was unfairly handicapped for flight. This impression, however, was due solely to his physical appearance; it was the deep bed of fat in which his eyes lay, that gave them this look of suspicion; the caution of his movements resulted from the exertion of keeping his balance and not from any embarrassment at his own clumsiness, for it had never occurred to him that he looked at all unusual.

Rather more than half Reggie St Cloud's time and income was spent abroad in modest archaelogical expeditions. His house in London was full of their fruit – fragmentary amphoras,[9] corroded bronze axe-heads, little splinters of bone and charred stick, a Graeco-Roman head in marble, its features obliterated and ground smooth with time. He had written two little monographs about his work, privately printed and both dedicated to members of the royal family. When he came to London he was regular in attendance at the House of Lords; all his friends were well over forty and for some years now he had established himself as a member of their generation; few mothers still regarded him as a possible son-in-law.

'This whole business of Brenda is *very* unfortunate,' said Reggie St Cloud.

Tony agreed.

'My mother is extremely upset about it, naturally. I'm upset myself. I don't mind admitting, perfectly frankly, that I think she has behaved very foolishly, foolishly and wrongly. I can quite understand your being upset about it too.'

'Yes,' said Tony.

'But all the same, making every allowance for your feelings, I do think that you are behaving rather vindictively in the matter.'

'I'm doing exactly what Brenda wanted.'

'My dear fellow, she doesn't know what she wants. I saw this chap Beaver yesterday. I didn't like him *at all*. Do you?'

'I hardly know him.'

'Well, I can assure you I didn't like him. Now you're just throwing Brenda into his arms. That's what it amounts to, as I see it, and I call it vindictive. Of course at the moment Brenda's got the idea that she's in love with him. But it won't last. It couldn't with a chap like Beaver. She'll want to come back in a year, just you see. Allan says the same.'

'I've told Allan. I don't want her back.'

'Well, that's vindictive.'

'No, I just couldn't feel the same about her again.'

'Well, why feel *the same*? One has to change as one gets older. Why, ten years ago I couldn't be interested in anything later than the Sumerian age and I assure you that now I find even the Christian era full of significance.'

For some time he spoke about some *tabulae execrationum*[10] that he had lately unearthed. 'Almost every grave had them,' he said, 'mostly referring to the circus factions,[11] scratched on lead. They used to be dropped in through a funnel. We had found forty-three up to date, before this wretched business happened, and I had to come back. Naturally I'm upset.'

He sat for a little eating silently. This last observation had brought the conversation back to its point of departure. He clearly had more to say on the subject and was meditating the most convenient approach. He ate in a ruthless manner, champing his food (it was his habit, often, without noticing it, to consume things that others usually left on their plates, the heads and tails of whiting, whole mouthfuls of chicken bone, peach stones and apple cores, cheese rinds and the fibrous parts of the artichoke). 'Besides, you know,' he said, 'it isn't as though it was all Brenda's fault.'

'I haven't been thinking particularly whose fault it is.'

'Well, that's all very well, but you seem rather to be taking the line of the injured husband – saying you can't feel the same again, and all that. I mean to say, it takes two to make a quarrel and I gather things had been going wrong for some time. For instance you'd been drinking a lot – have some more burgundy, by the way.'

'Did Brenda say that?'

'Yes. And then you'd been going round a bit with other girls yourself. There was some woman with a Moorish name you had to stay at Hetton while Brenda was there. Well, that's a bit thick, you know. I'm all for people going their own way, but if they do they can't blame others, if you see what I mean.'

'Did Brenda say that?'

'Yes. Don't think I'm trying to lecture you or anything, but all

I feel is that you haven't any right to be vindictive to Brenda, as things are.'

'She said I drank and was having an affair with the woman with a Moorish name?'

'Well, I don't know she actually said that, but she said you'd been getting tight lately and that you were certainly interested in that girl.'

The fat young man opposite Tony ordered prunes and cream. Tony said he had finished dinner.

He had imagined during the preceding weekend that nothing could now surprise him.

'So that really explains what I want to say,' continued Reggie blandly. 'It's about money. I understand that when Brenda was in a very agitated state just after the death of her child, she consented to some verbal arrangement with you about settlements.'

'Yes, I'm allowing her five hundred a year.'

'Well, you know, I don't think that you have any right to take advantage of her generosity in that way. It was most imprudent of her to consider your proposal – she admits now that she was not really herself when she did so.'

'What does she suggest instead?'

'Let's go outside and have coffee.'

When they were settled in front of the fire in the empty smoking room, he answered, 'Well, I've discussed it with the lawyers and with the family and we decided that the sum should be increased to two thousand.'

'That's quite out of the question. I couldn't begin to afford it.'

'Well, you know, I have to consider Brenda's interests. She has very little of her own and there will be no more coming to her. My mother's income is an allowance which I pay under my father's will. I shan't be able to give her anything. I am trying to raise everything I can for an expedition to one of the oases in the Lybian desert. This chap Beaver has got practically nothing and doesn't look like earning any. So you see –'

'But my dear Reggie, you know as well as I do that it's out of the question.'

'It's rather less than a third of your income.'

'Yes, but almost every penny goes straight back to the estate. Do you realize that Brenda and I together haven't spent half that amount a year on our personal expenses? It's all I can do to keep things going as it is.'

'I didn't expect you'd take this line, Tony. I think it's extremely unreasonable of you. After all, it's absurd to pretend in these days that a single man can't be perfectly comfortable on four thousand a year. It's as much as I've ever had.'

'It would mean giving up Hetton.'

'Well, I gave up Brakeleigh, and I assure you, my dear fellow, I never regret it. It was a nasty wrench at the time of course, old association and everything like that, but I can tell you this, that when the sale was finally through I felt a different man, free to go where I liked . . .'

'But I don't happen to want to go anywhere else except Hetton.'

'There's a lot in what these Labour fellows say, you know. Big houses are a thing of the past in England.'

'Tell me, did Brenda realize when she agreed to this proposal that it meant my leaving Hetton?'

'Yes, it was mentioned, I think. I daresay you'll find it quite easy to sell to a school or something like that. I remember the agent said when I was trying to get rid of Brakeleigh that it was a pity it wasn't Gothic, because schools and convents always go for Gothic. I daresay you'll get a very comfortable price and find yourself better off in the end than you are now.'

'No. It's impossible,' said Tony.

'You're making things extremely awkward for everyone,' said Reggie. 'I can't understand why you are taking up this attitude.'

'What is more, I don't believe that Brenda ever expected or wanted me to agree.'

'Oh yes, she did, my dear fellow. I assure you of that.'

'It's inconceivable.'

'Well,' said Reggie, puffing at his cigar, 'there's more to it than just money. Perhaps I'd better tell you everything. I hadn't meant to. The truth is that Beaver is cutting up nasty. He says he can't marry Brenda unless she's properly provided for. Not fair on her, he says. I quite see his point in a way.'

'Yes, I see his point,' said Tony. 'So what your proposal really amounts to, is that I should give up Hetton in order to buy Beaver for Brenda.'

'It's not how I should have put it,' said Reggie.

'Well, I'm not going to and that's the end of it. If that's all you wanted to say, I may as well leave you.'

'No, it isn't quite all I wanted to say. In fact I think I must have put things rather badly. It comes from trying to respect people's feelings too much. You see I wasn't so much asking you to agree to anything as explaining what our side propose to do. I've tried to keep everything on a friendly basis but I see it's not possible. Brenda will ask for alimony of two thousand a year from the Court and on our evidence we shall get it. I'm sorry you oblige me to put it so bluntly.'

'I hadn't thought of that.'

'No, nor had we, to be quite frank. It was Beaver's idea.'

'You seem to have got me in a fairly hopeless position.'

'It's not how I should have put it.'

'I should like to make absolutely sure that Brenda is in on this. D'you mind if I ring her up?'

'Not at all, my dear fellow. I happen to know she's at Marjorie's tonight.'

'Brenda, this is Tony . . . I've just been dining with Reggie.'

'Yes, he said something about it.'

'He tells me that you are going to sue for alimony. Is that so?'

'Tony, don't be so bullying. The lawyers are doing everything. It's no use coming to me.'

'But did you know that they proposed to ask for two thousand?'

'Yes. They did say that. I know it sounds a lot but . . .'

'And you know exactly how my money stands, don't you? You know it means selling Hetton, don't you? . . . hullo, are you still there?'

'Yes, I'm here.'

'You know it means that?'

'Tony, don't make me feel a beast. Everything has been so difficult.'

'You do know just what you are asking?'

'Yes . . . I suppose so.'

'All right, that's all I wanted to know.'

'Tony, how odd you sound . . . don't ring off.'

He hung up the receiver and went back to the smoking room. His mind had suddenly become clearer on many points that had puzzled him. A whole Gothic world had come to grief . . . there was now no armour glittering through the forest glades, no embroidered feet on the green sward; the cream and dappled unicorns had fled . . .

Reggie sat expanded in his chair. 'Well?'

'I got on to her. You were quite right. I'm sorry I didn't believe you. It seemed so unlikely at first.'

'That's all right, my dear fellow.'

'I've decided exactly what's going to happen.'

'Good.'

'Brenda is not going to get her divorce. The evidence I provided at Brighton isn't worth anything. There happens to have been a child there all the time. She slept both nights in the room I am supposed to have occupied. If you care to bring the case I shall defend it and win, but I think when you have seen my evidence you will drop it. I am going away for six months or so. When I come back, if she wishes it, I shall divorce Brenda without settlements of any kind. Is that clear?'

'But look here, my dear fellow.'

'Goodnight. Thank you for the dinner. Good luck to the excavations.'

On his way out of the club he noticed that John Beaver of Brat's Club was up for election.

'Who on earth would have expected the old boy to turn up like that?' asked Polly Cockpurse.

'Now I understand why they keep going on in the papers about divorce law reform,' said Veronica. 'It's *too* monstrous that he should be allowed to get away with it.'

'The mistake they made was in telling him first,' said Souki.

'It's so like Brenda to trust everyone,' said Jenny Abdul Akbar.

*

'I do think Tony comes out of this pretty poorly,' said Marjorie. 'Oh I don't know,' said Allan. 'I expect your ass of a brother put the thing wrong.'

Chapter Five

IN SEARCH OF A CITY

One

'Any idea how many times round the deck make a mile?'

'None, I'm afraid,' said Tony. 'But I should think you must have walked a great distance.'

'Twenty-two times. One soon gets out of sorts at sea if you're used to an active life. She's not much of a boat. Travel with this line often?'

'Never before.'

'Ah. Thought you might have been in business in the islands. Not many tourists going out this time of year. Just the other way about. All coming home, if you see what I mean. Going far?'

'Demerara.'[1]

'Ah. Looking for minerals perhaps?'

'No, to tell you the truth I am looking for a city.'

The genial passenger was surprised and then laughed. 'Sounded just like you said you were looking for a city.'

'Yes.'

'That *was* what you said?'

'Yes.'

'I thought it sounded like that . . . well, so long. I must do another few rounds before dinner.'

He paced off up the deck, straddling slightly in order to keep his balance and occasionally putting out a hand to the rail for support.

Regularly every three minutes for the last hour or so, this man had come by. At first Tony had looked up at his approach and then turned away again, out to sea. Presently the man had taken to nodding, then to saying 'Hullo' or 'Bit choppy' or 'Here we are again'; finally he had stopped and begun a conversation.

Tony went aft to break this rather embarrassing sequence. He descended the companion way which led to the lower deck. Here, in crates lashed to the side, was a variety of livestock – some stud

157

bulls, a heavily blanketed racehorse, a couple of beagles, being exported to various West Indian islands. Tony threaded a way between them and the hatches to the stern, where he sat against a winch watching the horizon mount above the funnels, then fall until they stood out black against the darkening sky. The pitch was more sensible here than it had been amidships; the animals shifted restlessly in their cramped quarters; the beagles whined intermittently. A lascar[2] took down from a line some washing which had been flapping there all day.

The wash of the ship was quickly lost in the high waves. They were steaming westward down the Channel. As it grew to be night, lighthouses appeared flashing from the French coast. Presently a steward walked round the bright, upper deck striking chimes on a gong of brass cylinders, and the genial passenger went below to prepare himself for dinner in hot sea water which splashed from side to side of the bath and dissolved the soap in a thin, sticky scum. He was the only man to dress that evening: Tony sat in the mustering darkness until the second bell. Then he left his greatcoat in the cabin and went down to dinner.

It was the first evening at sea.

Tony sat at the captain's table, but the captain was on the bridge. There were empty chairs on either side of him. It was not rough enough for the fiddles[3] to be out, but the stewards had removed the flower vases and damped the table-cloth to make it adhesive. A coloured archdeacon sat facing him. He ate with great refinement but his black hands looked immense on the wet, whitish cloth. 'I'm afraid our table is not showing up very well tonight,' he said. 'I see you are not a sufferer. My wife is in her cabin. *She* is a sufferer.'

He was returning from a Congress, he told Tony.

At the top of the stairs was a lounge named the Music and Writing Room. The light here was always subdued, in the day by the stained glass of the windows, at night by pink silk shades which hid the electric candles. Here the passengers assembled for their coffee, sitting on bulky, tapestry-covered chesterfields or on swivel chairs irremovably fastened before the writing tables. Here too the steward for an hour every day presided over the cupboardful of novels which constituted the ship's library.

'It's not much of a boat,' said the genial passenger, sitting himself beside Tony. 'But I expect things will look brighter when we get into the sun.'

Tony lit a cigar and was told by a steward that he must not smoke in this room. 'That's all right,' said the genial passenger, 'we're just going down to the bar. You know,' he said a few minutes later, 'I feel I owe you an apology. I thought you were potty just now before dinner. Honestly I did, when you said you were going to Demerara to look for a city. Well, it sounded pretty potty. Then the purser – I'm at his table. Always get the cheeriest crowd at the purser's table *and* the best attention – the purser told me about you. You're the explorer, aren't you?'

'Yes, come to think of it, I suppose I am,' said Tony.

It did not come easily to him to realize that he was an explorer. It was barely a fortnight ago that he had become one. Even the presence in the hold of two vast crates, bearing his name and labelled *not wanted on the voyage* – crates containing such new and unfamiliar possessions as a medicine chest, an automatic shot gun, camping equipment, pack saddles, a cinema camera, dynamite, disinfectants, a collapsible canoe, filters, tinned butter and, strangest of all, an assortment of what Dr Messinger called 'trade goods' – failed to convince him fully of the serious nature of his expedition. Dr Messinger had arranged everything. It was he who chose the musical boxes and mechanical mice, the mirrors, combs, perfumery, pills, fish hooks, axe heads, coloured rockets, and rolls of artificial silk, which were packed in the box of 'trade goods.' And Dr Messinger himself was a new acquaintance who, prostrate now in his bunk with what the negro clergyman would have called 'suffering,' that day, for the first time since Tony had met him, seemed entirely human.

Tony had spent very little of his life abroad. At the age of eighteen, before going to the University, he had been boarded for the summer with an elderly gentleman near Tours,[4] with the intention that he should learn the language. (. . . a grey stone house surrounded by vines. There was a stuffed spaniel in the bathroom. The old man had called it 'Stop' because it was chic at that time to give dogs an English name. Tony had bicycled along straight, white roads to visit the chateaux; he carried rolls of bread and cold veal tied to the back of the machine, and the soft dust seeped into them through the paper and gritted against his teeth. There were two other English boys there, so he had learned little French. One of them fell in love and the other got drunk for the first time on sparkling Vouvray[5] at a fair that had been held in the town. That evening Tony won a live pigeon at a tombola;[6] he set it free and later saw it being recaptured by the proprietor of the stall with a butterfly net . . .) Later he had gone to Central Europe for a few weeks with a friend from Balliol.[7] (They had found themselves suddenly rich with the falling mark and had lived in unaccustomed grandeur in the largest hotel suites. Tony had bought a fur for a few shillings and given it to a girl in Munich who spoke no English.) Later still his honeymoon with Brenda in a villa, lent to them, on the Italian Riviera. (. . . cypress and olive trees, a domed church half way down the hill, between the villa and the harbour, a café where they sat out in the evening, watching the fishing boats and the lights reflected in the quiet water, waiting for the sudden agitation of sound and motion as the speed boat came in. It had been owned by a dashing young official, who called it *Jazz Girl*. He seemed to spend twenty hours a day running in and out of the little harbour . . .) Once Brenda and he had gone to Le Touquet[8] with Brat's golf team. That was all. After his father died he had not left England. They could not easily afford it; it was one of the things they postponed until death duties were paid off; besides that, he was never happy away from Hetton, and Brenda did not like leaving John Andrew.

Thus Tony had no very ambitious ideas about travel, and when he decided to go abroad his first act was to call at a tourist agency and come away laden with a sheaf of brightly coloured prospectuses, which advertised commodious cruises among palm trees, negresses and ruined arches. He was going away because it seemed to be the conduct expected of a husband in his circumstances, because the associations of Hetton were for the time poisoned for him, because he wanted to live for a few months away from people who would know him or Brenda, in places where there was no expectation of meeting her or Beaver or Reggie St Cloud at every corner he frequented, and with this feeling of evasion dominant in his mind, he took the prospectuses to read at the Greville Club. He had been a member there for some years, but rarely used it; his resignation was only postponed by his recurrent omission to cancel the banker's order for his subscription. Now that Brat's and Brown's were distasteful to him he felt thankful that he had kept on with the Greville. It was a club of intellectual flavour, composed of dons, a few writers and the officials of museums and learned societies. It had a tradition of garrulity, so that he was not surprised when, seated in an armchair and surrounded with his illustrated folders, he was addressed by a member unknown to him who asked if he were thinking of going away. He was more surprised when he looked up and studied the questioner.

Dr Messinger, though quite young, was bearded, and Tony knew few young men with beards. He was also very small, very sun-burned and prematurely bald; the ruddy brown of his face ended abruptly along the line of his forehead, which rose in a pale dome; he wore steel-rimmed spectacles and there was something about his blue serge suit which suggested that the wearer found it uncomfortable.

Tony admitted that he was considering taking a cruise.

'I am going away shortly,' said Dr Messinger, 'to Brazil. At least it may be Brazil or Dutch Guiana. One cannot tell. The frontier has never been demarcated. I ought to have started last week only my plans were upset. Do you by any chance know a Nicaraguan calling himself alternately Ponsonby and FitzClarence?'

'No, I don't think I do.'

'You are fortunate. That man has just robbed me of two hundred pounds and some machine guns.'

'Machine guns?'

'Yes, I travel with one or two, mostly for show you know, or for trade, and they are not easy to buy nowadays. Have you ever tried?'

'No.'

'Well you can take it from me that it's not easy. You can't just walk into a shop and order machine guns.'

'No, I suppose not.'

'Still, at a pinch I can do without them. But I can't do without the two hundred pounds.'

Tony had, open on his knee, a photograph of the harbour at Agadir.[9] Dr Messinger looked over his shoulder at it. 'Ah yes,' he said, 'interesting little place. I expect you know Zingerman there?'

'No, I've not been there yet.'

'You'd like him – a very straight fellow. He used to do quite a lot, selling ammunition to the Atlas caids[10] before the pacification. Of course it was easy money with the capitulations,[11] but he did it better than most of them. I believe he's running a restaurant now in Mogador.'[12] Then he continued dreamily, 'The pity is I can't let the R.G.S.[13] in on this expedition. I've got to find the money privately.'

It was one o'clock and the room was beginning to fill up; an Egyptologist was exhibiting a handkerchief-ful of scarabs[14] to the editor of a church weekly.

'We'd better go up and lunch,' said Dr Messinger.

Tony had not intended to lunch at the Greville but there was something compelling about the invitation; moreover, he had no other engagement.

Dr Messinger lunched off apples and a rice pudding. ('I have to be very careful what I eat,' he said.) Tony ate cold steak and kidney pie. They sat at a window in the big dining room upstairs. The places round them were soon filled with members, who even carried the tradition of general conversation so far as to lean back in their chairs and chat over their shoulders from table to table – a practice which greatly hindered the already imperfect service. But Tony remained oblivious to all that was said, absorbed in what Dr Messinger was telling him.

'. . . You see there has been a continuous tradition about the City[15] since the first explorers of the sixteenth century. It has been variously allocated, sometimes down in Matto Grosso,[16] sometimes on the upper Orinoco[17] in what is now Venezuela. I myself used to think it lay somewhere on the Uraricuera.[18] I was out there last year and it was then that I established contact with the Pie-wie Indians;[19] no white man had ever visited them and got out alive.

And it was from the Pie-wies that I learned where to look. None of them had ever visited the City, of course, but they *knew about it.* Every Indian between Ciudad Bolivar[20] and Para[21] knows about it. But they won't talk. Queer people. But I became blood-brother with a Pie-wie – interesting ceremony. They buried me up to the neck in mud and all the women of the tribe spat on my head. Then we ate a toad and snake and a beetle and after that I was a blood brother – well, he told me that the City lies between the head waters of the Courantyne[22] and the Takutu.[23] There's a vast track of unexplored country there. I've often thought of visiting it.

'I've been looking up the historical side too, and I more or less know how the City got there. It was the result of a migration from Peru at the beginning of the fifteenth century when the Incas[24] were at the height of their power. It is mentioned in all the early Spanish documents as a popular legend. One of the younger princes rebelled and led his people off into the forest. Most of the tribes have a tradition in one form or another of a strange race passing through their territory.'

'But what do you suppose this city will be like?'

'Impossible to say. Every tribe has a different word for it. The Pie-wies call it the "Shining" or "Glittering," the Arekuna[25] the "Many Watered," the Patamonas[26] the "Bright Feathered," the Warau,[27] oddly enough, use the same word for it that they use for a kind of aromatic jam they make. Of course one can't tell how a civilization may have developed or degenerated in five hundred years of isolation . . .'

Before Tony left the Greville that day, he tore up his sheaf of cruise prospectuses, for he had arranged to join Dr Messinger in his expedition.

'Done much of that kind of thing?'

'No, to tell you the truth it is the first time.'

'Ah. Well, I daresay it's more interesting than it sounds,' conceded the genial passenger, 'else people wouldn't do it so much.'

The ship, so far as any consideration of comfort had contributed to her design, was planned for the tropics. It was slightly colder in the smoking room than on deck. Tony went to his cabin and retrieved his cap and greatcoat; then he went aft again, to the place where he had sat before dinner. It was a starless night and nothing was visible beyond the small luminous area round the ship, save for a single lighthouse that flashed short-long, short-long, far away on the port bow. The crests of the waves caught the reflection from the promenade deck and shone for a moment before plunging away into the black depths behind. The beagles were awake, whining.

For some days now Tony had been thoughtless about the events of the immediate past. His mind was occupied with the City, the Shining, the Many Watered, the Bright Feathered, the Aromatic Jam. He had a clear picture of it in his mind. It was Gothic in character, all vanes and pinnacles, gargoyles, battlements, groining and tracery, pavilions and terraces, a transfigured Hetton, pennons and banners floating on the sweet breeze, everything luminous and translucent; a coral citadel crowning a green hill top sewn with daisies, among groves and streams; a tapestry landscape filled with heraldic and fabulous animals and symmetrical, disproportionate blossom.

The ship tossed and tunnelled through the dark waters towards this radiant sanctuary.

'I wonder if anyone is doing anything about those dogs,' said the genial passenger, arriving at his elbow. 'I'll ask the purser tomorrow. We might exercise them a bit. Kind of mournful the way they go on.'

Next day they were in the Atlantic. Ponderous waves rising over murky, opaque depths. Dappled with foam at the crests, like downland where on the high, exposed places, snow has survived the thaw. Lead-grey and slate in the sun, olive, field blue and khaki like the uniforms of a battlefield; the sky overhead was neutral and steely with swollen clouds scudding across it, affording rare half hours of sunlight. The masts swung slowly across this sky and the bows heaved and wallowed below the horizon. The man who had made friends with Tony paraded the deck with the two beagles. They strained at the end of their chains, sniffing the scuppers; the man lurched behind them unsteadily. He wore a pair of race glasses with which he occasionally surveyed the seas; he offered them to Tony whenever they passed each other.

'Been talking to the wireless operator,' he said. 'We ought to pass quite near the Yarmouth Castle[28] at about eleven.'

Few of the passengers were on their feet. Those who had come on deck lay in long chairs on the sheltered side, pensive, wrapped in tartan rugs. Dr Messinger kept to his cabin. Tony went to see him and found him torpid, for he was taking large doses of chloral. Towards evening the wind freshened and by dinner time was blowing hard; portholes were screwed up and all destructible objects disposed on the cabin floors; a sudden roll broke a dozen coffee cups in the music and reading room. That night there was little sleep for anyone on board; the plating creaked, luggage shifted from wall to wall. Tony wedged himself firm in his bunk with the lifebelt and thought of the City.

. . . Carpet and canopy, tapestry and velvet, portcullis and bastion, water fowl on the moat and kingcups along its margin, peacocks trailing their finery across the lawns; high overhead in a sky of sapphire and swansdown silver bells chiming in a turret of alabaster.

Days of shadow and exhaustion, salt wind and wet mist, fog-horn and the constant groan and creak of straining metal. Then they were clear of it, after the Azores. Awnings were out and passengers moved their chairs to windward. High noon and an even keel; the blue water lapping against the sides of the ship, rippling away behind her to the horizon; gramophones and deck tennis; bright arcs of flying fish ('Look, Ernie, come quick, there's a shark.' 'That's not a shark, it's a dolphin.' 'Mr Brink said it was a porpoise.' 'There he is again. Oh, if I had my camera.'); clear, tranquil water and the regular turn and tread of the screw; there were many hands to caress the beagles as they went loping by. Mr Brink amid laughter suggested that he should exercise the racehorse, or, with a further burst of invention, the bull. Mr Brink sat at the purser's table with the cheery crowd.

Dr Messinger left his cabin and appeared on deck and in the dining saloon. So did the wife of the archdeacon; she was very much whiter than her husband. On Tony's other side at table sat a girl named Thérèse de Vitré.[29] He had noticed her once or twice during the grey days, a forlorn figure almost lost among furs and cushions and rugs; a colourless little face with wide dark eyes. She said, 'The last days have been terrible. I saw you walking about. How I envied you.'

'It ought to be calm all the way now,' and inevitably, 'Are you going far?'

'Trinidad. That is my home . . . I tried to decide who you were from the passenger list.'

'Who was I?'

'Well . . . someone called Colonel Strapper.'

'Do I look so old?'

'Are colonels old? I didn't know. It's not a thing we have much in Trinidad. Now I know who you are because I asked the head steward. Do tell me about your exploring.'

'You'd better ask Doctor Messinger. He knows more about it than I do.'

'No, *you* tell me.'

She was eighteen years old; small and dark, with a face that disappeared in a soft pointed chin so that attention was drawn to the grave eyes and the high forehead; she had not long outgrown her schoolgirl plumpness and she moved with an air of exultance, as though she had lately shed an encumbrance and was not yet fatigued by the other burdens that would succeed it. For two years she had been at school in Paris.

'. . . Some of us used to keep lipstick and rouge secretly in our bedrooms and try it on at night. One girl called Antoinette came to Mass on Sunday wearing it. There was a terrible row with Madame de Supplice[30] and she left after that term. It was awfully brave. We all envied her . . . But she was an ugly girl, always eating chocolates . . .

'. . . Now I am coming home to be married . . . No, I am not yet engaged, but you see there are so few young men I can marry. They must be Catholic and of an island family. It would not do to marry an official and go back to live in England. But it will be easy because I have no brothers or sisters and my father has one of the best houses in Trinidad. You must come and see it. It is a stone house, outside the town. My family came to Trinidad in the French Revolution. There are two or three other rich families and I shall marry into one of them. Our son will have the house. It will be easy . . .'

She wore a little coat, of the kind that was then fashionable, and no ornament except a string of pearls. '. . . There was an American girl at Madame de Supplice's who was engaged. She had a ring with a big diamond but she could never wear it except in bed. Then one day she had a letter from her young man saying he was going to marry another girl. How she cried. We all read the letter and most of us cried too . . . But in Trinidad it will be quite easy.'

Tony told her about the expedition; of the Peruvian emigrants in the middle ages and their long caravan working through the mountains and forests, llamas packed with works of intricate craftsmanship; of the continual rumours percolating to the coast and luring adventurers up into the forests; of the route they would take up the rivers, then cutting through the bush along Indian trails and across untravelled country; of the stream they might strike higher up and how, Dr Messinger said, they would make woodskin canoes and take to the water again; how finally they would arrive under the walls of the city like the Vikings at Byzantium.[31] 'But of course,' he added, 'there may be nothing in it. It ought to be an interesting journey in any case.'

'How I wish I was a man,' said Thérèse de Vitré.

After dinner they danced to the music of an amplified gramophone and the girl drank lemon squash on the bench outside the deck bar, sucking it through two straws.

A week of blue water that grew clearer and more tranquil daily, of sun that grew warmer, radiating the ship and her passengers, filling them with good humour and ease; blue water that caught the sun in a thousand brilliant points, dazzling the eyes as they searched for porpoises and flying fish; clear blue water in the shallows revealing its bed of silver sand and smooth pebble, fathoms down; soft warm shade on deck under the awnings; the ship moved amid unbroken horizons on a vast blue disc of blue, sparkling with sunlight.

Tony and Miss de Vitré played quoits and shuffle-board; they threw rope rings into a bucket from a short distance. ('We'll go in a small boat,' Dr Messinger had said, 'so as to escape all that hideous nonsense of deck games.') Twice consecutively Tony won the sweepstake on the ship's run; the prize was eighteen shillings. He bought Miss de Vitré a woollen rabbit at the barber's shop.

It was unusual for Tony to use 'Miss' in talking to anyone. Except Miss Tendril he could think of no one he addressed in that way. But it was Thérèse who first called him 'Tony,' seeing it engraved in Brenda's handwriting in his cigarette case. 'How funny,' she said, 'that was the name of the man who didn't marry the American girl at Madame de Supplice's'; and after that they used each other's Christian names to the great satisfaction of the other passengers who had little to interest them on board except the flowering of this romance.

'I can't believe this is the same ship as in those cold, rough days,' said Thérèse.

They reached the first of the islands; a green belt of palm trees with wooded hills rising beyond them and a small town heaped up along the shores of a bay. Thérèse and Tony went ashore and bathed. Thérèse swam badly with her head ridiculously erect out of the water. There was practically no bathing in Trinidad, she explained. They lay for some time on the firm, silver beach; then drove back into the town in the shaky, two-horse carriage he had hired, past ramshackle cabins from which little black boys ran out to beg or swing behind on the axle, in the white dust. There was nowhere in the town to dine so they returned to the ship at sundown. She lay out at some distance but from where they stood after dinner, leaning over the rail, they could just hear in the intervals when the winch was not working, the chatter and singing in the streets. Thérèse put her arm through Tony's, but the decks were full of passengers and agents and swarthy little men with lists of cargo. There was no dancing that night. They went above on to the boat deck[32] and Tony kissed her.

Dr Messinger came on board by the last launch. He had met an acquaintance in the town. He had observed the growing friendship between Tony and Thérèse with the strongest disapproval and told

him of a friend of his who had been knifed in a back street of
Smyrna, as a warning of what happened if one got mixed up with
women.

In the islands the life of the ship disintegrated. There were
changes of passengers; the black archdeacon left after shaking hands
with everyone on board; on their last morning his wife took round
a collecting box in aid of an organ that needed repairs. The captain
never appeared at meals in the dining saloon. Even Tony's first
friend no longer changed for dinner; the cabins were stuffy from
being kept locked all day.

Tony and Thérèse bathed again at Barbados and drove round
the island visiting castellated churches. They dined at an hotel high
up out of town and ate flying fish.

'You must come to my home and see what real creole cooking
is like,' said Thérèse. 'We have a lot of old recipes that the planters
used to use. You must meet my father and mother.'

They could see the lights of the ship from the terrace where they
were dining; the bright decks with figures moving about and the
double line of portholes.

'Trinidad the day after tomorrow,' said Tony.

They talked of the expedition and she said it was sure to be
dangerous. 'I don't like Doctor Messinger at all,' she said. 'Not
anything about him.'

'And you will have to choose your husband.'

'Yes. There are seven of them. There was one called Honoré I
liked but of course I haven't seen him for two years. He was
studying to be an engineer. There's one called Mendoza who's
very rich but he isn't really a Trinidadian. His grandfather came
from Dominica and they say he has coloured blood. I expect it
will be Honoré. Mother always brought in his name when she
wrote to me and he sent me things at Christmas and on my
fête.[33] Rather silly things because the shops aren't good in Port of
Spain.'[34]

Later she said, 'You'll be coming back by Trinidad, won't you?
So I shall see you then. Will you be a long time in the bush?'

'I expect you'll be married by then.'

'Tony, why haven't you ever got married?'

'But I am.'

'Married?'

'Yes.'

'You're teasing me.'

'No, honestly I am. At least I was.'

'Oh.'

'Are you surprised?'

'I don't know. Somehow I didn't think you were. Where is she?'

'In England. We had a row.'

'Oh . . . What's the time?'

'Quite early.'

'Let's go back.'

'D'you want to?'

'Yes, please. It's been a delightful day.'

'You said that as if you were saying goodbye.'

'Did I? I don't know.'

The negro chauffeur drove them at great speed into the town. Then they sat in a rowing boat and bobbed slowly out to the ship. Earlier in the day, in good spirits, they had bought a stuffed fish. Thérèse found she had left it behind at the hotel. 'It doesn't matter,' she said.

Blue water came to an end after Barbados. Round Trinidad the sea was opaque and colourless, full of the mud which the Orinoco brought down from the mainland. Thérèse spent all that day in her cabin, doing her packing.

Next day she said goodbye to Tony in a hurry. Her father had come out to meet her in the tender. He was a wiry bronzed man with a long grey moustache. He wore a panama hat and smart silk clothes, and smoked a cheroot; the complete slave-owner of the last century. Thérèse did not introduce him to Tony. 'He was someone on the ship,' she explained, obviously.

Tony saw her once next day in the town, driving with a lady who was obviously her mother. She waved but did not stop. 'Reserved lot, these real old creoles,'[35] remarked the passenger who had first made friends with Tony and had now attached himself again. 'Poor as church mice most of them but stinking proud. Time and again I've palled up with them on board and when we got to port it's been goodbye. Do they ever so much as ask you to their houses? Not they.'

Tony spent the two days with this first friend who had business connections in the place. On the second day it rained heavily and they could not leave the terrace of the hotel. Dr Messinger was engaged on some technical enquiries at the Agricultural Institute.

Muddy sea between Trinidad and Georgetown;[36] and the ship lightened of cargo rolled heavily in the swell. Dr Messinger took to his cabin once more. Rain fell continuously and a slight mist enclosed them so that they seemed to move in a small puddle of brown water; the foghorn sounded regularly through the rain. Scarcely a dozen passengers remained on board and Tony prowled disconsolately about the deserted decks or sat alone in the music room, his mind straying back along the path he had forbidden it, to the tall elm avenue at Hetton and the budding copses.

Next day they arrived at the mouth of the Demerara. The customs sheds were heavy with the reek of sugar and loud with the buzzing of bees. There were lengthy formalities in disembarking their stores. Dr Messinger saw to it while Tony lit a cigar and strayed out on to the quay. Small shipping of all kinds lay round them; on the further bank a low, green fringe of mangrove; behind, the tin roofs of the town were visible among feathery palm trees; everything steamed from the recent rain. Black stevedores grunted rhythmically at their work; East Indians trotted busily to and fro with invoices and bills of lading. Presently Dr Messinger pronounced that everything was in order and that they could go into the town to their hotel.

Two

The storm lantern stood on the ground between the two hammocks, which, in their white sheaths of mosquito net, looked like the cocoons of gigantic silk worms. It was eight o'clock, two hours after sundown; river and forest were already deep in night. The howler monkeys were silent but tree frogs near at hand set up a continuous, hoarse chorus; birds were awake, calling and whistling, and far in the depths about them came the occasional rending and reverberation of dead wood falling among the trees.

The six black boys who manned the boat squatted at a distance round their fire. They had collected some cobs of maize, three days back in a part of the bush, deserted now, choked and overrun with wild growth, that had once been a farm. (The rank second growth at that place had been full of alien plants, fruit and cereals, all gross now, and reverting to earlier type.) The boys were roasting their cobs in the embers.

Fire and storm lantern together shed little light; enough only to suggest the dilapidated roof over their heads, the heap of stores, disembarked and overrun by ants and, beyond, the undergrowth that had invaded the clearing and the vast columns of tree-trunks that rose above it, disappearing out of sight in the darkness.

Bats like blighted fruit hung in clusters from the thatch and great spiders rode across it astride their shadows. This place had once been a balata station.[37] It was the furthest point of commercial penetration from the coast. Dr Messinger marked it on his map with a triangle and named it in red 'First Base Camp.'

The first stage of the journey was over. For ten days they had been chugging up stream in a broad, shallow boat. Once or twice they had passed rapids (there the outboard engine had been reinforced by paddles; the men strained in time to the captain's count; the bo'sun stood in the bows with a long pole warding them off the rocks). They had camped at sundown on patches of sand-bank or in clearings cut from the surrounding bush. Once or twice they came to a 'house' left behind by balata bleeders or gold washers.

All day Tony and Dr Messinger sprawled amidships among their stores, under an improvised canopy of palm thatch; sometimes in the hot hours of the early afternoon they fell asleep. They ate in the boat, out of tins, and drank rum mixed with the water of the river which was mahogany brown but quite clear. The nights seemed interminable to Tony; twelve hours of darkness, noisier than a city square with the squealing and croaking and trumpeting of the bush denizens. Dr Messinger could tell the hours by the succession of sounds. It was not possible to read by the light of the storm lantern. Sleep was irregular and brief after the days of lassitude and torpor. There was little to talk about; everything had been said during the day, in the warm shade among the stores. Tony lay awake, scratching.

Since they had left Georgetown there had not been any part of his body that was ever wholly at ease. His face and neck were burned by the sun reflected from the water; the skin was flaking off them so that he was unable to shave. The stiff growth of beard pricked him between chin and throat. Every exposed part of his skin was bitten by cabouri fly.[38] They had found a way into the buttonholes of his shirt and the laces of his breeches; mosquitoes had got him at the ankles when he changed into slacks for the evening. He had picked up bêtes rouges[39] in the bush and they were crawling and burrowing under his skin; the bitter oil which Dr Messinger had given him as protection, had set up a rash of its own wherever he had applied it. Every evening after washing he had burned off a few ticks with a cigarette end but they had left irritable little scars behind them; so had the djiggas[40] which one of the black boys had dug out from under his toe nails and the horny skin on his heels and the balls of his feet. A marabunta[41] had left a painful swelling on his left hand.

As Tony scratched he shook the framework from which the hammocks hung. Dr Messinger turned over and said, 'Oh, for God's sake.' He tried not to scratch; then he tried to scratch quietly; then in a frenzy he scratched as hard as he could, breaking the skin in a dozen places. 'Oh, for God's sake,' said Dr Messinger.

'Half past eight,' thought Tony. 'In London they are just beginning to collect for dinner.' It was the time of year in London when there were parties every night. (Once, when he was trying to get engaged to Brenda, he had gone to them all. If they had dined in different houses, he would search the crowd for Brenda and hang about by the stairs waiting for her to arrive. Later he would hang about to take her home. Lady St Cloud had done everything to make it easy for him. Later, after they were married, in the two years they had spent in London before Tony's father died, they had been to fewer parties, one or two a week at the most, except for one very gay month, when Brenda was well again, after John Andrew's birth.) Tony began to imagine a dinner party assembling at that moment in London, with Brenda there and the surprised look with which she greeted each new arrival. If there was a fire she would be as near it as she could get. Would there be a fire at the end of May? He could not remember. There were nearly always fires at Hetton in the evening, whatever the season.

Then, after another bout of scratching it occurred to Tony that it was not half past eight in England. There was five hours' difference[42] in time. They had altered their watches daily on the voyage out. Which way? It ought to be easy to work out. The sun rose in the east. England was east of America so he and Dr Messinger got the sun later. It came to them at second hand and slightly soiled after Polly Cockpurse and Mrs Beaver and Princess Abdul Akbar had finished with it . . . Like Polly's dresses which Brenda used to buy for ten or fifteen pounds each . . . he fell asleep.

He woke an hour later to hear Dr Messinger cursing, and to see him sitting astride his hammock working with bandages and iodine at his great toe.

'A vampire bat got it. I must have gone to sleep with my foot against the netting. God knows how long he had been at it, before I woke up. That lamp ought to keep them off but it doesn't seem to.'

The black boys were still awake, munching over the fire. 'Vampires plenty bad this side, Chief,' they said. 'Dat for why us no leave de fire.'

'It's just the way to get sick, blast it,' said Dr Messinger. 'I may have lost pints of blood.'

Brenda and Jock were dancing together at Anchorage House.[43] It was late, the party was thinning, and now for the first time that evening, it was possible to dance with pleasure. The ball room was hung with tapestry and lit by candles. Lady Anchorage had lately curtsied her farewell to the last royalty.

'How I hate staying up late,' Brenda said, 'but it seems a shame to take my Mr Beaver away. He's so thrilled to be here, bless him, and it was a great effort to get him asked . . . Come to think of it,' she added later, 'I suppose that this is the last year *I* shall be able to go to this kind of party.'

'You're going through with the divorce?'

'I don't know, Jock. It doesn't really depend on me. It's all a matter of holding down Mr Beaver. He's getting very restive. I have to feed him a bit of high life every week or so, and I suppose that'll all stop if there's a divorce. Any news of Tony?'

'Not for some time now. I got a cable when he landed. He's gone off on some expedition with a crook doctor.'

'Is it *absolutely* safe?'

'Oh, I imagine so. The whole world is civilized now, isn't it – charabancs[44] and Cook's offices[45] everywhere.'

'Yes, I suppose it is . . . I hope he's not *brooding*. I shouldn't like to think of him being unhappy.'

'I expect he's getting used to things.'

'I do hope so. I'm very fond of Tony, you know, in spite of the monstrous way he behaved.'

There was an Indian village a mile or two distant from the camp. It was here that Tony and Dr Messinger proposed to recruit porters for the two hundred mile march that lay between them and the Pie-wie country. The niggers were river men and could not be taken into Indian territory. They would go back with the boat.

At dawn Tony and Dr Messinger drank a mug each of hot cocoa and ate some biscuits and what was left over from the bully beef[46] opened the night before. Then they set out for the village. One of the blacks went in front with a cutlass to clear the trail. Dr Messinger and Tony followed, one behind the other; another black came behind them carrying samples of trade goods – a twenty dollar Belgian gun, some rolls of printed cotton, hand-mirrors in coloured celluloid frames, some bottles of highly scented pomade.

It was a rough, unfrequented trail, encumbered by numerous fallen trunks; they waded knee deep through two streams that ran to feed the big river; underfoot there was sometimes a hard network of bare root, sometimes damp and slippery leaf mould.

Presently they reached the village. They came into sight of it quite suddenly, emerging from the bush into a wide clearing. There were eight or nine circular huts of mud and palm thatch. No one was visible, but two or three columns of smoke, rising straight and thin into the morning air, told them that the place was inhabited.

'Dey people all afeared,' said the black boy.

'Go and find someone to speak to us,' said Dr Messinger.

The nigger went to the low door of the nearest house and peered in.

'Dere aint no one but women dere,' he reported. 'Dey dressing deirselves. Come on out dere,' he shouted into the gloom. 'De chief want talk to you.'

At last, very shyly, a little old woman emerged, clad in the filthy calico gown that was kept for use in the presence of strangers. She waddled towards them on bandy legs. Her ankles were tightly bound with blue beads. Her hair was lank and ragged; her eyes were fixed on the earthenware bowl of liquid which she carried. When she was a few feet from Tony and Dr Messinger she set the bowl on the ground, and still with downcast eyes, shook hands with them. Then she stooped, picked up the bowl once more and held it to Dr Messinger.

'Cassiri,'[47] he explained, 'the local drink made of fermented cassava.'

He drank some and handed the bowl to Tony. It contained a thick, purplish liquid. When Tony had drunk a little, Dr Messinger explained, 'It is made in an interesting way. The women chew the root up and spit it into a hollow tree trunk.'

He then addressed the woman in Wapishiana.[48] She looked at him for the first time. Her brown, mongol face was perfectly blank, devoid alike of comprehension and curiosity. Dr Messinger repeated and amplified his question. The woman took the bowl from Tony and set it on the ground.

Meanwhile other faces were appearing at the doors of the huts. Only one woman ventured out. She was very stout and she smiled confidently at the visitors.

'Good morning,' she said. 'How do you do? I am Rosa. I speak English good. I live bottom-side two years with Mr Forbes. You give me cigarette.'

'Why doesn't this woman answer?'

'She no speak English.'

'But I was speaking Wapishiana.'

'She Macushi[49] woman. All these people Macushi people.'

'Oh. I didn't know. Where are the men?'

'Men all go hunting three days.'

'When will they be back?'

'They go after bush pig.'

'When will they be back?'

'No, bush pig. Plenty bush pig. Men all go hunting. You give me cigarette.'

'Listen, Rosa, I want to go to the Pie-wie country.'

'No, this Macushi. All the people Macushi.'

'But we want to go Pie-wie.'

'No, *all* Macushi. You give me cigarette.'

'It's hopeless,' said Dr Messinger. 'We shall have to wait till the men come back.' He took a packet of cigarettes from his pocket. 'Look,' he said, 'cigarettes.'

'Give me.'

'When men come back from hunting you come to river and tell me. Understand?'

'No, men hunting bush pig. You give me cigarettes.'

Dr Messinger gave her the cigarettes.

'What else you got?' she said.

Dr Messinger pointed to the load which the second nigger had laid on the ground.

'Give me,' she said.

'When men come back, I give you plenty things if men come with me to Pie-wies.'

'No, *all* Macushi here.'

'We aren't doing any good,' said Dr Messinger. 'We'd better go back to camp and wait. The men have been away three days. It's not likely they will be much longer ... I wish I could speak Macushi.'

They turned about, the four of them, and left the village. It was ten o'clock by Tony's wrist watch when they reached their camp.

*

Ten o'clock on the river Waurupang was question time at West-minster. For a long time now Jock had had a question which his constituents wanted him to ask. It came up that afternoon.

'Number twenty,' he said.

A few members turned to the order paper.

No. 20.

'*To ask the Minister of Agriculture whether in view of the dumping in this country of Japanese pork pies, the right honourable member is prepared to consider a modification of the eight-and-a-half-score basic pig from two and a half inches of thickness round the belly as originally specified, to two inches.*'

Replying for the Minister, the under-secretary said: 'The matter is receiving the closest attention. As the honourable member is no doubt aware, the question of the importation of pork pies is a matter for the Board of Trade, not for the Board of Agriculture. With regard to the specifications of the basic pig, I must remind the honourable member that, as he is doubtless aware, the eight-and-a-half-score pig is modelled on the requirements of the bacon curers and has no direct relation to pig meat for sale in pies. That is being dealt with by a separate committee who have not yet made their report.'

'Would the honourable member consider an increase of the specified maximum of fatness on the shoulders?'

'I must have notice of that question.'

Jock left the House that afternoon with the comfortable feeling that he had at last done something tangible in the interest of his constituents.

Two days later the Indians returned from hunting. It was tedious waiting. Dr Messinger put in some hours daily in checking the stores. Tony went into the bush with his gun, but the game had all migrated from that part of the river bank. One of the black boys was badly injured in the foot and calf by a stingray; after that they stopped bathing and washed in a zinc pail. When the news of the Indians' return reached camp, Tony and Dr Messinger went to the village to see them, but a feast had already started and everyone in the place was drunk. The men lay in their hammocks and the women trotted between them carrying calabashes of cassiri. Everything reeked of roast pork.

'It will take them a week to get sober,' said Dr Messinger.

All that week the black boys lounged in camp; sometimes they washed their clothes and hung them out on the gunwales of the boat to dry in the sun; sometimes they went fishing and came back with a massive catch, speared on a stick (the flesh was tasteless and rubbery); usually in the evenings they sang songs round the fire. The fellow who had been stung kept to his hammock, groaning loudly and constantly asking for medicine.

On the sixth day the Indians began to appear. They shook hands all round and then retired to the margin of the bush where they stood gazing at the camp equipment. Tony tried to photograph them but they ran away giggling like schoolgirls. Dr Messinger spread out on the ground the goods he had brought for barter.

They retired at sundown but on the seventh day they came again, greatly reinforced. The entire population of the village was there. Rosa sat down on Tony's hammock under the thatch roof.

'Give me cigarettes,' she said.

'You tell them I want men to go Pie-wie country,' said Dr Messinger.

'Pie-wie bad people. Macushi people no go with Pie-wie people.'

'You say I want ten men. I give them guns.'

'You give me cigarettes . . .'

Negotiations lasted for two days. Eventually twelve men agreed to come; seven of them insisted on bringing their wives with them. One of these was Rosa. When everything was arranged there was a party in the village and all the Indians got drunk again. This time, however, it was a shorter business as the women had not had time to prepare much cassiri. In three days the caravan was able to set out.

One of the men had a long, single-barrelled, muzzle-loading gun; several others carried bows and arrows; they were naked except for red cotton cloths round their loins. The women wore grubby calico dresses – they had been issued to them years back by an itinerant preacher and kept for occasions of this kind; they had wicker panniers on their shoulders, supported by a band across the forehead. All the heaviest luggage was carried by the women in these panniers, including the rations for themselves and their men. Rosa had, in addition, an umbrella with a dented, silver crook, a relic of her association with Mr Forbes.

The negroes returned down stream to the coast. A dump of provisions, in substantial tin casing, was left in the ruinous shelter by the bank.

'There's no one to touch it. We can send back for it in case of emergency from the Pie-wie country,' said Dr Messinger.

Tony and Dr Messinger walked immediately behind the man with the gun who was acting as guide; behind them the file straggled out for half a mile or more through the forest.

'From now onwards the map is valueless to us,' said Dr Messinger with relish.

(Roll up the map – you will not need it again for how many years, said William Pitt . . .[50] memories of Tony's private school came back to him at Dr Messinger's words, of inky little desks and a coloured picture of a Viking raid, of Mr Trotter who had taught him history and wore very vivid ties.)

Three

'Mumsy, Brenda wants a job.'

'Why?'

'Just like everybody else, short of money and nothing to do. She wondered if she could be any use to you at the shop.'

'Well . . . It's hard to say. At any other time she is exactly the kind of saleswoman I am always looking for . . . but I don't know. *As things are* I'm not sure it would be wise.'

'I said I'd ask you, that's all.'

'John, you never tell me *anything* and I don't like to seem inter-fering; but what *is* going to happen between you and Brenda?'

'I don't know.'

'You never tell me *anything*,' repeated Mrs Beaver. 'And there are so many rumours going round. Is there going to be a divorce?'

'I don't know.'

Mrs Beaver sighed. 'Well, I must get back to work. Where are you lunching?'

'Brat's.'

'Poor John. By the way, I thought you were joining Brown's.'

'I haven't heard anything from them. I don't know whether they've had an election yet.'

'Your father was a member.'

'I've an idea I shan't get in . . . anyway I couldn't really afford it.'

'I'm not happy about you, John. I'm not sure that things are working out as well as I hoped about Christmas time.'

'There's my telephone. Perhaps it's Margot. She hasn't asked me to anything for weeks.'

But it was only Brenda.

'I'm afraid mother's got nothing for you at the shop,' he said.

'Oh well. I expect something will turn up. I could do with a little good luck just at the moment.'

'So could I. Have you asked Allan about Brown's?'

'Yes, I did. He says they elected about ten chaps last week.'

'Oh, does that mean I've been blackballed?'

'I shouldn't know. Gentlemen are so odd about their clubs.'

'I thought that you were going to make Allan and Reggie support me.'

'I asked them. What does it matter anyway? D'you want to come to Veronica's for the weekend?'

'I'm not sure that I do.'

'*I*'d like it.'

'It's a beastly little house – and I don't think Veronica likes me. Who'll be there?'

'I shall be.'

'Yes . . . well, I'll let you know.'

'Am I seeing you this evening?'

'I'll let you know.'

'Oh dear,' said Brenda as she rang off. 'Now he's taken against me. It isn't my fault he can't get into Brown's. As a matter of fact I believe Reggie *did* try to help.'

Jenny Abdul Akbar was in the room with her. She came across

every morning now in her dressing gown and they read the news-paper together. Her dressing gown was of striped Berber[51] silk.

'Let's go and have a cosy lunch at the Ritz,' she said.

'The Ritz isn't cosy at lunch time and it costs eight and six. I daren't cash a cheque for three weeks, Jenny. The lawyers are so disagreeable. I've never been like this before.'

'What wouldn't I do to Tony? Leaving you stranded like this.'

'Oh, what's the good of knocking Tony? I don't suppose he's having a packet of fun himself in Brazil or wherever it is.'

'I hear they are putting in bathrooms at Hetton – while you are practically starving. And he hasn't even gone to Mrs Beaver for them.'

'Yes, I *do* think that was mean.'

Presently Jenny went back to dress. Brenda telephoned to a delicatessen store round the corner for some sandwiches. She would spend that day in bed, as she spent two or three days a week at this time. Perhaps, if Allan was making a speech somewhere, as he usually was, Marjorie would have her to dinner. The Helm-Hubbards had a supper party that night but Beaver had not been asked. 'If I went there without him it would be a major bust-up . . . Come to think of it, Marjorie's probably going. Well, I can always have sandwiches for dinner here. They make all kinds. Thank God for the little shop round the corner.' She was reading a biography of Nelson[52] that had lately appeared; it was very long and would keep her going well into the night.

At one o'clock Jenny came in to say goodbye (she had a latch key of Brenda's), dressed for a cosy lunch. 'I got Polly and Souki,' she said. 'We're going to Daisy's joint. I *wish* you were coming.'

'Me? Oh, I'm all right,' said Brenda and she thought 'It might occur to her to sock a girl a meal once in a while.'

They walked for a fortnight, averaging about fifteen miles a day. Sometimes they would do much more and sometimes much less; the Indian who went in front decided the camping places; they depended on water and evil spirits.

Dr Messinger made a compass traverse of their route. It gave him something to think about. He took readings every hour from an aneroid.[53] In the evening, if they had halted early enough, he employed the last hours of daylight in elaborating a chart. '*Dry watercourse, three deserted huts, stony ground . . .*'

'We are now in the Amazon system of rivers,' he announced with satisfaction one day. 'You see, the water is running South.' But almost immediately they crossed a stream flowing in the opposite direction. 'Very curious,' said Dr Messinger. 'A discovery of genuine scientific value.'

Next day they waded through four streams at intervals of two miles, running alternately North and South. The chart began to have a mythical appearance.

'Is there a name for any of these streams?' he asked Rosa.

'Macushi people called him Waurupang.'[54]

'No, not river where we first camped. *These rivers.*'

'Yes, Waurupang.'

'*This river here.*'

'Macushi people call him all Waurupang.'

'It's hopeless,' said Dr Messinger.

When they were near water they forced their way through blind bush; the trail there was grown over and barred by timber; only Indian eyes and Indian memory could trace its course; sometimes they crossed little patches of dry savannah, dun grass growing in tufts from the baked earth; thousands of lizards scampered and darted before their feet and the grass rustled like newspaper; it was burning hot in these enclosed spaces. Sometimes they climbed up into the wind, over loose red pebbles that bruised their feet; after these painful ascents they would lie in the wind till their wet clothes grew cold against their bodies; from these low eminences they could see other hill tops and the belts of bush through which they had travelled, and the file of porters trailing behind them. As each man and woman arrived he sank on to the dry grass and rested against his load; when the last of them came up with the party Dr Messinger would give the word and they would start off again, descending into the green heart of the forest before them.

Tony and Dr Messinger seldom spoke to one another, either when they were marching or at the halts, for they were constantly strained and exhausted. In the evenings after they had washed and changed into dry shirts and flannel trousers, they talked a little, mostly about the number of miles they had done that day, their probable position and the state of their feet. They drank rum and water after their bath; for supper there was usually bully beef stewed with rice and flour dumplings. The Indians ate farine,[55] smoked hog and occasional delicacies picked up by the way – armadillo,[56] iguana,[57] fat white grubs from the palm trees. The women had some dried fish with them that lasted for eight days; the smell grew stronger every day until the stuff was all eaten; then it still hung about them and the stores, but grew fainter until it merged into the general, indefinable smell of the camp.

There were no Indians living in this country. In the last five days of the march they suffered from lack of water. The streams they came to were mostly dry; they had to reconnoitre up and down their beds in search of tepid, stagnant puddles. But after two weeks they came to a river once more, flowing deep and swift to the South East. This was the border of the Pie-wie country and Dr Messinger marked the place where they stopped, Second Base Camp. The cabouri fly infested this stream in clouds.

'John, I think it's time you had a holiday.'

'A holiday what from, mumsy?'

'A change . . . I'm going to California in July. To the Fischbaums – Mrs Arnold Fischbaum, not the one who lives in Paris. I think it would do you good to come with me.'

'Yes, mumsy.'

'You *would* like it, wouldn't you?'

'Me? Yes, I'd like it.'

'You've picked up that way of talking from Brenda. It sounds ridiculous in a man.'

'Sorry, mumsy.'

'All right then, that's settled.'

At sunset the cabouri fly disappeared. Until then, through the day, it was necessary to keep covered; they settled on any exposed flesh like house flies upon jam; it was only when they were gorged that their bite was perceptible; they left behind a crimson, smarting circle with a black dot at its centre. Tony and Dr Messinger wore cotton gloves which they had brought for the purpose, and muslin veils, hanging down under their hats. Later they employed two women to squat beside their hammocks and fan them with leafy boughs; the slightest breeze was enough to disperse the flies, but as soon as Tony and Dr Messinger dozed the women would lay aside their work, and they woke instantly, stung in a hundred places. The Indians bore the insects as cows bear horse-flies; passively with occasional fretful outbursts when they would slap their shoulders and thighs.

After dark there was some relief, for there were few mosquitoes at this camp, but they could hear the vampire bats all night long nuzzling and flapping against their netting.

The Indians would not go hunting in this forest. They said there was no game, but Dr Messinger said it was because they were afraid of the evil spirits of the Pie-wie people. Provisions were not lasting as well as Dr Messinger had calculated. During the march it had been difficult to keep a proper guard over the stores. They were short of a bag of farine, half a bag of sugar and a bag of rice. Dr Messinger instituted careful rationing; he served them himself, measuring everything strictly in an enamel cup; even so the women managed to get to the sugar behind his back. He and Tony had finished the rum, except for one bottle which was kept in case of emergency.

'We can't go on breaking into tinned stores,' said Dr Messinger peevishly. 'The men must go out and shoot something.'

But they received the orders with expressionless, downcast faces and remained in camp.

'No birds, no animals here,' explained Rosa. 'All gone. May be they get some fish.'

But the Indians could not be persuaded to exert themselves. They could see the sacks and bales of food heaped on the bank; it would be plenty of time to start hunting and fishing when that had been exhausted.

Meanwhile there were canoes to be built.

'This is clearly Amazon water,' said Dr Messinger. 'It probably flows into the Rio Branco or the Rio Negro. The Pie-wies live along the bank, and the City, from all accounts, must be downstream of us, up one of the tributaries. When we reach the first Pie-wie village we will be able to get guides.'

The canoes were made of woodskin. Three days were spent in finding trees of suitable age and straightness and in felling them. They cut four trees and worked on them where they lay, clearing the bush for a few feet round them. They stripped the bark with their broad-bladed knives; that took another week. They worked patiently but clumsily; one woodskin was split in getting it off the trunk. There was nothing Tony and Dr Messinger could do to help. They spent that week guarding the sugar from the women. As the men moved about the camp and the surrounding bush, their steps were soundless; their bare feet seemed never to disturb the fallen leaves, their bare shoulders made no rustle in the tangled undergrowth; their speech was brief and scarcely audible, they never joined in the chatter and laughter of their women; sometimes they gave little grunts as they worked; only once they were merry, when one of them let his knife slip as he was working on the tree trunk and cut deeply into the ball of his thumb. Dr Messinger dressed the wound with iodine, lint and bandages. After that the women constantly solicited him, showing him little scratches on their arms and legs and asking for iodine.

Two of the trees were finished on one day, then another next day (that was the one which split) and the fourth two days after that; it was a larger tree than the others. When the last fibre was severed four men got round the trunk and lifted the skin clear. It curled up again at once making a hollow cylinder, which the men carried down to the waterside and set afloat, fastening it to a tree with a loop of vinerope.

When all the woodskins were ready it was an easy matter to make canoes of them. Four men held them open while two others fixed the struts. The ends were left open, and curled up slightly so as to lift them clear (when the craft was fully laden it drew only an inch or two of water). Then the men set about fashioning some single-bladed paddles; that, too, was an easy matter.

*

Every day Dr Messinger asked Rosa, 'When will the boats be ready? Ask the men,' and she replied, 'Just now.'

'How many days – four? – five? – how many?'

'No, not many. Boats finish just now.'

At last when it was clear that the work was nearly complete, Dr Messinger busied himself with arrangements. He sorted out the stores, dividing the necessary freight into two groups; he and Tony were to sit in separate boats and each had with him a rifle and ammunition, a camera, tinned rations, trade goods and his own luggage. The third canoe which would be manned solely by Indians was to hold the flour and rice, sugar and farine, and the rations for the men. The canoes would not hold all the stores and an 'emergency dump' was made a little way up the bank.

'We shall take eight men with us. Four can stay behind with the women to guard the camp. Once we are among the Pie-wies everything will be easy. These Macushis can go home then. I don't think they will rob the stores. There is nothing here that would be much use to them.'

'Hadn't we better keep Rosa with us to act as interpreter with the Macushis?'

'Yes, perhaps we had. I will tell her.'

That evening everything was finished except the paddles. In the first exhilarating hour of darkness, when Tony and Dr Messinger were able to discard the gloves and veils that had been irking them all day, they called Rosa across to the part of the camp where they ate and slept.

'Rosa, we have decided to take you down the river with us. We need you to help us talk to the men. Understand?'

Rosa said nothing; her face was perfectly blank, lit from below by the storm lantern that stood on a box between them; the shadow of her high cheek bones hid her eyes; lank, ragged hair, a tenuous straggle of tattooing along forehead and lip, rotund body in its filthy cotton gown, bandy brown legs.

'Understand?'

But still she said nothing; she seemed to be looking over their heads into the dark forest, but her eyes were lost in shadow.

'Listen, Rosa, all women and four men stay here in camp. Eight men come in boats to Pie-wie village. You come with boats. When we reach Pie-wie village, you and eight men and boats go back to camp to other women and men. Then back to Macushi country. Understand?'

At last Rosa spoke. 'Macushi peoples no go with Pie-wie peoples.'

'I am not asking you to *go with* Pie-wie people. You and the men take us as far as Pie-wies, then you go back to Macushi people. Understand?'

Rosa raised her arm in an embracing circle which covered the camp and the road they had travelled and the broad savannahs behind them. 'Macushi peoples there,' she said. Then she raised the other arm and waved it down stream towards the hidden country. 'Pie-wie peoples there,' she said. 'Macushi peoples no go with Pie-wie peoples.'

'Now listen, Rosa. You are sensible, civilized woman. You lived two years with black gentleman, Mr Forbes. You like cigarettes –'

'Yes, give me cigarettes.'

'You come with men in boats, I give you plenty, plenty cigarettes.'

Rosa looked stolidly ahead of her and said nothing.

'Listen. You will have your man and seven others to protect you. How can we talk with men without you?'

'Men no go,' said Rosa.

'Of course the men will go. The only question is, will you come too?'

'Macushi peoples no go with Pie-wie peoples,' said Rosa.

'Oh God,' said Dr Messinger wearily. 'All right, we'll talk about it in the morning.'

'You give me cigarette . . .'

'It's going to be awkward if that woman doesn't come.'

'It's going to be much more awkward if none of them come,' said Tony.

Next day the boats were ready. By noon they were launched and tied in to the bank. The Indians went silently about the business of preparing their dinner. Tony and Dr Messinger ate tongue, boiled rice and some tinned peaches.

'We're all right for stores,' said Dr Messinger. 'There's enough for three weeks at the shortest and we are bound to come across the Pie-wies in a day or two. We will start tomorrow.'

The Indians' wages, in rifles, fish hooks and rolls of cotton, had been left behind for them at their village. There were still half a dozen boxes of 'trade'[58] for use during the later stages of the journey. A leg of bush-pig was worth a handful of shot or twenty gun caps in that currency; a fat game bird cost a necklace.

When dinner was over, at about one o'clock, Dr Messinger called Rosa over to them. 'We start tomorrow,' he said.

'Yes, just now.'

'Tell the men what I told you last night. Eight men to come in boats, others wait here. You come in boats. All these stores stay here. All these stores go in boats. You tell men that.'

Rosa said nothing.

'Understand?'

'No peoples go in boats,' she said. 'All peoples go this way,' and she extended her arm towards the trail that they had lately followed. 'Tomorrow or next day all people go back to village.'

There was a long pause; at last Dr Messinger said, 'You tell the men to come here . . . It's no use threatening them,' he remarked to Tony when Rosa had waddled back to the fireside. 'They are a queer, timid lot. If you threaten them they take fright and disappear leaving you stranded. Don't worry, I shall be able to persuade them.'

They could see Rosa talking at the fireside but none of the group moved. Presently, having delivered her message, she was silent and squatted down among them with the head of one of the women between her knees. She had been searching it for lice when Dr Messinger's summons had interrupted her.

'We'd better go across and talk to them.'

Some of the Indians were in hammocks. The others were squatting on their heels; they had scraped earth over the fire and extinguished it. They gazed at Tony and Dr Messinger with slit, pig eyes. Only Rosa seemed incurious; her head was averted; all her attention went to her busy fingers as she picked and crunched the lice from her friend's hair.

'What's the matter?' asked Dr Messinger, 'I told you to bring the men here.'

Rosa said nothing.

'So Macushi people are cowards. They are afraid of Pie-wie people.'

'It is the cassava[59] field,' said Rosa. 'We must go back to dig the cassava. Otherwise it will be bad.'

'Listen. I want the men for one, two weeks. No more. After that, all finish. They can go home.'

'It is the time to dig the cassava. Macushi people dig cassava before the big rains. All people go home just now.'

'It's pure blackmail,' said Dr Messinger. 'Let's get out some trade goods.'

He and Tony together prised open one of the cases and began to spread out the contents on a blanket. They had chosen these things together at a cheap store in Oxford Street. The Indians watched the display in unbroken silence. There were bottles of scent and pills, bright celluloid combs set with glass jewels, mirrors, pocket knives with embossed aluminium handles, ribbons and necklaces and barter of more solid worth in the form of axe heads, brass cartridge cases and flat, red flasks of gunpowder.

'You give me this,' said Rosa picking out a pale blue rosette, that had been made as a boatrace favour. 'Give me this,' she repeated, rubbing some drops of scent into the palm of her hands and inhaling deeply.

'Each man can choose three things from this box if he comes in the boats.'

But Rosa replied monotonously, 'Macushi peoples dig cassava field just now.'

'It's no good,' said Dr Messinger after half an hour's fruitless negotiation. 'We shall have to try with the mice.[60] I wanted to keep them till we reached the Pie-wies. It's a pity. But they'll fall for the mice, you see. I *know* the Indian mind.'

These mice were comparatively expensive articles; they had cost three and sixpence each, and Tony remembered vividly the embarrassment with which he had witnessed their demonstration on the floor of the toy department.

They were of German manufacture; the size of large rats but conspicuously painted in spots of green and white; they had large glass eyes, stiff whiskers and green-and-white-ringed tails; they ran on hidden wheels, and inside them were little bells that jingled as they moved. Dr Messinger took one out of their box, unwrapped the tissue paper and held it up to general scrutiny. There was no doubt that he had captured his audience's interest. Then he wound it up. The Indians stirred apprehensively at the sound.

The ground where they were camping was hard mud, inundated at flood time. Dr Messinger put the toy down at his feet and set it going; tinkling merrily it ran towards the group of Indians. For a moment Tony was afraid that it would turn over, or become stuck against a root but the mechanism was unimpaired and by good chance there was a clear course. The effect exceeded anything that he had expected. There was a loud intake of breath, a series of horrified, small grunts, a high wail of terror from the women, and a sudden stampede; a faint patter of bare brown feet among the fallen leaves, bare limbs, quiet as bats, pushed through the undergrowth, ragged cotton gowns caught and tore in the thorn bushes. Before the toy had run down, before it had jingled its way to the place where the nearest Indian had been squatting, the camp was empty.

'Well, I'm damned,' said Dr Messinger, 'that's better than I expected.'

'More than you expected anyway.'

'Oh it's all right. They'll come back. I know them.'

But by sundown there was still no sign. Throughout the hot afternoon Tony and Dr Messinger, shrouded from cabouri fly, sprawled in their hammocks. The empty canoes lay in the river; the mechanical mouse had been put away. At sundown Dr Messinger said, 'We'd better make a fire. They'll come back when it is dark.'

They brushed the earth away from the old embers, brought new wood and made a fire; they lit the storm lantern.

'We'd better get some supper,' said Tony.

They boiled water and made some cocoa, opened a tin of salmon and finished the peaches that were left over from midday. They lit their pipes and drew the sheaths of mosquito netting across their hammocks. Most of this time they were silent. Presently they decided to go to sleep.

'We shall find them all here in the morning,' said Dr Messinger. 'They're an odd bunch.'

All round them the voices of the bush whistled and croaked, changing with the hours as the night wore on to morning.

Dawn broke in London, clear and sweet, dove grey and honey, with promise of good weather; the lamps in the streets paled and disappeared; the empty streets ran with water, and the rising sun caught it as it bubbled round the hydrants; the men in overalls swung the nozzles of their hoses from side to side and the water jetted and cascaded in a sparkle of light.

'Let's have the window open,' said Brenda. 'It's stuffy in here.'

The waiter drew back the curtains, opened the windows.

'It's quite light,' she added.

'After five. Oughtn't we to go to bed?'

'Yes.'

'Only another week and then all the parties will be over,' said Beaver.

'Yes.'

'Well, let's go.'

'All right. Can you pay? I just haven't any money.'

They had come on after the party, for breakfast at a club Daisy had opened. Beaver paid for the kippers and tea. 'Eight shillings,' he said. 'How does Daisy expect to make a success of the place when she charges prices like that?'

'It does seem a lot . . . So you really *are* going to America?'

'I must. Mother has taken the tickets.'

'Nothing I've said tonight makes any difference?'

'Darling, don't go on. We've been through all that. You know it's the only thing that *can* happen. Why spoil the last week?'

'You *have* enjoyed the summer, haven't you?'

'Of course . . . well, shall we go?'

'Yes. You needn't bother to see me home.'

'Sure you don't mind? It *is* miles out of the way and it's late.'

'There's no knowing what I mind.'

'Brenda, darling, for heaven's sake . . . It isn't like you to go on like this.'

'I never was one for making myself expensive.'

The Indians returned during the night, while Tony and Dr Messinger were asleep; without a word spoken the little people crept out of hiding; the women had removed their clothes and left them at a distance so that no twig should betray their movements; their naked bodies moved soundlessly through the undergrowth; the glowing embers of the fire and the storm lantern twenty yards away were their only light; there was no moon. They collected their wicker baskets and their rations of farine, their bows and arrows, the gun and their broad-bladed knives; they rolled up their hammocks into compact cylinders. They took nothing with them that was not theirs. Then they crept back through the shadows, into the darkness.

When Tony and Dr Messinger awoke it was clear to them what had happened.

'The situation is grave,' said Dr Messinger. 'But not desperate.'

Four

For four days Tony and Dr Messinger paddled down stream. They sat, balancing themselves precariously, at the two ends of the canoe; between them they had piled the most essential of their stores; the remainder, with the other canoes, had been left at the camp, to be called for when they had recruited help from the Pie-wies. Even the minimum which Dr Messinger had selected overweighted the craft so that it was dangerously low; any movement brought the water to the lip of the gunwale and threatened disaster; it was heavy to steer and they made slow progress, contenting themselves for the most part, with keeping end on, and drifting with the current.

Twice they came to stretches of cataract, and here they drew in to the bank, unloaded, and waded beside the boat, sometimes plunging waist deep, sometimes clambering over the rocks, guiding it by hand until they reached clear water again. Then they tied up to the bank and carried their cargo down to it through the bush. For the rest of the way the river was broad and smooth; a dark surface which reflected in fine detail the walls of forest on either side, towering up from the undergrowth to their blossoming crown a hundred or more feet above them. Sometimes they came to a stretch of water scattered with fallen petals and floated among them, moving scarcely less slowly than they, as though resting in a flowering meadow. At night they spread their tarpaulin on stretches of dry beach, or hung their hammocks in the bush. Only the cabouri fly and rare, immobile alligators menaced the peace of their days.

They kept a constant scrutiny of the banks but saw no sign of human life.

Then Tony developed fever. It came on him quite suddenly, during the fourth afternoon. At their midday halt he was in complete health and shot a small deer that came down to drink on the opposite bank; an hour later he was shivering so violently that he had to lay down his paddle; his head was flaming with heat, his body and limbs frigid; by sunset he was slightly delirious.

Dr Messinger took his temperature and found that it was a hundred and four degrees, Fahrenheit. He gave him twenty-five grains of quinine and lit a fire so close to his hammock that by morning it was singed and blacked with smoke. He told Tony to keep wrapped up in his blanket, but at intervals throughout that night he woke from sleep to find himself running with sweat; he was consumed with thirst and drank mug after mug of river water. Neither that evening nor next morning was he able to eat anything.

But next morning his temperature was down again. He felt weak and exhausted but he was able to keep steady in his place and paddle a little.

'It was just a passing attack, wasn't it?' he said. 'I shall be perfectly fit tomorrow, shan't I?'

'I hope so,' said Dr Messinger.

At midday Tony drank some cocoa and ate a cupful of rice. 'I feel grand,' he said.

'Good.'

That night the fever came on again. They were camping on a sand bank. Dr Messinger heated stones and put them under Tony's feet and in the small of his back. He was awake most of the night fuelling the fire and refilling Tony's mug with water. At dawn Tony slept for an hour and woke feeling slightly better; he was taking frequent doses of quinine and his ears were filled with a muffled sound as though he were holding those shells to them in which, he had been told in childhood, one could hear the beat of the sea.

'We've got to go on,' said Dr Messinger. 'We can't be far from a village now.'

'I feel awful. Wouldn't it be better to wait a day till I am perfectly fit again?'

'It's no good waiting. We've got to get on. D'you think you can manage to get into the canoe?'

Dr Messinger knew that Tony was in for a long bout.

For the first few hours of that day Tony lay limp in the bows. They had shifted the stores so that he could lie full length. Then the fever came on again and his teeth chattered. He sat up and crouched with his head in his knees, shaking all over; only his forehead and cheeks were burning hot under the noon sun. There was still no sign of a village.

It was late in the afternoon when he first saw Brenda. For some time he had been staring intently at the odd shape amidships where the stores had been piled; then he realized that it was a human being.

'So the Indians came back?' he said.

'Yes.'

'I knew they would. Silly of them to be scared by a toy. I suppose the others are following.'

'Yes, I expect so. Try and sit still.'

'Damned fool, being frightened of a toy mouse,' Tony said derisively to the woman amidships. Then he saw that it was Brenda. 'I'm sorry,' he said. 'I didn't see it was you. *You* wouldn't be frightened of a toy mouse.'

But she did not answer him. She sat as she used often to sit when she came back from London, huddled over her bowl of bread and milk.

Dr Messinger steered the boat in to the side. They nearly capsized as he helped Tony out. Brenda got ashore without assistance. She stepped out in her delicate, competent way, keeping the balance of the boat.

'That's what poise means,' said Tony. 'D'you know I once saw a questionnaire that people had to fill in when they applied for a job in an American firm, and one of the things they had to answer was "Have you poise?"'

Brenda was at the top of the bank waiting for him. 'What was so absurd about the question was that they only had the applicant's word for it,' he explained laboriously. 'I mean – is it a sign of poise to think you have it?'

'Just sit quiet here while I sling your hammock.'

'Yes, I'll sit here with Brenda. I am so glad she could come. She must have caught the three-eighteen.'

She was with him all that night and all the next day. He talked to her ceaselessly but her replies were rare and enigmatic. On the succeeding evening he had another fit of sweating. Dr Messinger kept a large fire burning by the hammock and wrapped Tony in his own blanket. An hour before dawn Tony fell asleep and when he awoke Brenda had gone.

'You're down to normal again.'

'Thank God. I've been pretty ill, haven't I? I can't remember much.'

Dr Messinger had made something of a camp. He had chopped a square clear of undergrowth, the size of a small room. Their two hammocks hung on opposite sides of it. The stores were all ashore, arranged in an orderly pile on the tarpaulin.

'How d'you feel?'

'Grand,' said Tony, but when he got out of his hammock he found he could not stand without help. 'Of course, I haven't eaten anything. I expect it will be a day or two before I'm really well.'

Dr Messinger said nothing, but strained the tea clear of leaves by pouring it slowly from one mug into another; he stirred into it a large spoonful of condensed milk.

'See if you can drink this.'

Tony drank it with pleasure and ate some biscuits.

'Are we going on today?' he asked.

'We'll think about it.' He took the mugs down to the bank and washed them in the river. When he came back he said, 'I think I'd better explain things. It's no use your thinking you are cured because you are out of fever for one day. That's the way it goes. One day fever and one day normal. It may take a week or it may take much longer. That's a thing we've got to face. I can't risk taking you in the canoe. You nearly upset us several times the day before yesterday.'

'I thought there was someone there I knew.'

'You thought a lot of things. It'll go on like that. Meanwhile we've provisions for about ten days. There's no immediate anxiety there but it's a thing to remember. Besides, what you need is a roof over your head and constant nursing. If only we were at a village . . .'

'I'm afraid I'm being a great nuisance.'

'That's not the point. The thing is to find what is best for us to do.'

But Tony felt too tired to think; he dozed for an hour or so. When he awoke, Dr Messinger was cutting back the bush further. 'I'm going to fix up the tarpaulin as a roof.'

(He had marked this place on his map *Temporary Emergency Base Camp*.)

Tony watched him listlessly. Presently he said, 'Look here, why don't you leave me here and go down the river for help?'

'I thought of that. It's too big a risk.'

That afternoon Brenda was back at Tony's side and he was shivering and tossing in his hammock.

When he was next able to observe things, Tony noted that there was a tarpaulin over his head, slung to the tree trunks. He asked, 'How long have we been here?'

'Only three days.'

'What time is it now?'

'Getting on for ten in the morning.'

'I feel awful.'

Dr Messinger gave him some soup. 'I am going downstream for the day,' he said, 'to see if there's any sign of a village. I hate leaving you but it's a chance worth taking. I shall be able to get a long way in the canoe now it's empty. Lie quiet. Don't move from the hammock. I shall be back before night. I hope with some Indians to help.'

'All right,' said Tony and fell asleep.

Dr Messinger went down to the river's edge and untied the canoe; he brought with him a rifle, a drinking cup and a day's provisions. He sat in the stern and pushed out from the bank; the current carried the bows down and in a few strokes of the paddle he was in midstream.

The sun was high and its reflection in the water dazzled and scorched him; he paddled on with regular, leisurely strokes; he was travelling fast. For a mile's stretch the river narrowed and the water raced so that all he had to do was to trail the blade of the paddle as a rudder; then the walls of forest on either side of him fell back and he drifted into a great open lake, where he had to work heavily to keep in motion; all the time he watched keenly to right and left for the column of smoke, the thatched dome, the sly brown figure in the undergrowth, the drinking cattle, that would disclose the village he sought. But there was no sign. In the open water he took up his field glasses and studied the whole wooded margin. But there was no sign.

Later the river narrowed once more and the canoe shot forward in the swift current. Ahead of him the surface was broken by rapids; the smooth water seethed and eddied; a low monotone warned him that beyond the rapids was a fall. Dr Messinger began to steer for the bank. The current was running strongly and he exerted his full strength; ten yards from the beginning of the rapids his bows ran in under the bank. There was a dense growth of thorn here, overhanging the river; the canoe slid under them and bit into the beach; very cautiously Dr Messinger knelt forward in his place and stretched up to a bough over his head. It was at that moment he came to grief; the stern swung out downstream and as he snatched at the paddle the craft was swept broadside into the troubled waters;

there it adopted an eccentric course, spinning and tumbling to the falls. Dr Messinger was tipped into the water; it was quite shallow in places and he caught at the rocks but they were worn smooth as ivory and afforded no hold for his hands; he rolled over twice, found himself in deep water and attempted to swim, found himself among boulders again and attempted to grapple with them. Then he reached the falls.

They were unspectacular as falls go in that country – a drop of ten feet or less – but they were enough for Dr Messinger. At their foot the foam subsided into a great pool, almost still, and strewn with blossom from the forest trees that encircled it. Dr Messinger's hat floated very slowly towards the Amazon and the water closed over his bald head.[61]

Brenda went to see the family solicitors.

'Mr Graceful,' she said, 'I've got to have some more money.'

Mr Graceful looked at her sadly. 'I should have thought that was really a question for your bank manager. I understand that your securities are in your own name and that the dividends are paid into your account.'

'They never seem to pay dividends nowadays. Besides it's really very difficult to live on so little.'

'No doubt. No doubt.'

'Mr Last left you with power of attorney, didn't he?'

'With strictly limited powers, Lady Brenda. I am instructed to pay the wage bill at Hetton and all expenses connected with the upkeep of the estate – he is putting in new bathrooms and restoring some decorations in the morning room which had been demolished. But I am afraid that I have no authority to draw on Mr Last's account for other charges.'

'But Mr Graceful, I am sure he didn't intend to stay abroad so long. He can't possibly have meant to leave me stranded like this, can he? . . . Can he?'

Mr Graceful paused and fidgeted a little. 'To be quite frank, Lady Brenda, I fear that *was* his intention. I raised this particular point shortly before his departure. He was quite resolved on the subject.'

'But is he *allowed* to do that? I mean, haven't I got any rights under the marriage settlement or anything?'

'Nothing which you can claim without application to the courts. You *might* find solicitors who would advise you to take action. I cannot say that I should be one of them. Mr Last would oppose any such order to the utmost and I think that, in the present circumstances, the courts would undoubtedly find for him. In any case it would be a prolonged, costly and slightly undignified proceeding.'

'Oh, I see . . . well, that's that, isn't it?'

'It certainly looks as though it were.'

Brenda rose to go. It was high summer and through the open windows she could see the sunbathed gardens of Lincoln's Inn.⁶²

'There's one thing. Do you know, I mean, can you tell me whether Mr Last made another will?'

'I'm afraid that is a thing I cannot discuss.'

'No, I suppose not. I'm sorry if it was wrong to ask. I just wanted to know how I am with him.'

She still stood between the door and the table, looking lost, in her bright summer clothes. 'Perhaps I can say as much as this to guide you. The heirs presumptive to Hetton are now his cousins, the Richard Lasts at Princes Risborough. I think that your knowledge of Mr Last's character and opinions will tell you that he would always wish his fortune to go with the estate, in order that it may be preserved in what he holds to be its right condition.'

'Yes,' said Brenda, 'I ought to have thought of that. Well, goodbye.'

And she went out alone into the sunshine.

All that day Tony lay alone, fitfully oblivious of the passage of time. He slept a little; once or twice he left his hammock and found himself weak and dizzy. He tried to eat some of the food which Dr Messinger had left out for him, but without success. It was not until it grew dark that he realized the day was over. He lit the lantern and began to collect wood for the fire, but the sticks kept slipping from his fingers and each time that he stooped he felt giddy, so that after a few fretful efforts he left them where they had fallen and returned to his hammock. And lying there, wrapped in his blanket, he began to cry.

After some hours of darkness the lamp began to burn low; he leant painfully over, and shook it. It needed refilling. He knew where the oil was kept, crept to it, supporting himself first on the hammock rope and then on a pile of boxes. He found the keg, pulled out the bung and began to refill the lamp, but his hand trembled and the oil spilled over the ground, then his head began to swim again so that he shut his eyes; the keg rolled over on its side and emptied itself with slow gurglings. When he realized what had happened he began to cry again. He lay down in his hammock and in a few minutes the light sank, flickered and went out. There was a reek of kerosene on his hands and on the sodden earth. He lay awake in the darkness crying.

Just before dawn the fever returned and a constant company of phantoms perplexed his senses.

Brenda awoke in the lowest possible spirits. The evening before she had spent alone at a cinema. Afterwards she felt hungry – she had had no proper meal that day – but she had not the strength to go alone into any of the supper restaurants. She bought a meat pie at a coffee stall and took it home. It looked delicious but, when she came to eat she found that she had lost her appetite. The remains of that pie lay on the dressing table when she awoke.

It was August and she was entirely alone. Beaver was that day landing in New York. (He had cabled her from mid-ocean that the crossing was excellent.) It was for her the last of Beaver. Parliament was over and Jock Grant-Menzies was paying his annual visit to his elder brother in Scotland; Marjorie and Allan at the last moment had made Lord Monomark's yacht and were drifting luxuriously down the coast of Spain attending bullfights (they had even asked her to look after Djinn). Her mother was at the chalet Lady Anchorage always lent her on the Lake of Geneva.[63] Polly was everywhere. Even Jenny Abdul Akbar was cruising in the Baltic.[64]

Brenda opened her newspaper and read an article by a young

man who said that the London Season was a thing of the past; that everyone was too busy in those days to keep up the pre-war routine; that there were no more formal dances but a constant round of more modest entertaining; that August in London was the gayest time of all (he rewrote this annually in slightly different words). It did not console Brenda to read that article.

For weeks past she had attempted to keep a fair mind towards Tony and his treatment of her; now at last she broke down and turning over buried her face in the pillow, in an agony of resentment and self-pity.

In Brazil she wore a ragged cotton gown of the same pattern as Rosa's. It was not unbecoming. Tony watched her for some time before he spoke. 'Why are you dressed like that?'

'Don't you like it? I got it from Polly.'

'It looks so dirty.'

'Well, Polly travels about a lot. You must get up now to go to the County Council meeting.'

'But it isn't Wednesday?'

'No, but time is different in Brazil; surely you remember?'

'I can't get as far as Pigstanton. I've got to stay here until Messinger comes back. I'm ill. He told me to be quiet. He's coming this evening.'

'But all the County Council are here. The Shameless Blonde brought them in her aeroplane.'

Sure enough they were all there. Reggie St Cloud was chairman. He said, 'I strongly object to Milly being on the committee. She is a woman of low repute.'

Tony protested. 'She has a daughter. She has as much right here as Lady Cockpurse.'

'Order,' said the Mayor. 'I must ask you gentlemen to confine your remarks to the subject under discussion. We have to decide about the widening of the Bayton–Pigstanton road. There have been several complaints that it's impossible for the Green Line buses to turn the corner safely at Hetton Cross.'

'Green Line *rats*.'[65]

'I said Green Line rats. Mechanical green line rats. Many of the villagers have been scared by them and have evacuated their cottages.'

'I evacuated,' said Reggie St Cloud. 'I was driven out of my house by mechanical green rats.'

'Order,' said Polly Cockpurse. 'I move that Mr Last address the meeting.'

'Hear, hear.'

'Ladies and gentlemen,' said Tony. 'I beg you to understand that I am ill and must not move from the hammock. Dr Messinger has given the clearest instructions.'

'Winnie wants to bathe.'

'No bathing in Brazil. No bathing in Brazil.' The meeting took up the cry. 'No bathing in Brazil.'

'But you had two breakfasts.'

'Order,' said the Mayor. 'Lord St Cloud, I suggest you put the question to the vote.'

'The question is whether the contract for the widening of the corner at Hetton Cross shall be given to Mrs Beaver. Of the tenders submitted hers was by far the most expensive but I understand that her plans include a chromium plated wall on the south side of the village . . .'

'. . . and two breakfasts,' prompted Winnie.

'. . . and two breakfasts for the men engaged on the work. Those in favour of the motion will make a clucking sound in imitation of hens, those against will say bow-wow.'

'A most improper proceeding,' said Reggie. 'What will the servants think?'

'We have got to do something until Brenda has been told.'

'. . . Me? I'm all right.'

'Then I take it the motion is carried.'

'Oh, I *am* glad Mrs Beaver got the job,' said Brenda. 'You see I'm in love with John Beaver, I'm in love with John Beaver, I'm in love with John Beaver.'

'Is that the decision of the committee?'

'Yes, she is in love with John Beaver.'

'Then that is carried unanimously.'

'No,' said Winnie. 'He ate two breakfasts.'

'. . . by an overwhelming majority.'

'Why are you all changing your clothes?' asked Tony, for they were putting on hunting coats.

'For the lawn meet. Hounds are meeting here today.'

'But you can't hunt in summer.'

'Time is different in Brazil and there is no bathing.'

'I saw a fox yesterday in Bruton Wood. A mechanical green fox with a bell inside him that jingled as he ran. It frightened them so much that they ran away and the whole beach was deserted and there was no bathing except for Beaver. He can bathe every day, for the time is different in Brazil.'

'I'm in love with John Beaver,' said Ambrose.

'Why, I didn't know you were here.'

'I came to remind you that you were ill, Sir. You must on no account leave your hammock.'

'But how can I reach the City if I stay here.'

'I will serve it directly, Sir, in the library.'

'Yes, in the library. There is no point in using the dining hall now that her Ladyship has gone to live in Brazil.'

'I will send the order to the stables, Sir.'

'But I don't want the pony. I told Ben to sell her.'

'You will have to ride to the smoking room, Sir. Dr Messinger has taken the canoe.'

'Very well, Ambrose.'

'Thank you, Sir.'

The committee had moved off down the avenue; all except Colonel Inch who had taken the other drive and was trotting towards Compton Last. Tony and Mrs Rattery were all alone.

'Bow-wow,' she said, scooping in the cards. 'That carries the motion.'

Looking up from the card table, Tony saw beyond the trees the ramparts[66] and battlements of the City; it was quite near him. From the turret of the gatehouse a heraldic[67] banner floated in the tropic breeze. He struggled into an upright position and threw aside his blankets. He was stronger and steadier when the fever was on him. He picked his way through the surrounding thorn-scrub; the sound of music rose from the glittering walls; some procession or pageant was passing along them. He lurched into tree trunks and became caught up in roots and hanging tendrils of bush-vine; but he pressed forward unconscious of pain and fatigue.

At last he came into the open. The gates were before him and trumpets were sounding along the walls, saluting his arrival; from bastion to bastion the message ran to the four points of the compass; petals of almond and apple blossom were in the air; they carpeted the way, as, after a summer storm, they lay in the orchards at Hetton. Gilded cupolas[68] and spires of alabaster[69] shone in the sunlight.

Ambrose announced, 'The City is served.'

Chapter Six

DU CÔTÉ DE CHEZ TODD

Although Mr Todd[1] had lived in Amazonas for nearly sixty years, no one except a few families of Pie-wie Indians was aware of his existence. His house stood in a small savannah, one of those little patches of sand and grass that crop up occasionally in that neighbourhood, three miles or so across, bounded on all sides by forest.

The stream which watered it was not marked on any map; it ran through rapids, always dangerous and at most seasons of the year impassable, to join the upper waters of the river where Dr Messinger had come to grief. None of the inhabitants of the district, except Mr Todd, had ever heard of the governments of Brazil or Dutch Guiana,[2] both of which from time to time claimed its possession.

Mr Todd's house was larger than those of his neighbours, but similar in character – a palm thatch roof, breast-high walls of mud and wattle, and a mud floor. He owned the dozen or so head of puny cattle which grazed in the savannah, a plantation of cassava, some banana and mango trees, a dog and, unique in the neighbourhood, a single-barrelled, breech-loading shotgun. The few commodities which he employed from the outside world, came to him through a long succession of traders, passed from hand to hand, bartered for in a dozen languages at the extreme end of one of the longest threads in the web of commerce that spreads from Manáos[3] into the remote fastness of the forest.

One day while Mr Todd was engaged in filling some cartridges, a Pie-wie came to him with the news that a white man was approaching through the forest, alone and very sick. He closed the cartridge and loaded his gun with it, put those that were finished into his pocket and set out in the direction indicated.

The man was already clear of the bush when Mr Todd reached him, sitting on the ground, clearly in a very bad way. He was without hat or boots, and his clothes were so torn that it was only by the dampness of his body that they adhered to it; his feet were cut and grossly swollen; every exposed surface of skin was scarred by insect and bat bites; his eyes were wild with fever. He was talking to himself in delirium but stopped when Todd approached and addressed him in English.

'You're the first person who's spoken to me for days,' said Tony. 'The others won't stop. They keep bicycling by . . . I'm tired . . . Brenda was with me at first but she was frightened by a mechanical mouse, so she took the canoe and went off. She said she would come back that evening but she didn't. I expect she's staying with one of her new friends in Brazil . . . You haven't seen her, have you?'

'You are the first stranger I have seen for a very long time.'

'She was wearing a top hat when she left. You can't miss her.' Then he began talking to someone at Mr Todd's side, who was not there.

'Do you see that house over there? Do you think you can manage to walk to it? If not I can send some Indians to carry you.'

Tony squinted across the savannah at Mr Todd's hut.

'Architecture harmonizing with local character,' he said, 'indigenous material employed throughout. Don't let Mrs Beaver see it or she will cover it with chromium plating.'

'Try and walk.' Mr Todd hoisted Tony to his feet and supported him with a stout arm.

'I'll ride your bicycle. It *was* you I passed just now on a bicycle, wasn't it? . . . except that your beard is a different colour. His was green . . . green as mice.'

Mr Todd led Tony across the hummocks of grass towards the house.

'It is a very short way. When we get there I will give you something to make you better.'

'Very kind of you . . . rotten thing for a man to have his wife go away in a canoe. That was a long time ago. Nothing to eat since.' Presently he said, 'I say, you're English. I'm English too. My name is Last.'

'Well, Mr Last, you aren't to bother about anything more. You're ill and you've had a rough journey. I'll take care of you.'

Tony looked round him. 'Are you all English?'

'Yes, all of us.'

'That dark girl married a Moor[4]. . . It's very lucky I met you all.
I suppose you're some kind of cycling club?'

'Yes.'

'Well, I feel too tired for bicycling . . . never liked it much . . .
you fellows ought to get motor bicycles, you know, much faster
and noisier . . . Let's stop here.'

'No, you must come as far as the house. It's not very much
further.'

'All right . . . I suppose you would have some difficulty getting
petrol here.'

They went very slowly, but at length reached the house.

'Lie there in the hammock.'

'That's what Messinger said. He's in love with John Beaver.'

'I will get something for you.'

'Very good of you. Just my usual morning tray – coffee, toast,
fruit. And the morning papers. If her Ladyship has been called I
will have it with her . . .'

Mr Todd went into the back room of the house and dragged a
tin canister from under a heap of skins. It was full of a mixture of
dried leaf and bark. He took a handful and went outside to the fire.
When he returned his guest was bolt upright astride the hammock,
talking angrily.

'. . . You would hear better and it would be more polite if you
stood still when I addressed you instead of walking round in a
circle.[5] It is for your own good that I am telling you . . . I know
you are friends of my wife and that is why you will not listen to
me. But be careful. She will say nothing cruel, she will not raise
her voice, there will be no hard words. She hopes you will be great
friends afterwards as before. But she will leave you. She will go
away quietly during the night. She will take her hammock and her
rations of farine . . . Listen to me. I know I am not clever but that
is no reason why we should forget all courtesy. Let us kill in the
gentlest manner. I will tell you what I have learned in the forest,
where time is different. There is no City. Mrs Beaver has covered
it with chromium plating and converted it into flats. Three guineas

a week, each with a separate bathroom. Very suitable for base love. And Polly will be there. She and Mrs Beaver under the fallen battlements . . .'

Mr Todd put a hand behind Tony's head and held up the concoction of herbs in the calabash. Tony sipped and turned away his head.

'Nasty medicine,' he said, and began to cry.

Mr Todd stood by him holding the calabash. Presently Tony drank some more, screwing up his face and shuddering slightly at the bitterness. Mr Todd stood beside him until the draught was finished; then he threw out the dregs on to the mud floor. Tony lay back in the hammock sobbing quietly. Soon he fell into a deep sleep.

Tony's recovery was slow. At first, days of lucidity alternated with delirium; then his temperature dropped and he was conscious even when most ill. The days of fever grew less frequent, finally occurring in the normal system of the tropics, between long periods of comparative health. Mr Todd dosed him regularly with herbal remedies.

'It's very nasty,' said Tony, 'but it does do good.'

'There is medicine for everything in the forest,' said Mr Todd; 'to make you well and to make you ill. My mother was an Indian and she taught me many of them. I have learned others from time to time from my wives. There are plants to cure you and give you fever, to kill you and send you mad, to keep away snakes, to intoxicate fish so that you can pick them out of the water with your hands like fruit from a tree. There are medicines even I do not know. They say that it is possible to bring dead people to life after they have begun to stink, but I have not seen it done.'

'But surely you are English?'

'My father was – at least a Barbadian. He came to Guiana as a missionary. He was married to a white woman but he left her in Guiana to look for gold. Then he took my mother. The Pie-wie women are ugly but very devoted. I have had many. Most of the men and women living in this savannah are my children. That is why they obey – for that reason and because I have the gun. My father lived to a great age. It is not twenty years since he died. He was a man of education. Can you read?'

'Yes, of course.'

'It is not everyone who is so fortunate. I cannot.'

Tony laughed apologetically. 'But I suppose you haven't much opportunity here.'

'Oh yes, that is just it. I have a *great* many books. I will show you when you are better. Until five years ago there was an Englishman – at least a black man, but he was well educated in Georgetown. He died. He used to read to me every day until he died. You shall read to me when you are better.'

'I shall be delighted to.'

'Yes, you shall read to me,' Mr Todd repeated, nodding over the calabash.

During the early days of his convalescence Tony had little conversation with his host; he lay in the hammock staring up at the thatched roof and thinking about Brenda. The days, exactly twelve hours each, passed without distinction. Mr Todd retired to sleep at sundown, leaving a little lamp burning – a handwoven wick drooping from a pot of beef fat – to keep away vampire bats.

The first time that Tony left the house Mr Todd took him for a little stroll around the farm.

'I will show you the black man's grave,' he said, leading him to a mound between the mango trees. 'He was very kind. Every afternoon until he died, for two hours, he used to read to me. I think I will put up a cross – to commemorate his death and your arrival – a pretty idea. Do you believe in God?'

'I suppose so. I've never really thought about it much.'

'I have thought about it a *great* deal and I still do not know . . . Dickens[6] did.'

'I suppose so.'

'Oh yes, it is apparent in all his books. You will see.'

That afternoon Mr Todd began the construction of a headpiece for the negro's grave. He worked with a large spokeshave in a wood so hard that it grated and rang like metal.

At last when Tony had passed six or seven consecutive nights without fever, Mr Todd said, 'Now I think you are well enough to see the books.'

At one end of the hut there was a kind of loft formed by a rough platform erected in the eaves of the roof. Mr Todd propped a ladder against it and mounted. Tony followed, still unsteady after his illness. Mr Todd sat on the platform and Tony stood at the top of the ladder looking over. There was a heap of small bundles there, tied up with rag, palm leaf and raw hide.

'It has been hard to keep out the worms and ants. Two are practically destroyed. But there is an oil the Indians make that is useful.'

He unwrapped the nearest parcel and handed down a calf bound book. It was an early American edition of *Bleak House*.[7]

'It does not matter which we take first.'

'You are fond of Dickens?'

'Why, yes, of course. More than fond, far more. You see, they are the only books I have ever heard. My father used to read them and then later the black man . . . and now you. I have heard them all several times by now but I never get tired; there is always more to be learned and noticed, so many characters, so many changes of scene, so many words . . . I have all Dickens's books here except those that the ants devoured. It takes a long time to read them all – more than two years.'

'Well,' said Tony lightly, 'they will well last out my visit.'

'Oh, I hope not. It is delightful to start again. Each time I think I find more to enjoy and admire.'

They took down the first volume of *Bleak House* and that afternoon Tony had his first reading.

He had always rather enjoyed reading aloud and in the first year of marriage had shared several books in this way with Brenda, until one day, in a moment of frankness, she remarked that it was torture to her. He had read to John Andrew, late in the afternoon, in winter, while the child sat before the nursery fender eating his supper. But Mr Todd was a unique audience.

The old man sat astride his hammock opposite Tony, fixing him throughout with his eyes, and following the words, soundlessly, with his lips. Often when a new character was introduced he would say, 'Repeat the name, I have forgotten him,' or 'Yes, yes, I remember her well. She dies, poor woman.' He would frequently interrupt with questions; not as Tony would have imagined about the circumstances of the story – such things as the procedure of the Lord Chancellor's Court[8] or the social conventions of the time, though they must have been unintelligible, did not concern him – but always about the characters. 'Now why does she say that? Does she really mean it? Did she feel faint because of the heat of the fire or of something in that paper?' He laughed loudly at all the jokes and at some passages which did not seem humorous to Tony, asking him to repeat them two or three times; and later at the description of the sufferings of the outcasts in 'Tom-all-alone's'[9] tears ran down his cheeks into his beard. His comments on the story were usually simple. 'I think that Dedlock[10] is a very proud man,' or, 'Mrs Jellyby[11] does not take enough care of her children.'

Tony enjoyed the readings almost as much as he did.

At the end of the first day the old man said, 'You read beautifully, with a far better accent than the black man. And you explain better. It is almost as though my father were here again.' And always at the end of a session he thanked his guest courteously. 'I enjoyed that *very* much. It was an extremely distressing chapter. But, if I remember rightly, it will all turn out well.'

By the time that they were in the second volume, however, the novelty of the old man's delight had begun to wane, and Tony was feeling strong enough to be restless. He touched more than once on the subject of his departure, asking about canoes and rains and the possibility of finding guides. But Mr Todd seemed obtuse and paid no attention to these hints.

One day, running his thumb through the pages of *Bleak House* that remained to be read, Tony said, 'We still have a lot to get through. I hope I shall be able to finish it before I go.'

'Oh yes,' said Mr Todd. 'Do not disturb yourself about that. You will have time to finish it, my friend.'

For the first time Tony noticed something slightly menacing in his host's manner. That evening at supper, a brief meal of farine and dried beef, eaten just before sundown, Tony renewed the subject.

'You know, Mr Todd, the time has come when I must be thinking about getting back to civilization. I have already imposed myself on your hospitality far too long.'

Mr Todd bent over the plate, crunching mouthfuls of farine, but made no reply.

'How soon do you think I shall be able to get a boat? . . . I said how soon do you think I shall be able to get a boat? I appreciate all your kindness to me more than I can say but . . .'

'My friend, any kindness I may have shown is amply repaid by your reading of Dickens. Do not let us mention the subject again.'

'Well, I'm very glad you have enjoyed it. I have, too. But I really must be thinking of getting back . . .'

'Yes,' said Mr Todd. 'The black man was like that. He thought of it all the time. But he died here . . .'

Twice during the next day Tony opened the subject but his host was evasive. Finally he said, 'Forgive me, Mr Todd, but I really must press the point. When can I get a boat?'

'There is no boat.'

'Well, the Indians can build one.'

'You must wait for the rains. There is not enough water in the river now.'

'How long will that be?'

'A month . . . two months . . .'

They had finished *Bleak House* and were nearing the end of *Dombey and Son*,[12] when the rain came.

'Now it is time to make preparations to go.'

'Oh, that is impossible. The Indians will not make a boat during the rainy season – it is one of their superstitions.'

'You might have told me.'

'Did I not mention it? I forgot.'

Next morning Tony went out alone while his host was busy, and, looking as aimless as he could, strolled across the savannah to the group of Indian houses. There were four or five Pie-wies sitting in one of the doorways. They did not look up as he approached them. He addressed them in the few words of Macushi he had acquired during the journey but they made no sign whether they understood him or not. Then he drew a sketch of a canoe in the sand, he went through some vague motions of carpentry, pointed from them to him, then made motions of giving something to them and scratched out the outlines of a gun and a hat and a few other recognizable articles of trade. One of the women giggled but no one gave any sign of comprehension, and he went away unsatisfied.

At their midday meal Mr Todd said, 'Mr Last, the Indians tell me that you have been trying to speak with them. It is easier that you say anything you wish through me. You realize, do you not, that they would do nothing without my authority. They regard themselves, quite rightly in many cases, as my children.'

'Well, as a matter of fact, I was asking them about a canoe.'

'So they gave me to understand . . . and now if you have finished your meal perhaps we might have another chapter. I am quite absorbed in the book.'

They finished *Dombey and Son*; nearly a year had passed since Tony had left England, and his gloomy foreboding of permanent exile became suddenly acute when, between the pages of *Martin Chuzzlewit*,[13] he found a document written in pencil in irregular characters.

Year 1919

I James Todd of Brazil do swear to Barnabas Washington of Georgetown that if he finish this book in fact Martin Chuzzlewit I will let him go away back as soon as finished.

There followed a heavy pencil *X* and after it: *Mr Todd made this mark signed Barnabas Washington.*

'Mr Todd,' said Tony, 'I must speak frankly. You saved my life, and when I get back to civilization I will reward you to the best of my ability. I will give you anything within reason. But at present you are keeping me here against my will. I demand to be released.'

'But, my friend, what is keeping you? You are under no restraint. Go when you like.'

'You know very well that I can't get away without your help.'

'In that case you must humour an old man. Read me another chapter.'

'Mr Todd, I swear by anything you like that when I get to Manáos I will find someone to take my place. I will pay a man to read to you all day.'

'But I have no need of another man. You read so well.'

'I have read for the last time.'

'I hope not,' said Mr Todd politely.

That evening at supper only one plate of dried meat and farine was brought in and Mr Todd ate alone. Tony lay without speaking, staring at the thatch.

Next day at noon a single plate was put before Mr Todd but with it lay his gun, cocked, on his knee, as he ate. Tony resumed the reading of *Martin Chuzzlewit* where it had been interrupted.

Weeks passed hopelessly. They read *Nicholas Nickleby*[14] and *Little Dorrit*[15] and *Oliver Twist*.[16] Then a stranger arrived in the savannah, a half-caste prospector, one of that lonely order of men who wander for a lifetime through the forests, tracing the little streams, sifting the gravel and, ounce by ounce, filling the little leather sack of gold dust, more often than not dying of exposure and starvation with five hundred dollars' worth of gold hung round their necks. Mr Todd was vexed at his arrival, gave him farine and *tasso*[17] and sent him on his journey within an hour of his arrival, but in that hour Tony had time to scribble his name on a slip of paper and put it into the man's hand.

From now on there was hope. The days followed their unvarying routine; coffee at sunrise, a morning of inaction while Mr Todd pottered about on the business of the farm, farine and *tasso* at noon, Dickens in the afternoon, farine and *tasso* and sometimes some fruit for supper, silence from sunset to dawn with the small wick glowing in the beef fat and the palm thatch overhead dimly discernible; but Tony lived in quiet confidence and expectation.

Sometime, this year or the next, the prospector would arrive at a Brazilian village with news of his discovery. The disasters of the Messinger expedition would not have passed unnoticed. Tony could imagine the headlines that must have appeared in the popular press; even now, probably, there were search parties working over the country he had crossed; any day English voices must sound over the savannah and a dozen friendly adventurers come crashing through the bush. Even as he was reading, while his lips mechanically followed the printed pages, his mind wandered away from his eager, crazy host opposite, and he began to narrate to himself incidents of his homecoming – the gradual re-encounters with civilization (he shaved and bought new clothes at Manáos, telegraphed for money, received wires of congratulation; he enjoyed the leisurely river journey to Belem, the big liner to Europe; savoured good claret and fresh meat and spring vegetables; he was shy at meeting Brenda and uncertain how to address her . . . 'Darling, you've been much longer than you said. I quite thought you were lost . . .')

And then Mr Todd interrupted. 'May I trouble you to read that passage again? It is one I particularly enjoy.'

The weeks passed; there was no sign of rescue but Tony endured the day for hope of what might happen on the morrow; he even felt a slight stirring of cordiality towards his jailer and was therefore quite willing to join him when, one evening after a long conference with an Indian neighbour, he proposed a celebration.

'It is one of the local feast days,' he explained. 'and they have been making *piwari*.[18] You may not like it but you should try some. We will go across to this man's home tonight.'

Accordingly after supper they joined a party of Indians that were assembled round the fire in one of the huts at the other side of the savannah. They were singing in an apathetic, monotonous manner and passing a large calabash of liquid from mouth to mouth. Separate bowls were brought for Tony and Mr Todd, and they were given hammocks to sit in.

'You must drink it all without lowering the cup. That is the etiquette.'

Tony gulped the dark liquid, trying not to taste it. But it was not unpleasant, hard and muddy on the palate like most of the beverages he had been offered in Brazil, but with a flavour of honey and brown bread. He leant back in the hammock feeling unusually contented. Perhaps at that very moment the search party was in camp a few hours' journey from them. Meanwhile he was warm and drowsy. The cadence of song rose and fell interminably, liturgically. Another calabash of *piwari* was offered him and he handed it back empty. He lay full length watching the play of shadows on the thatch as the Pie-wies began to dance. Then he shut his eyes and thought of England and Hetton and fell asleep.

He awoke, still in the Indian hut, with the impression that he had outslept his usual hour. By the position of the sun he knew it was late afternoon. No one else was about. He looked for his watch and found to his surprise that it was not on his wrist. He had left it in the house, he supposed, before coming to the party.

'I must have been tight last night,' he reflected. 'Treacherous drink that.' He had a headache and feared a recurrence of fever. He found when he set his feet to the ground that he stood with difficulty; his walk was unsteady and his mind confused as it had been during the first weeks of his convalescence. On the way across the savannah he was obliged to stop more than once, shutting his eyes and breathing deeply. When he reached the house he found Mr Todd sitting there.

'Ah, my friend, you are late for the reading this afternoon. There is scarcely another half hour of light. How do you feel?'

'Rotten. That drink doesn't seem to agree with me.'

'I will give you something to make you better. The forest has remedies for everything; to make you awake and to make you sleep.'

'You haven't seen my watch anywhere?'

'You have missed it?'

'Yes. I thought I was wearing it. I say, I've never slept so long.'

'Not since you were a baby. Do you know how long? Two days.'

'Nonsense. I can't have.'

'Yes, indeed. It is a long time. It is a pity because you missed our guests.'

'Guests?'

'Why, yes. I have been quite gay while you were asleep. Three men from outside. Englishmen. It is a pity you missed them. A pity for them, too, as they particularly wished to see you. But what could I do? You were so sound asleep. They had come all the way to find you, so – I thought you would not mind – as you could not greet them yourself, I gave them a little souvenir, your watch. They wanted something to take back to England where a reward is being offered for news of you. They were very pleased with it. And they took some photographs of the little cross I put up to commemorate your coming. They were pleased with that, too. They were very easily pleased. But I do not suppose they will visit us again, our life here is so retired . . . no pleasures except reading . . . I do not suppose we shall ever have visitors again . . . well, well, I will get you some medicine to make you feel better. Your head aches, does it not? . . . We will not have any Dickens today . . . but tomorrow, and the day after that, and the day after that. Let us read *Little Dorrit* again. There are passages in that book I can never hear without the temptation to weep.'

Chapter Seven

ENGLISH GOTHIC — III

A light breeze in the dewy orchards; brilliant, cool sunshine over meadows and copses; the elms were all in bud in the avenue; everything was early that year for it had been a mild winter.

High overhead among its gargoyles and crockets the clock chimed for the hour and solemnly struck fourteen. It was half past eight. The clock had been irregular lately. It was one of the things that Richard Last intended to see to, when death duties were paid and silver foxes began to show a profit.

Molly Last bowled up the drive on her two-stroke[1] motor cycle; there was bran mash on her breeches and in her hair. She had been feeding the Angora rabbits.

On the gravel in front of the house the new memorial stood, shrouded in a flag. Molly propped the motor cycle against the wall of the drawbridge and ran in to breakfast.

Life at Hetton was busier but simpler since Richard Last's succession. Ambrose remained but there were no longer any footmen; he and a boy and four women servants did the work of the house. Richard Last called them his 'skeleton staff.' When things were easier he would extend the household; meanwhile the dining hall and the library were added to the state apartments which were kept locked and shuttered; the family lived in the morning room, the smoking room and what had been Tony's study. Most of the kitchen quarters, too, were out of use; an up-to-date and economical range had been installed in one of the pantries.

The family all appeared downstairs by half past eight, except Agnes, who took longer to dress and was usually some minutes late; Teddy and Molly had been out for an hour, she among the rabbits, he to the silver foxes. Teddy was twenty-two and lived at home. Peter was still at Oxford.

They breakfasted together in the morning room. Mrs Last sat at one end of the table, her husband at the other; there was a constant traffic from hand to hand to and fro between them of cups, plates, honey jars and correspondence.

Mrs Last said, 'Molly, you have rabbit-feed on your head again.'

'Oh well, I shall have to tidy up anyway before the jamboree.'

Mr Last said, '*Jamboree?* Is nothing sacred to you children?'

Teddy said, 'Another casualty at the stinkeries. That little vixen we bought from the people at Oakhampton got her brush bitten off during the night. Must have got it through the wire into the next cage. Tricky birds, foxes.'

Agnes came next; she was a neat, circumspect child of twelve, with large, grave eyes behind her goggles. She kissed her father and mother and said, 'I'm sorry if I'm late.'

'*If* you're late . . .' said Mr Last tolerantly.

'How long will the show last?' asked Teddy. 'I've got to run over to Bayton and get some more rabbits for the foxes. Chivers says he's got about fifty waiting for me. We can't shoot enough here. Greedy little beggars.'

'It will be all over by half past eleven. Mr Tendril isn't going to preach a sermon. It's just as well really. He's got it into his head that cousin Tony died in Afghanistan.'

'There's a letter here from Cousin Brenda. She's very sorry but she can't get down for the dedication.'

'Oh.'

There was a general silence.

'She says that Jock has a three-line whip[2] for this afternoon.'

'Oh.'

'She could have come without him,' said Molly.

'She sends her love to us all and to Hetton.'

There was another pause.

'Well, I think it's a jolly good thing,' said Molly. '*She* couldn't show much widowly grief. It didn't take *her* long to get hitched up again.'

'*Molly!*'

'And you know you think the same.'

'I will not allow you to talk like that about Cousin Brenda, whatever we think. She had a perfect right to marry again and I hope she and Mr Grant-Menzies are very happy.'

'She was always jolly decent to us when she used to live here,' said Agnes.

'Well, I should hope so,' said Teddy. 'After all it's *our* place.'

The day was still fine at eleven o'clock, though the wind had got up, fluttering the papers on which the order of the service was printed and once threatening to unveil the memorial prematurely. Several relatives were present, Lady St Cloud, Aunt Frances, and the family of impoverished Lasts who had not profited by Tony's disappearance. All the household and estate servants were there, several tenants and most of the village; there were also a dozen or so neighbours, among them Colonel Inch – Richard Last and Teddy had hunted regularly that season with the Pigstanton. Mr Tendril conducted the brief service in resonant tones that were clearly audible above the blustering wind. When he pulled the cord the flag fell away from the memorial without mishap.

It was a plain monolith of local stone, inscribed:

ANTHONY LAST OF HETTON
EXPLORER
BORN AT HETTON, 1902
DIED IN BRAZIL, 1934

When the local visitors had left and the relatives had gone into the house to be shown the new labour-saving arrangements, Richard Last and Lady St Cloud remained for a short time on the gravel.

'I'm glad we put that up,' he said. 'You know, I should never have thought of it, if it had not been for a Mrs Beaver. She wrote to me as soon as the news of Tony's death was published. I didn't know her at the time. Of course we knew very few of Tony's friends.'

'It was her suggestion?'

'Yes, she said that as one of Tony's closest friends she knew he would wish to have some monument at Hetton. She was most considerate – even offering to arrange with the contractors for it. Her own plans were more ambitious. She proposed that we should have the Chapel redecorated as a chantry.[3] But I think this is what he would have preferred. The stone comes from one of our own quarries and was cut by the estate workmen.'

'Yes, I think he would have preferred this,' said Lady St Cloud.

Teddy had chosen Galahad for his bedroom. He disengaged himself from the family and hurried up to change out of his dark clothes. Within ten minutes he was in his car driving to Chivers' farm. Before luncheon he was back with the rabbits. They were skinned and tied round the feet into bundles of four.

'Coming to the stinkeries?'[4] he asked Agnes.

'No, I'm looking after cousin Frances. She got rather on mother's nerves through crabbing[5] the new boiler.'

The silver-fox farm was behind the stables; a long double row of wire cages; they had wire floors covered with earth and cinders to prevent the animals digging their way out. They lived in pairs; some were moderately tame but it was unwise to rely upon them. Teddy and Ben Hacket – who helped with them – had been badly bitten more than once that winter.

They ran up to the doors when they saw Teddy come with the rabbits. The vixen who had lost her brush seemed little the worse for her accident.

Teddy surveyed his charges with pride and affection. It was by means of them that he hoped one day to restore Hetton to the glory that it had enjoyed in the days of his cousin Tony.

NOTES

The majority of the factual notes are drawn, with the author's permission, from Paul A. Doyle's *A Reader's Companion to the Novels and Short Stories of Evelyn Waugh* (Pilgrim Books, 1988). Additional annotations were provided by Edmund A. Hennessy. Iain Gale's *Waugh's World: A Guide to the Novels of Evelyn Waugh* (Sidgwick and Jackson, 1990) lists places and characters but gives no explanation outside the context of the novels.

A Handful of Dust: for the source of the title and the epigraph, see the Introduction and note 1

Contents: chapter one, 'Du Côté de Chez Beaver': French for 'In the Direction of Beaver's Place'; that is, where Beaver lives. The reference is to Marcel Proust's title 'Du Côté de Chez Swann.' In chapter six the same words are used, with the substitution of 'Todd' for 'Beaver'. In the earliest editions, 'À Côté' appears in chapter one and six instead of 'Du Côté'. This may help to explain why, in 1925, Waugh did not get a position as secretary to C. K. Scott Moncrieff, who was translating Proust into English. Chapter five, 'Hard Cheese': tough luck; bad fortune.

[frontispiece]: in a letter of September 1934, to Tom Dreiberg, Waugh said that he had ' "instructed the architect to design the worst possible 1860 and I think he has done well".'

Chapter One: Du côté de chez Beaver

1. *Sussex Gardens*: just south of Paddington Station. Later, when Beaver says that Brenda's flat in Belgravia is 'miles out of the way', he is talking about the width of Hyde Park.

2. *jockeys*: bottles of scent for men.

3. *the slump*: the economic depression of the 1930s.

4. *Chasm*: Viola, Lady Chasm, appears in *Vile Bodies* as the mother of Agatha Runcible and as an off-stage character in 'Period Piece', *Scoop* and *Brideshead Revisited*. Because of the presence of Polly, Lady Cockpurse, the sexual pun on Lady Chasm's name is more obvious in *A Handful of Dust* than in her other appearances.

5. *Bond Street*: in the fashionable area of West Central London.

6. *demobilized*: discharged from military service.

7. *New Yorker*: fashionable and literate American weekly magazine, filled with advertisements for luxury goods.

8. *paper games*: games played with pencil and paper, such as Consequences, or listing as many items beginning with the same letter in a category, such as rivers or birds, the longest list winning.

9. *Hill Street*: in Mayfair, on the other side of Berkeley Square from Bond Street.

Chapter Two: English Gothic

1. *Abbey*: a monastery or convent under the rule of an abbot or abbess. In England, religious foundations of this type were dissolved in 1536–9 by Henry VIII and the property given to his secular supporters.

2. *Mr Pecksniff*: the famous hypocrite who appears in Charles Dickens's novel *Martin Chuzzlewit* (1843–4). Pecksniff was an architect and a surveyor.

3. *death duties*: inheritance taxes. The supposed death of Tony, coming roughly five years after that of his father, would impose a heavy burden of taxation on the estate.

4. *groined*: a groin, in architecture, is the point at which two vaults meet.

5. *diapers*: repeated geometric figures.

6. *lancet windows*: high, narrow windows, pointed at the top.

7. *Malory*: Sir Thomas Malory (d. 1471), author of the great Arthurian saga *Le Morte d'Arthur* (*c*. 1469–70), popularized in Victorian times in Alfred, Lord Tennyson's *Idylls of the King* (1859–85). The names that follow are those of characters in the Arthurian legend. *Yseult*: Better known as Iseult or Isolde, the wife of King Mark of Cornwall. As a result of a magic potion she and Tristram (Tristan) fall in love, and their relationship proves tragic. *Elaine*: although there are several women with this name in the Arthurian sagas, the most prominent is the daughter of King Pelles. In one version she is the mother of Galahad by Lancelot. The room here was probably named after the Elaine in Tennyson's poem. *Mordred*: both the son and the nephew of King Arthur. He and Arthur die in combat with each other. *Merlin*: the magician and seer of Arthurian legend. *Gawaine*: nephew of King Arthur and one of his knights. *Bedivere*: one of King Arthur's most devoted knights. He transports King Arthur's body to the three Queens on the barge and watches as the Avalon-bound vessel slowly disappears. *Lancelot*: the most talented warrior among King Arthur's knights. He commits adultery with Arthur's wife, Guinevere. *Perceval*: one of the Arthurian knights who seeks the Holy Grail. In some versions of the saga he manages to gain sight of it. *Tristram*: see Yseult, above. *Galahad*: the most honourable of King Arthur's knights, he finds the Holy Grail. The least comfortable room at Hetton is, of course, named ironically. *Morgan le Fay*: King Arthur's fairy sister, one of the principal mischief-makers in the Arthurian romances. *Guinevere*: the adulterous wife of King Arthur, a particularly appropriate name for Brenda Last's bedroom, though Beaver is no Lancelot.

8. *Chums*: an adventure magazine for boys, published in England.

9. *Bevis*: a novel (1882) by Richard Jefferies (1848–87).

10. *The Young Visiters*: a novel (1919) by Daisy Ashford, supposedly written when

she was nine years old but socially and, though less obviously, sexually quite sophisticated. Waugh encountered ant-eaten copies of this book and *Practical Joinery* – very close to Tony's *Woodwork at Home* – at the Hart ranch in British Guiana. See *Diaries*, 22 January 1933.

11. *[A] Farewell to Arms*: Ernest Hemingway's novel (1929) about a doomed love affair on the Italian front in the First World War.

12. *nereid*: a sea nymph. See Mrs Beaver's reference to Brenda's 'very fair, underwater look' [serial: 'fair, half-drowned look'].

13. *Life-Guard*: a member of one of the regiments in the Household Cavalry.

14. *Christabelle*: perhaps a suitable name for a hound because, in Samuel Taylor Coleridge's poem 'Christabel' (1816), 'Sir Leoline, the Baron rich, / Hath a toothless mastiff bitch'.

15. *Jimmy-o-goblins*: slang for sovereigns, gold coins worth two pounds, eighteen shillings in the former system of English coinage.

16. *Aintree*: site of the racetrack where the Grand National steeplechase is run each year.

17. *protein and starch*: Tony later tells Ambrose that he will have two courses at meals when he is alone. Eating Mr Todd's farine and tasso, he mixes protein and starch.

18. *Badders*: bad news.

19. *Great Western*: a railway that departed from Paddington Station for the West and the North, including Warwickshire, probably the location of Hetton Abbey.

20. *grog tray*: a tray of alcoholic beverages, mixes, glasses, and so on.

21. *A.B.C.*: railway timetable.

22. *Wipers*: anglicization of Ypres, the name of a town in Belgium, the scene of several especially destructive battles in the First World War.

23. *'Enter not into judgment with Thy servant, O Lord'*: Psalm 143:2, which continues with a petition to be delivered from enemies.

24. *half-crown*: two shillings and sixpence under the old system of English coinage.

25. *Queen Empress*: Queen Victoria, who reigned from 1837 to 1901 and was proclaimed Empress of India in 1876. The gardener's wife thinks that the Reverend Tendril refers to the queen then on the throne.

26. *uttermost parts of the earth*: possible allusion to Joseph Conrad's *Heart of Darkness*, which near the beginning and at the end describes a 'waterway leading to the uttermost ends of the earth'.

27. *Tendril*: literally, the shoot of a plant by which it supports itself on another structure. Here the implications of parasitism seem intentional.

28. *Jellalabad*: a reference to the siege of Jellalabad, in which the British defeated the army of Akbar Khan during the first Afghan War (1842). In many editions the word is misspelled 'Jalalabad'.

29. *Coldstream Guards*: one of the guards divisions of the Infantry.

30. *Sidmouth, Mentone, Winchester, Leicester, Bournemouth*: places no more suitable than Hetton for the Reverend Tendril's sermon.

31. *cat*: vomit.

32. *lych gate*: in a cemetery, the roofed structure under which the corpse rests at the beginning of the funeral ceremony.

33. *oriel*: large bay window.

34. *gules*: in heraldry, red.

35. *azure*: in heraldry, blue.

36. *yashmak*: a veil, covering the lower part of the face but not the eyes, worn in public by women who observe Muslim custom.

37. *bitching*: flirting with, acting seductively.

38. *battlements*: walls atop a fortification with open spaces through which the defenders can use weapons or projectiles.

39. *ormolu*: gilded metal, usually brass or bronze.

40. *cloisonné*: enamelwork in which thin metal bands are used to separate different colours.

41. *Vanbrugh*: Sir John Vanbrugh (1664–1726), English dramatist and architect. His most famous play was *The Relapse* (1697). Among the buildings he designed were Blenheim Palace and Castle Howard (the mansion representing Brideshead Castle in the television production of *Brideshead Revisited*). American editions spell the name 'Vanburgh'.

42. *'Analogies'*: a game in which the players write down descriptions that relate to particular set categories, e.g. listing a particular jewel, flower, animal, food, scent, that they associate with the person being analysed. The game is described in Waugh's biography of *Monsignor Ronald Knox*, pp. 223–4, and is played in Waugh's first professionally published story, 'The Balance', in *Georgian Stories, 1926*, ed. Alec Waugh (Chapman and Hall, 1926), pp. 253–91.

43. *bone-setting*: adjustment of the spine and other joints by an osteopath.

44. *prospective Conservative candidate for a South London constituency of strong Labour sympathies*: that is, hopeless for a Conservative, as too, apparently, is the Clydeside district. Allan's dim prospects help to establish Jock Grant-Menzies as the most successful politician in the novel.

45. *Portman Square*: north-east of Hyde Park.

46. *Paddingon Station*: the terminus for the Great Western Railway, the line for Hetton.

47. *Djinn*: according to Waugh's letter of early 1934 to Lady Mary Lygon, Marjorie's Pekinese was based on Lulu, Phillis de Janzé's dog.

48. *Watt's Physical Energy*: an equestrian statue entitled *Physical Energy*, in London's Kensington Gardens, sculptured by George Watts (1817–1904).

49. *Cruttwell*: this is one of a number of fairly discreditable characters by this name, chosen because Waugh disliked his Oxford history tutor, C. R. M. F. Cruttwell. See *A Little Learning*.

50. *Morecambe Bay*: an inlet of the Irish Sea in Lancashire.

51. *Albemarle Street*: just off Old Bond Street and Piccadilly.

52. *Belgravia*: in the vicinity of Belgrave Square, south of Hyde Park.

53. *slap-up*: elegant, high-class.

54. *Barnardo case*: down and out. Dr Thomas J. Barnardo (1845–1905) ran homes

for destitute children. He was the father of Syrie Barnardo, who later married W. Somerset Maugham and became a well-known interior decorator. Some scholars regard her as the person on whom the character of Mrs Beaver was based. See Donald Greene, *Evelyn Waugh Newsletter*, 21, 1 (Spring 1987), 1–2.

55. *Camberwell*: south of the Thames, hopelessly unfashionable, and far from any other London setting in the novel.

56. *made love*: not, as in modern usage, having sexual intercourse; here, and until the end of the 1930s, used of somewhat more restrained physical demonstrations of affection or sexual desire.

57. *Marble Arch*: at the corner of Oxford Street and Park Lane, slightly south-west of Marjorie's house in Portman Square.

58. *walk out*: casual romantic affair.

59. *Conservative Central Office*: the party's governing body, thus in control of Allan's prospects as a candidate for Parliament.

60. *sock*: treat.

61. *croûte*: literally, French for 'crust'.

62. *crackers*: party favours enclosed in paper holders that pop when pulled.

63. *charades*: parlour game in which one person mimes a well-known word or phrase and the audience tries to guess a syllable or a word at a time.

64. *standing on the Clydeside*: the implication is that this Scottish constituency is as solidly Labour as the one for which Allan is standing in south London.

Chapter Three: Hard Cheese on Tony

1. *Chucked*: cancelled an engagement at the last minute or failed to turn up at the appointed place and time.

2. *I've been drinking a whole lot*: Waugh told Broder Cartensen that he had 'a deep admiration for Mr Hemingway's books and was certainly influenced by *The Sun Also Rises (Fiesta)* in writing the dialogue of *Vile Bodies*' (*Archiv für Studium der Neueren Sprachen*, vol. 190, February 1954, p. 203). This scene demonstrates that Hemingway's influence persisted.

3. *Pig Scheme*: see Jock's question in Parliament, the effect of which is to suggest a reduction in the amount of fat in bacon. The question is addressed to the wrong minister and is irrelevant to the issue on the floor.

4. *Regent Street*: runs between Oxford Street and Piccadilly. In the American edition, the text reads Shaftesbury Avenue, and the taxi turns down Wardour Street and into Sink Street. No Sink Street is listed in any London street guide, but Gerrard Street, the site of the club on which the Old Hundredth is based, runs east from Wardour Street, too close for the comfort of libel lawyers.

5. *Golden Square*: east of Regent Street and, from a libel lawyer's point of view, safely west of Gerrard Street.

6. *Home Secretaries*: the Home Secretary is among other things in charge of the Metropolitan Police District.

7. *100 Sink Street*: the location of an identical night club in *Brideshead Revisited*.

American editions use the address '64 Sink Street'. Based on the night club at 43 Gerrard Street. See Alec Waugh, *The Fatal Gift*, (New York, Farrar, Straus and Giroux, 1973), p. 16.

8. *Sloane number*: a former London telephone exchange.

9. *Sandhurst*: site of the Royal Military College.

10. *county council*: elected body governing local affairs at county level. Tony Last would regard membership as obligatory for a large landowner.

11. *dado*: 'the lower part of the wall of a room when visually distinct from the upper part' (*OED*).

12. *backgammon*: board game for two people.

13. *Sedobrol*: the trademark of a sedative drink. The trademark was registered in 1913 by John Henry Land of Coalville, Leicestershire.

14. *Sybil*: perhaps an allusion to the Cumean sybil referred to in the epigraph to *The Waste Land*.

15. *bimetallism*: the theory that a country's monetary system should be based on the circulation of both gold and silver, coined by the country's mint and circulating at a fixed ratio. This theory is opposed to the single standard based on gold.

16. *Teddy*: Jenny's misnaming Tony can be thought of as prophetic, since Teddy Last is in line to inherit Hetton at the end of the novel.

17. *Moulay*: variant of 'mullah', or lord; usually applied to an Islamic religious leader, but also added to the names of noblemen in the Arabic world.

18. *battle of Marston Moor*: where Cromwell defeated the Loyalists in 1644.

19. *lawner*: a lawn or garden party; here, refreshments before the hunt served outside rather than inside the house.

20. *oxer*: rail.

21. *Cottesmore country*: in Leicestershire, a popular fox-hunting region.

22. *Biarritz*: French resort town near the Spanish border.

23. *rat-catcher*: rather casual hunting attire consisting of knickerbocker trousers and a Norfolk jacket – loose-fitting, single-breasted and box-pleated.

24. *nobody's fault*: these words were the original title of Charles Dickens's novel *Little Dorrit*, which figures in the final Brazilian scene in chapter six. See Brooke Allen, 'The Man Who Didn't Like Dickens', *Dickens Quarterly*, 4 (December 1991), 155–62 on this and other points about Waugh's use of Dickens. See also Jerome Meckier, 'Why the Man Who Liked Dickens Read Dickens Instead of Conrad: Waugh's *A Handful of Dust* ', *Novel*, 13 (Winter 1980), 171–87. One reason is that Waugh did not think very highly of Conrad. See *Catalogue*, E74.

25. *crockets*: architectural ornaments attached to gables or spires.

26. *finials*: ornamental features at the top of gables or pinnacles.

27. *Aylesbury or Tring*: towns north-north-west of London. If Jock is half-way to London, Hetton must be located near Fenny Compton in Warwickshire.

28. *bezique*: game played with a deck of sixty-four cards.

29. *piquet*: game played with a deck of thirty-two cards.

30. *Bokhara*: also spelled Bukhara. A city in the Uzbek Republic of the former Soviet Union.

31. *Yokohama*: Japanese port city on Tokyo Bay.

32. *Port Said*: city on the Mediterranean end of the Suez Canal. Waugh describes his visit in *Labels*.

33. *Bombay*: island and city in west India.

34. *Lalique*: René Lalique (1860–1945), French designer of art nouveau jewellery and glass. In American editions, spelled 'Lallique'.

35. *Senegal*: West African country. At the time in which the novel is set, a territory of French West Africa.

36. *golliwog*: a doll dressed to represent a small black man.

37. *fumed oak*: wood darkened by ammonia fumes. Presumably rather garish.

38. *Tudor*: late sixteenth century in style.

39. *pencil case*: propelling pencil.

40. *Empire chair*: made in, or in the style of, early nineteenth-century France, the Napoleonic empire.

41. *thank God*: words spoken by Rachel, Lady Castlewood, of one Harry, misunderstood by a listener to be another character of the same name, in William Makepeace Thackeray's novel *Henry Esmond*. See Donald Greene, *Evelyn Waugh Newsletter*, vol. 21, no. 1 (Spring 1987), p. 2.

42. *Princes Risborough*: town south of Aylesbury and north-west of London. In American editions, Great Missenden. In view of the lawyer's later remark about the heirs to Hetton, 'Great Missenden' was probably an inadvertent authorial error.

43. *stained glass windows*: an echo of the scene in which Brenda descends to meet John Beaver in chapter one.

Chapter Four: English Gothic – II

1. *gêne*: uneasiness, difficulty.

2. *King's Proctor*: a court official who watched over divorce cases to prevent unlawful collusion between the parties. At the time in which this novel was set, adultery was the only grounds for divorce in England; thus fake adulteries were sometimes staged so that a couple could be divorced. About 1938 desertion and insanity were added as acceptable legal reasons for the termination of marriage.

3. *Finchley*: in north-west London. In Edwardian times, often considered the residence of kept women.

4. *fairy cycle*: 'a small-wheeled low bicycle for children' (*OED*).

5. *Dieppe*: Atlantic port city in northern France.

6. *put the kybosh on it*: put an end to it.

7. *ostlers*: people who tend to horses.

8. *atavistic*: reverting to a previous, usually primitive, type of physical structure or, as here, behaviour.

9. *amphoras*: clay pots with handles, used in ancient times for storing wine and other liquids.

10. *tabulae execrationum*: Latin for ancient 'tablets of curses'.

11. *circus factions*: in the Roman Empire, the circus was an area used for games, chariot races and similar events. Factions were groups who supported various contestants or teams, analogous to modern football fans.

Chapter Five: In Search of a City

1. *Demerara*: a river basin in British Guiana, now Guyana, at the mouth of which Georgetown, the capital, lies.

2. *lascar*: a sailor from the East Indies.

3. *fiddles*: devices, usually of cord or wood, to keep dishes on the table at sea.

4. *Tours*: a city in France.

5. *Vouvray*: a wine of the Loire Valley, north of Tours.

6. *tombola*: a type of bingo.

7. *Balliol*: a college of Oxford University.

8. *Le Touquet*: French resort town on the English channel.

9. *Agadir*: seaport city in south-western Morocco.

10. *Atlas caids*: Muslim chiefs among the Berber tribes in northern Africa.

11. *capitulations*: articles of agreement in a treaty.

12. *Mogador*: a city on the south-western coast of Morocco; now called Essaouira.

13. *R. G. S.*: Royal Geographical Society.

14. *scarabs*: the sacred dung-beetle of ancient Egypt, symbol of resurrection.

15. *the City*: Waugh may have conceived the idea for this lost city from the account of Boa Vista and Manáos given him by Mr Bain. See *Ninety-Two Days*, p. 68.

16. *Matto Grosso*: a town and state in north-western Brazil; now spelled Mato Grosso. Also the name of a plateau in this region.

17. *Orinoco*: river flowing through Venezuela from the Brazilian border to the Caribbean.

18. *Uraricuera*: river in northern Brazil; also spelled Uraricoeia. It joins the Takutu River to form the Rio Branco.

19. *Pie-wie*: apparently a corruption, for comic effect, of 'Wie-wie', a tribe Waugh heard of but did not visit during his trip to British Guiana because they 'still live in absolute seclusion'. See *Ninety-Two Days*, p. 28.

20. *Ciudad Bolivar*: A city on the Orinoco River in central Venezuela.

21. *Para*: a state in northern Brazil; also the name given to the eastern mouth of the Amazon River.

22. *Courantyne*: river forming the boundary between British Guiana (Guyana) and Dutch Guiana (Surinam).

23. *Takutu*: a river in British Guiana and Brazil; it unites with the Uraricuera River to form the Rio Branco.

24. *Incas*: the dominant tribe and culture in what is now Peru before the Spanish invasion. After Waugh had written 'The Man Who Liked Dickens' but before he began to work on the novel, he noted in *Ninety-Two Days* (p. 199) that 'The Guiana

Indians so far as is known, never participated at all, or had any contact, with the high civilization of the Indians in medieval Peru.'

25. *Arekuna*: tribe of South American Indians.

26. *Patamonas*: tribe of Indians. Waugh describes meeting two of its members in *Ninety-Two Days*, pp. 102–3.

27. *Warau*: tribe of South American Indians.

28. *Yarmouth Castle*: a ship of the Union Castle Line, a British shipping company. All of its ships had names ending in 'Castle'.

29. *Thérèse de Vitré*: some commentators believe that her first name is taken from that of Teresa Jungman, who refused Waugh's offer of marriage in 1934. Her last name is taken from the masculine form of the French word for 'glazed' or 'made of glass'. This may indicate her unfitness, in a way very different from Tony's, to live in the modern world.

30. *Madame de Supplice*: from the French word meaning 'corporal punishment'. Appropriate to the character of the mistress of the school.

31. *Byzantium*: Istanbul.

32. *boat deck*: the deck from which lifeboats hang.

33. *fête*: birthday or feast of one's patron saint.

34. *Port of Spain*: the capital and principal city of Trinidad.

35. *creoles*: in *Ninety-Two Days*, pp. 25–6, Waugh defines creoles as all people, 'black, coloured, or white, born in the West Indies, and also of animals bred there.'

36. *Georgetown*: capital and chief seaport of British Guiana.

37. *balata station*: a timber plantation on which balata trees are grown. The gum of these trees is used as a substitute for gutta-percha. In *Ninety-Two Days*, p. 62n., Waugh wrote that 'The Indians bleed it from trees, and exchange it with representatives of a local company for cloth, hardware, etc.'

38. *cabouri fly*: Waugh writes in *Ninety-Two Days*, p. 101, that these insects are 'so small that they easily penetrate any ordinary mosquito curtain ... You cannot feel their bite until they have finished sucking; then they leave a little black spot behind them and a circle of burning flesh.'

39. *bêtes rouges*: in *Ninety-Two Days*, p. 101, Waugh describes the insect as 'a minute red creature which brushes off the leaves of the bush onto one'sclothes and finds its way below one's skin where it causes unendurable itching.'

40. *djiggas*. In *Ninety-Two Days*, pp. 213–14, Waugh describes them as 'small insects which ... work their way through one's boots to the soles of one's feet where they drill holes and lay their eggs, preferably under the toenails or any hard piece of skin ... if allowed to remain, [the eggs] hatch out into maggots in the foot and serious poisoning sets in.' He goes on to describe the process of removing them.

41. *marabunta*: a Guyanan wasp. Waugh's use of the term is cited in the *OED*.

42. *five hours' difference*: the fact behind the echoed phrase, 'Time is different'.

43. *Anchorage House*: the London house of Lady (and presumably the never-mentioned Lord) Anchorage. Lady Anchorage appears as a minor character, representing the highest social levels, in a number of Waugh's stories and novels up through to *Brideshead Revisited*.

NOTES TO CHAPTER 5

44. *charabancs*: sightseeing buses.

45. *Cook's offices*: offices of Thomas Cook and Son, the travel agency.

46. *bully beef*: corned beef.

47. *cassiri*: in *Ninety-Two Days*, pp. 190–91, Waugh says that 'It is made from sweet cassava roots, chewed up by the elder members of the community and spat into a bowl. The saliva starts fermentation, and the result is a thick, pinkish liquor of mildly intoxicating property.'

48. *Wapishiana*: one of the tribes of Indians Waugh encountered in British Guiana.

49. *Macushi*: tribe Waugh encountered in British Guiana. See *Ninety-Two Days*, pp. 82, 182 ff.

50. *Roll up the map – you will not need it again for how many years, said William Pitt*: an allusion to a statement made by Prime Minister William Pitt (1759–1806) about a map of Europe upon hearing of Napoleon's victory in the Battle of Austerlitz (1805). The actual quotation was, 'Roll up that map; it will not be wanted these ten years'.

51. *Berber*: Arabic peoples and culture of Africa, west of Tripoli.

52. *Nelson*: Admiral (and Viscount) Horatio Nelson (1758–1805), hero of the battle of Trafalgar, at which he was killed. In American editions, Brenda reads a biography of Louis Thiers (1797–1877), a French political figure and historian. Waugh may have changed Thiers to Nelson in order to underline the contrast between John Beaver and a more famous and more enterprising adulterer.

53. *aneroid*: barometer.

54. *Waurupang*: river, identifiable only by context.

55. *farine*: in *Ninety-Two Days*, pp. 64–5, Waugh defines it as 'a vegetable product made from cassava root ... It is like coarse sawdust in appearance; a granulated, tapioca-coloured substance of intense hardness and a faint taste of brown paper.'

56. *armadillo*: armour-plated mammal of the Americas.

57. *iguana*: large lizard.

58. *'trade'*: see Waugh's diary for 4 March 1933, where he learned something about the system of barter.

59. *cassava*: staple crop in South America. See 'farine' and 'cassiri' above.

60. *mice*: based on the trade goods imported by Mr Winter, whom Waugh met in British Guiana. See *Ninety-Two Days*, p. 230.

61. *the water closed over his bald head*: see *The Waste Land*, 'Fear death by water' (line 55).

62. *Lincoln's Inn*: site of many law offices, near the Courts of Justice.

63. *Lake of Geneva*: also called Lac Leman by the French – beside the waters of which one of the speakers in *The Waste Land* 'sat down and wept' (line 182). Eliot wrote the poem while in Lausanne, which is on the lake.

64. *Baltic*: sea dividing Scandinavia from Denmark, Germany and Poland.

65. *Green Line buses/rats*: a conflation, in Tony's delirium, of the indirect causes of his abandonment in England and in Brazil.

66. *ramparts*: broad embankment used in fortification.

67. *heraldic*: the designs of armorial insignia.

68. *cupolas*: structure, usually rounded, built on top of a roof.

69. *alabaster*: white gypsum which can be carved into decorative shapes.

Chapter Six: Du côté de chez Todd

1. *Todd*: the pun on the German *Tod*, or death, is obvious, but an additional allusion to Beatrix Potter's *The Tale of Mr Tod* seems probable. Tod, a fox, lives in 'something between a prison, a cave and a tumbledown pigsty'. If so, there are obvious connections between death and foxes, most notably in the death of John Andrew and in the foxes, 'Tricky birds, foxes', raised by Tony's successors. See Eric Korn, 'Remainders', *Times Literary Supplement* (July 23–8 1988), p. 803.

2. *Dutch Guiana*: now Surinam, it lies on the eastern border of British Guiana.

3. *Manáos*: Brazilian city in the Amazon basin. In *Ninety-Two Days*, p. 68, the city is described by Waugh as incomparably splendid.

4. *Moor*: technically, a person from Morocco. At the time of the novel, commonly used by English whites for any black person. There may be a veiled reference to Shakespeare's *Othello the Moor of Venice*.

5. *walking round in a circle*: see *The Waste Land*, 'I see crowds of people, walking round in a ring,' (line 56).

6. *Dickens*: Charles Dickens (1812–70). Chapman and Hall publishing company, which Waugh's father, Arthur Waugh, directed for years, owned the Dickens copyrights; Arthur Waugh edited the Nonesuch Edition of Dickens; he also read Dickens and other writers aloud to his family.

7. *Bleak House*: published 1852–3.

8. *Lord Chancellor's Court*: a major setting and thematic centre of Dickens's point about legal delay and obscurantism in *Bleak House*.

9. *'Tom-all-alone's'*: the hideous London slum in *Bleak House*.

10. *Dedlock*: Sir Leicester Dedlock, the excessively proud aristocrat and owner of a large estate in *Bleak House* whose wife has, in the Victorian sense of the term, 'a past'. Unlike Brenda, she comes to a painful end.

11. *Mrs Jellyby*: in *Bleak House*, she neglects her family, devoting her attention to a plan to colonize a section of Africa. The resemblance to Brenda is slight but unmistakable.

12. *Dombey and Son*: Waugh reread this novel while in British Guiana. See his diary for 27 February 1933.

13. *Martin Chuzzlewit*: Waugh reread this novel in British Guiana. See his diary for 4 and 29 March 1933. In this novel, the hero makes a trip to North America, but his adventures end happily.

14. *Nicholas Nickleby*: Waugh rediscovered the pleasure of reading while in British Guiana. He borrowed a copy of this novel from Father Mather 'and read it with avid relish during the ensuing journey, bit by bit while the light lasted, grudging the night every hour of her splendour and the day its toil, which kept me from this new and exciting hobby.' *Ninety-Two Days*, p. 182.

15. *Little Dorrit*: the central theme of this novel is imprisonment, both literal and metaphorical.

16. *Oliver Twist*: Oliver, the hero, is fed very bad food in very small portions.

17. *tasso*: dried beef. In *Ninety-Two Days*, pp. 65–6, Waugh describes it as 'the incarnation of every joke ever made about meat at schools or messes or charitable institutions. It would certainly cause a mutiny in any English prison.' To prepare, it 'is sliced into thin slabs, rolled in salt and hung up to dry. A few days of sun and hot savannah wind reduce it to a black, leathery condition in which it will remain uncorrupt indefinitely. Even the normally omnivorous ants will not touch it.'

18. *piwari*: in *Ninety-Two Days*, p. 190, Waugh notes that piwari is a drink similar to cassiri.

Chapter Seven: English Gothic – III

1. *two-stroke*: a two-cycle piston engine which runs on a mixture of petrol and oil; it makes a sound distinctively different from a four-stroke cycle engine.

2. *three-line whip*: an order given by the party leaders to members of Parliament notifying them how they must vote on an issue. To emphasize its importance, the order is underlined three times. Members who do not follow the order or do not vote at all are regarded as disloyal to their party.

3. *chantry*: a chapel in which masses are sung for a dead person's soul. Ironically, Mrs Beaver proposes a structure which would return at least part of Hetton to its original purpose as a religious foundation.

4. *stinkeries*: slang for the cages in which silver foxes were kept on breeding farms. Silver-fox farms were especially popular in England between the First World War and the Second World War.

5. *crabbing*: complaining about.

APPENDIX I
Alternative Ending

Preface

This book found favour with the critics who often date my decline from it. It had confused origins. In January 1933 I was travelling alone in the borderlands of British Guiana and Brazil and during the journey spent a night at the little Indian settlement dominated by a mulatto evangelist whose eccentricities I described in *Ninety-Two Days*. A few weeks later I came to an impasse at the Brazilian village of Boa Vista and spent the tedious days of waiting for a non-existent boat in writing a short story which was later published under the title 'The Man Who Liked Dickens'. That story was substantially the chapter of this book named 'Du Côté de Chez Todd'.

A year passed. I was wintering at Fez in Morocco and there I wrote this novel, on the theme of the betrayed romantic, affording an explanation of my hero's presence in the South American bush.

An American magazine wished to serialize it (under the title of their choosing, 'A Flat in London') but could not do so while it incorporated 'The Man Who Liked Dickens'. I accordingly provided the alternative ending which is here included as a curiosity.

E. W.
Combe Florey 1963

One

The liner came into harbour at Southampton, late in the afternoon.

They had left the sun three days behind them; after the Azores there had been a high sea running; in the Channel a white mist. Tony had been awake all night, disturbed by the fog signals and the uncertainty of home-coming.

They berthed alongside the quay. Tony leant on the rail looking for his chauffeur. He had cabled to Hetton that he was to be met and would drive straight home. He wanted to see the new bathrooms. Half the summer workmen had been at Hetton. There would be several changes to greet him.

It had been an uneventful excursion. Not for Tony were the ardours of serious travel, desert or jungle, mountain or pampas; he had no inclination to kill big game or survey unmapped tributaries. He had left England because, in the circumstances, it seemed the correct procedure, a convention hallowed in fiction and history by generations of disillusioned husbands. He had put himself in the hands of a travel agency and for lazy months had pottered from island to island in the West Indies, lunching at Government Houses, drinking swizzles on club verandahs, achieving an easy popularity at Captains' tables; he had played deck quoits and ping-pong, had danced on deck and driven with new acquaintances on well-laid roads amid tropical vegetation. Now he was home again. He had thought less and less of Brenda during the passing weeks.

Presently he identified his chauffeur among the sparse population of the quay. The man came on board and took charge of the luggage. The car was waiting on the other side of the customs sheds.

The chauffeur said, 'Shall I have the big trunk sent on by train?'

'There's plenty of room for it behind the car, isn't there?'

'Well, hardly, sir. Her ladyship has a lot of luggage with her.'

'Her ladyship?'

'Yes, sir. Her ladyship is waiting in the car. She telegraphed that I was to pick her up at the hotel.'

'I see. And she has a lot of luggage?'

'Yes, sir, an uncommon lot.'

'Well . . . perhaps you *had* better send the trunks by train.'

'Very good, sir.'

So Tony went out to the car alone, while his chauffeur was seeing to the trunks.

Brenda was in the back, shrunk into the corner. She had taken off her hat – a very small knitted hat, clipped with a brooch he had given her some years ago – and was holding it in her lap. There was deep twilight inside the car. She looked up without moving her head.

'Darling,' she said, 'your boat was *very* late.'

'Yes, we had fog in the channel.'

'I got here last night. The people in the office said you'd be in early this morning.'

'Yes, we *are* late.'

'You can never tell with ships, can you?' said Brenda.

There was a pause. Then she said, 'Aren't you going to come in?'

'There's a fuss about the luggage.'

'Blake will see to that.'

'He's sending it by train.'

'Yes, I thought he would have to. I'm sorry I brought so much . . . You see, I brought everything. I've turned against that flat . . . It never quite lost the smell. I thought it was just newness, but it got worse. You know – *radiator smell*. So what with one thing and another I thought, how about giving it up.'

Then the chauffeur came back. He had settled everything about the luggage.

'Well, we'd better start right away.'

'Very good, sir.'

Tony got in beside Brenda, and the chauffeur shut the door on them. They ran through the streets of Southampton and out into the country. The lamps were already alight behind the windows they passed.

'How did you know I was coming this afternoon?'

'I *thought* you were coming this morning. Jock told me.'

'I didn't expect to see you.'

'Jock said you'd be surprised.'

'How *is* Jock?'

'Something awful happened to him, but I can't remember what. I think it was to do with politics – or it may have been a girl. I can't remember.'

They sat far apart, each in a corner. Tony was very tired after his sleepless night. His eyes were heavy and the lights hurt them when the car passed through a bright little town.

'Have you been having a lovely time?'

'Yes. Have you?'

'No, rather lousy really. But I don't expect you want to hear about that.'

'What are your plans?'

'Vague. What are yours?'

'Vague.'

And then in the close atmosphere and gentle motion of the car, Tony fell asleep. He slept for two and a half hours, with his face half hidden in the collar of his overcoat. Once, as they stopped at a level crossing, he half woke up and asked, deep down in the tweed, 'Are we there?'

'No, darling. *Miles* more.'

And then he fell asleep again and woke to find them hooting at the lodge gates. He woke, too, to find that the question which neither he nor Brenda had asked, was answered. This should have been a crisis; his destinies had been at his control; there had been things to say, a decision to make, affecting every hour of his future life. *And he had fallen asleep.*

Ambrose was on the drawbridge to greet them. 'Good evening, my lady. Good evening, sir. I hope you have had an agreeable voyage, sir.'

'Most agreeable, thank you, Ambrose. Everything quite all right here?'

'Everything *quite* all right, sir. There are one or two small things, but perhaps I had better mention them in the morning.'

'Yes, in the morning.'

'Your correspondence is all in the library, sir.'

'Thank you. I'll see to all that tomorrow.'

They went into the great hall and upstairs. A large log fire was burning in Guinevere.

'The men only left last week, sir. I think you will find their work quite satisfactory.'

While his suitcase was being unpacked, Tony and Brenda examined the new bathrooms. Tony turned on the taps.

'I haven't had the furnace lighted, sir. But it was lit the other day and the result was quite satisfactory.'

'Let's not change,' said Brenda.

'No. We'll have dinner right away, Ambrose.'

During dinner, Tony talked about his trip; of the people he had met, and the charm of the scenery, the improvidence of the negro population, the fine flavour of the tropical fruits, the varying hospitality of the different Governors.

'I wonder if we could grow Avocado pears, here, under glass,' he said.

Brenda did not say very much. Once he asked her, 'Have you been away at all?' and she replied, 'Me? No. London all the time.'

'How is everybody?'

'I didn't see many people. Polly's in America.'

And that set Tony talking about the excellent administration in Haiti. 'They've made a new place of it,' he said.

After dinner they sat in the library. Tony surveyed the substantial pile of letters that had accumulated for him in his absence. 'I can't do anything about that tonight,' he said. 'I'm so tired.'

'Yes, let's go to bed soon.'

There was a pause, and it was then that Brenda said, 'You aren't still in a rage with me, are you? . . . over that nonsense with Mr Beaver, I mean?'

'I don't know that I was ever in a rage.'

'Oh yes you were. Just at the end you were, before you went away.'

Tony did not answer.

'You aren't in a rage, *are* you? I hoped you weren't when you went to sleep in the car.'

Instead of answering, Tony asked, 'What's become of Beaver?'

'It's rather a sad story, do you really want to hear it?'

'Yes.'

'Well, I come out of it in a very small way. You see, I just couldn't hold him down. He got away almost the same time as you.

'You see, you didn't leave me with very much money, did you? And that made everything difficult because poor Mr Beaver hadn't any either. So everything was *most* uncomfortable ... And then there was a club he wanted to join – Brown's – and they wouldn't have him in, and for some reason he held *that* against me, because he thought I ought to have made Reggie help more instead of what actually happened, which was that Reggie was the chief one to keep him out. Gentlemen are so funny about their clubs, I should have thought it was heaven to have Mr Beaver there, but they didn't.

'And then Mrs Beaver turned against me – she was always an old trout anyway – and I tried to get a job with her shop, but no, she wouldn't have me on account she thought I was doing harm to Beaver. And then I had a job with Daisy trying to get people to go to her restaurant, but that wasn't any good, and those I got didn't pay their bills.

'So there was I living on bits from the delicatessen shop round the corner, and no friends much except Jenny, and I got to hate her.

'Tony, it was a lousy summer.

'And then, finally, there was an American vamp called Mrs Rattery – *you know*, the Shameless Blonde. Well, my Mr Beaver met her and from that moment I was nowhere. Of course she was just his ticket and he was bats about her, only she never seemed to notice him, and every time he met her she forgot she'd seen him before, and that was hard cheese on Beaver, but it didn't make him any more decent to me. And he wore himself to a shadow chasing after her and getting no fun, till finally Mrs Beaver sent him away and he's got some job to do with her shop buying things in Berlin or Vienna.

'So that's that ... *Tony*, I believe you're falling asleep again.'

'Well, I didn't get any sleep at all last night.'

'Come on, let's go up.'

Two

That winter, shortly before Christmas, Daisy opened another restaurant. Tony and Brenda were in London for the day, so they went there to lunch. It was very full (Daisy's restaurants were often full, but it never seemed to make any effect on the resulting deficit). They went to their table nodding gaily to right and left.

'All the old faces,' said Brenda.

A few places away sat Polly Cockpurse and Sybil with two young men.

'Who was that?'

'Brenda and Tony Last. I wonder what's become of them. They never appear anywhere now.'

'They never did much.'

'I had an idea they'd split.'

'It doesn't look like it.'

'Come to think of it, I *do* remember some talk last spring,' said Sybil.

'Yes, I remember. Brenda had a fancy for someone quite extra-ordinary. I can't remember who it was, but I know it was someone quite extraordinary.'

'Wasn't that her sister Marjorie?'

'Oh no, *hers* was Robin Beaseley.'

'Yes, of course ... Brenda's looking pretty.'

'Such a waste. But I don't think she'd ever have the energy now to get away.'

At Brenda and Tony's table they were saying, 'I wish *you'd* see her.'

'No, you *must* see her.'

'All right, I'll see her.'

*

Tony had to go and see Mrs Beaver about the flat. Ever since his return they had been trying to sublet it. Now Mrs Beaver had informed them that there was a tenant in sight.

So while Brenda was at the doctor's (she was expecting a baby) Tony went round to the shop.

Mrs Beaver was surrounded with a new sort of lampshade made of cellophane and cork.

'*How* are you, Mr Last?' she said, rather formally. 'We haven't met since that *delightful* weekend at Hetton.'

'I hear you've found a tenant for the flat.'

'Yes, I think so. A young cousin of Viola Chasm's. Of course I'm afraid you'll have to make some slight sacrifice. You see the flats have proved *too* popular, if you see what I mean. The demand was so brisk that a great many other firms came into the market and, as a result, rents have fallen. *Everyone* is taking flats of the kind now, but the speculative builders are letting them at competitive rents. The new tenant will only pay two pounds fifteen a week and he insists on its being entirely repainted. *We* will undertake that, of course. I think we can make a very nice job of it for fifty pounds or so.'

'You know,' said Tony, 'I've been thinking. It's rather a useful thing to have – a flat of that kind.'

'It is *necessary*,' said Mrs Beaver.

'Exactly. Well I think I shall keep it on. The only trouble is that my wife is inclined to fret a little about the rent. My idea is to use it when I come to London instead of my club. It will be cheaper and a great deal more convenient. But my wife may not see it in that light . . . in fact . . .'

'I *quite* understand.'

'I think it would be better if my name didn't appear on that board downstairs.'

'Naturally. A number of my tenants are taking the same precaution.'

'So that's all right.'

'That's quite satisfactory. I daresay you will want some little piece of extra furniture – a writing-table, for instance.'

'Yes, I suppose I had better.'

'I'll send one round. I think I know just what will suit you.'

The table was delivered a week later. It cost eighteen pounds; on the same day there was a new name painted on the board below.

And for the price of the table Mrs Beaver observed absolute discretion.

Tony met Brenda at Marjorie's house and they caught the evening train together.

'Did you get rid of the flat?' she asked.

'Yes, that's all settled.'

'Mrs Beaver decent?'

'*Very* decent.'

'So that's the end of that,' said Brenda.

And the train sped through the darkness towards Hetton.

APPENDIX II

Variant Readings

A selection from the substantive variant readings in the first British (Chapman and Hall, 1934) and first American (Farrar and Rinehart, 1934) editions. Edmund A. Hennessy provided valuable help in preparing these notes.

The entries before the vertical dash are from the first British edition, and those after it are from the first American edition. The figures refer to page and then line numbers (of this edition).

7.5	never reached | never properly reached
10.21	Mrs Tipping | Lady Tipping
11.22	or, more simply, | or simply
17.22	with vine-wreathed capitals | with carved capitals
18.7	could count, on days of exceptional clearness, the spires | could count the spires
19.2	desultory hobbies | desultory collections
19.34	I needn't, need I? | Please, needn't I?
24.4	altogether unlike | so unlike
26.3	keep it | keep him
27.7	J would | I would
28.9	into Galahad | into Sir Galahad
36.11	buttonholes | button-hole
37.33	his treasures. / They saw it all | his treasures. / It was a huge building conceived in the late generation of the Gothic revival, when the movement had lost its fantasy and become structurally logical and stodgy. / They saw it all
38.28	Vanbrugh | Vanburgh
38.37	really lovely house | really lively house
40.24	hard up and popular | hard up and smart
48.9	Then, her eyes still fixed | Then still fixed
49.17–18	just as Brenda had meant him to feel. | exactly as Brenda had meant him to.
53.8	what's the dirt | what's the diet
54.22	I daresay | I expect
60.4	That evening as usual she | That evening she

60.32	I'm not awfully fond of Tony | I'm awfully fond of Tony
63.6−7	Brenda felt a little sick when she read this letter but she showed it to Marjorie, saying, 'I can't complain, he's | Brenda showed it to Marjorie who was still at Hetton. 'I can't complain,' she said. 'He's
64.19	seems | seemed
72.27	lousy joint | low joint (repeated several times)
72.30	made towards Regent Street | made towards Shaftesbury Avenue
72.34	turned into Golden Square | turned down Wardour Street
72.34	down Sink Street | into Sink Street
72.36	Old Hundredth | old Sixty-four
74.5	the bottle | a whole bottle
74.7	*Liqueur* | *Liquor*
74.7	came there was a label | came it had a label
74.36−7	gentlemen's?' Milly asked. | gentlemen's?'
75.34	postmen's hats | postman's hats
76.1	I've got | I got
76.5	'You told her we weren't coming, didn't you?' | 'I told her we weren't coming, didn't I?'
79.29	This time tomorrow | Tomorrow this time
80.7	car. Perhaps Daisy Maids | car. Maids
80.11	morning room. Polly bringing chauffeur. | morning room. Only Polly bringing maid. Also chauffeur.
82.7	between Morgan le Fay and | between Mordred and
82.33	between the women | between the four women
83.36	some almost black | four almost black
85.19	Gin. No, Djin – how? – has | Cin no Djinñ how? has
85.28	called Jenny Abdul Akbar | called Abdul Akbar
91.12	When they were dressing | When she was dressing
91.21	a Jewess | Jewish
92.36	come in. | come.
96.11	rather flushed | rather hurried
97.31	other married couple | other married couples
98.13−14	they start walking out | they have affaires
102.7	an arrow slit | a narrow slit
102.15	titupping | titapping
103.18	which, while all | which, though all
103.33	at a gallop | at a canter
104.11	stood in the corner | stood at the corner
105.11	twenty minutes after her disappearance | twenty minutes since her disappearance
106.6	Miss Ripon's horse | the horse
109.32	"Gone to ground" | "Gone Away"
110.12	she'd got nothing else | she's got nothing else
113.15	'I'll buy it.' | 'Well you come show me that.'

113.17   'Show me.' | 'I'll learn it.'

113.19   I'm a dog and you're a hen. | I'm a hen and you're a dog.

121.8—9   Princes Risborough | Great Missenden

121.29   Tony and Brenda to leave the room. | Tony and Brenda to reach their car.

122.1   When everyone had gone | When they were in the car

123.15   at the corner | at its corner

124.35   and of my dear | and my dear

129.14   Instead Tony and Jock went | Instead they went

130.16   flattering to find | flattering to her to find

133.7   a Hundred Sink Street | 64 Sink Street

133.35   at an hotel | at a hotel

134.21   have to work. | have to work for a living.

134.26   fairy cycle | fairy bicycle

135.8   detectives were there earliest | detectives were the first

138.18   James and me | James and I

141.36   So also, Tony noticed | So, Tony noticed

142.33   with Dan, who said, 'Nice kid, Milly.' | with Dan. 'Nice kid, Milly,' he said.

144.23   Now my knickers are wet | Now I'm all wet

145.18   You've had | You have had

147.34   was due solely to | was made solely by

148.1   eyes lay, that | eyes lay, which

151.1   goes straight back to the estate | goes on the estate

151.8   It's as much as I've ever had | It's more than I've ever had

153.7   glittering through the forest | glittering in

153.35   said Jenny Abdul Akbar. | said Jenny.

157.29   embarrassing sequence | embarrassing recurrence

158.23   on the bridge. | on the bridge that evening.

161.19   brown of his face ended | brown of his face and hands ended

164.11   His mind was occupied | His thoughts were occupied

166.22   drawn to the grave eyes | drawn to the large, grave eyes

166.34   engaged | affiancée

167.4   marry into one of them | marry one of them

171.20—21 formalities in disembarking their stores. | formalities in getting their stores ashore.

171.26   trotted busily to and fro | trotted to and fro busily

172.8   (The rank | (The gross

172.10   all gross | all rank

172.13   roof over | roof about

174.13   so he and Dr Messinger got | so they got

174.26   Dat for why | Dat why for

175.4   through with the divorce? | through with it?

175.27   with a cutlass | with cutlass

178.4–7   'Number twenty,' he said. / A few members turned to the order paper. / *No. 20.* / *To ask the Minister* | 'I should like to ask the Minister

179.5   gunwales | bulwarks

179.23   I want ten men | I want the men

182.24   biography of Nelson | biography of Thiers

183.18–19   'It's hopeless,' said Dr Messinger. / When they | 'It's hopeless,' said Dr Messinger. / 'Don't you think that, possibly we *have* struck the upper waters of the Waurupang?' suggested Tony, 'and have crossed and recrossed the stream as it winds down the valley.' / 'It is a hypothesis,' said Dr Messinger. / When they

184.1   into dry shirts | into clean shirts

184.14   lack of water. The streams | lack of water. They had left the Waurupang behind and the streams

185.19–20   They were short a bag of farine, half a bag of sugar and a bag of rice. | There was a bag of farine, half a bag of sugar and a bag of rice short.

186.2   from all accounts, must | must from all accounts

187.37   Eight men | Six men

188.15   sensible, civilized woman | sensible woman

190.6   It is the cassava | It's the cassava

193.26   low; any movement | low; and movement

194.5   their blossoming crown | their flowering crown

194.9   a flowering meadow | a blossoming meadow

194.10   beach, or hung | beach, and hung

194.17   health and shot | health and had shot

195.32   frightened of a toy mouse,' Tony | frightened of a toy,' Tony (repeated)

198.12   the bows | the bow (repeated)

198.21   thatched dome | thatched domes

198.35   up to a bough | up to a bow

199.11   strewn with blossom | strewn with blossoms

203.5   said Polly Cockpurse | said Lady Cockpurse

203.20   her plans include | her plans included

205.1   gates were before | gates were open before

211.34   forget all courtesy | forget courtesy

212.1   a week, each with | a week with

227.13–14   conducted the service in resonant tones that were clearly audible | conducted the service in his clear, resonant voice that was clearly audible

228.8   into bundles of four | into four bundles